LAST OF THE GOOD GUYS

LAST OF THE GOOD GUYS

JOHN CARBONE

headline

First published in 2007
by HEADLINE PUBLISHING GROUP

1

Cataloguing in Publication Data is available from the British Library

978 0 7553 3579 4 (hardback)
978 0 7553 3580 0 (trade paperback)

Typeset in AGaramond by Avon DataSet Ltd,
Bidford on Avon, Warwickshire

Printed and bound in Great Britain by
Mackays of Chatham plc, Chatham, Kent

HEADLINE PUBLISHING GROUP
A division of Hachette Livre UK Ltd
338 Euston Road
London NW1 3BH

www.headline.co.uk

For my parents

Prologue

When I was young I thought my life would be special. Maybe I'd be a successful entrepreneur. My father would have liked that. Or maybe a famous musician. My mother would have liked that. Or maybe just a good person, a good friend, someone people trusted and respected, an adoring husband and doting father. I would have liked that. But the things you think about in the waning years of adolescence don't always come to fruition.

For most of us, we experience a life quite different from the one we hoped for. We marry the wrong people for the wrong reasons or we don't take life seriously and let opportunities slip through our hands, thinking that something better awaits us.

Then there are the pitfalls: drugs, alcohol, gambling – any of which can destroy us. And what about the psychological disorders and phobias that many of us harbour? Anxiety, megalomania, paranoia ... Any of these can slowly erode our self-confidence until we become just shadows, ghosts of the people we once were. Am I a ghost? A shadow of the man I once was?

I feel my soul is drifting in and out of dimensions, unable to find peace because of the injustices committed by my body. It's as if my soul is trapped in some karmic void, wandering, until the wrongs are finally righted. Maybe then peace can come to my body, which only wants rest.

It's been thirty-five years since I sat at my school desk and

1

dreamed of a love and a life that would descend upon me and fulfil my intuition of being special, a dream that I have yet to realise. I write this story in an attempt to exorcise my demons and to learn to forgive, so that maybe I can be forgiven and the ghosts can rest and stop haunting me through my painful days and sleepless nights.

I'm sure a sense of self-pity ebbs from my words, begging the reader to understand and forgive me for what I'm about to disclose. No person should forgive a man who immersed himself in a life of crime and fast money. But maybe they can forgive the boy, the boy who only wanted to be loved and accepted.

For this story starts when I was no more than a boy: one of seven boys actually. Seven streetwise kids who wanted to find a way out. Boys who would form a bond so strong that only death would separate them. *A bond so strong that only death would separate them?* How's that possible? When I sit back and absorb the enormity of those words, I can't help but question my lucidity . . . but then I remember.

I can still see the faces of four of those boys – the Italians. So young, full of promise, still unaware of our capabilities as we ran wild through the streets. We four aggravated shop owners and stole the occasional piece of fruit from the market vendors with the same detached emotion as the Dickens characters that I had read about in the books given to me by my Uncle Tony. But the rest of the country in 1962 was consumed with the impending doom of the Cuban missile crisis.

The threat of a Third World War didn't bother us though. Our neighbourhoods were consumed with a different kind of war – the war of the streets. Gangs of young people fighting turf wars that were heated by ethnic differences and invisible borders that only we could see. Old, cultural differences driven by the insist-ence for respect and recognition in a jungle city that was commonly known to the rest of the world as the Melting Pot. But we were young, valiant knights, or so we perceived ourselves. We took up our wooden swords, handmade by Uncle Tony, and spent endless hours in competition with each other, preparing ourselves for the inevitable battles that we would soon inherit, never giving a second thought to those faceless Russians that frightened our parents.

Our parents? Many people, mostly people who grew up someplace that was more like the land of Oz than our neighbourhoods, often place the blame on the parents when they hear someone recount yet another tragic chapter in the ongoing saga of the streets. But the truth is, our parents were as impotent as UN delegates are in the Middle Eastern turf wars. How could they keep us safe from the shrapnel that rained down around us every day without warning? Shrapnel that's been exploding from the melting pot since the fire was first ignited almost two hundred years ago.

I was eight years old when Uncle Tony came home for good and married Francesca Rimaldi; it was 1964. Before that, Tony was away in the service and I'd only see him a couple of weeks a year. He would always take me fishing or to a ball game; I think he felt bad that I didn't see my dad much. At that time my dad had to support my mom and us four kids by working long days in the shipyard as a boat builder; he didn't have a lot of free time. So Tony picked up the slack for his kid brother and helped out with the father thing.

The other three boys didn't come along until later. They were from another part of the city and a different ethnic background: they were Irish – the Micks. They, too, were busy fighting turf wars, trying to cut out a small piece of ground that they could call their own. It would be another six years before our destinies collided.

Sometimes I wonder if I could have changed our destiny. I think of all the bad choices I made early on. Could one altered choice have made a difference? Maybe two better choices? I don't know how cause and effect works, but I assume that there's a proverbial line that one crosses that ensures a certain path. Like I said, I don't know how it works. What I do know is, once you've set yourself on the wrong side of the rainbow-coloured path that supposedly leads to the pot of gold, you're torn away from everything you once held sacred as a child. Family, friends, happy endings – gone forever, swept away in a torrent that few survive. I often wonder how I survived. Maybe it's my fate. Maybe it's my Herculean grip on the desire to live, and live free. Who knows? Maybe it's just God's idea of a little thrilling Saturday-night entertainment . . .

There's one more thing I know. There's no pot of gold at the end of the rainbow path. There's only the path, which might have a little gold along the way, but the end of the rainbow and happily ever after? It's a load of shit. I don't think anyone ever makes it. Because the toll you must pay to travel that deceptive path exceeds the value of any potential gold that may be found. There's no free rides in life, you pay one way or another – but I'm getting ahead of myself.

Like I said, when Uncle Tony got home in 1964, he helped out with the father thing. Not just with me, but with the other three Italian boys as well; all of their fathers were in prison at the time.

He taught us to play chess and encouraged us to read the classics. He would also tell us great stories about the legendary King Arthur and the formidable Lancelot. It was those stories, and the wooden swords made by Tony, that drew us into the magical realm of chivalry. Honour, loyalty and courage were the themes that we embraced in those tender years Unfortunately, the river of change, polluted by the Vietnam War and our bad choices, would eventually dilute those pure and good values.

We considered ourselves knights, or as Tony would call us in our mother tongue, *cavaliere*. That became the title we used to indoctrinate all the members of our brotherhood. We four Italians and the three Irish would be our brotherhood, our gang. Together we would defend ourselves from the hordes of overlords who would try to control us and occupy our turf. Together we would break free from the chains of mediocrity that humbly subdued our parents and loved ones. Together we would stand, or together we would die.

In the beginning, we were just boys. Boys who grew to be hardened men, violent men, men without fear and only one desire: to rise above the foul stench of the Brooklyn streets that had taken away our souls, souls that may have been brave knights or valiant warriors in some long ago forgotten time. We became men bound together so tightly that no one was able to save us from ourselves. For in the end it was our bond that destroyed us and left us as shadows, lost souls unable to find peace from a life of wanting more.

I'm writing this as a testimony to those men, my friends, who tore apart many lives and stopped at nothing to achieve the power and success they desired. Men who became warriors, hardened warriors, capable of unimaginable atrocities, as you will soon see. I write this story with the hope of finding peace and becoming a man again, alive in the world of men. But then again I'm not just a man, I'm the last Cavallo. And this is my story.

1
Uncle Tony

Tony Bolzani was the fifth born of eleven children and the last born in Sicily. In 1937, when Tony was just a young boy, my grandfather, Guido, took his young family and went to America in hopes of finding a better life. That 'better life' consisted of a small apartment and seventy hours a week working in the shipyard. The hard work didn't bother my grandfather. He saw it as a way to ensure a stable life for his children and, most importantly, their education. In school Tony excelled and my grandfather had high hopes for him.

Then at the age of sixteen Tony heard the call of the streets. I can only compare it to the sound of a dog whistle: most people can't hear it but those that do are pulled away from their lives and their souls in the hope of finding recognition, riches and power. It's a life that only few survive.

Tony greeted the call with enthusiasm. Like many young soldiers, he started his new life with great vigour. However, unlike most other recruits, he became a good earner quickly, using his sharp mind, good looks, and natural charm to pull off profitable scams that paved the way to what seemed like a sure and fast rise to the top of his crew. When Tony was twenty-one, he hijacked a truck full of televisions out of LaGuardia Airport. The weather was bad that night and it snowed heavily. When he was just two blocks from the warehouse where he was supposed to deliver the goods, he hit a patch of ice, lost control of the truck and crashed into a tree. The impact knocked him out and when the cops arrived he was still behind the wheel, unconscious. He woke up in the hospital later that night, handcuffed to the bed.

When he went to court, the district attorney offered a deal: plead guilty and get three to five years in Sing Sing for theft of a motor vehicle, or plead innocent and face a possible twenty years for hijacking if found guilty. Since Tony was still in the truck when the cops arrived, his lawyer advised he plead guilty and he did. Upon sentencing, the judge took account of Tony's young age and clean record and gave him a choice: take five in the big house or enlist in one of the armed services. Tony chose the army. These types of deals were common in the 1950s and 1960s, and usually giving a young man a second chance was the best thing for everyone concerned. But in the case of Tony Bolzani it was a bad mistake.

When he arrived at the recruiting centre, Tony, like all recruits, took an IQ test to determine where he'd best be placed. To their surprise, he scored 188, twenty-eight points above the level of genius. After Tony finished boot camp he was sent to take a series of psychological tests. He did well and the army decided he was an ideal candidate for special operations and 'black operations'. They put him through one of the most intense training regimes any man can endure.

He was educated in the art of war and assassination, taught to be one of the finest tuned killing machines. And this is how a Brooklyn thug, after four years of successful missions, ended up in a Third World airport, ready to complete one last mission. He was met by two CIA liaisons: Robert Stockland and David Simms. They quietly greeted him and led him to a waiting car which took him off to a safe house outside the centre of the city. Tony was then informed that they had to sit and wait for word from higher up, which could take a couple of weeks. Tony, Stockland and Simms sat and played cards for almost two weeks, during which time they formed a solid base for a long-term relationship. It turned out that the three men shared a common trait: they all hated to lose.

Stockland, who was in charge of all the operations that he and Simms worked on together, lorded it over Simms with no care for his feelings. His plan was to advance as far as possible as fast as possible, no matter how many Dave Simms he had to step on to get there. The only problem was this: men like Robert Stockland and David Simms aren't naturally gifted, they have to cheat and play dirty to get anywhere, which, with regard to their common culpability in any of their rogue enterprises, left them wide open to each other's subterfuge. This inharmonious partnership left them both in stalemate. They were like Siamese twins joined at the hip, with two minds vying to control one pair of legs.

Unlike Stockland, Simms was prepared to play the waiting game. He figured that Stockland might have the upper hand at the moment, but the odds were in his favour that Stockland would fuck up at some point in the game, which was when Simms would cut off his head and claim total control.

It took them only a couple of nights playing cards and drinking whisky to size up the new kid on the block. Tony had already made a name for himself as a brilliant executioner and he made no secret of his plans for his future – as soon as his time was done, he'd be straight back to civilian life; the military could 'go fuck their mothers'. The twins saw a lot of potential in having a guy like this on the outside and they wanted to make friends.

Tony, who read both guys on the first night like a dime novel, knew that having a couple of rogue agents on the other side of the fence could be very profitable. So he lay back on the intensity and let them feel like they were picking his brain, but he'd actually got two land sharks hooked and he was gently reeling them in. 'Come into my humble web and rest,' the spider said to the tired fly.

Finally the orders arrived and the details needed to be worked out. Tony's mission was to assassinate some poor bastard and leave it to Simms and Stockland to make it look like a coup attempt, perpetrated by an internal compartment of the target's regime.

As usual Tony worked out the details for the hit alone. He credited his perfect success rate to this one principle. From the beginning of his career he had never followed the plans laid out before him. Normally this would have led to a long, fruitless term in some far-off military base in the middle of nowhere, or the brig. But not in Tony's case; he simply explained the flaws in the so-called intelligence reports and mission plan. Fatal flaws that he proved would have resulted in disaster. That, along with a track record of successful missions, gained him total control in every facet of his future operations.

After careful consideration, Tony concluded that this particular mission would be easy, with success an absolute sure bet which would leave him with a perfect track record. This mission in particular was the most sensitive to date and its success would open any doors he wanted in the world of military intelligence, an opportunity most guys would kill for. But Tony didn't have any desire for that kind of future. His future was back on the streets in the city that he called home; a home that he planned on making his personal kingdom when he got out of the military.

After considering all the angles, Tony decided on a strategy. He formulated a plan that was perfect except for one flaw. Tony saw it clearly, and with his help Stockland would see it too. If he stuck with this plan he could get as close to success as possible without succeeding at all.

Now why would he want to fail? Because success made his future plans much harder to achieve. If he did this thing right, the government could spend months or even years making offers and threats that would make it almost impossible to go back to civilian existence and engage in the plans he'd set out for himself. If he failed, his superiors would be disenchanted and Stockland would get to say 'I told you so', which would give him a false sense of superiority over Tony.

Tony liked that part the best; let the guy you're controlling actually believe that you're being controlled by him. Machiavelli could have learned something from Tony. But Machiavelli was a novice when it came to the art of war. His ideas were not conceived in the mystical pool of imagination and creation, which only true genius can spawn, but in the dirty waters of plagiarism. He took ideas from the Far East written thousands of years before and rewrote them in a way that would imply they were his own.

Tony knew this, which was why he always went to the source when it came to understanding an idea or an issue that he deemed important to his future plans. Tony's ideas and thoughts, right or wrong, immoral or vile, were always spawned in the pool of imagination and creation, using others' thoughts and ideas as stepping stones, building blocks and a psychological exercise room. Strength comes from within.

This last operation and its outcome took place when 'the boys' were just that, boys. I only mention it to illustrate how the partnership of these three men came into being. This is the story of how the bishop, Tony, controlled the king and queen, Stockland and Simms, and finally the boys – the seven pawns that would play such a unique role in a most deadly game.

2
The Italian Four

Brooklyn isn't the best place to grow up but it isn't the worst either. By the summer of 1970, a few months before I turned fourteen, I was out of my father's house and on my own, which I preferred. My father and I didn't see eye to eye and spent more time knocking each other around than being civil to one another. Not to mention, my father's house wasn't exactly what you'd call big, and with three sisters and two baby brothers, there wasn't much room and even less privacy. I was the oldest, with two sisters close behind, and I couldn't deal with all the shit that comes with that particular scenario, so I left.

Well, I guess it wasn't that abrupt. I guess the problems that led to my early departure began a few years earlier. I think a lot of it had to do with the fact that most of the kids that I hung with had fathers that were either in prison or dead. Not to mention they were all older than I was. So when it came to going to church or school when I was supposed to, I'd find it easier to play hooky and run with the crowd. There were so many things changing in the late sixties, how could I not go on those amazing expeditions into the concrete jungle? Vietnam protests and the hippie generation in full bloom were just a train ride away; we were all drawn into that new world emerging before our eyes just over the East River in Manhattan.

At first my father tried talking to me, explaining the

13

importance of school and the church, but I wasn't interested. Then he tried setting strict regulations and made me come to the shipyard to work with him every weekend. I did that for two summers before I left. I began to resent my father and sometimes we would argue and I'd just leave the shipyard, but soon the arguments became heated and he started knocking me around a bit.

It started with just the occasional slap, but became much worse after I delivered my first retaliatory punch. The last three or four months I was with him we had a couple of real bad scraps that left a lot of unsettled tension between us and a few more scars on my face. Then in August of 1970 he slapped me and I let off with a right punch that actually rocked him harder than he expected.

He volleyed with a shot to the face that broke my nose and sent me to the ground. I suppose I should've stayed there, down on the ground, I was just as guilty as he was in the whole affair, but my temper got the best of me and I grabbed an oak plank, got up and hit him across the side of his head. He went down and out.

I didn't wait around for him to get up. I went straight home where I found my mother waiting at the front door holding my baby brother. She was crying. She had just got off the telephone with my dad and knew the situation.

'Marco, are you all right?' The concern was for the blood that was still on my shirt and my swollen, broken nose.

'Yeah, I'm fine,' I said in a detached tone as I walked by her and into my small room.

She followed and watched as I started to pack a small bag with the few clothes that I owned.

'Where will you go?'

I shrugged my shoulders. 'I don't know. As far away from him as I can get, I suppose.'

My mother cried, lost for words and unable to choose between the son she loved and the husband who tried so hard to provide for his family. She turned and went out to the kitchen and put the baby in his high chair. She returned with a small wad of cash in the palm of her hand. She walked over to me as I was pulling the strings that tightened the old duffel bag Tony had returned from the service with.

'Here. It isn't much . . . it's everything I have from the cookie jar.'

I took the money and gave her a hug, trying not to let the torrent of tears that were welling up inside flow. 'Thanks, Mom. Don't worry about me, I'll be fine.'

'Maybe you can stay with your cousin Tommaso for a couple of days. I'm sure everything will be fine then. We'll all sit down and talk.'

I grabbed my bag and slung it over my shoulders. 'I'm not talking to him any more, Mom. I hate him and he hates me.'

This of course just made my mother cry even more. She followed me to the door and watched me walk out into the cold, hard world. I didn't know where I was going, but I knew I'd never go home again, and I didn't.

I started hanging with the local bugadha full time. In the beginning there were twelve of us, but my cousin Tommaso Capaccioni, Giuseppe Giaconi, Cristobal Maggio and I were the closest. We spent a lot of time together making plans for our glorious futures in the crime world.

Next door to Tommaso's house stood an old building that used to be a corner store owned by his grandparents who had died. Tommaso's father, who married my father's sister, refused to sell it and kept it empty. This became our hideout, and no one outside our circle of four was allowed in; it also doubled as my first home away from home. When I left my father's house, the clubhouse and TC were the first stop on my shortlist; TC didn't hesitate in letting me stay.

It wasn't bad really; the décor was shit, but the living room had a couple of big couches and two comfortable armchairs. Towards the back was a dividing wall that led to the kitchen and bathroom. Just before entering the rear kitchen area was a large, wooden oval table. It would have been the dining table for normal people but we never used it as such. That table was where we spent most of our time, playing cards, drinking wine and discussing business. The only meals we ever ate at it were take-away hero sandwiches, pizzas or the ever coveted takeaway Chinese, a real favourite among the immigrant Italian men who found themselves making a living on the wrong side of the law.

At first it was just Tommaso, Giuseppe, and Cristo who hung there. I was a few years younger than the others and TC didn't let me take part in any of the illegal activities until I turned fourteen, just a few months after I left home.

Tommaso didn't let me in the gang because I was his cousin; he recruited me, as well as the others, for two reasons. One: we all had fathers or uncles that were legendary gangsters. Two: we had no fear of the streets or the danger that pervaded them. There were a lot of 'turf'-related shakedowns going on in those days, and if you wanted to move freely you had to walk tall and take what came your way. We had all proved ourselves at a young age – you only have to stomp on a handful of wannabes before the word gets out.

I'm sure a lot of Tommaso's motivation for the gang came from his burning desire to become a wise guy, but his father, who was a respected member of the Cosa Nostra, put the word on the street about his son. If anyone involved Tommaso Capaccioni in any part of the rackets, they would pay with their lives.

Salvatore Capaccioni had big plans for his son: college, law degree, then run the family business on the safe side of the game. But Tommaso's ideas were different. His plan was to handpick the best of the lot and start his own crime family. Not anything as big or powerful as the Cosa Nostra, but a small handful of young men who would build their empire on the new frontier: drugs.

Tommaso Capaccioni, a.k.a. Top Cat, or 'TC' as I called him, was more like a brother to me. Being almost five years older and one of the toughest guys in the neighbourhood, TC tended to look after me and teach me things. I never questioned him. He made his 'bones', first hit, by the time he was twenty-one, and he didn't do it for the money – he didn't get any for it. TC did it because he believed people should have respect for certain things.

This guy Vinnie was from our neighbourhood and he was a real piece of shit. He'd made his bones but he wasn't a made guy and he was real pissed off about it. He was a twisted fuck, he'd come down on anybody that 'needed it'. Vinnie regularly went to this local store where Joey Dagostino worked; it was his mom's store and he was a decent guy. But when Vinnie's bill got up to two thousand dollars and it became clear that he wasn't going to pay it, Mrs Dagostino shut Vinnie off and told him he wasn't welcome in the store any more.

Vinnie decided he was going to have to teach her a lesson so he shook down Joey. Vinnie got carried away and turned Joey into a vegetable for life. Then, just to be a hard ass, Vinnie burned down Mrs Dagostino's store, leaving her totally broke because all the money she'd saved was hidden in the store and destroyed in the fire. As a result, she was unable to take care of her crippled son.

Now you're probably wondering why anyone would do that. Well, Vinnie's thing was pushing people around, people who didn't have protection or the ability to retaliate.

Now we all figured it was Vinnie, but no one wanted to get involved because Vinnie was a loose cannon and you never knew what was coming next. But TC figured the guy had no respect and had to be dealt with.

One rainy night, after a couple of months had passed, TC called Vinnie and told him he'd got a line on a small arsenal of stolen guns and ammo, and if he was interested, to meet him in one hour in an out-of-the-way neighbourhood. TC gave him the address and told Vinnie to bring ten thousand dollars in cash. Vinnie got the money and showed up at the designated spot.

TC got into Vinnie's car and said, 'You got the green, Vinnie?' 'Sure I do,' was all Vinnie said.

TC gave him the address and they made the ten-minute trip without any conversation. The address TC gave Vinnie was a very dark street behind a park.

TC pointed to a house and said, 'There's the place, park over there.'

Vinnie backed into the spot and shut the car off. As he reached for the keys, TC put a bullet in Vinnie's temple.

With all the rain, no one saw the flash. With a silencer, no one heard the shot. TC put his gun away and went through Vinnie's suit jacket pockets and found the money. He not only found the ten Gs, he found seven thousand more in Vinnie's right front pants pocket. It was wet and stank of piss but seven Gs is seven Gs.

TC sat there for a minute and smoked a butt and looked around to be sure no one had seen him. When the stench of Vinnie's bowels got really bad, TC got out of the car and locked the door then walked half a block away to a stolen car that Giuseppe, Cristo and I were waiting in. Even though TC knew that we'd never talk, he wanted us all to be there to pick him up; it made us accessories to murder, and less likely to talk.

Later that night, TC put the seventeen thousand dollars into an envelope and dropped it into Joey's mom's letterbox with a note inside that read:

Dear Mrs Dagostino,
    I'm sorry about Joey. I know it's not much, but here's a little something to help you get the store open again.
    Yours truly,
    Vinnie

P.S. I would have given it to you in person, but I'm dead.

P.P.S. I'm sorry if the money smells like piss but I lost my bladder when the bullet tore through my frontal lobe, but it's still legal tender.

After Joey's mom reopened the store, she always had a special smile and hug for TC. I think she knew that TC was Vinnie's judge, jury, and executioner. TC would have been a legendary gangster, but ironically enough his father's attempts to keep him out of the Mafia catapulted TC down a violent path that would dead-end at a young age. If Tommaso couldn't be part of the mob, he'd surely be an independent operator who would demand respect.

Giuseppe Giaconi, a.k.a. GG, was fourteen and I was thirteen when we had our first real knockdown fight, one of many to come. We were already close friends and spent a lot of time together. While TC and Cristo were honing their skills as potential gangsters, GG and I, both upset that the two older boys wouldn't include us, made our own plans and shared our dreams with each other.

We were about the same size, but he was a little bit tougher at that time. One day I called him a faggot for wearing the white dress shoes he always wore – his father was a wise guy making real money and was grooming his son for the job. I was jealous, I guess. My father worked in the shipyard and I was lucky just to have shoes. So, I called him a faggot, and with that a two-hour fight ensued with no real victor, but I was the worse for wear.

After that fight we became inseparable, more like brothers really. We always competed for the best looking girls and tried to outdo each other when it came down to earning the respect of TC and Cristo. For all our similarities, we were very different; GG had a sense of security that had always eluded me, he tended to take things for granted. He was a small boy who had no fear of the dark, the boogie man or five guys with baseball bats. I suppose he got it from his dad, who was a hard-hitting wise guy

19

who took no prisoners; but he adored his son, and he made sure GG had the best of everything.

From as far back as I can remember, long before adolescence, G wanted to be just like his dad, and always tried to impress him. When he got on his first baseball team, he tried his hardest to be a starter, but the coach didn't think he was ready to be a starter, so when he didn't start the first game, his dad put a word in the coach's ear. After that, G started every game for the next three years. So as the little boy grew, he just kept trying as hard as he could; if it wasn't good enough, tell Dad. Don't get me wrong, it's nice to have a dad go to bat for you, but you shouldn't count on it.

As far as G was concerned, he was invincible. Like I said, when I was thirteen, he was fourteen, and there was a lot of racial tension in the city. So one day we're heading home from school and we cross paths with four Puerto Rican kids, probably our age, and they want to beef with us. We didn't think twice. The biggest one pushed me first and I kicked him in the balls, a dead shot, and he went down for the count. From there it was three on two and G and I made easy work of them. When they were limping away, G just kept running his mouth and one of the kids yelled back, 'We'll be back, man, you'll see.' The fact that we were still ten blocks from our neighbourhood and had a couple of cuts on our faces should have been enough to let it go and get out of harm's way, but not for G, he was determined to wait for them. I think he really believed they wouldn't come back. So we waited. I knew it was stupid, but I didn't want to lose face.

About twenty minutes passed and my nose had stopped bleeding, I was calling it a day.

'G, come on, let's get out of here, I have to get home.'

'Yeah, all right . . . I told you they were faggots.'

As we turned and headed back towards our neck of the woods, three of the original four and six more came out of a side street. They had backtracked and came up on us from the opposite direction. Before we knew it, they were on us and it was only minutes before we were on the ground catching boots in the face and ribs. The only thing that came to my mind was to make a move on the biggest one of the gang. He was just to my right and kicking me. I got my feet firm on the pavement, which opened me up for direct kicks to the ribs, then let out a loud roar and lunged for him.

As I married my body to his, I grabbed his balls and the momentum of my body sent him sprawling backwards. The upside was it stunned everyone there and gave G a chance to run for help. Once I was on the big guy, no one butted in, they let us go. I grabbed the kid by his hair and started banging his head on the pavement; I felt like I might get out of this thing if I could just knock the kid out. Well, it might have been a good idea, except that the big guy grabs a discarded Knickerbocker bottle out of the gutter, smashes the bottom, and sticks it into the side of my hip. Now I figure I'm fucked, but it actually worked in my favour. As soon as the others see all the blood, they panic and run. I rolled off the big kid and he got to his feet and followed the rest.

By the time G and a handful of the gang found me, I was back on our own turf and on the home stretch, limping towards the clubhouse. I had a broken rib, a broken nose and a hell of a hole in the side of my hip. G's face was a bit fucked up and he had some body bruises, but he wasn't too bad.

When I got out of the hospital, I had nineteen internal stitches and thirty-six external stitches. I never cried once and took the beating in my stride. G caught a lot of shit for running off; I got all the respect for standing, even if I did get the shit kicked out of me.

G didn't learn anything from that whole episode. His dad sent a few young street punks into the other guy's neighbourhood and they kicked some ass – big fucking deal. There has to come a point in any man's life when he realises that all actions have consequences and Daddy can't bail you out, and sometimes, when the odds are stacked against you, you have to suck it up and walk away. If you can't walk, you give it your all and hope for the best. Maybe if G had learned something that day he'd still be alive today.

And let's not forget about Cristo. I can't start this story without a little introduction to Cristobal Maggio, a.k.a. Cristo, or Face, which is what most people called him. He got the name Face because of his looks. His features weren't delicate but chiselled and stoic. There was something about him that made men fear him instantly and women crave him just as quickly. It wasn't his size that captivated people – he was six foot three with a barrel chest – but his face; it was as impassive as a stone wall.

When I think of Cristo, and I often do, I remember the good times we had, and I choose to forget the bad. One night, when I was about eighteen, Cristo and I went to this fraternity party at one of the out-of-town colleges where he knew some girls. That wasn't the only reason for going though. We were trying to expand our distribution points and colleges are a great outlet for drugs. So anyway, we spent a couple of hours 'doing business', then had a few drinks and talked to the chicks.

As it turned out we got two of the best lookers in the joint and asked them if they wanted to go to our place for our own little party. They were all for it. So we say our goodbyes to our prospective clients and head for the door with our two honeys at our side, where we're met by a wall of jock-type jerks blocking the way out. So this big Joey Jamoke says to me, 'Where the fuck do you think you're going?'

'I'm going home. What the fuck's it to you?' I said without an ounce of emotion.

And he says, 'Not with them,' and he nods to the two chicks with us.

Now I know two things these fucks don't. One, I've got a 9mm with a full clip holstered under my jacket in the event this thing gets ugly. Two, even more lethal, I've got Face behind me. So I say, 'Says who, fuck face?'

So Joey Jamoke crosses his arms over his chest, spreads his legs a little, and real tough like he says, 'Me and my fifty-two brothers, that's who.' He nods towards the wall of fraternity guys surrounding him.

I casually turn to Cristo and say, 'Hey, Face, this guy's got fifty-two brothers.'

Cristo, who doesn't show any concern, says, 'Fifty-two brothers? Geez, Marco, his mother must be a real fucking whore.'

Well, that's all it took. Joey Jamoke punches me in the face and busts my lip, I rally with my palm to his nose from the side, which puts his nose about an inch to the left and him out cold.

I figure it's gonna get hairy, but almost instantly Cristo lets out this roar like a lion and grabs the two guys closest to him by the neck and slams their heads together, rendering them fucked, and then proceeds to work his way into the crowd, punishing anyone in his way with a barrage of punches that would have cowed the hardiest of men. It's not just Cristo's ability to hurt people that scared the crowd, but the violent force, like that of an erupting volcano.

It wasn't even two minutes later and I was standing over Joey Jamoke, frozen, mesmerised by Cristo's onslaught. That's when they all backed off and left Cristo by himself amidst the bodies on the floor. He can see that no one wants to toe the line with him, but he's pissed off now and he doesn't want to let it go. So he kicks this guy that's lying on the floor and holding his broken nose. It's enough to knock the guy out.

Cristo yells, at the top of his voice, to the bunch of guys standing up by the wall, well away from the door now, 'Come on, you bunch of faggots, after I finish here I'm gonna go fuck that whore mother of yours in the ass! So what are ya gonna do about that? Nothing, that's what you gonna do, because you're the biggest bunch of pussies that I ever met. But I'll tell you what. I'm gonna be back here next Friday on business. If any you fucks got the balls, you come see me and we can finish this. Actually, if you can't wait until Friday, come over to Brooklyn and look me

23

up. I'm on Broadway, just ask around for Cristobal Maggio, you'll find me.'

The chick that was with Cristo looked horrified and backed into the crowd. But the chick that was with me had real nerve, she just walks over grabs my arm and says, 'Shall we?'

So we left and Cristo drops us at my place. He didn't say a word on the way home. He just drove the car and quietly hummed to the radio. I don't think it bothered him that his chick didn't go home with him. For him, this night was already a good one.

The first two summers, 1971–2, we spent most of our time pulling two-bit scams. Then, at the end of the summer of '73, we made a connection that would change our lives forever. These Micks on the other side of town were moving a shit load of reefer, about a hundred pounds a week of Panama Red at two to three hundred dollars a pound, depending on the quantity bought, with about $150 per pound profit. Now that's only $15,000 profit, not much by today's standards, but then it bought a modest house or seven brand-new Chevy Malibus, or 2.5 new Cadillacs, and that was per week. So we saw the tremendous potential the Micks had to offer, to get to where we wanted to go, not to mention, with our help, we could triple it. And so this is how it started. A series of events that would lead to an inescapable reality. Could we have changed it? Could I have changed it? Yeah, sure, no one was putting a gun to our heads and making us do it. Do I wish I had changed it? Every day for more than twenty-five years I've dreamt about the possibilities that could have been for all of us.

I guess it comes down to this: we knew we were doing something wrong, but we were young and independent, getting more and more addicted to that life with each successful business deal.

We were surrounded by guys who were the real thing, bank robbers and murderers. Compared to them we were just a couple of small-time hoods who weren't making any real noise. I don't think any one of us would have continued down that path if we'd known ten per cent of what was coming later, and I guess that's how people fall into pitfalls every damn day.

We'd all change our past to some degree if we could. And we'd all avoid the minefields ahead if we knew where they were. But we don't, the future's a grab bag, some people pull the million-dollar lottery ticket at the age of twenty, others get leukaemia Everything else in between, it's just life.

3
The Micks

Shawn McDonald, Steven O'Leary and John O'Connell were the three Irish guys who would complete our gang.

Shawn was the mind behind the dope operation those guys were running. He was also one of the greediest men I've ever met. Physically, he wasn't the toughest or biggest guy, but he had heart, I guess. If you offended his family or his girlfriend, he'd most likely let it slide, but if you threatened his financial world, you'd have a fight on your hands. He and Steven had been friends since childhood and were now brothers-in-law; Steven had married Shawn's sister Susan five years earlier.

Steven, or Paws as we called him – a reference to the massive hands that went along with the six-foot-five frame – was one of the toughest men I've ever met. Whereas Shawn was shrewd and not so tough, Paws was mean, tough and dumb as they come, which made them a good pair. Paws was the only son of a traditional Irish New York cop, whose father's father and father before him were cops as well.

Paws left home at seventeen as a result of being beaten by his father, who was a big man as well. Like Shawn Paws was twenty-five when we met (eight years older than myself), and had not returned to see his parents since his departure. Paws had a sense of decency that seemed a bit oxymoronic; like most people, he just wanted to be married and have a family.

The first time I really spent any time with Paws I didn't know much about him. I had seen him around and heard from other guys that he was a solid guy but he was a lot older and our paths didn't cross much.

One Sunday, after we started doing business together, Paws and I drove down to Pittsburgh to catch a Steelers football game. They were on their way to becoming a dynasty team in those days and well worth going out of the way for. We had to leave earlier than usual to get there because the weather was shit and the driving was slow and dangerous.

About an hour before kick-off, we were only twenty minutes away from the stadium, no problem. Then we pass this car on the side of the road with two old ladies standing beside it. They were covered with sleet and looked as if they were freezing to death.

Paws pulled over straightaway and put on the flashers. When we got out of the car I think they were a bit frightened. With Paws being six foot five and the size of a mountain and me looking like a rough street kid, I couldn't blame them. They had a flat tyre and had been standing outside for almost an hour. When we offered our assistance they reluctantly accepted. We figured ten minutes to change the tyre and still plenty of time to catch the kick-off. It didn't work out that way.

The spare tyre was flat and they were from out of town as well, so none of us knew where the closest place to get a tyre fixed on a Sunday was. We invited them to come with us in search of a garage, but they declined. They were probably scared.

So off we go with the flat spare, in search of an open garage. To make a long story short, it took us almost an hour to find one and by the time we got back, the old dears were just about frozen through.

Changing the tyre didn't take long, but I knew Paws was dying inside because we were missing the game. When we finished, we put the flat tyre and the jack in the trunk and told the women we'd be on our way. They tried to pay Paws for the cost of the garage plus money for gas and changing the tyre. He just smiled, like he didn't have a care in the world or anywhere to go, and said, 'No, ma'am, I couldn't take that, I just hope someone helps my mom some day if she needs it.'

The women were really taken aback and almost in tears. We said goodbye and got in the car and went to the game. We had missed most of the first half.

From that day forward I always had a lot time for Paws, truly a gentle giant – unless provoked. I think his plan was to make a bundle quick, get out, and buy a house for Susan and Jessica, his wife and baby daughter. Paws' plan was as futile as communism; it looked great on paper, but it didn't work.

John O'Connell was a small man, five-feet-eight inches tall, and weighed about 130 pounds and was probably as tough as any man his size that I ever met. He got the nickname 'Ace' because of his love of poker – he never seemed to lose.

We spent endless nights in the clubhouse playing cards and talking shit. Usually this was a good thing, but after a while things started to get tense. Ace had been winning consistently for a month and everyone was getting the shits with it. It's one thing to lose a couple of grand a week when you're making lots of money, but the bottom line is, no one likes to lose all the time.

So one night Ace is on fire and up about six grand, and he's rubbing it in a little, not a very smart thing to do when you have four other guys' money, they're all packing guns and you're the odd man out. I was getting ready to call it a night and go visit this chick that I was seeing once in a while, but I thought it would be better to stay. Cristo was down two grand, getting real quiet and talking to himself, which is not a good sign. So everyone took their draw cards, and the bet's to Ace: 'I'll bet three hundred.'

Everyone looks pissed; that's a big fucking bet. The thing with poker is, if a guy's hot and all the cards are coming his way, you should lay off and just ride it out until the cards turn in your favour. You lose as little as possible and stay in the game until you

29

can make a score on a few big hands. If you're the guy on fire, and the cards stop coming your way, you can try to buy a couple of hands by bidding big right off the bat, bluffing. No one else knows the cards stopped coming your way; you might get to buy a couple of pots before anyone's on to you. Well, that was the story at that point of the night; Ace had been on fire too long, and we figured he was trying to buy a couple of pots.

I was the next bidder.

'I'm in. I think you're trying to rough that kitty off and I'm going to keep you honest, you prick.'

I threw my three hundred into the kitty and lit a smoke. I was holding a queen high straight, not an amazing hand but more than good enough to keep him honest. TC was next bidder.

'I think you're right, kid, he's trying to get some free pussy. I'm in.'

The bid went to GG.

'I fold. I'm not going on this crusade with two small pairs.' He chucked his cards in and now it's up to Cristo.

'Yeah, I'm going to see that, and I'll raise it another three hundred.' Cristo threw the six hundred into the kitty. There was almost two grand in there.

I wasn't sure what was going through Cristo's mind. If you just want to keep a guy honest, you don't raise, because then he can fold and doesn't have to show his hand, unless of course you're holding some cards and want to make a legit run for the pot. I thought for sure Ace would fold, even if he was holding half-decent cards. Everyone was getting a bit scratchy and he was the itch.

'I'll see that and raise another five.' Ace was nervous, but he was holding his ground. I wasn't risking another five hundred on a straight, queen high or not.

'I'm out.'

TC was hot with anger – the vibes at the table were so intense you could have cut them with a knife. 'No way, that's too fucking rich for these cards, I'm out.' He chucked his cards in with a look that could've killed.

It was up to Cristo, who was talking quietly to himself in Italian again. When he stopped talking to himself he gave Ace a stare that would have made Hercules shit himself. 'Even if I was holding a shit hand I'd be in, just to see what the fuck you got.'

Cristo counted out the five hundred, but before he put it in, he stopped and gave Ace another nasty glare and said, 'Yo, John, if you ain't holding some pretty damn good cards, I'm going to stuff all fifty of these cards straight up your ass, even if I do win!'

Now you know and I know that there's fifty-two cards in a deck, and I'm sure Cristo did as well, when he was more rational, but I wasn't about to make a point of it at that particular moment in time; nor was anyone else.

Cristo chucked in the last bet. 'I call. Let's see what you got.'

Ace, for the first time that night, looked like he was about to shit his pants, but he made an attempt at composure and put his cards on the table so everyone could see them.

'I've got a full boat, kings over nines.'

By the way he said it I think he was afraid he might have the better hand of the two and was a bit concerned about Cristo's tack. Cristo just looked at the cards and nodded as if in agreement with someone else he was talking with that we couldn't see.

'Well, at least he's got the fucking cards.'

I assumed that meant he was beaten, but then he calmly placed his cards on the table with a slight air of triumph.

'Read and weep, you fuck. Four fours. Ha ha ha, we got you.'

Everyone de-tensed and all the anger we were feeling turned to relief. As Cristo pulled the huge pot towards himself, he and his invisible buddy were talking away congratulating each other in Italian.

I've never seen a guy lose a pot that big and look as relieved as Ace did. Those fours that Cristo had probably saved Ace's life that night; like I said, he was one of the luckiest guys I've ever met.

As dangerous as that night got, one great thing came from it. Whenever we played cards from then on, which we did all the time, we always had more fun with it and were careful never to put someone in a position that would make them feel the fool. At the end of the day, it's all about respect.

Within six months of the new partnership, we all let our guard down. Instead of the four of us and the three of them, it became the seven of us and business was good. TC was a brilliant businessman. Every week he would send two of us out as scouts to a new potential place of business: colleges, parties, small pubs on the outskirts of the city. By the fall of '76, we were moving about four hundred pounds of pot a week and had money to burn. That's about the time that cocaine started to really make a presence on the street. Prior to that, cocaine was more or less a rich man's drug. It wasn't really prevalent in the blue-collar crowd, but times where changing. That's where Uncle Tony, Robert Stockland, and David Simms come into the story.

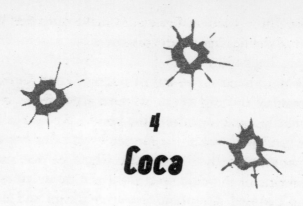

4
Coca

Robert Stockland and Dave Simms were still with the agency when they came to New York to visit their old friend Tony Bolzani, to make him a business proposition. The deal, Stockland's brainchild, resulted from a new task force being launched by the Drug Enforcement Administration. The DEA, in conjunction with the Federal Aviation Administration, were putting together a task force aimed at stopping the influx of cocaine into the United States. The reason for bringing the FAA into it was to give the DEA a broader reach of jurisdiction. This meant that all international airports operating under the guidelines of the FAA could now be targeted and controlled by the DEA.

The strategy was this: the DEA send undercover men into South America with the hopes of getting information on any shipments being made to the US. When they get a tip on something, the DEA send in an agent, accompanied by an FAA agent, after the aircraft has been boarded and loaded, to search the cargo hold for any narcotics.

Now Bobby and Dave have a friend on the inside and the ability to get proper documentation. So the plan was to get two sets of papers – DEA badge and FAA badge, along with authorisation – and put Tony's picture and false name on one and Tony's future accomplice on the other. Once this was done,

Bobby and Dave could get the inside info on any potential activity in any one area. So if all the heat was in Peru, and nothing was happening in Bogota, they would give the green light to Tony to make a run out of Bogota. Then Tony, and his as yet unnamed accomplice, could take a private Lear Jet into Bogota, pick up ten kilograms of the best cocaine available, drive into the airport and out to the tarmac – with diplomatic plates and the immunity that goes with them – without being searched. Then they would wait until the intended plane was loaded and boarded, and then casually walk up and flash their identification, demanding to inspect the cargo hold. While they make their so-called inspection, they plant their drugs. They pronounce the plane uncontaminated, officially seal it and clear it for take-off, which means no one else can enter the cargo area until the plane has reached its destination, which in most cases was Miami.

Then they drive across the airport, reboard their jet and fly on to the plane's intended destination, arriving there first so that they can perform the same show in Miami. By doing this, they are the first to enter the cargo hold and are able to get the drugs without incident. When they leave the cargo hold, they clear the plane for unloading.

You have to keep in mind that back in the mid-seventies there was none of the sophistication and technology available today. With no cell phones and limited computers, these guys could virtually walk in and out of most major airports totally unchecked. The only problem that faced Bobby and Dave was distribution. So they called their old friend Tony Bolzani.

Now this all sounded good to Tony, who was always up for a profitable operation. However, there was one problem: Tony's pact with the Fratellanza. In many families a made man was forbidden to get directly involved in the drugs business. Death was usually the penalty for breaching this family policy. This of course didn't sway Tony. He knew he could pull it off. He just needed the right guys, guys he could trust.

The first call for a sitdown came the week before Thanksgiving, 1976. Tony called me and said he wanted to talk, and I should stop by the house for a coffee. Now my first thought was that he'd got wind of the amount of business we were doing and wanted to discuss 'rent', a sum of money levied by the mob on anyone operating in their territory. When you paid rent, you got protection. If someone fucked with you and you couldn't deal with it yourself, you made a call and it was taken care of. If you got busted, they could pull some strings, but that cost extra of course. Tony could collect rent from drug dealers, but he couldn't be a drug dealer himself.

As it turned out I was wrong about the rent. I got to Tony's and rang the doorbell and he answered the door with a warm smile.

'Marco! *Come va? Tutto bene?*' he said.

'Yeah, sure, Uncle Tony, everything's all right, *grazie*.' I walked in the door and hugged him.

'Let me take your jacket for you, Marco.'

'Thanks, Uncle Tony.'

'*Prego*, go into the kitchen and get a cup of coffee, I'll be with you in a minute. I got someone on the phone in the other room.'

'Yeah, OK, thanks.' I walked down the well-lit hallway that led into the kitchen.

For me, Tony's house was picture perfect. Everything was modern and the best. The kitchen was fitted out with handmade Pecan cabinets, stainless-steel appliances and black marble counter tops.

At that point in my life I hadn't done a lot of cooking, but I had the desire to make it a big part of my future. So every time I found myself in Tony's kitchen alone, I would stare at the oversized, Vulcan Gas stove and dream about the amazing home that I would build for myself when I made the big time.

My thoughts were interrupted when Tony entered the kitchen. 'Hey, kid, this call's going to take a couple of minutes. You OK for a couple of minutes?'

'Yeah, sure, Uncle, take as long as you need . . . Hey, where's Aunt Francesca?'

'Shopping, what else? She's making the calamari and lasagne for Thanksgiving this year.'

'Hey, that's great, she makes it the best,' I said, and I meant it. No one could cook like Zia Francesca.

It was always like that when I saw Tony in his not working mood around the house. The guy could've won Grammy awards for his acting ability. He always had a smile and very simple and pleasant things to say when there wasn't any real business on the table or if we were out and about town in public. I was his favourite nephew. Even when I was small, Tony had time for me. He and Francesca didn't have any children, so I guess I was the son he never had. The other side of Tony, the one that few people knew, was truly terrifying.

I suppose there was more than one reason for his affection for me, and maybe a reason or reasons I'll never know. What I do know is that Tony was the eldest son and felt responsible for everyone else in his family. My father, on the other hand, was younger and chose an honest and respectable way to make his living.

This meant he worked long hours to sustain the simple lifestyle that he chose for his family, leaving me and the rest of us with no real quality time. I didn't have a dad to throw a baseball with or go fishing, or any of that great stuff that sons and dads do. The truth of it is in working class America, even back then, you had to give up a lot of the pearls in life just to support your family.

Tony took me to backroom crap games and boxing matches as well as baseball and football games. He taught me to shoot the dice and play poker, the art of betting on a horse and how to spot a dick, an undercover detective.

As early as seven I can remember him saying, 'Watch out for the dicks, they're everywhere.' It wasn't difficult. They weren't very clever in those days. They all wore cheap five and dime trench coats, drove black or grey cars of the same make and model, and wore cheap sunglasses and stupid hats, not to mention their robotic mannerisms.

I was the kid. All of Tony's pals looked at me like I was the team mascot. They always had a smile, and lots of words of wisdom. Things like how to take a guy down in two shots, or how to pick the right trifecta at the horse track, endless shit like that.

A lot of those guys, years later, became the most serious characters on the East Coast, and they had all the time in the world for me. I could go into back rooms and private clubs that were off limits to most everyone; even TC couldn't walk into some of those places. In a sad sense, I probably would have fared better if I'd had an alcoholic, torpid Neanderthal as a father, as opposed to Tony as my surrogate.

Anyway, just about the time I finished my second cup of coffee, Tony came into the kitchen and sat down across from me. As he sipped his coffee his face tensed, all warmth disappeared, and he became the other Uncle Tony I knew. It was very scary the way he could become so cold, so intense, in just an instant.

'I hear you been moving a lot of dope around town the last few months.' That was all he said, and he looked at me – no, not at me, right through me, in a way I find impossible to describe, except that it always made me feel cold and very alone.

'Yeah, me and TC were gonna come see you and take care of things. No disrespect or anything, Uncle Tony, we were just getting things set up and—'

Tony cut me off like he always did when he was like this, and said, 'Relax, I'm not looking for rent, I just want to know how things are going. And what's the scoop on the Micks? Can you trust them?'

Something in his tone calmed me instantly. I'm not sure why I was scared in the first place, Tony had never hurt me before. In fact, it was just the opposite; he'd never refused me help that I asked for. 'Everything's good, real good, we haven't had any problems, and the Micks are solid as can be. Why, did you hear something?'

'No, I haven't heard anything. But I think I might have something for you – well, something for all of us, something big. Let's say I could get you an endless supply of high-grade cocaine and a couple of the distribution outlets you need. Do you think you guys could handle it? Of course I can help, with a long hand, that is.'

This wasn't what I had expected. But I liked the sound of it.

Now I know that by saying 'no' at that juncture I probably could have changed the outcomes of a lot of our lives. But the problem in these situations is that when you reach the 'fork in the road', you've already bought the car, fuelled it up and now you're going to take it for a spin at high speed. You just put the accelerator to the floor and take the path that looks good, no matter what your better judgement is telling you.

That's just the sad reality of it. A lot of the mistakes we make in our lives are generally set in motion by a series of much smaller mistakes that were made at a much earlier juncture. I was optimistic in my response to Tony because I knew the rest of the guys would be excited about this.

'Sure, Uncle, I think we could do something great together, it fits with what we're trying to do. I'll have a talk with the others and get back to you.'

'No . . . Now listen to me,' he said very quietly, in a low tone, the same tone used by all the great Mafia dons when discussing business plans, plans well thought out, involving cunning and deception. 'This is what I want you to do. Don't mention anything to the others, except TC. Now, you and TC know what you can handle. If you decide to do this, I want you to run it by the rest of the crew, but the thing is I don't want you to name me as your guy, not yet. TC tells the crew he's got a guy, a guy that's been vouched for. This guy has a solid connection, he just needs the people to move the product. The upside is endless and everyone scores big. When TC runs the deal by the others, you make like you're just hearing this for the first time. Then you say to TC you like it, but you want me to come to the meeting as a non-involved player, just as an outside observer and a heavy. This will make everyone more comfortable with getting involved with a stranger and keep the rest of them honest. Most of all, it keeps you safe. If this thing gets out of hand, you're the last one to get whacked, and if someone takes a pinch, they're not gonna talk, they do their bid and I help where I can. Are you with me so far?'

'Yeah, pretty much, Uncle, but who's this other guy?'

'He's just a front. He's a guy I know from Florida, a guy that TC met briefly last year when he came to Florida with me. If anyone looks into this thing from the family, it has to check out. Now this guy I pay out of my profit, plus he gets all distribution in Florida. And, by bringing him to the table as the front man, it takes me out of the hot seat. It makes me look like an uncle looking out for his nephew's interests and a good capo collecting rent for his don.'

I hated interrupting Tony, because he didn't like being interrupted, but I took the chance. 'But if the family looks into this thing, they're going to whack him for fucking with the hard drugs.'

'No, this guy is not a made guy, he's just connected. If this thing goes sideways, I can whack him without asking anybody's permission. Then I shut this thing down. That way the family doesn't know I'm directly involved, and your guys don't know I'm directly involved. Which leaves you and TC, and I know I can count on the both of you to keep it to yourselves. Now, are there any more questions?'

I got off light. 'Just one. Shouldn't TC meet up with this guy first, so they get their stories straight?'

'First run this thing by TC. If he agrees, have him call me and we'll work that out. Now, any problems?'

'No, Uncle Tony. I got it, no problem.'

'Good! That's that then. Now you get it arranged with TC and I'll work out the details. *Capsici?*'

'*Ho capito!*' I walked out the door taking two steps at a time.

For Tony, as well as us, it was a match made in heaven. Tony trusted me and TC implicitly and we trusted Cristo and GG. As far as the Micks went, we trusted them and we knew we didn't have to worry about them. They had proved themselves loyal and very capable. If they stepped out of line, we could come at them with an army. As for moving the product, we had a well-oiled machine moving pot around. With those well-established distribution points in place, making the switch to cocaine would be easy.

An incredible exhilaration was running through my body. I was heading for the big time. I couldn't wait to tell TC the news.

TC reacted just as I expected. He called Uncle Tony and met with Paulie Martini, the Florida guy, and then set a meeting with the others right away. He explained about this connection he had and that he expected us to do a million the first year. Everyone was all ears and no questions. I was the only one to show any doubt, as part of Tony's plan. So when I said I would bring Uncle Tony along, everyone agreed. We all knew this was the beginning of something big, but we couldn't have known how big. So we set the meeting for the Sunday after Thanksgiving and continued with business as usual until the meeting.

The time passed quickly and Sunday arrived without any major incident. The warehouse wasn't insulated well and the November freeze was upon us so I thought I'd go by early and put the heat on and clean up a bit.

The warehouse was an old lumber company that went out of business with the recession brought on by the oil shortage of 1972. It consisted of two big corrugated tin buildings and about an acre and a half of land. One of the buildings had about three hundred square feet of office space on the ground floor and an additional three hundred on the first floor, which was tucked away in one corner of the warehouse. There were large overhead garage doors at both ends, big enough to drive a tractor trailer truck through. The other building was identical in size but had no office space; it was possible to drive in one end and out the other as well.

The property was owned by one of TC's great-uncles, on his father's side, who had been in the olive oil business many years before. After he sold his interest in the business he rented the property to the lumber company. When they folded, we made a deal with TC's cousin to rent the place for $700 a month, cash, which he pocketed tax free, while getting a tax break for the building being vacant. It was a perfect arrangement that gave us an ideal staging area for our operation at a very affordable price.

It was TC that had the idea to get the warehouse. We were moving so much pot that storing it became a problem. Not to mention, the guys we were getting it from offered us a great deal: if we would store a bulk of product for them, we would get a better price – about $10 per pound less. It doesn't sound like much, but when you're buying 1,500 pounds a month it's $15,000 a month. That was a hell of a lot of money in the mid-seventies.

For us the only downside was that if we took a pinch, we were probably gonna be doing some time. But we already had enough pot around to take a bad hit. What was the difference between one thousand pounds and four thousand pounds? When you're talking about time in jail, nothing, zip. We figured it was a small risk for a big return. So that was where the warehouse came into play, it gave a good front, an ample working area and a second hangout.

Along with the warehouse, we needed a false company that suited the likes of us and didn't demand regular hours. Construction. It was perfect, it made sense on every level. Moving that much pot required trucks, and it was realistic that a couple of young guys could start a home repair business; it gave us a perfect cash-based business that could lend itself to laundering some of the money. Instead of being flashy and obvious, we dressed like construction guys and even acted like construction guys. In some senses we were construction guys, except we didn't work construction, which could have been a problem because our trucks could always be seen driving around, but never at any construction site. But TC and I worked that out as well. We figured we could buy a couple of old rundown Victorian houses for about ten grand apiece and fix them up using subcontractors. It did two things: it gave us a job site for our trucks to be at, and it was a great investment.

So that's where we were when the meeting with Uncle Tony and the Florida front guy took place. Just seven guys in the construction business, quietly moving a lot of pot around the city and making what we thought then was a lot of money. It would look like small change compared to what we were about to make.

When I got to the warehouse, I checked on Paws – he was in the building without the office, the one where we stored the pot for the other guy as well as our own. We all took turns guarding the building at night because with three thousand pounds of someone else's pot around we didn't take any chances.

Paws took it very seriously; he was the only one of us who actually stayed in the building with the pot. The rest of us would go next door and watch television or listen to music because you could see the whole yard and storage building from the office. Plus we had the storage building wired for sound. If there was the smallest noise, it would come echoing over the intercom in the office. But Paws felt that if someone tried to come in, he was gonna be there waiting.

'Hey, Paws, how ya doing?' I said before I opened the door the whole way, just to be safe.

'Hey, Marco, what's going on, pal?'

'Not much, buddy. I thought I'd come by and put on the heat and clean up the office. I don't want Uncle Tony to think we're a bunch of pigs. Hey, why don't you go home and grab a nap and a shower? I'll hold the fort.'

'That sounds good, buddy. I'll see you at noon.' He started for the door.

'Actually, TC says to be here for eleven forty-five. I think he wants to cover a couple of things before the meeting.' I shrugged my shoulders, knowing that it was Uncle Tony who requested we all be there early. Tony didn't like anyone arriving after him; a meeting never started after Tony arrived, it started when he arrived.

'Eleven forty-five it is. I'll see you then, kid.'

While I got the place cleaned up and put on the coffee, I got a bit nervous about all the pot that we had down there. If Uncle Tony knew he was coming to a meeting in a place with enough pot to put us all away, he'd probably kill us.

The thing is, if you get busted with any kind of drugs, and the DA can link you to racketeering, the charge becomes organised crime. But I thought, fuck it, life's full of chances, and opened a bottle of wine. In keeping with customs, after we finished the meeting, if all went well, we'd have a small glass of wine to celebrate the business, followed by a coffee.

The upstairs office was where we always discussed business. The furniture was sparse, consisting of two couches along the wall, and a large oval table that could comfortably accommodate ten people, maybe fourteen if you squeezed them in, and two old desks. It also served as a great card table, something we all spent a lot of time doing.

TC was the first to show; as usual he was early. 'Is everything on target?'

'I talked to everyone this morning, they're all gonna be here any minute,' I said without looking up from my newspaper.

'That's good, *molto bene*. We need this to go off smooth.' That's all TC said. He wasn't a man of words, he was a man of action.

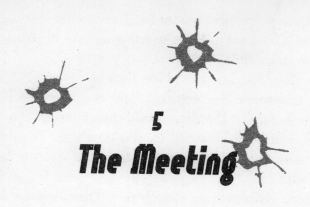

5
The Meeting

The meeting went off without a hitch and nobody suspected for a minute that Tony was there for his own interest. Paulie Martini came in and played his part. Paul was a tall, dark, thin guy in his early thirties – an old man to me at the time – who wasn't what I'd call a rocket scientist but he was even-keeled and reliable; everyone felt comfortable doing business with him. The only unexpected event was at the end of the meeting.

Uncle Tony asked everyone to leave because he wanted a word with TC, GG and me. Paulie was leaving anyway and the Micks didn't care, but Cristo looked like someone cut his heart out. But, being Cristo, he just got up from the table and gave us all a stoic look and a raise of the chin. I couldn't figure it so I just sat there with my mouth shut and waited for Uncle Tony to let us know the purpose of all this.

'Marco.'

'Yeah, Uncle?'

'Go down and make sure no one hangs around and tell my driver I'll be down in ten minutes.'

I got up and went into the warehouse. Everyone was in their cars and pulling out. I checked the garage door to make sure it was locked and put on the second lock that's only unlockable from the inside and gave Tony's message to the driver. When I got back inside, everyone was quiet; I hadn't missed anything. I sat back in my chair and waited for Tony.

'Right. GG, what I'm going to tell you is not to go any further than this room, *capisci*?'

GG just nodded and waited for Tony to continue.

'I put this whole deal together, and as you know, if anyone leaks it to the family, I'm dead. I told my nephews here, whom I have all the faith in the world in, and now you. The reason I'm telling you is because you're going to make the runs to South America with me.'

GG didn't give anything away, he acted like a good soldier and just sat there, never losing eye contact with Tony, and waited for instructions without interrupting. Then Tony began to fill GG in on how he would be wingman on the trips to South America as a DEA officer.

GG looked a bit confused. 'How we supposed to get all this diplomatic paperwork?'

'You don't ask questions, right?' The glare and heat that emanated from Tony's persona were as forceful as a sledgehammer to the face. GG didn't stir; not even to nod. 'You listen to me and it'll all go smooth, right?'

'Yeah, yeah . . . sure, Tony, you're the boss.' GG looked a bit lost, but no one went against Tony. Once you got this deep in the pool with Tony, you either swam or were drowned.

Tony lit his cigar, stood up and filled each of our wine glasses. Tony's tall, lean frame, chiselled face, penetrating green eyes and catlike grace upstaged the thousand-dollar suit he was wearing. His energy was so electric that he could have been wearing jeans and a tattered shirt and he'd still be the guy that everyone looked at in any room. 'All right, boys, *salute!*'

We all made the toast and drank the half-filled glasses down. 'GG, we'll talk more soon, all right? Call me at the restaurant Wednesday at noon. *Capisci?*'

'*Si, ho capito*, Tony.'

'Good. Now I'd like to have a word with my nephews.' Tony sat down and looked at me. 'Marco, show GG out.'

Tony wasn't usually that authoritarian with us. I guess it was his way of quietly letting us know that this was his new kingdom and he was God. GG gave TC a nod and I walked him out to the warehouse. I opened the small door in the garage and shook his hand.

'Marco, what the fuck just happened in there? I feel like I just got thrown into the deep end.'

'We all did, G. Take care of yourself,' I said with no expression and a slight nod before turning to go back into the lion's den.

When I went back in the office, Tony and TC were having another glass of wine. I noticed my glass was full as well, so I sat down, took a sip and waited for Tony to begin.

'Now I know you had no idea I was bringing GG into the big play. Eventually, if things work out, they'll all know. But I'm going to tell you something I want you both to take to heart. My two partners, who I don't want you to meet, for your own good, are guys that walk with big fucking sticks. They got pull like you couldn't believe, and they ain't like us, they got no respect. They'd kill your sister for fun on a Friday night.' Tony hesitated, gave us both a short stare and sipped his vino. 'I normally wouldn't do business with these guys, but hey, I figure what the fuck, everyone we do business with is dangerous. Even you two, you're fucking dangerous . . . Now listen to me, I'm trying to teach you something here.'

Tony leaned forward and started speaking lower and slower, and his eyelids, more the right than the left, closed about halfway, so the right one was just about down on the pupil, covering most of the green iris. 'You never let anyone too close that can outthink you. Fuck trust, that comes second. And that doesn't mean don't get involved.' Tony sat up straight and spoke a little louder, 'Just not too close.' He sipped his wine and slowly leaned forward again. He quietened to a whisper and his eyes did the eerie same thing as the moment before. 'Now, you two, well, you both already fucked up.'

TC looked concerned. 'How's that, Uncle Tony?' he asked sheepishly.

'Well, if you shut the fuck up I'll tell you. What are you, stupid? With two ears, two eyes and one mouth, see and hear twice as much as you speak; then maybe you'll learn something.'

TC took the chide like a good soldier and just nodded.

Tony continued. 'You fucked up by getting into this thing with me. You fucked up first getting into the drug business selling truckloads of pot.'

I must have given something away in my face because he stopped and looked at me.

'What? You don't think I know about that? You don't think I know you got a couple tons of that fat Irish Denni's pot sitting in this building right now?'

I wasn't saying a word, I got two ears and two eyes and I want to keep them; I just nodded and waited for Tony to continue.

'Listen to me. You're both pretty good kids, you're smart as whips and you should've known better than to get in the drug business in the first place. I couldn't have stopped either one of you. And I've been watching your backs for a couple of years now. But there's only so much I can do from the outside. So this thing comes up with the cocaine, I figure that maybe it's a fast means to the end. I'm chasing nickels and dimes and taking the chance of getting pinched, or whacked. The way I'm seeing this thing, we all take the same risk for the big score and walk away, disappear with a bundle big enough for three lifetimes.'

Tony stopped and gave us both a stare. I think he was daring us to say something. TC and I just sat and stared back with mouths shut. TC actually looked unnerved; it was the only time I've ever seen fear in him.

'All right, the reason you don't want to get in business with someone like me is I'm not only the most dangerous guy in the room, I'm the smartest guy as well. I've already thought of every possible scenario available to you. Speaking of that, I want you to slowly back off that fat Irish fucker Denni. He's out of your league, and he's a dangerous man. He may be just moving pot now, but that'll change. We'll talk more of that later.'

He stopped for another refill of his wine and went right back into his dialogue. 'As you both know, you never tell your right hand what your left hand's doing. Then again, you keep your friends close and your enemies closer. Now I'm not saying GG's the enemy, I'm saying he's the weakest link in this chain. Not that I'm giving the Micks more credit than they deserve. I'm just saying we have the Micks in check. If they take a pinch, they'll never rat, they know we can get to them and their families without even trying. Now Cristo, he's got more character then most men I've ever met; he's a rock and a good soldier. As you know, his dad was one of my best friends, may God rest his soul. But G, he's dumb enough to believe his father can bail him out of anything. And his old man might even be stupid enough to try to bring me down if he knew I was involved in this thing that the family forbids. That's why I have to have him close to me. I'll know before he does if he's going to do anything stupid. If he gets out of line, I'll whack him and his old man so fast no one will ever think a thing.' Tony eased up, paused for a second.

'All right, boys, lesson one's over. Take it to heart. You don't get second chances in this game. Make sure your crew keeps strong. Loyalty is the most important quality any crew can have, you need to unite as one. It's what keeps the Fratellanza strong.'

Uncle Tony stood up and raised his glass.

'*Salute!* Never take your eye off the ball, boys.' Tony started for the door and kept talking. 'I'll call in a few days . . .' He stopped and turned to us. 'By the way, you better go change your underwear, because if you haven't shit your pants, you're not as smart as I thought you were.'

TC and I both felt the chill that Tony sent out with this casual statement. We walked out with him and I couldn't stop myself from asking one question.

'Hey, Uncle, if you knew we had all that pot here, why'd you come?'

Tony just laughed. 'I had dinner with the chief of police at his house last night. If he knew anything, he would have told me.'

With that he walked out into the garage and signalled Guido, his driver, to pull the Mercedes up to the door. I opened the garage. Tony got in and didn't wave; he was too busy giving Guido instructions. I shut the door and followed TC inside and up to the office.

TC went to the cupboard and pulled out another bottle of red wine, opened it and gestured to me with it. I nodded and grabbed my glass, he filled them both in silence and we sat down.

TC sipped his wine and asked. 'So, what'd you think of that?'

'I think we better drink this bottle and open another.'

'Why is that?'

'Because I think the party's over.' That meeting was the first time I'd listened to Tony from the perspective of someone who'd have to answer for anything that upset him. It's not that I wasn't aware of how dangerous and calculating he could be. It's just that I had always been on the observer's side of Tony's wrath and cunning, never the receiving end; I was his nephew, his team mascot.

'Maybe the party's just starting.'

'TC, you heard him. He just told us we were getting into bed with some heavy motherfuckers for the big show. We better toe the line.'

'I'm not worried about that. We got a solid crew. It's the other thing he said that bugs me.'

'What thing?'

'You know what keeps the Mafia strong? Loyalty, a bond – you know, cutting the finger and the blood and fire, all that shit.'

'So what? You want us to make a pact?'

'Yeah, that's it . . . maybe. I don't know. I'll think about it.'

6
Sealing Our Fate

Ten days later GG arrived with the ten kilos of coke we had been promised. Paulie Martini showed up as well. He had agreed to teach us how to handle, package and cut the product, because we had no idea. 'Pure' cocaine is only about eighty-two per cent cocaine, the rest is ether. I'm certainly no expert, but I understand that approximately eighteen per cent of ether is needed to bring cocaine to a crystallised state. What we had to do was cut the blow with twenty per cent of whatever was available at the time for cut. Within two years there were several products available over the counter at head shops. In the beginning we used Mannitol and within a few days we had the process figured out and Paulie went back to Florida to take care of his own distribution.

Moving the product proved to be a lot easier than we had anticipated. We put the word out to the customers that we sold pot too and got good feedback. But the real movers and shakers in the beginning were the bikers that we had sold pot to in the past. They took seven kilos the first week and wanted more the next week. It looked like it was going to be a real moneymaker.

The third shipment came in a few days after Christmas and was out the door again before New Year's Eve. TC decided to call a meeting at the warehouse on New Year's Eve. We figured it was for a small celebration, just between us, and then we'd all go and hit the parties around town.

Like usual, TC didn't explain, he just said, 'I want everyone there for eleven thirty. By twelve thirty they can get back to their parties.'

So I passed it on to the rest of the crew. Some of the guys moaned about having to interrupt their plans an hour before midnight, but in the end they all agreed. Things were going so well, no one wanted to rock the boat.

News Year's Eve was so cold I brought two extra electric heaters to the office, just to get it comfortable enough to take off our jackets. When TC arrived it was almost eleven thirty. We were all there and seated at the large oval card table in the centre of the room. The table had a small mirror on it, with a couple of grams of blow in a small pile ... Actually, I think I should probably mention the scenario before TC arrived.

Cristo, GG and I were already at the warehouse when Paws first arrived with Shawn and John; they walked into the office like it was a bar room. The three of them were dressed in jeans and leather jackets; Paws had a leather hat on that made him look like an Irish version of Rocky. GG, Cristo and I had on new suits we had got from the Louis Men store in Manhattan.

A week before Christmas, TC had taken the three of us downtown for some new suits. With the money that was coming in we could afford nine hundred dollar suits no problem.

So the Micks walk in and sit down, but then Paws gets up and takes the mirror off the wall and says, 'Let's party!' and proceeds to draw lines out on the mirror for everyone.

I knew TC wouldn't like it, but I didn't say anything. Paws snorted the first line, then, Shawn, followed by John. I was next in the circle and just said, 'Not for me,' and passed it to my left to Cristo. He slid it over to GG without a word, just a slight shake of his head. When the mirror got to GG, he picked up the tooter and looked at Cristo and snorted the two biggest lines on the mirror, put the tooter down and looked at Cristo again and said, 'You're getting to be a boring bastard, Face. Lighten up, it's fucking New Year's Eve.'

Cristo didn't acknowledge GG, he just picked up the pint can of beer in front of him and chugged it down in one long swig, looked at GG and let out a large belch. And then, as fast as lightning, he smashed the can onto the table with a deafening crash that made the large oak table, and everything on it, jump, spilling a couple of the drinks.

After a brief death glance at GG, Cristo picked up the can, which was as flat as a pancake, and tossed it into the trash. John and Shawn grabbed cloths to wipe up the mess from the spilled drinks while Paws just sat in his chair, not knowing if he should shit or go blind. GG, trying not to look afraid, was trying to regain his composure.

GG was a fast talker and usually could handle any situation with bravado or reverse psychology, but just then he was a bit tongue-tied. Cristo turned to me and said, 'Kid, grab me a beer, would ya?'

I was the closest to the refrigerator so I just nodded and got up for the beer. Truth be told, if I'd been the furthest away and had to pack an overnight bag for the trip, I would have got the beer.

Without one word Cristo had made it clear to everyone in the room what his position was. He didn't think we should be snorting blow, but if we did, he wasn't going to say anything. He definitely didn't like the idea of anyone, especially one of the Italians, doing blow before a meeting.

Shawn and John had wiped off the table and sat back down. I handed the beer to Cristo *'Grazie mille, fratello mio!'* he said and drank his beer.

'Prego,' was the only reply that seemed safe at that point. When Cristo's been angry, and he's speaking in Italian, you know he's not over it and it's best not to say anything.

So that's when TC walks in. I was relieved in one sense, but a bit nervous in another. The mirror with the blow was still on the table and he probably wasn't going to be impressed. He walked in and sat in the seat between Cristo and me. I saw him eye the mirror and then slowly make a quick inspection of everyone's face and eyes.

When he looked at Cristo, who was still red and a bit agitated, he knew he'd walked into the middle of something. TC just sat there quietly for a full minute or so. It seemed more like an eternity.

It was exactly eleven thirty when I got up and grabbed a clean glass, another bottle of Barbosa and opened it. I handed the glass of wine to TC, who was now standing and pulling a small black leather bag out of the pocket of his suit jacket.

He took a long, slow sip of wine, put down his glass and sat down. He spoke evenly. 'The reason I called this meeting tonight is because it's the end of a year that's finished. When we leave here tonight, it's going to be a new year, a new beginning, and we all want it to be a good one, right?'

He glanced around the table. Everyone just nodded in agreement. I don't think anyone else saw it, but I knew he was trying real hard to be like Uncle Tony and his dad, a well-respected mob guy who was wrapping up the last two years of a fifteen-year jail bid.

'Now, this new business, this cocaine thing, it looks fucking great. But we don't want to end up like the coloured dealers up there in Harlem, shooting each other for fucking nickels, ratting on each other when we get pinched just to keep our own asses out of jail.'

TC stood up and slowly took off his black suit jacket and hung it on the back of the chair. As usual, he had his gun, a .38 calibre snub nose revolver, holstered on his left side, under his shoulder. Now we all had guns, but as far as I knew at that time, TC was the only one who had ever killed anyone. That made him a little more frightening. He took the gun out of the holster, very slowly, and placed it on the table between himself and me.

'So, like I said, when we leave here tonight, it's going be a new year. And we're going to do things differently now.' He paused for a moment, glanced at the blow on the mirror, and pointed at it. 'That shit's poison. If ever I see anyone, *anyone*, do that shit in here or around me again, I'll kill him. If anyone gets fucked up on this shit and brings this whole thing down because of it, I'll kill him. And if it's one of you fucking Micks, I'll kill you so slow you'll beg me like a fucking dog to end you quick.'

Everyone was as still and quiet as a corpse in a coffin. TC spoke so quietly, so evenly, without emotion, that it was clear to all of us he meant every word. Then he looked everyone in the eyes – Cristo, GG, Paws, Shawn, John and then me.

I think he was daring someone to disagree, but no one did. I knew the Micks were shitting in their pants and might've felt singled out if TC hadn't given everyone the stare. TC's antics were a bit caveman and over the top, but they were necessary.

If we learned one thing growing up around the Mafia, it was chain of command. No one went against orders from above. If you did, you paid. I didn't like TC giving me this shit, especially since I was the one that had put this thing together. What no one knew, not even TC, was that without me Uncle Tony wouldn't have taken the chance on this thing. He knew I was the most loyal guy in his fold, and if things went funny, I'd let him know before they got past the point of repair. But I sat there and took it like everyone else.

TC slowly sipped his glass of wine. I wanted to light a cigarette, but thought better of it. TC set his glass down and began again. 'OK, so we're all in agreement?'

Everyone was quick to nod. TC leaned across the table, picked up the mirror and blew the coke off into the air behind him. No one said a word.

He said, '*Tutto bene*,' and handed the mirror to me. Without a word I got up and walked over to the wall, rehung it, and placed the razor blade in my pocket. As I walked back to the table TC pulled out a piece of writing paper and put it next to the small black leather bag that he had pulled out earlier.

I knew right away what he had in mind. When a new guy is

enlisted in the mob, it's called being made. The new guy is brought to a meeting place, could be someone's cellar, or maybe the back room of a private club. There, other members of the family that's taking him in have a ritual, like a rite of passage.

TC had his own ritual in mind. He lit the candle and asked me to turn the light off.

'If anybody wants out, do it now,' TC glanced at his watch, 'because in sixteen minutes it's a new year and we're going to be inseparable. Does anybody want out?' He looked around the room. Everyone shook their head.

TC pulled a small envelope out of the little black bag and spilled the contents on the table. They were tailor's pins.

'All right, grab a pin and prick your right index finger so it bleeds.'

Everyone grabbed a pin except me, I grabbed the razor blade in my pocket. They all sterilised the pins on the candle's flame. Paws hesitated and looked around to check which finger everyone else was holding out. He didn't want to fuck up, and he certainly wasn't going to ask.

I didn't bother to try and sterilise the razor blade, I just made a quick gentle pass down my finger towards myself. It didn't cut. Everyone else was waiting for me so I gave it another quick pass with a little more pressure. I cut it all right, I had blood pouring out in abundance. I had made a thin slash about an inch and a half long.

TC didn't say anything, but he wasn't impressed, he just grabbed the piece of paper on the table and put his fingerprint in blood on the paper and passed it on to Shawn, who did the same. The paper then went to Cristo and the rest of the guys, and finally to me. I left a huge mark because of the oversized slash in my finger, passed the paper to TC and wrapped my finger in my dark green silk hankie that had cost me twenty bucks.

TC then placed the paper in front of himself and began his speech. 'If anyone ever fucks with one of you, they fuck with me and the rest of us. This pact is what's going to separate us from the rest. Tonight we become one, and no one can get between us. If one of us fucks one of us, we kill them slow, no questions, no exceptions, because after tonight anyone who fucks with you, fucks with me, and I'll honour the pact and so will the rest of us. Agreed?'

Everyone nodded in silence. TC took the paper, lit it from the candle and placed it in the ashtray. As it burned, he opened another bottle of wine and filled all our glasses; then we toasted. 'We win together, or we die together. *Salute!*'

We all drank and GG put his glass down. He wanted to get his own two cents in. 'So what, we going to meet every New Year's Eve? That fucks the festivities up . . . doesn't it?'

TC was a little put out with GG, but he shook it off. 'No, not every year. We'll have our first meeting in seven years, New Year's Eve nineteen eighty-three. That's when we'll decide if we're still going to do this thing. Maybe then someone wants out.'

I was a guy that liked history and I'd really enjoyed all the parties earlier in the year for the 1976 bicentennial. I'd read a piece in a newspaper about the next real big event being the millennium New Year's Eve bash and thought I'd interject.

'Hey, T, how about we fix our second meeting for the New Year's Eve millennium party?'

Cristo stood up and raised his glass again. 'Sounds right to me. Seven years, seven brothers. And then another meeting for the thing that Marco said. *Salute.*'

Everyone toasted and Cristo looked at me. 'So, kid, when's this helium party?'

'The year two thousand. It's called the millennium, Face.'

'Oh yeah, right.'

TC just shook his head at Cristo. 'One last thing. We put the lion's share of the profits into a kitty and buy property, and our construction company fixes them up. That way we make a big investment in our futures, and we set up a good solid front that makes us look legit and good honest taxpayers.' He looked around. 'All in agreement?'

Everyone nodded, although I think they all had slight reservations. But no one would have given TC any shit at this point. Bottom line, he was straight and everyone believed in him.

'There's one catch. Anyone who fucks up not only gets the beating, but they lose their share in the pie. All agreed?'

Once again everyone nodded. I knew there were lots of questions everyone had, but they would come later. We all toasted and drank up. It was a good moment.

TC got up, looked around and said, 'Good. I'll see you all in four days. Make the most of it because we're going to get busy. Happy New Year! *Salute!*'

That was the real beginning, when we all became closer than brothers. I thought nothing could ever change that but I was just twenty back then, what did I know?

After everyone left I called Brenda, a nice girl I spent some time with on occasions. I had made arrangements with her earlier that day. I didn't feel like going to any of the parties, I went to her place and spent a quiet night by a warm fire.

The next morning I took Brenda to Fort Lauderdale for a few days of sun and sailing. That's how I dealt with change and new prospects. I escaped and rethought things so they made sense in my head. The seven-year commitment was an unexpected turn in the path and I wondered if we had enough gas to get to that distant place and if we would all arrive in one piece. For me, it didn't matter where I was as long as there was a small boat to escape on, if only for a short while so I could try to out-think the possibilities.

7
The Mathematics of Success

That first year things took off fast. We made connections for distribution as far north as New Hampshire and as far south as Philadelphia. It was incredible. Guys that took 2Ks the first week wanted three or four the next. The big problem was keeping up with the demand.

Tony and GG had to make a trip every week and started taking 12Ks each trip. That was as much as they could get on the plane without carrying oversized briefcases, which would have looked too suspicious. The whole idea was to be as risk-free as possible. Going once a week was more than Tony had bargained for, but the money was so good he did it. The answer to lack of product came from Tony. 'Add another twenty per cent of cut,' he said. 'Fuck them, they'll buy it.'

Things were growing fast and we had to make adjustments at a geometric rate, but the key to any successful operation is to never lose sight of what got you up and running in the first place. If you have a system that works, don't change it, reinvent it maybe, but you have to find a way of growing in a way that keeps the natural rhythm of the beat that got you there in the first place. One of the keys to our success was if Uncle Tony said jump, we didn't even ask how high, we just jumped.

So when Uncle Tony told us to add more cut, that's what we did. Instead of twenty per cent cut, we started putting forty per cent, which meant the 12Ks a week became 17. No one, except the bikers, bitched. They were probably whacking the piss out of it themselves and threatened not to buy any more. We told them we understood and there was nothing we could do about it. 'That's how we're getting it,' TC explained to Chop, the guy who represented the bikers and did the buying for them. I had foreseen this and mentioned it to TC before we met with Chop and his guy.

'TC,' I said, 'this guy knows more about this shit than we ever will. He's some kind of chemist, or some shit like that; he's going to know it's been stepped on hard.'

'You're right. What do you have in mind?'

'We tell him this is the way it's coming to us but if he takes fifteen Ks instead of ten, we can charge him three hundred and fifty grand instead of three seventy-five; they get a K free.'

'We don't do charity, kid. If they don't want it, fuck him!'

'TC, you're wrong. These guys are in our backyard. They're coming to us to buy, we take no risk moving the shit to them, and they'd never fuck us, they know Tony's our uncle. As fucked up as these guys are, they're the surest bet we got. I'd rather they take the extra five Ks and we cut those angel dust freaks down in Philly out of the loop. It's only a matter of time before something gets stupid with those guys, they're not connected to shit and Uncle Tony's a couple hundred miles north. I know I shit my pants driving that far south with five Ks in the trunk, and Face doesn't like it either.'

'Yeah, but twenty-five grand, kid, I don't like it.'

'TC, twenty-five grand on fifteen Ks is less than eight per cent. We're cutting this shit with twenty per cent more then we were. We still come out twelve per cent on top, they take five extra Ks and me and Face don't have to drive to Philly to off the other five. If they go for it, it's good fucking business!'

'I'll think about it . . . Twenty-five fucking grand, mingya.'

I knew that meant he'd go for it. It didn't take a rocket scientist to figure this one out. So, back to the deal with Chop.

'I'll tell you what I can do,' TC offered Chop. 'I'll give you the fifteen Ks for three sixty-five Gs. You save ten grand; go have a fucking party.'

Chop didn't even think about it. 'Not a chance, three forty-five Gs or no deal.'

Now TC puts on his 'I don't give a fuck' face and says, 'Three fifty. Take it or leave it. I'm getting fucking hungry here.'

Chop thought about it for a minute. 'Deal. I'll need a couple of hours to get the extra money. Can we meet tonight and do the deal then?'

I had to step in here. 'Chop, you got the two hundred and fifty grand now? Right?'

'Yeah, sure, of course.'

'Great, you give us that and take the fifteen Ks. We'll see you tonight for the other hundred grand. We know you're good for it. Say you drop by about midnight?'

'Yeah, no problem, that's great.'

TC gave me a look that could kill, but I didn't care, I was right and Tony would've agreed. You don't let two hundred and fifty grand in cash walk out the door when you know these guys are good for the rest. And it made them feel like we respected them.

TC never said a word to me about it; if they didn't pay us he would have thrown a fucking nutty. But they paid us, just like I knew they would. The bottom line, they were still getting high-grade cocaine in their backyard. They didn't have to worry about moving the shit four thousand miles. If they'd been taking that risk, they would've put on the dancing shoes and cut the shit out of it as well.

When things grow that fast, so do the number of headaches. The first line of business was to get our customers to come to us. We were spending a lot of time driving all over the north-east, which was risky, and it took up too much time. Not to mention we had a new problem: money.

We started accumulating a lot of cash in small denominations;

we needed to think about that. Then we needed a place that was set up for cutting the blow and meeting with customers.

The warehouse was our hangout and where we stashed the blow when it came in, so we decided we didn't want any outsiders getting that close to us. Not to mention, Tony told us to quit storing the pot for Denni the Mick. We had stopped buying it, but he was paying us in pot for the storage fee. We told Denni we wouldn't be able to buy any more or store it any longer. He didn't like it, but he said he'd find a place of his own and to give him a couple of months. Well, a couple of months passed and he was dragging his feet, it was only a matter of time before Tony was going to bitch about the risk.

Getting people to come to us turned out to be pretty easy. A friend of ours owned a small bar and we used his back room for meetings with clients. We cut a lot of the original connections just because we didn't need them. We only had 17Ks a week to move. It might sound like a lot but in the drug world it wasn't much; and the bikers were taking 30Ks a month like clockwork. That gave us the luxury of picking and choosing our clientele. We only kept three out-of-state connections. The rest were nice and local.

Money: most people can't get enough of it to live. We had so much, we had no place to put it. But this story isn't about how much money we made because, relatively speaking, we weren't even close to the front runners in the cocaine business. Our whole plan was conceived around safe and steady, not greed. Now I know I said 17Ks a week wasn't much, but it's 74Ks a month, 884Ks a year. Nine hundred is more like it because 3Ks a week were being made up in pieces (ounces), and those were cut more than the whole Ks. So let's say we were getting twenty-five grand per K.

Now, when you have almost two mil a month in twenties, fifties and hundreds, it takes up a lot of time and space — especially by the third and fourth month. Where do you put that kind of money and feel comfortable about it?

The first thing we did each week was to give Tony his cut and the cut for Simms and Stockland; we didn't like holding their cash, it was too much responsibility. And they wanted all their cash in one hundred dollar bills.

I guess Tony met with them in Florida every week to settle; I didn't know and I didn't ask. The deal was set like this: Simms and Stockland gave Tony 12Ks a week, which they probably didn't pay a dime for. I'd guess it was just a small part of their payment from their Colombian connection for whatever doors they opened for them. So that was $120,000 a week to them. Then Tony got a flat $25,000 a week for his trip to South America. Then he got twenty per cent of our net, before we cut the blow; ten for him and ten for 'rent'.

Now, with having to pay the overheads to Tony and the others in hundreds, we were stuck with about half a mil a month in twenties and fifties, and another half a mil in hundreds. Like I said, after three or four months, where do you put it all? The bank? I don't think so.

The bathroom in the warehouse was quite big and the far end wall had a door that went out to a small storage area, on the upper loft, where there used to be filing cabinets. I removed the cabinets and installed an oversized jeweller's safe. Then I took out the door and frame and built a sliding door that, from the inside of the bathroom, looked like the old tongue-and-groove panelling that was throughout the whole office area. You never would have guessed it if you didn't know. We weren't worried about getting robbed; we just wanted an extra edge in the event we took a pinch. Not that the cops were that bright, but if they'd seen the safe they would have emptied it and kept most of it for themselves.

Back then some of the cops used to do 'shakedowns'. They would come in and act like they were going to bust you, but if they found a good score they just took it and you got to stay out of jail. A real fucking scam but what could you do? Call the cops?

We didn't worry about that because of Tony, but you never

really knew. If the DEA or the Feds were in on the bust, there was a chance Tony wouldn't be able to do anything to help so it was still a risk. The beauty of having Stockland and Simms in the game with us was that they used their connections to find out if something was happening in our city with the FBI or the DEA.

The new safe could have probably held about nine, ten mil if you had crispy new hundreds, still wrapped in the original Federal Reserve bands. We, of course, never had crispy hundreds. We had stacks of beat-up cash that we banded after we counted it. We never had more than three mil in that safe, that was just a staging area until we could find a better way of downsizing.

I had a lot of ideas when it came to hiding money and cleaning it up. One of the better ones was running it through the construction company, let's call it, AAAA-1 QUALITY BUILDERS INC. I never liked the name, but TC didn't want anything too catchy.

We knew guys that owned second-hand car dealerships, auto repair shops, furniture warehouses etc. We'd give them contracts for new roofs or structural repair, underpinning and sill rot – big money work. But we didn't do any work. They'd sign a pre-dated contract for $30,000, give us a cheque for thirty grand and we'd give them thirty grand in dirty money, plus a grand for incentive. They'd got a good tax break and a few bucks to take to the dog track, and we'd got 30Gs in revenue that ran through the business and came out clean as a whistle on the other side.

We didn't do it with all the cash, but we did enough so that if we took a pinch the cops couldn't seize all of our assets. Plus, running 900Gs a year through the business made us respectable businessmen and successful, tax-paying, credit-worthy entrepreneurs in the eyes of any financial institution.

It was moves like this that separated us from the average drug dealers. With TC's anal need to be safe and smart and with my creative ideas, we made a great team.

TC and I always handled the money. TC because he was the leader, and me for the back-up in case something happened to

TC, because I was the most loyal and trustworthy, no one ever doubted that.

I might've been the youngest of the crew but, even at eighteen, I was more of a man than a lot of guys will ever be, at any age. And they all knew I had Uncle Tony's approval and confidence; that went a long way.

When it was only pot, everyone just did what they had to do. If one of the guys needed twenty pounds of pot and no one else was around, they just took it and marked twenty on the calendar with their initial on the day it was taken, then gave TC the money that night or the next day.

We never had a problem with that system. But with the blow thing, that was different. No one just took what they needed and made their mark. You had to sit down with TC and tell him who, how much and what time you and the money would be back.

I didn't blame him, we were on the line with Tony and Co. and couldn't afford a fuck-up. The Micks handled all the pieces (the smaller amounts, like ounces and half-ounces) and the reefer. A normal take for any one of them might have been four, five ounces in pieces, and whatever pot they needed. Face and I usually made all the four, five kilo deliveries. The big deals, like the bikers, were always handled by TC and myself and some-times, especially in the beginning, Cristo; he was the best back-up we had. GG, he might take a K or two if he felt like it. But his position was he was making the runs with Tony every week, and that, in his mind, was more than his share of the graft.

G was the first one you could actually see a change in. No one said anything, but we all noticed it. TC even went so far as to play up the importance of GG's runs with Tony. A couple of times GG offered to make a five kilo deal and TC just said, 'Don't worry about it, G, you're doing plenty. Besides, I got Face and Marco on it.' It was an easy way to diffuse a situation.

A couple of times, when G took a kilo for a supposed one-shot deal for 27Gs, he was gone for three days. Now we're not stupid, he's taking the K and cutting the shit out of it and making pieces.

I don't know, but my guess is he got 40 or 50Gs and pocketed the extra coin. That's not exactly team play, is it?

The thing with G, he always had to be one up on everyone else. If I bought a new Lincoln, he'd have to buy a new Cadillac and a new Corvette. It was some competition thing with him. But we weren't supposed to be out and about flashing $30,000 cars in the first place. Not to mention he always had to drop all the real big dough on every broad he met. You add a cocaine habit, and you know he's spending amounts of money that most people only dream about.

TC, Cristo and I had a talk about it. We were going to have to watch G and keep him closer than ever.

Looking back, I suppose we should have dealt with G and his fucking problems right there and then. But we didn't want to upset the apple cart. If we told the Micks, we looked weak, like we couldn't keep our house together. If we told Tony, who knew, maybe he'd shut the whole thing down and give G a beating or, worse, whack him. It was a tough call to make. The bottom line, you don't rat out your buddy, even if he's hanging on the edge of reality and teetering on a real, deep and dark precipice.

9
Denni's Pot

Cutting the blow and bagging it turned out to be a lot of fucking work and after a while we knew we were going to need help. Face's sister, Lena, was a widow and had two kids and a huge house to support. She had been used to a great lifestyle and found things difficult without the seemingly endless cash that her husband Sal used to bring in.

Sal had been an uptown bookie. Things were going good until he got into it with some Arab guy who loved betting on long shots. Long shots are called long shots because they don't have a prayer of winning – unless the fix is in.

So this Arab guy's into Sal for about a 100Gs. The guy has the money, but he's lost over 300Gs already and his pride's hurt. So the stupid fuck gets high and goes looking for Sal late one night. He spots Sal's car in the parking lot of Sal's restaurant and waits. When Sal and his brother Jimmy come out and get in the car, Jimmy is driving, as per usual.

So this crazy Arab waits until they're out on the highway and runs Sal's car off the road, killing Sal. The guy might've got away with it if Jimmy hadn't lived and fingered him. Two days later the crazy Arab was found dead in his house. I don't know, I never asked, but I figure Uncle Tony took care of that himself.

Lena didn't like the idea of getting caught up in the drug thing. But it didn't have a bad social stigma back then and we told her we'd set it up so that she couldn't ever get pinched. That's where my creativity came in.

I found two apartments for sale that were next to each other, like a townhouse, and bought them in separate names. They both had a large attic space above, which was divided by a wall.

In the attic of Place A I built a large, walk-in closet with a normal sized, flat-panelled door that led to the attic in Place B. Then I built a wall of shelves from the floor to the ceiling in the closet. The door could only be locked from Place B. We never used the living quarters of Place B. We left the 'For Sale' sign in the window so even the neighbours thought it was empty. No one saw any lights on in Place B or any activity.

Place B was there just for an escape route and the neighbours only knew what they saw: a young Italian guy bought Place A and fixed it up. I rented it out to Lena who they assumed became my lover and I would drop in a couple of nights a week for our romantic interludes.

Lena introduced herself and told the neighbours she was a live-in nurse for an elderly woman and wasn't home some nights. A couple of the neighbours assured Lena they'd keep an eye on the place for her. It was perfect.

Lena would stay there at weekends and I would bring 6Ks of uncut blow in two brown paper shopping bags that had 3Ks each at the bottom and bread, cereal and other basic groceries hanging out of the top. I'd take them upstairs, to the attic of Place A, and enter the attic of Place B through the unlocked false door. I'd put on the lights, take out the Ks and put them on the big work table and then put my groceries away. I would sleep on the couch or watch television while Lena did her magic.

We had a plan worked out in the event of a bust. If the cops came through the door, Lena would hear it and she would bolt the panel door from Place B, locking herself, the blow and all the paraphernalia (bags, gloves, masks, etc., that we never kept in Place A) in Place B. She would then just walk out of Place B through the back door and I would deal with the cops. Most likely they would never find Place B, and I could throw the cops out empty-handed. If they did find it, I would take the rap and Lena would walk. When she finished her work, I'd take the cut and packaged blow out in a large trash bag and toss it in the back of my truck with the rest of the construction debris that was always in it.

I actually got pulled over once by the cops with almost 9Ks of blow in the back. It was early in the morning and I forgot to put on my headlights. The first thing I did when I pulled over was reach over to the glove box and pull out my paperwork and the half-full box of 'it's a boy' cigars, which I always carried, just for this purpose. When the cop got up to the window I handed him my paperwork and he said, 'Do you know why I pulled you over?'

'Yeah, headlights. I'm sorry, sir. My wife just had a baby.' I reached down and pulled out the box of blue banded cigars and offered him one. He took one and immediately became the nicest guy on the planet.

'Hey, congratulations. Your first?'

'Yeah. Anthony, I'll call him Tony. Fucking A,' I said with a big 'I'm so happy I could just shit' smile on my face.

The guy gave me my paperwork back and said, 'That's great, pal. Take care of that Tony. Hey, don't forget the lights.'

He never even looked at the bag full of blow sitting there in the back.

Tony always said the best way to do anything was right out in the open, and I agreed. The other thing was, cops are generally just nice guys doing a difficult job. I always treated them with a lot of respect, it goes a long way.

Getting the pot out of our lives was more difficult. Denni kept saying, 'Another two months.' So six months after Tony told us to call it a day we had more than a thousand pounds in the warehouse. The thing that made it hard to say no was that Denni kept upping his storage fees. But Tony started getting pissy and we had to pull the plug.

TC made a call to Denni and told him they had to meet for a talk. Denni said to meet him the next day for lunch at his sister's restaurant on the waterfront and TC agreed. Paws drove TC, Cristo and me to the restaurant, and waited outside to keep an eye on things while we met with Denni.

Denni was sitting alone at a large round table that could have seated eight or maybe ten; it was set for four. Denni was in the seat with his back to the wall. He made eye contact with TC and pointed to the seat right across from himself. Cristo sat to TC's left, I was on the right. There were no customers in the restaurant; it opened nights, lunch was only served on the weekends. The only people there, that I could see, were Denni's sister and the barman, who looked more like a thug to me. Denni was already eating and just greeted us with a nod and said, 'Sit down and eat.'

Denni's sister brought a bottle of wine over and took our orders; we all had lobster and steak. While we were eating, we just made small talk, keeping it simple. But when Denni finished eating he started getting into the business side of things while we were still enjoying our meals.

Denni was about forty and a big guy. Six foot two maybe, and probably weighed three hundred pounds, but he wasn't fat. He wasn't overly muscular either. He was just a solid wall of sinewy flesh. He had an air about him that suggested he wasn't afraid of anyone or anything.

He was one of the few people I've met that I couldn't read. His blue eyes were bright as stars and when he stared at you it was impossible to get in his head, but you felt like he had just read you like an old newspaper. He took a sip from his glass of beer, pushed his plate away from himself and wiped his mouth with his napkin, then he began the dialogue.

'How's things, boys?' he said.

We all nodded, our mouths were full. TC was the only one to reply, but he got right to the point.

'The thing is, Denni, we can't take any more product for you. We're out of that business now.'

70

'Well, we got another three thousand pounds coming tomorrow, and after that I got a place worked out.' Now he looked TC right in the eyes, daring him to refuse. TC stared right back at Denni without an ounce of fear.

'Like I said, Den, we can't help you out.'

Denni sat back in his chair and broke the stare with a wipe of his mouth. He knew he could walk the line close here, but he shouldn't cross it. That would be bad for everyone.

'So what about the thousand pounds you're holding for me? You going to throw them in the fucking street then?'

Denni was getting edgy and I didn't like it. I drank my wine, refilled the glass again and attempted to finish the rest of my meal.

TC pulled an envelope out of his pocket and placed it on the table in front of him.

'Here's the money for the thousand units. That covers our usual price, less our storage fee.'

'And what if I got those sold already?' he said in a cocky way that was intended to get TC uptight. TC didn't bite.

'No problem. We'll keep our money and deliver your pot to your place tonight by six.' TC reached to pick up the envelope.

Denni gave TC another stare and re-routed his attitude.

'No. That's all right. You keep the product. Like I said, I've got more coming tomorrow.'

TC nodded and put the envelope back on the table.

Denni took a new tack.

'So, you're out of that business . . . What line of business are you getting into now then?'

I was a bit pissed off that he wasn't letting us enjoy our meals and had to get my two cents in.

'We're getting in the none-ya business.'

TC shot a look at me that was meant to kill. But Denni intervened.

'Don't worry about it, TC. The kid's got balls. I wouldn't have done business with you guys if you weren't serious.'

71

Then he looks at me and says, 'No disrespect, kid. I was just curious.'

I backed off and tried to speak easy. 'We're getting into the real estate business, Denni. There's a lot of good deals out there.'

Denni just nodded his head and hesitated. TC and I were on edge, it was hard to say where this was going. Cristo just kept eating his meal without a care in the world.

'Ah, real estate. Where's that now, Colombia or Peru?' Denni's tone was sarcastic.

No one answered right away. So Denni came right back.

'Come on, guys. The pot I stored at your place wasn't even twenty per cent of what I've been moving. You don't think I'm connected? I hear everything.'

We all went quiet for a minute. He was right. We'd already moved over 400Ks of blow in the last six months; he was bound to have heard something. He could sense we were hesitant, and he relaxed his demeanour.

'You know, I was thinking maybe we could do some of that business together.'

I just sat there and tried to appear calm. Cristo was eating much quicker than his relaxed manner suggested. He had already finished his lobster and was now working on his steak, and his head and hands were moving around a bit, like he was talking to himself. His knife and fork were working in short, angry movements as if the steak was the potential threat. If you didn't know Cristo, you wouldn't think nothing about it. But I knew him better than his own family; he was getting hot and was trying to talk himself out of something.

The silence started to become uncomfortable and I was getting a knot in my stomach. TC broke the silence.

'Yeah, Denni, we'll see. It's early days, who knows what tomorrow brings. But we can't commit to anything right now.' TC's tone was calm, and I thought things were going to relax a bit.

'I understand, got to talk to your partners?'

Denni was trying to bait us into saying something that he

might find useful. But the way I saw it was, let him ask questions, it was the best way for us to figure two things. One: by learning what he didn't know, we'd know what he wanted to know. Two: by learning what he wanted to know, we'd know what he wanted.

'We don't have any partners, Denni. We work alone.' My tone was flat and off the cuff, almost flippant.

Denni leaned forward and drank the last of his beer. He held it up to his sister and pointed to the empty bottle of wine. She went for the bar. Denni looked at TC, as if trying to find the right tack.

'Look, I've moved over two hundred tons of pot from Mexico and Panama. I've been doing it for years. I know what it takes, who has to be greased and whose toes not to step on. I even know who's making that nose candy shit.'

Denni paused for a moment while his sister delivered his beer and the wine. She quickly wiped the smile off her face and aborted whatever dippy comment she was about to make. She felt the tension and just walked away quietly and quickly. No one even thanked her. Denni got right back into it.

'And I'll tell you something else interesting. Nobody down there knows any of you guys. You guys are ghosts. So don't insult my sensibilities and tell me you don't have any fucking partners. And I know it's not your Uncle Tony or any other grease ball; they're not that stupid to go against their fucked-up code. And I'll tell you something else—'

Without warning Cristo shot up out of his chair, grabbed the table with enormous speed and power, and pushed it into Denni's abdomen. It sent him back on his chair, which would have gone over backwards if the wall hadn't stopped him. Instead, Denni was pinned against the wall. Everything on the table crashed to the floor and TC jumped up to grab Cristo, who started yelling at Denni in a very loud voice.

'Insult your sensibilities? I'll kill you and your whole fucking family, and then fuck you all in the ass when I'm done. That's my code, you piece of shit . . .'

73

TC was trying to subdue Cristo, but he's one powerful guy and it's like trying to move a two-ton safe. I couldn't help TC, I was more worried about the guy behind the bar, and I went on the offensive. I jumped up and drew my 9mm out of its shoulder holster and put my back against the wall, just a couple of feet to the left of Denni.

That gave me a visual advantage. I could see the front door across the room directly in front of me, the bar to my left, and the kitchen and the bathroom doors on the left wall, down from the bar. I saw the guy behind the bar reach for something, I figured a gun, at the same time the chef came out of the kitchen. The only move was to put my gun to Denni's temple and take control of the room.

'Everybody fucking stop or I'm going to blow his fucking brains out of his head,' I yelled at the top of my lungs.

Cristo quit shouting but kept Denni pinned against the wall. TC pulled out his gun and pointed it first at the barman, then at the guy in the kitchen door and back to the barman. 'Drop your fucking guns and come out from there.'

They looked at Denni for instructions – they were clearly shitting their pants. To be honest, I think everyone in the room was.

TC looked at Denni with a stern face and said, 'Denni. Tell these guys to drop their guns and I give you my word, we'll all get out of this thing. We can figure what to do next later on.'

I couldn't see Denni's face because I was busy watching the two guys and Denni's sister, who was just standing near the bar crying; her pants were wet with piss. But when Denni spoke I could tell from his voice he wasn't scared, or if he was, he wasn't advertising.

'Listen, TC, your only card is the gun against my head. But your big problem is the kid isn't a killer . . . Are you, kid?'

He said it with a sense of compassion and understanding that, I must admit, eased me a little. But I knew I couldn't let him get inside my head, so I just got hard and said, 'Go fuck your mother, Denni.'

74

That's when things took a turn. Paws came walking in to use the bathroom and make sure everything was all right. If he was freaked out by what he walked into, he didn't show it. He calmly drew his gun and said with a sardonic smile on his face, 'Jeez, guys, is the food that bad?'

TC looked at Denni. 'Looks like I got two big cards now, Denni. Now tell these guys to put their guns down, and we'll all get out of this.'

Denni knew two things. One: he was in a bad fucking spot. Two: TC was a man of his word; everyone knew that. He looked over at his guys.

'Drop your guns.' The bar guy slowly tossed his over the bar and the other guy dropped his in front of his feet and then kicked it away.

TC looked at Paws. 'Paws, grab those guns and check Denni.' Paws picked up the pieces on the floor and went over to the opposite side of Denni. Cristo was still holding the table and pushing Denni against the wall with it.

Denni didn't wait for him to search him. 'It's under my left shoulder.' Paws tried but couldn't reach the gun; the table was in the way.

TC, who didn't put anything past Denni, was pretty calm. 'Face, ease off the table and pull out your gun and watch those two.' Cristo let go of the table, drew his gun and took a bead on the guy behind the bar. TC aimed at Denni with one hand and pulled the table out about six inches. I still had my cold barrel against Denni's temple. Paws reached in and got Denni's gun.

TC now controlled the room totally. 'Paws, you and Marco go to the door and check outside.'

I pulled my gun away from Denni's temple and walked to the door with Paws. Everything looked clear. 'It's good here,' I said.

TC and Cristo started backing out of the restaurant. Paws and I held a bead on Denni. TC was the last out and I followed him to the car with my gun out and one eye on the restaurant door.

75

As I got to the car, Denni popped out the door and yelled, 'You should've fucking killed me, kid. Big mistake!'

Paws, who was already behind the wheel, pulled his gun out and drew a bead on Denni so I could put my gun down and get in the car. Denni went back inside and we drove off.

'What do you want me to do with those?' Paws asked and pointed to the three guns on the front seat that he'd taken from Denni and Co.

'Don't worry about it. We got real problems to deal with.' TC lit a cigarette and didn't say another word the whole way home.

9

The Rock and the Hard Place

The first thing we did when we got back was call Tony. We knew he was going to be pissed off, but we had to tell him about Denni. He told us to meet him at the old clubhouse. When Tony arrived, all seven of us were there sitting at the card table in the middle of the room. I told him, word for word, what happened. When I finished the story, he just shook his head.

'That's fucking great. How many times do I . . . Oh, fuck it.' Tony knocked back his glass of wine and reached in his pocket for another cigar.

He was clearly heating up and we all started getting nervous. He got the cigar lit and gave Cristo a nasty stare. 'There's no sense talking to morons.' He got up from the table and began pacing the room and then turned and directed his stare on Cristo again. 'What the fuck were you thinking, Cristobal?'

Cristo looked up at Tony. 'The guy was out of line. What was I suppose to do? I couldn't—'

'You were supposed to sit there and keep your mouth shut. You're just like your father, if someone said something he didn't like, badda bing, baddaa boom. It's not the answer, kid.' Tony walked over and bent down so he was inches from Cristo's face. 'Do you want to hit me, kid? Knock me around a little?'

Cristo looked shocked. I suppose we all did. He replied tersely,

'No, of course not, Uncle Tony.' Cristo had always called Tony that since he was a kid.

'Why not? I'm giving you a load of shit, aren't I? So why not hit me?' Tony was pissed off and picking up momentum; we were all getting more than a little nervous. Cristo thought for a moment before he replied.

'Because that'd be crazy.'

Tony stood erect again and resumed pacing the room. 'No. Not crazy. If you three were crazy, I'd call this guy and ask him to give you all a pass. I'd tell him, "The poor fuckers are re-tarded, Denni; I'll up their Thorazine." And that might work, because people tend to forgive crazy. But they don't forgive stupid. For stupid you get whacked. And I'll tell you another fucking thing, Denni isn't stupid. You guys aren't made guys. If he whacks you out, I'm the only one he's got to worry about, and you want to know something? I might have to give him a pass. Do you know why?'

No one offered a response.

'I'll tell you why. Politics! This guy's got a lot of paid officials in his pocket. The same people the family does business with. The first thing this guy's going to do is retaliate. Then he's going to pick up the phone and call everyone he knows in the city, and then they're going to call the people I have to answer to and have them put pressure on me to stand down. Not wanting to disrupt millions of dollars of business, they'd have no choice. So don't tell me about crazy, no one kills retards.' Tony stopped pacing and gave us all another hard look. 'But they kill stupid fucks just like you guys every fucking day.'

No one said a word. The Micks had never seen him this mad before. To tell you the truth, neither had I. After a couple of minutes he started again. He was a little bit calmer.

'If we have another fuck-up like this I'm shutting it all down, *capisci?*' We all nodded. 'All right, let's fix this thing. Marco, get that piece of shit Denni on the phone. We have to end this thing before it gets out of control.'

I dialled the number and Denni picked up on the third ring. Not knowing what to say, I handed the phone to Tony. He introduced himself and then listened.

'Yeah, I heard about that; that's why I'm calling.' Tony paused again. 'Hey, Denni, listen to me. You all got a little stupid out there today and I don't give a fuck about who was more stupid. I just want to sit down and figure this thing out without any more fucking headaches, before we all get really stupid.'

Ever since I was a kid, Tony taught me things. One of those things was, 'Always listen with all your attention when people talk to you. That way you can hear what they're really saying.' The older I got the more I realised that he was right; people use words in a funny way. You just have to listen; the truth's there if you can just hear it.

Tony's face was emotionless as he listened to Denni. 'Well, I can give you my word, Denni, it'll be just a sitdown. This thing doesn't call for any bad shit. I'm sure you can all work it out. I'm just there to make sure none of you get stupid again.' Tony paused again briefly.

'Don't worry about it, Denni. I'll work out someplace neutral with lots of exposure. I'll get back to you with the details.' Tony handed the phone back to me to hang up.

'All right, I'm going to set this up for tomorrow afternoon. Marco, Cristo, you two are going with me.'

TC looked up at Tony, puzzled. 'What about me and Paws, Uncle Tony?'

'Denni's beef isn't with you two. You guys just backed up your crew. He wants an apology from these two,' he said, pointing to me and Cristo. 'And he's going to get one. And I'm sure that's just for starters.'

Paws looked at John and Shawn with relief; GG just sat there trying to be hard, he wasn't in the shit so he wasn't worried. But TC looked concerned. 'What else does he want?'

Tony grabbed his jacket off of the coat rack and turned to us as he put it on. 'We'll talk about that in the morning. Right now

I want you to do whatever it takes to get all that pot off your hands, quick-discount it cheap if you have to. And if you have any blow, get rid of it immediately. It's better to be safe than sorry. I'll work out this meeting and call you later.'

We all said goodbye and waited until the door closed before we started talking. TC was the first to start.

'Tony's right. We have to be smarter now. We fix this thing tomorrow, and concentrate on just moving blow and cleaning up cash. That way we don't get too close to anyone again. But first, any ideas on who we can offload large quantities of pot to?'

GG was busting to get a nickel's worth of time. 'I don't see why we have to apologise to that fuck Denni. Who does he think he is?'

I jumped right in on that. 'For starters, G, you don't have to say shit to anyone. Me and Face have to eat the shit, not you. Talking that fucking shit of yours, that's exactly what Tony was saying. He's got to play by a lot more rules then we do. He can't just whack out everyone we have a beef with.'

'I'm not saying he should.'

'Then what are you saying, G?'

'I'm saying we should whack Denni ourselves.' The look on G's face was one of self-importance and ignorance.

That's when I first realised just how stupid GG really was. I had to count to ten to regain my composure, which was quickly slipping away. 'G . . . Tony just got done telling you, Denni's not an easy guy to whack. Weren't you listening? I don't know who he's in bed with, but it's someone fucking heavy way up high. If Tony's thinking twice about it, we shouldn't even consider it.'

TC came in right behind me. 'He's right, G. Forget about it.'

GG didn't say anything. He just lit a cigarette and leaned back in his chair and folded his arms – back to the hard guy. It was obvious that he hated the fact that I had more clout than he did.

'Why don't we call Jose over in Spanish Harlem and offer him a good deal and some credit if he can take five hundred pounds off us?' That was the first thing John the Ace had said all day, which wasn't a surprise, he never said much.

TC, who was in deep thought, looked at me, and then everyone else. We were all in agreement. TC stood up and reached over towards me and slid the phone across the table to Johnny. 'He's good for it, Ace?'

'He'd never fuck us. He's solid.'

TC nodded in agreement. 'Give him a call and set up a meeting.'

While Johnny talked with Jose, TC turned to Paws. 'Paws, what about that guy you know in Queens that usually takes hundred-pound lots? Do you think if we drop forty a pound he'll take five hundred in one shot?'

Paws shrugged. 'I don't know, T, he's a pretty low-key guy, doesn't like to flash or shout too loud. I'll take a ride by and see him this afternoon. He's always got plenty of cash on hand.'

Before TC replied, Shawn sounded off. 'What about that rich kid from Providence? He moves a lot of weed, and money's definitely not a problem for him.'

TC nodded. 'That's a good idea, Shawn.'

John hung up the phone. 'He says he's interested. He'll meet me in thirty minutes, so I better split.'

TC stood up. 'Listen, Shawn, you go with John and check with Jose. Then stop at a payphone and call the rich kid. Get back to me on this tonight. Paws, you go and see your guy and call me later. Let's try to put this shit to bed as quick as we can. Tony's going to be expecting it gone in the morning and we've already pissed him off enough. Oh yeah, G, that Jewish guy you know in Manhattan. You think he might take the last K of blow?'

GG shrugged his shoulders. 'I don't know. I'll run by his restaurant and have a chat with him.'

'All right, great. If we can move all this in the next twenty-four hours then we'll have three days before the next shipment of blow. I think we should all go down to Atlantic City and have a little party.' That put a spring in everyone's step. Atlantic City was always a good time, and I loved going, but first we had to deal with the Denni problem.

Later that night Tony called me. 'I want you and TC to meet me at the clubhouse tonight. Ten o'clock sharp. Make sure you have a good bottle of wine. *Ciao.*'

TC and I took care of our business, left the warehouse and made sure we were at the clubhouse ten minutes early; enough time for a couple of glasses of wine to ease the stress that always rose inside us before one of those meetings with Tony.

'You know, TC, we need to get a safe for this place as well.'

TC didn't give it much thought. 'Yeah, sounds good.'

'It's going to have to be an in-the-floor model,' I said to myself aloud. TC was in his own world. 'Maybe I'll pick one up tomorrow after we meet Denni.' TC shrugged his shoulders.

There was a slight knock on the rear door. It was Tony. As usual, he scanned the room as he walked to the table, taking notice of every corner of the room. 'Why don't you clean this place up? A new coat of paint, some art on the walls . . . quit being Neanderthals.'

TC grabbed the bottle of wine off the counter and sat down at the table to pour. 'We've moved most of that pot today and have a guy lined up to take the last three hundred pounds tomorrow.'

'That's good news.' Tony raised his glass. '*Salute.*' After he sipped his wine we got straight to business. 'I spoke to Denni again a few hours ago.' TC and I didn't say anything, we just waited. 'To make this thing all right he's looking for an apology from Marco and Face . . . and an introduction to your guy in South America.'

TC looked incredulous. 'We can't give him an introduction. He'd know you're in the middle of this thing.'

Tony just sipped his wine and calmly replied, 'I thought about that. I'm going to take Paulie with me next time and introduce him to my guy. Then you can introduce Denni to Paulie. It's the only way we can make this thing fly.'

I didn't like the idea at all. I didn't like the idea of this guy giving us demands. 'Who the fuck is he that we have to give up our connection?' I started strong and ended meekly, trying not to upset Tony.

'He isn't anybody. But the guys he's greasing, and the guys he's doing business with are serious guys. This cocaine thing is taking off like wild fucking fire, and everybody wants in. Denni figures he can bring boatloads of this shit in.'

TC took a different tack. 'Why does he need our connection? He said he knew everyone down there.'

Tony gave TC a look. 'What, you believe everything you hear now?'

'No, I'm just saying.'

'Listen to me.' Tony paused. 'I'm sure he asked around with some heavy hitters down there. And the fact that he couldn't make your connection probably impressed him, and pissed him off. Forget about it. We're going to have to bring Paulie into the middle of this thing. We just don't let him, or Denni, find out how we're moving this shit. I'll have my guy down there introduce Paulie to a reliable local guy, that way we don't give too much up.'

It all sounded right but I didn't see why we should spend all that money for Paulie and one of us, probably G, to fly to South America to make an introduction. I felt we should be compensated for it.

'And what do we get out of it? For our trouble?' TC nodded at me. He was thinking the same thing.

Tony agreed. 'That's a fair question. It's going to cost some money and time. I don't know, tell Denni the price for this introduction is two uncut Ks, delivered up here. You guys whack it up with some cut and piece it into ounces. That should give us about a hundred grand; we'll all go to Vegas for a couple of days for the next big fight. Sound good?'

I nodded and TC tapped the table. 'Sounds real good, Uncle.'

TC loved Atlantic City, but he was crazy about Vegas. Heavyweight title fights were the hottest events on the planet. If TC had one weakness, it was a title fight. To be honest I liked them myself, but Cristo and I were the ones that had to go apologise the next day. I just wanted to get this thing out of the way, then I could get jazzed about Atlantic City or Vegas.

Meeting with Denni the next day wasn't as bad as I thought it would be. Cristo, Tony and me arrived ten minutes early at a small diner downtown and ordered a coffee. When Denni came in, Tony got up and went to the phone. I'm sure he did it so we wouldn't have to apologise in front of him. Denni just sat down like nothing ever happened.

'What's up, boys?'

I spoke up first. I didn't want to waste time.

'About that thing the other day, I just wanted to say sorry and hope there's no hard feelings.' I extended my hand to shake his. Denni nodded, smiled and shook my hand.

'No hard feelings, kid. You got balls the size of a tank; you both do If you ever need work, you call me.'

I just nodded.

Cristo jumped in, he wanted to get this over with as well. 'Ah, yeah, you know, ah, sorry about that thing.' And he stuck his hand out and they shook.

Denni might not have liked what happened at his sister's place but I think the fact that he was old enough to be our father took the edge off. Bottom line, he was a businessman. 'Now, about that connection.'

I didn't hesitate. 'Yeah, Denni, we can help you out with that. We can take you down to our guy – we'll pick up the expense of the trip. You meet our guy and give us a one-time three Ks of uncut blow, payment for our troubles.'

Denni wasn't smiling any more. 'Three fucking Ks? That's pretty fucking steep, isn't it?'

I wasn't moving on this one. I knew Tony might get pissed that I upped it from two to tree Ks, but I didn't care. I just didn't like the guy.

'Listen, Denni. There's a river of white gold getting ready to flow out of South America. By giving you the connection, it cuts into our business. The way we see it, three Ks, we're doing you a fucking favour here. That's the only deal we can offer you.'

I actually amazed myself. Guys like Tony, TC and Cristo, they would never hurt me, but I always backed down from them and tried to avoid confrontations. But over the years, guys like Denni, who were capable of crushing me, I never backed down from. I guess I didn't like the idea of someone like that making me do something I didn't want to.

He just looked at me hard and tried to see through me. I stared straight back at him. He slowly eased and nodded slightly. 'All right, kid, deal. When do I meet this guy?'

'We'll make the appointment in the next couple of days and let you know; probably a week, ten days on the outside.' That seemed to please him.

'Good. That's good. Call me when you get it fixed up.' Denni shook my hand and then Cristo's, and got up and stood over by the door. Tony walked over to the door as well.

Denni shook his hand. 'Take care of yourself, Anthony.'

Tony nodded. 'Yeah, you too.'

I don't know what it was, but something gave me the impression that this wasn't the first time they'd met. I didn't say anything, I had to think that one out. Tony left almost immediately, and then, Cristo. I said my goodbyes to them and then stayed there for another coffee.

I was trying to fit the pieces of the puzzle together, but they weren't fitting. One thing I was almost sure of, Tony and Denni were running some deal on the side. But what was it? I was going to have to pay attention and watch close. Tony was the rock and Denni was the hard place. The last thing I wanted was to be caught up between the two.

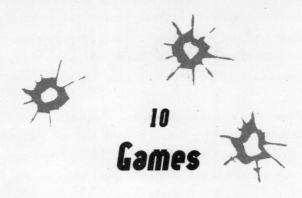

10
Games

Since time immemorial, people have loved games. Some people play games their whole lives, others stop once they've had enough losses and realise that the energy needed to play the games leaves them empty and unable to fulfil their intended dreams.

After a few years we were strong and seemed invincible. We hadn't changed much; not really. Better cars, better clothes, but mostly the same guys doing exactly the same thing.

One big difference was we had all the pistons firing and things were going pretty smooth. But by the third year of the operation we were all playing games. Some of us were playing honest games, spawned out of self-preservation and a 'happy ending'. Others were playing games of duplicity, motivated by greed and the desire to ensure they were the eventual winner of all of the games.

Paws was the easiest guy to read. The Micks – Shawn, Ace and Paws – had always felt a bit threatened because they knew that if we wanted to cut them out of the loop and stick it to them, we could, and there wasn't a damn thing they could do about it. But we never would have done that.

Paws' game was simple, he just wanted to make sure things went smooth and that Shawn and Ace didn't fuck up. He figured if they didn't give us an excuse, we wouldn't fuck them. So his game was to try and control as much as he could in his own group, and play us sweet, to keep the peace and ensure a winning position among all the winners at the end of the game. Game or not, Paws' motivations were as honest as anybody's. He just wanted to finish the game and walk into a new life with his wife and child.

Ace's game was a little different. He didn't want to fuck anyone. He loved the drug business, not just for the money but for the exalted position it put him in. If Ace had any ulterior motive, it was to walk away from the pact with us and head his own operation.

But on his own, as he was, he just didn't have the mind for the business. He didn't realise that the drug business was an endless money pit. The more money you made, the more you needed to spend on outside assistance and protection. Anyone can make a big splash of quick money in a short time and then get out. But to do it for years you need to buy all the help you can get. Which means you need heavy connections, and connections like that weren't going to get in bed with a two-bit street punk like him.

Now Shawn, he was driven by the dollar. This guy had a great mind, but it was always clouded with that thick fog that greed generates. His game was always optimising scenarios, calculating the odds. He asked a lot of questions, and never offered any information about what he'd hear on the street. I think he was just buying time, waiting for the big meeting so he could go his own way.

We still had more than three years to go of our seven-year pact. I think Shawn was the only one who was actually counting the days at that point; the rest of us just were getting on with what we had to do and enjoying all the fringe benefits. If he could have put his hands on the money we invested, which was more than half of what we were earning, I think he might've tried to pull one fast score and make a run. But I knew we had him in check and we didn't give any real worry to Shawn's game. As cloudy as his judgement was, he wasn't stupid. He wouldn't pull any shit until he had his cut of the assets stashed away somewhere safe.

Cristo was as straight as you could get, his game was self-preservation, and the preservation of our brotherhood. He got obsessed with knowing what everyone was doing. It was two years before TC and I found out that Cristo, along with one of his cousins, was keeping an eye on the Micks and GG. We only found out about his obsession when he came to us in the third year and told us he was worried about GG

It was already clear to me that GG was running on a bad path. His game was all fucked up. He was dealing dirty hands everywhere. When we were hesitant about giving him Ks – because he was disappearing for days on end – he started paying cash before he took them. He said he had a guy who was giving him the money up front. We figured he was probably using his own money and then cutting the K and selling it off that way; a dirty accusation that none of us wanted to prove.

GG's physical appearance had changed; he was getting thin and drawn. There was no doubt he was snorting, and maybe smoking a lot of product. We figured that was the motivation for piecing out one K a month – a free stash.

When Cristo came to TC and me, he told us GG was spending most of his time in the presidential suite at a swanky, uptown Manhattan hotel and dining out at all the high-end restaurants. GG was off the reservation and becoming a liability. As a result, the chances of us doing this thing for three more years without it blowing up were looking slim. We were going to have to talk with Tony; we just had to find the right time – we didn't want to get GG whacked.

TC's game was straightforward. He had to play the hard guy who kicked ass if anyone slipped up. His game was straight and he was great at it, even if he was getting a little carried away with the safety thing. He was always double-checking everyone to make sure they stuck with the procedures that I invented. It was probably one of the reasons we went as far as we did.

My game was simple. I was always trying to figure out who was playing what game. This took up a lot of my time and energy and it took me a couple of years to figure out Tony's game. What I learned about the game Uncle Tony was playing was a real eye-opener.

I learned that Uncle Tony had more games than Milton Bradley. He was juggling officials, gangsters, us, and who knows what else. But he was straight, he never played anyone dirty. If Uncle Tony was going to fuck someone, they had it coming. The game Tony was playing with Denni was one that I didn't like, but when I found out what it was, I understood why he made us apologise to Denni and share our connections.

I had been downtown Manhattan to meet this girl I'd been seeing. I was meeting her at a ritzy restaurant for lunch. I had brought her to my house the night before, and I never brought anyone to my place. I had just over a million dollars of my personal cash in a safe there and I didn't like the idea of anyone knowing where I lived. TC, Tony and Cristo were the only ones who had ever come to my place prior to that. Everyone else assumed I lived in one of the two houses we bought for cutting the blow and storing some of the cash. So it came as a surprise to me when I found myself inviting her to my house for dinner after just a handful of dates. There was something different about Julia D'Angelo and I was compelled to know more.

When I met Julia, she was working as a waitress at her parents' small Italian restaurant. When she came over to my table, I was instantly taken with her. It wasn't because she was the most beautiful woman I'd ever seen; don't get me wrong, she was very attractive, but that's not what struck me.

Her brown hair was tied back in a ponytail and the waitress's uniform she was wearing didn't exactly show off her great figure. As she approached the table she caught my eye and I was taken with her smile and her gracefulness. Her smile became somehow warmer and more knowing the nearer she got to the table, almost as if she was seeing an old friend.

Before I could gather my thoughts, she started speaking, 'Hi, I'm Julia. Today's special of the day is stuffed shells and meatballs. But everything on the menu is great; my dad's a great chef.'

Her blue eyes had a sparkle that seemed generated by some unidentifiable power source which was also transmitting great energy through her whole persona.

A bit off guard, I replied, 'I'm Marco . . . The special sounds great.'

I guess I looked as dazed as I felt because she let out a small laugh, wrote out my order and replied in the same sweet tone, 'It's nice to meet you, Marco. Is there anything else you'd like?'

Not sure what to say, I just looked into her eyes, smiled and replied casually, 'Yes, I'd like a glass of Coke, a cup of coffee after the meal and your phone number to go.'

She blushed and put her pen and her small pad in her apron without writing down the rest of my order and said, 'A man who knows what he wants, how unusual.' Then she turned and went off.

I figured I'd blown it by being too forward and tried not to make too much eye contact with her as she brought me my meal and coffee; I didn't want to make her feel uncomfortable.

When I finished my coffee, I gave her a small wave to catch her attention. She put up her index finger and said, 'One minute.'

I watched her as she carried a tray of discarded dishes across the room and into the back. She had an amazing glow about her and I was regretting saying something so stupid so quickly.

When she returned from the back, she went behind the counter briefly and returned carrying my bill. She looked at me with the same big smile and intensity as when I first set eyes on her. 'Here's your bill, Marco. It was nice to meet you, I hope you come in and see us again.'

I glanced at the bill so that I could pay her and noticed a

phone number written at the bottom of the page. 'Not only is the food great, the service is sensational,' I said calmly.

'I'm glad. We try to keep all of our customers happy, especially the ones we like.'

'Does that mean they all have your number, or is this the wrong number?'

Julia shook her head gently and bit her lip in the most attractive manner. 'Nope, they don't all have my number. We've been here two years and you're the first customer that I've given it to. And nope, it's not the wrong number . . . The best time to call is between four and six thirty. I work nights as well.'

From that moment on, Julia D'Angelo slowly made her way into my heart. And that's how I ran into Tony and Denni, they were having lunch in the restaurant where I had made plans to meet Julia. They didn't see me and I could have left without saying a word, but I was curious.

Now I had always thought Tony and Denni were doing something on the side, but I wasn't sure and I couldn't ask what it was. I figured if I walked by, and they saw me, they'd have to say hello. So I walked by and I heard Tony's voice. 'Marco, what are you doing here?'

I didn't want Tony to think I was keeping tabs on him or that I was staging this encounter. I approached the table casually and Tony got up and gave me a hug and a kiss on the cheek. I turned and offered my hand to Denni.

'Hey, Denni, how's things?'

'Yeah, I'm all right, kid. You want some wine?'

I accepted the offer and sat down at their table. 'I won't stay, you guys probably have business to discuss. Anyways, I'm meeting this chick here for lunch.' They both looked at me a bit suspiciously which made me really hope that Julia showed up or they might think I really had staged this thing.

We chatted for a few minutes and I really wanted to go to the payphone and call Julia, but that might look like I'm calling some bimbo to cover a deception. Now I know it sounds like paranoid thinking, but it's not. That's exactly how these types of guys are. They pay attention to detail better than Sherlock Holmes did. If Julia didn't show, they were going to have concerns, maybe even doubts.

About ten minutes later I saw Julia walk into the reception area. Relieved, I stood up and gave her a wave; she smiled and headed over to Tony's table. As she approached, I couldn't take my eyes off her. Everything inside me seemed to come alive and I tried to compose myself.

I got up and gave her a big kiss and turned to Tony, who was looking at me with one of those looks that said, 'I don't want to know.' I think he knew I was falling for Julia then. At that time I wasn't thinking about the future, I was just enjoying the time I spent with her.

'Listen, guys, thanks for the drink. I'll call you next week and we'll look at those blueprints. Take it easy.'

I didn't wait for a reply. I just grabbed Julia's hand and headed towards the hostess. I was feeling relieved. Tony and Denni would never doubt my story now, and the next time I saw Tony, I could throw out a question about him having lunch with Denni, which was exactly what I did, two weeks later.

Tony had invited me over to his house for lunch one afternoon, as he did from time to time. Aunt Francesca was very old-fashioned, she would make something nice and then leave the two of us in his study to eat and talk. After we finished our lunch, Francesca cleared away the debris and left us in peace, closing the door behind her.

Sitting alone in any room with Tony can be intimidating. But sitting in Tony's study, that was overwhelming because, unlike the rest of the house which had been decorated by Aunt Francesca, everything in Tony's study was there by Tony's design.

Three of the walls were lined with walnut bookshelves that were shaped and detailed to perfection. And the books, they were the 'right books', as Tony would often say. First editions of the classics, ancient editions of the great Greek, Chinese and Italian philosophers, the most complete collection of books on history that I'd ever personally seen, a complete wall of shelves dedicated to astronomy, alchemy and physics; a collection that took Tony years to complete and would be almost impossible to duplicate today.

The wall that wasn't lined with books was used as a display for Tony's collection of ancient weapons. In the middle of the wall were two original Japanese Shogun swords, and surrounding them several different types of revolvers and old muskets. Add Tony to the setting and you can be intimidated instantly.

As per usual, Tony started the conversation. 'So how's things going, kid? You taking care of yourself?'

'Yeah, I'm good. TC wants to have a chat with you, though.' Tony knew that meant something was up.

'Anything that needs to be dealt with right away?'

'No, not today. It's just, ah, GG's running a bit fucked up lately. We're concerned. We think maybe GG needs a kick in the ass from you. TC might take it too far if he starts.'

'Right. Tell TC I'll be at the clubhouse tomorrow night at seven. I want to stay away from that warehouse as much as I can. You don't need any extra attention over there. Everything else OK? I hope you're putting away most of the coin you're making?'

'Yeah, it's all good. I got my cash stashed away, plus my cut of the investments we've made.'

'Good. That's real good, kid. Now, what's the story with that little honey you had at the restaurant a couple of weeks ago? She a regular fixture yet?'

'Julia? No, she's just a nice girl who wants to have some fun. I told her I was self-employed and couldn't offer her too much of my time. It's perfect really, she never asks questions.' This wasn't exactly the truth. I was actually spending a lot of time with Julia, but I was nervous about how Tony would take it; 'Love can cloud the mind,' he always said.

Tony nodded. 'So, how did you meet this girl?'

94

'She works at a little diner her parents run across town. She's just a real nice girl, Uncle Tony; no story.'

'That's good. Bring her by for Sunday dinner next week, I want to know who this broad is.'

I gave Tony a look like he was crazy. 'What are you talking about, Uncle?'

'Either you're not telling me the whole truth about how you feel for this girl, or you're fucking stupid. I could see it a mile away, that day in the restaurant; the girl's in love with you and you're a fucking goner – which is probably a good thing for you.'

I didn't want to discuss Julia and decided it was a good chance for me to change the subject. 'So what's up with you and Denni, Uncle?'

Tony paused, looked me straight in the eyes. 'I knew you'd ask, eventually, that's why I asked you over today.' He paused briefly. 'This is strictly between you and me. *Capisci?*'

'Absolutely.'

'Denni's been moving some arms for me to Central America. The deal's worth a boatload to me and my partners. We put a couple of deals together a couple of years ago, before you and Cristo got heavy with Denni. I couldn't let it fall apart, too much money involved. Not to mention, I've got plans. In the next four, five years I want out, from everything. I'll have plenty put away, and then I just want things to be easy.'

'That sounds great. But how you going to pull that off?'

'I don't know yet. Maybe I'll get my doctor to say I've got cancer and only a couple of years left. I've made a lot of money for the family, they'll give me their blessings, and I'll go to some country for special treatment, and when I don't die within two years, who's going to bother me?'

I nodded my head. 'Sounds like a plan. Why wait four years? You have more money than God.'

'Because this thing is rolling big right now. And it's not just about the money, kid. It's about taking this thing the whole way. A king doesn't give up his castle just because he's got an army at the gate; he goes out and does battle. He holds the reins of power for as long as he can.'

I didn't like the sound of that. I was wondering how many knights had to die to ensure the battle.

I guess Tony sensed my uneasiness. He grabbed a cigar, eased up on the intensity and said, 'I'm thinking, next spring, we'll start slowing it down; let it peter out. It'll take a year or two after that to wrap it all up.'

'To be honest with you, Uncle Tony, I think it's going to be difficult making the next two years. I think it's starting to come undone now.'

'We're going to have to kick some ass and get this thing right. We have partners to consider. When you're at the table playing poker with these guys, you can't just quit when you're ahead, can you? You have to be smart, kid. *Capisci?*

'Yeah, I understand everything. I'm just saying that we have to kick some ass in our own house.'

'You just leave that to me, kid. I'll keep them straight, even if I have to set an example or two.'

I didn't like the sound of 'setting an example', but I didn't say anything. It was time to wrap up our little meeting.

'Listen, Uncle, I have to go, but I'll see you soon.'

'I'll see you next Sunday for dinner, with the girl. Right?'

'Right.'

I left and pondered where this whole thing was going but, like anyone else, I couldn't see what waited around the corner.

Like always, Tony was true to his word. He met with TC, myself and Cristo. We gave him the skinny and he said he'd straighten GG out. I don't know what he said to him, maybe it was a couple of scary words, or even the cold barrel of a gun in his mouth, but for the next six months GG seemed to pull his shit together.

Looking back, I should have known the game was about to change, like all games do when the stakes change. I felt like the centre just couldn't hold much longer. But I had always trusted

Tony and he'd never let me down. Then again, I hadn't seen this side of Tony before – the Tony that was more concerned with the reins of power than getting from point A to point B. I just put my head down and played hard for the coach, even if I didn't agree.

It's like any great football or basketball dynasty riding on the clouds of glory for a few years. The big players get tired, the less talented get greedy and the whole industry is full of hot-blooded young rookies trying to knock the champs off the top of the hill for their own fifteen minutes of fame and fortune.

I suppose it's a nightmare for any coach to hold all that together. But the thing is, even if I had seen it all coming, I couldn't have stopped it. Tony made it clear we were all in this thing until the game was over. I wasn't even thinking about winning the game, I just wanted to make sure I survived long enough to see the finish line.

11
We Got Problems

It was the summer of 1982 and life hadn't really changed much. We were still moving our 17 Ks a week like clockwork. The truth is, if we'd had 100 Ks a week coming in, we still could have moved it all, no problem. The Micks and GG felt we should be bringing in more, we were losing a lot of fucking money, according to them. But TC, Cristo and I were happy with the arrangement.

As it was, I was spending forty to fifty hours a week moving money around and finding property to invest in, plus all the other, business-related work that I had to do. I didn't have a lot of free time. I guess that's when the constant knot in my stomach arrived. I was counting the days until I could walk away.

Julia and I were solid as could be and I still hadn't told her about my real business. Saturdays and Sundays were the days when I usually had time to spend with her and we often shared it with my sister Maria and her husband.

Maria's husband, Danny, was a hard-working construction guy and I helped them with the money to buy their first house. Danny spent six months fixing the place up and made a real nice home for them all. Unlike my other sisters, Maria was the only one to move back down to the city, and my little brothers were still at home with the folks.

Whenever I had time off, Julia and I would get together with

Maria and Danny at their place. Danny was a real family guy and loved staying home with his wife and two young sons. I really enjoyed the time spent with them. Not that we did anything fancy. It was just good home cooking, a lot of card playing, usually whist because the girls preferred it to bridge. Sometimes Julia and Maria would try to persuade me to pick up the telephone and call my folks, but I couldn't do that.

Once, while Julia and I were at Maria's, my mother called and Maria gave the telephone to me. I tried to talk to her but she just cried and cried, and that didn't give me any confidence to attempt a reunion with my dad.

My mother was very sweet and loved all of her children. But the bottom line was she had to choose between me and my dad. And I was relieved she chose my dad; I was a risky bet and I knew it. My whole life could come crashing in at any moment and I was more than aware of that.

The deeper I fell in love with Julia, the more the knot in my stomach tightened. As far as I was concerned, that was as much emotion as I could risk. If I attempted to bridge the gap with my dad, and got pinched, or killed, it would be like they were losing me again. I just couldn't do that to them, so it was easier to keep my distance.

The property market was starting to wake up and it seemed a good idea to do a little speculation development. This turned out to be real good for us. The thing is, if we had been smart, we could have quit moving blow and still made an easy $200,000 a year each through our property portfolio. But try and explain that one to Uncle Tony or the others.

In the beginning we bought tired old houses that needed a lot of work. We were buying them cheap because the real estate market was in the toilet. The motivation, at first, was just to have a legitimate front, an air of respectability.

The guys bitched at the expenses: taxes, accountants, overheads. But all of a sudden, houses that cost us $60,000, including the remodelling, had market values of $200,000. That should have been good news for us, but it only caused more unrest. A few guys wanted to sell. Once again, it was GG and the Micks against TC, Cristo and me.

TC wasn't going to give in on that one, and neither was I. TC figured it was all that money tied up in property, money the others couldn't touch without TC and me approving, that kept everyone straight. If we sold up and split the money, which would have been about six million apiece, it would have been a free-for-all. Including our weekly pay from the construction company, we were all bringing in more than twenty thousand a week, and we spent a lot of it on extravagances that weren't needed.

When we first decided on using a construction company for a front, we had no idea how perfect it would be. We chose it because TC and I knew something about it and we'd always been told to stick with what we knew.

As it turned out, there was an amazing amount of money to be made in construction if you did it right, though in our case our profits were shit in reality. Unlike some contractors, who cheat to hide profits, we padded our profits by paying cash for goods and services and throwing away the receipts. It sounds crazy, but in doing so we created a huge tax deficit which we paid to keep the IRS off our backs. You have to pay taxes – just look at what happened to Al Capone.

In the five and a half years since we started moving blow, we took in over five million dollars each, which didn't include the real estate investments. We had a bit of a party and didn't save as much as we should have. I only managed to stash away about $1.3 million, which is not very good. But I had a beautiful four thousand square foot Victorian home that took a bite out of my savings, and a fleet of vehicles. The trucks were owned by the business but the two luxury cars were mine. On top of all that, I helped out my three sisters with their houses as well.

The scary thing is I wasn't even close to being the worst offender. Cristo spent all his free time at the track, dog *and* horse.

101

Aside from the nice home and two sports cars he owned, I'd be surprised if he had a hundred grand to his name.

TC, he was solid, but he bought everyone in his family a house with a swimming pool. For his friends, they just got pools; he had a thing for swimming pools. The pool contractor loved him. One summer every pool he did was for TC, and that was a fair amount of pools. The pool guy not only did all of our pools, he became one of the family; he ended up marrying one of TC's sisters and becoming the godfather to one of my nephews.

GG was a real nightmare, he was Mr GQ. His thing was the big flash, the twenty-four-hour limousines, presidential suites, first-class tickets. Nothing was ever too flash for GG, he wouldn't think twice about dropping fifty grand for tickets for him and his cousins to go to the Super Bowl. They'd fly first class, get thousand-dollar a night hookers, stay at the best of best hotels – totally over the top. If it was his idea, it had to be the best. The real kicker was, if he owed you a hundred bucks on a bet from a football game, he'd piss and moan about having to pay you.

Paws, well he half tried. He would never take more than twenty grand to Atlantic City for a weekend, and he never bet the horses or dogs. His real problem was his wife. She spent more money shopping than any woman I've ever seen.

In all fairness, Susan didn't spend it all on herself. She took care of the kid real good and made sure Paws had everything he needed. She took care of her widowed mom as well. Susan was just a shopping junky, it didn't matter who she was buying for. At the end of the day, they lived a lifestyle as good, if not better, than an uptown attorney. It didn't seem to bother Paws though; he loved her a lot and was glad he could do that for her. As far as I knew, he never cheated on her. Whatever his shortcomings were, infidelity wasn't one of them. Paws found a great life and was truly content. He loved his wife and daughter more than he loved life itself. And he had us, his friends; that was all he needed. He was a solid guy who kept his mouth shut, did what he was told and played the Steady Eddy to a T.

Ace was a nonstop party and card game. He'd win a hundred grand in a thirty-hour card game, and then go lose twice as much with the local bookies and the horse track. And he was the only one who didn't own a home. Ace was actually a more degenerate gambler than the Chinese, and the Chinese are the worst fucking degenerate gamblers that ever came down the pike. Bottom line, Ace's biggest and darkest demon was gambling.

Now Shawn, he was the exception to the rule. I'd be willing to bet he probably had at least ten million dollars at that time. The more he made, the more he wanted. Shawn only gambled when we went to a big fight; he never bet on horses, dogs or sporting events. Shawn's two big things were the stock market . . . and Shawn.

One of Shawn's customers was a Wall Street lawyer with a drug problem. Shawn was cuffing him blow without any problems. When the guy got in deep, Shawn, apparently told the guy he'd squash the bill for a little inside information. I only know that because Ace and I got shit-faced one night and he told me about it. Ace was pissed off that Shawn didn't cut us in. I just said, 'Forget about it.' I knew if we told TC and the guys, we'd have a big problem. I just wanted to get through the next eighteen months.

Some guys are born selfish, some guys become that way as a result of being mistreated. With Shawn, I think he was just fucking angry with himself because he didn't like himself.

I think the fact that his father, who had abandoned him, his sister and mother, left a sizeable fortune to charity and not a dime to him or his mother when he died was probably the beginning of a cancer that would grow inside Shawn and eat away anything good that once may have been there.

Unlike the rest of the guys, I knew that Tony was getting out. We'd be without his protection moving the product from South America and I didn't want anything to do with that. I was starting to enjoy the construction business and figured that's what I would do. I just had to get through the last leg of this thing.

There was something else on my mind. I was almost twenty-six years old and hadn't seen my dad or mom in almost twelve years, I was in love with Julia and I really wanted to settle down, get married and have a family of my own. I guess I was starting to realise that this life that I was leading probably didn't include happy ever after.

The best chance I had to rebuild my life and the bridge to my family was to get myself out the drug business and completely immersed in an honest living. Then I could look my father in the eye and say, 'Dad, everything I'm involved in is legal and I'm sorry for all the shit.' At least then maybe dialogue could begin.

Later that summer we got a call from Tony saying he wanted to see all of us. He set a meeting at the clubhouse and I made sure everyone was there. I had no idea what was up, I just figured he was going to give us one of those 'don't fuck up now, things are good' talks.

I was the first guy to arrive at the clubhouse that night and I grabbed a cold beer, took a seat at the card table and quietly sat alone with my thoughts for a minute. As I scanned the room I realised that the clubhouse had become a mausoleum to our lives.

After all of these years, the four wooden swords that we used to do battle with as kids still hung in the same spot on the wall. Five empty bottles of Barbosa still sat on the same shelf collecting dust, each representing the five New Year's Eve celebrations that had passed since our pact. Two more bottles to go. In less than two years I'd be able to walk away and start a new life, a desire that had been gnawing at my soul for a long time.

As my eyes passed over all the baseball and football memorabilia, thousands of great memories the seven of us had had together went through my mind in a flash. But then my attention was caught by a familiar sight that didn't fit.

The deck of cards was sitting right where it always did, but it had a light coat of dust covering it. That wasn't right. In the previous years a week wouldn't go by without a couple of nights of cards. The dust made me realise that it had been a couple of months since any of us had sat down together for a night of cards, booze and amusement. These thoughts were going through my head when TC and Cristo arrived. They were in the middle of a disagreement.

'Listen, Face, I don't want to hear about it, not tonight. We still have a long way to go before we start looking at Italy. Just forget about it for now, will you?'

'*Dimenticarto!*' Cristo muttered to himself in Italian. He gave me a nod by way of greeting and sat to my left. *Dimenticarto*, means 'forgotten'.

I knew he had been at TC for more than a year to go to Italy with him to buy a place there, and TC had promised to do it, but after three trips to Italy, two with me and one with Cristo, TC still hadn't made the commitment. I was staying out of it. They had asked me if I was interested in buying a place there and I'd declined. I loved the old country, but I wasn't ready to take that big step until I rebuilt the bridge with my parents.

TC looked around the room and was visibly pissed off that no one else had shown up yet.

'Where the fuck is everybody?'

I was sitting with my back to TC and turned my chair around enough so that I could see him out of the corner of my eye. Then I casually shrugged my shoulders and didn't bother with a reply. TC had been on edge for a few months and these days I just dismissed the bullshit when he started up.

When he didn't get any reaction out of me, he picked up the telephone and dialled a number. As he waited for someone to pick up at the other end, he shot me a glare. I knew he was pissed off and was looking to start with anyone who would engage with him; I wasn't playing into that hand.

For a while now TC had been acting a bit nuts – stressed out is more like it. He saw it as his duty to hold our worlds together. Plus, on top of that, every time one of his sisters had financial problems they'd call him and expect him to save the day, and he'd do it. That wasn't what was bothering him though.

For a couple of years now there had been a lot of stories floating around the streets. Stories of small dealers getting busted, going missing or just showing up dead. The cocaine trade was turning in on itself and no one could stop it. Junkies were robbing dealers, dirty cops were busting junkies, making them talk and then robbing the dealers, dealers were robbing each other. It was getting like the Wild West. Everyone was packing a gun and trying to knock the king off the mountain for a little bit of white gold.

TC was still giving me the evil eye and I just pretended I didn't notice.

'What the fuck's with you these days?'

I didn't like TC's tone, but I knew it wasn't me he was upset with; he was just burnt out, so I tried not to overreact.

'What are you talking about, T? I'm sitting here minding my fucking business.'

'Your sister, Maria. She's called me three times this week, says she can't get hold of you.'

'That's not my fucking problem. If it was important she'd leave a message.'

'Well, it must be important or she wouldn't keep calling me.'

'She thinks she's my fucking mother. Asks me a million fucking questions and wants me to call in and let her know that I'm all right . . . I don't answer to anybody, T. I do what I'm supposed to do so leave me the fuck alone, all right? You know, T, why don't you go get yourself laid and I'll drink my beer here, and we'll both be fucking happy.' I was starting to get angry and T was getting even worse, partly because I was giving him shit back, and partly because the Micks weren't here and he couldn't get them on the phone.

TC put the telephone receiver down in its cradle and turned to me. I knew he didn't really want to beef with me, and I definitely didn't want to beef with him; we were all just feeling the strain of the constant pressure that our chosen way of life breeds. He took a few steps towards me, stopped and gave me a real hard look.

'What, you don't have to answer to no one, huh? Not your partners? Not your fucking family? So I guess you must be ready to go solo now that you're such a big fucking man!'

I got up off my seat and put my can of beer on the table. Cristo instantly jumped up and stood between us.

'Tommaso! *Basta!* You're being an asshole here.' Cristo's tone was formidable, but TC didn't flinch.

'Stay out of this, Face, this ain't your game.'

'I can't do that, T. You're out of line.'

Now TC started to get really angry and I'm not sure how it would have gone down if we hadn't been interrupted by the door opening and the sound of Uncle Tony's voice; he was obviously pissed off as well and in mid-conversation.

'What the fuck is going on here? You think this is a fucking game?'

With that, John, Shawn and Paws meekly entered the clubhouse with Tony right behind them giving them shit for being late. He would have continued his tirade, but when he saw TC and me looking fired up, with Cristo between us, he dropped the verbal assault on the Micks and started in on us.

'What the fuck is this?' Tony was looking right at TC when he said it, so I just sat down and continued drinking my beer. Cristo sat down as well.

TC casually turned to Tony and nodded. 'Hey, Uncle, how are you?'

'I'm just fucking dandy. Now that you know how I'm feeling, how about answering my question. What in the fuck is going on here?'

'It's nothing, Uncle. I was being an asshole, it's nothing.'

'An asshole?'

I guess Cristo thought he'd continue his diplomatic efforts because he leaned back in his chair with a serious, fatherly expression and said, 'That's exactly what I was telling T just before you come in, Tony. He was being a real asshole here. But everything's fine now . . . so that's good, right?' As Cristo finished

107

he was nodding in a knowing way that suggested he held a day job at the UN and only sold drugs in his spare time, you know, part of his get out and feel the pulse of the people venture.

Tony just shot him a 'you must have a mountain of shit between your ears' look and then turned his attention to everyone else in the room.

'I don't know what the fuck is going on here but you silly fucks better get it together. And I mean right fucking now. Because if you stupid fucks think I'm going down because you couldn't hold it together, you're mistaken. I'll whack you all out and shut it down before that happens.' Tony took a long pause and eyeballed all of us, then continued. 'Now listen to me, and listen to me good. We've got some real problems to deal with. My connections in the agency tell me there's a couple of undercover DEA agents working the city and they're getting ready to close in on a bust. We're going to shut down for a couple of months.'

Everyone was shocked because it was the last thing we expected.

I was the first to speak up. 'Do we have any idea who they're going to pinch?'

'No. The only thing we got so far is that it's a couple of gangster types. Which could be just about anyone in the city. My guys are doing their best to get more information.' Tony poured a glass of wine. 'It probably wouldn't be a bad idea for you guys to take a vacation, get out of town for a couple of weeks, enjoy yourselves. In a month or so we'll see where we are.'

No one responded right away. As for myself, I liked the idea of taking some time off. I'd been getting uneasy about our whole operation. The fact was, we were losing our edge and we just weren't as sharp as we had been. Then GG decided to share some of his wisdom with us.

'It's simple. We have these connections of yours, Tony, so we find out who these guys are and we whack them.' He tried looking important as he said it. I think Paws was the only one in the room who didn't see just how stupid the idea was. He nodded in agreement and was about to speak but Tony interrupted him.

'GG, if I hear you say anything that fucking stupid again I'm going to give you a lobotomy.' GG shrunk down in his chair, he hated being ridiculed. 'If we whack out those guys, the fucking city will be crawling with undercover assholes from agencies you've never even heard of. The smart move is to sit tight and keep clean. We need to find out who they're going to nab. If it's no one we know, we let them have them. If it's a friend of ours, we let them know they've got trouble coming. If it's one of your customers, we whack him. That will cut any ties to your crew.' Tony got up and finished his wine, he was getting ready to leave.

'Like I said, take some time, enjoy yourselves and get your heads back in the game. And make sure you keep TC or Marco updated on how to get in touch with you. And TC, Marco, you two check in with me every day this week.' Tony grabbed his hat and turned to GG. 'Tomorrow's run is off – all runs are off at the moment, just in case you didn't get that part, G. I'll see you guys later.'

As soon as Tony walked out the door, I spoke right up, mostly so GG wouldn't dwell on the last hard comment Tony had given him; I could see in his eyes he was pissed off, no one wants to look stupid.

'Well, I don't know about you girls, but when I finish up this property deal next week I'm going upstate for some R and R. I've got to get away from this fucking city.'

GG once again had to get his two cents in.

'What piece of shit property did you buy for us now, kid?'

I was feeling the strain of spending too much time with the guys in a high-stress environment. I still hadn't calmed down from the conflict with TC and GG was being a prick. I was on my feet and standing over him so fast no one had a chance to stop what was now in motion.

'Get the fuck up off your ass, G!' He tried to look hard, but I could see the fear in his eyes. He stood up, probably thinking someone was going to grab me before it got too far. As he was getting up he started running his mouth.

'Give it a fucking rest, Mar—'

Before he finished saying my name I punched him in the face and sent him back into the sofa. The punch dazed him and put a deep cut on his left cheekbone that bled profusely. But that wasn't enough for me. I reached over, grabbed him by his hair and lifted him off the sofa with my left, then punched him in the face three more times with my right. 'You got a fucking problem with me, G? You want to be a tough guy?'

TC grabbed me by the shoulder but I pulled away and threw another shot at GG. Then I was ripped backwards with an amazing force and lost my grip on GG. I knew for sure it had to be Cristo tearing me away. Aside from Paws, who I could see standing against the wall at the far side of the room, Cristo was the only guy with enough power to pull me off of my feet and send me halfway across the room. I knocked over two chairs before I hit the wall. Cristo, who was now in front of me, grabbed me by the chest and held me against the wall; he knew I had a bad temper and was taking precautions.

'Marco, it's me, Cristo. Take it easy, buddy. It's over!'

I came back to my senses and dropped my guard, but I was still pissed off. TC, who always took control of situations, went over to GG, who was sitting on the couch holding his broken nose. 'Are you all right G?'

'Yeah. Fuck this shit!'

That was it. TC's patience left the building. 'GG, cut the fucking shit right fucking now before I finish what the kid started. *Capisci?*

GG calmed down immediately. The last thing he wanted was TC starting on him. 'All right, T, take it easy.'

I had calmed down but still had something to say. 'G, if you or anybody got a problem with any of the properties, I'll buy your share out, cash, tomorrow, you fucking idiot.'

Cristo grabbed my arm and I quieted down again. 'Just so you know, GG, I've made more legal money for us on those properties then you could make in three lifetimes.'

GG, who didn't know when to just shut his mouth, still had to throw a little shit. 'Yeah, whatever, Marco, we'll see.' The way he said it was like a veiled threat.

Cristo let go of my arm and calmly walked over to GG. 'Listen, G, you let this go right fucking now or I'll cut you and feed you to the fish. You got a fucking attitude lately, and you been acting stupid. You asked for your face to be all fucked up.' He paused. No one said anything. 'Now, G, we've all been friends a long time. We got this thing, this business here. You have to suck it up and let it go.' Then he turned to me. 'What do you say, kid? You got a problem with G?'

'No, I got no problem, I never did.'

'Right. Well, why don't you tell G here you're sorry for fucking up his face.'

I didn't want to apologise, but the truth was, I loved G like a brother, he was just getting a bit stupid. I suppose all of us were getting a little stupid in those days. Making that kind of money when you're young can be bad medicine, especially when you have two guys like G and myself who had been in competition with each other since we were just boys. I knew the right thing to do was apologise. 'Hey, G, I'm sorry. I just feel like you've been breaking my balls lately.'

GG looked up and shook his head. 'Yeah, it's probably my fault, kid.' When he said 'kid', he smiled, the way he used to when we were just kids. I laughed and walked over and shook his hand. For the moment everything was fine. We were all looking forward to a bit of a holiday and taking a break from cleaning money, running drugs, and fighting with each other.

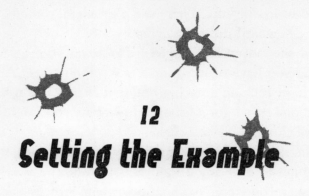

12
Setting the Example

We all went off in different directions for our mandatory vacation. Cristo and GG went to Atlantic City with G's two cousins, Vito and Donato. They were from Sicily and had come to visit G in the Big Apple. I think Cristo wanted to keep an eye on GG and rebuild any damaged bridges.

Ten days later TC and I closed the deal on two new buildings we'd bought and I dropped him at the airport. He was going to Italy for a month and asked me to join him, but I declined. I just wanted to get away on my own with Julia. I had asked her to move in with me a couple of months before, and this was the first time we would spend any real quality time together, away from the city and all the shit that came with it.

I took Julia up to Newport to go sailing for a week on my new sailboat. Then we were going to upstate New York because Uncle Tony had a big house on seven acres of land that he said I could use, and I really liked it up there. It was a place where nothing from my life back in the city could touch me.

It was hard to describe but something inside me changed during those six weeks of vacation. I knew that it was Julia who was responsible for the newfound glow in my soul, but that wasn't all of it. What was new was that for the first time in my life I actually wanted to share my life with someone completely.

I wanted to marry Julia. There was a problem, though; Julia still had no idea what I did for a living.

Before she moved in, there were a lot of questions. Things like, 'Why did you have to stay out so late some nights?' And, 'Why do you have such an amazing house at such a young age?' And then the one that I got a lot of: 'How come you can afford such expensive clothes and nice cars?'

At first, I found ways to satisfy her curiosity by simply bringing her to a closing on a piece of property I was buying; it was all very legit. Not to mention, when someone really loves you, they want to believe everything.

Asking Julia to move in was very difficult for me. I didn't want her to know what I was up to, but I didn't want to lose her either. She had made her position very clear, if I was serious about our relationship, it had to move further along. And moving in together is one of those natural steps you take on that journey.

Once she moved in, I made it a point to bring her along with me to meet with contractors when it was time to pay them. Then she offered to help out with some of the day-to-day book-keeping that took up so much of my time. It was perfect, within a month she was sold, hook, line and sinker – I was a very successful contractor who stayed out late playing poker a few nights a week.

Julia was a poorly paid waitress from a poor immigrant Italian family, but she gave me more than any person I had known in my past. She had a quality that you couldn't equate with any monetary value; she was the light that I was drawn to.

She smiled a lot and found an extraordinary amount of happiness in the simple things that life offered. The most important goal in Julia's life was to be married and have a family. Don't get me wrong, Julia liked the big house and the nice perks that went along with it, but if I had lost it all she would have stuck it out and made do with almost anything – she was down-to-earth, warm-hearted and as real as any human being I've ever met.

Sailing in Newport was great, but when we went upstate to Tony's place on the lake, we felt we belonged there. It just seemed like a perfect place to start a family and a new honest life.

So, one morning, while we were out for a quiet drive, we saw a two-acre parcel of land for sale and I bought it. I decided that the following year, when we started to slow down the drug business and get out, I'd build myself a big house and I hoped that Julia would still be around to help make it a home; I just had to keep myself focused and Julia in the dark about the cocaine trade for a little longer.

The other upside to buying and building upstate was my father and the rest of my family only lived thirty minutes away. Not long after I left home, he decided to get his family out of the city; he had already lost one son to the streets, there wouldn't be any more 'street casualties' from his brood if he could help it.

Two days before we were supposed to head back to the city, Tony called. He didn't tell me what was up, he just said that we had some things to take care of. The dread that had been exorcised from my soul during the time with Julia was suddenly back again. I explained to Julia that there was a problem with one of my construction projects and I needed to get back right away.

It was an outright lie and bothered me more than a little, but that's one of the prices you have to pay when you cross the line and run on the wrong side of the law. At least that's where it starts; how far you can fuck up your sense of morality from there is anyone's guess. The only thing that's sure is if lying to your girlfriend is the worst thing you did on any given day, you were doing pretty fucking good.

I dropped Julia at her place, called Tony and went straight to his house. 'What's going on, Uncle Tony?' I could see from his eyes he was pissed off.

'That stupid, overgrown Mick, Paws. He's gone off the reservation.'

My stomach knotted. 'What do you mean? How?'

'A week after I told you fuckers to lay low, that dumb fuck went to Denni and bought five Ks of blow, and started moving it around town – with different connections, guys he didn't know.'

'How could he be that stupid?'

'Well, he doesn't have any idea that Denni and I are moving guns to Central America. As far as he knows, I only met Denni through you guys that one time. I've known him for years.'

This admission about Denni didn't come as a surprise, and I figured there was more to it than running guns with him, but now wasn't the time to ask questions. 'I still can't believe Paws could be that stupid.'

'Well, that's the problem, he is that stupid. And wait till you hear the rest. He sold a couple of ounces to Louie's kid, Angelo, who's a fat shit anyway and thinks he can fuck anyone around who he wants, because his dad's a made guy.' Tony paused and lit a cigar. I didn't want to hear the rest of this shit, I knew where it was going, but I had to sit there and accept what I knew was coming. Once Tony got his cigar rolling he continued.

'So anyway, Angelo and his cousin, Joey Mazzero, another fucking beauty, tried to stiff Paws. Well, I guess it got out of hand and Paws went for them and now Angelo and Joey are in the hospital. Angelo might not make it.'

'What about Paws, is he all right?'

'What, are you kidding me? You can't hurt that stupid fuck. He's got some bruises, I hear, but he's all right . . . for now.' It was the way Tony said 'for now' that confirmed my worst fears. Paws was going to get whacked.

'So where are we, Uncle. Can we fix this thing?'

'There's nothing I can do, kid. That's why I called you as soon as TC came by and gave me the news. He's at the warehouse with Paws and the rest of your crew. I told him to keep that overgrown retard out of sight.' Tony put his cigar in the ashtray and began massaging his jaw with his right thumb and forefinger. This was where he had to lay down the law.

'I seen Louie this morning, he wants to whack Paws and there's no way out of it. I can't get him a pass, kid, it's not going to happen.'

I was getting stressed. I couldn't believe how fucked up this thing was getting. The only thing I did know was that I had to sit back and do what I was told. 'What if he gets out of town, Tony, just disappears? Will that work?'

'Listen, kid, I told Louie I was going take care of this thing myself, as a favour to him.'

'Oh fuck that, Uncle Tony, this is fucking crazy!'

Tony tensed and leaned in towards me. 'Listen to me, I told you guys before, you step out of line, make a mistake or just get unlucky in this game, you're going to go down.'

I just sat there feeling angry, lost and confused. Tony could see I wasn't happy with any of this and eased up a little.

'Listen, kid, don't get all emotional about this. I'm going to cut you guys a small break. In two hours I'm going to have my driver pick up one of Louie's guys, and then me. Then we're going to come looking for Paws. If we find him, I'm going to whack him. If I don't find him, I can't whack him. Can I? So you tell that stupid fuck I'm giving him a head start. That's the best I can do. If he's smart, he'll find a little town in bum-fuck Idaho and start farming, or some shit like that. Because the truth is, I don't care if I don't find him, but I have to save face and make it look like I put the press on for this guy. And I can't afford for Louie or any other fucking made guy to find him, he knows too fucking much. Now that's it, that's the best I can offer you, kid.'

The drive over to the warehouse was one of the worst trips I ever had to make. The idea that I had to tell Paws that he had to leave or die – it was a difficult message to give someone that was like a big brother. Don't get me wrong, I was pissed off at him for going against Tony's demands, but the truth is I could understand it to a point.

Paws wasn't trying to fuck anyone, we were all away on some kind of holiday and he probably had nothing to do. Someone approached him and was looking for some product, and he knew he could get it. I'm sure he did it more for the status than the money. What a lot of people don't realise is, once you get that kind of respect on the streets, you have a hard time letting go of it; it's almost like an addiction in itself.

When I got to the warehouse all the guys were there. I didn't waste any time, I told them what Tony had said. Paws was shitting his pants and I didn't blame him. The only thing to do was to go, but Paws didn't have any real cash to go with. What cash he did have he was leaving with the wife and daughter.

The thing was, his share of the property was worth five or six million dollars and he figured he should get it. He tried to make his point without getting too pushy.

'Listen, all I'm saying is, you guys can't let me walk out of here, off to who the fuck knows where, without something in my pocket.'

That greedy fucking Mick, Shawn, was the first to jump in. 'Hey, fuck you, Paws. You knew the deal: you fuck up, you lose.'

What everyone else was thinking, I'm not sure. But GG sat there and nodded in agreement with Shawn. I was pretty disappointed with G, you don't kick a dog when it's down, never mind a friend. And that fucking Shawn, I couldn't believe what a lowlife he was being. Not only were Shawn and Paws best friends since they were kids, but Shawn's sister Susan was Paws' wife. I was going to get that prick one day, this injustice wouldn't go unpunished.

I had to say something in support of Paws, 'Paws, I just had to ask a favour of Tony, to not kill you right now and give you a head start. The more we sit here and argue, the smaller your window of opportunity is. So this is what I think.'

Everyone got quiet. I guess it was that tone in my voice that I get when I don't give a fuck. I might not have been the toughest guy in the room, but I wasn't a guy who just talked shit to blow off steam; when I got edgy, anyone who knew me didn't take it lightly.

I stood up and put my gun on the table as a sign of resolve. 'I'm going to go into the safe in the toilet and I'm going to take out a million in tens and twenties that I don't feel like cleaning up anyway.' I paused and looked at everyone. No one said a word so I continued. 'Then I'm going put it in a bag and give it to our good friend here, our brother. Then I'm going to wish him all the best and reassure him that I'm personally going to check in on his family until he can get settled and send for them. So if anyone's got a problem with that, we can take care of it right now. If not, then I think you fuckers should help me count the cash. The clock's ticking, boys. Any problems?'

TC was the first to say something. 'The kid's right. Fuck the agreement. What kind of shitbag turns his back on his friend and partner, even if he did fuck up big time?' TC shot a hard glance at Paws, who just put his head down; he knew he'd fucked up and was getting a break.

TC's vote was all I needed. If anyone was thinking of going against my decision, they dropped it real quick. Not to mention, Cristo stood up and looked at me and nodded in agreement; that iced it for sure. We counted out banded stacks of tens, and some banded stacks of twenties – it only took twenty minutes with all of us working together.

As we were packing the two duffel bags, I noticed Paws looking at me. The expression on his face said that I had a brother for life. I was just hoping he could beat this thing and find a life.

We all said our goodbyes to Paws and went out into the garage. TC pulled his car keys out of his pocket. 'Here you go, pal. It's probably safer to take my car. Leave it in some airport in a few days. Put a postcard in the mail with the details and I'll send someone for it.'

Paws took the keys, got in and started the car. He just sat there looking out the window at us. No one said a word, it was like being at a funeral. In some ways it was worse than a funeral, he was still alive, but we couldn't do a thing to catch him a break; it was a feeling of helplessness.

I opened the big garage door and gave him a nod as he drove by. Paws just winked and said, 'Take care of yourself, kid.'

Two weeks later TC got a postcard that had a simple message. 'St Louis. Level 5. H-3. Thanks.' So we knew he made it as far as the St Louis. Where he went from there we couldn't even guess. As long as he kept his head down and didn't get into any shit, he'd be fine.

As we grow up, not just as children, but our whole life, we learn, or we're supposed to. Sometimes it's experience that shows us the way, sometimes the school of hard knocks or maybe someone sets an example, some decisive action that's designed to keep us on the straight and narrow, a scare tactic. I just figured this whole thing with Paws was something he had to do and learn from, and somehow it would work itself out in time.

We never talked about Paws when we were all together, it would have brought up bad vibes amongst us. But TC and I would talk about him frequently; we'd joke about Paws spending so many nights guarding the warehouse. For a while we called him Duke, after John Wayne. He kind of had that air about himself. He was a man's man.

Four months after Paws left, Tony called TC and me and told us to stop by his house. When we arrived, Tony was behaving in a distant kind of way and we quietly followed him into his study. We sat down and Tony poured three Scotches. He drank his down before he started.

'Well, I thought you should know that Paws is dead.'

TC and I both sat quiet, I wasn't about to show my emotions in front of Tony. I was angry and had an idea that Tony might be the one who killed him. I'm sure TC was feeling as bad as I was. There really wasn't much we could say. I had a couple of questions though.

'Where'd you find him?'

'The dumb shit showed up in Vegas a couple of weeks ago. A bookie from the Bronx, who was in Vegas for a few days, recognised him and called me, he owed me a favour. The stupid bastard – Vegas! It's his own doing.'

'What about the body? Is that ever going to find its way back here to his family?'

Tony poured another Scotch. 'No. He won't be coming back. He's buried in the desert.'

I wanted to ask Tony who killed him, but thought better of it. I was afraid of what the answer would be.

TC and I left Tony's and drove back to our world without saying a word to each other.

I couldn't stop thinking of Paws. It was the little things that kept running through my mind. Like when I was younger, in the early days, he'd always take me with him to the football games; something that meant a lot to me back then. And how he always took his daughter to the park and worried about her if she went too high on the swing. How in the world was I supposed to tell his wife? I wasn't sure I knew the words.

I guess you could say that Tony made an example of Paws. This was a game and the rules had to be followed. I was getting tired of Tony and the game.

13
Shooting Stars

Shooting stars are not really stars at all. They're just lumps of assorted ores that break free from a passing comet. Unlike the comet, which tends to keep a constant and predictable schedule and course, these lumps of ore soar through the sky on a path that cannot be charted or predicted. They recklessly shoot straight for earth's atmosphere, where they begin to disintegrate, causing that amazing sight that has earned them the name of 'shooting stars'.

This extraordinary display is, in fact, the destruction of the 'shooting star'. Most of these celestial seekers burn out on entry, long before they touch down. Paws had burnt out before touching down, and it seemed to me that the rest of us were burning up too; I didn't believe a safe touchdown was possible.

In the spring of 1983, with the seven-year reunion only eight months away, I started feeling tense every day. It was like a weight upon my shoulders that only got heavier.

I guess I just wanted a simple life with Julia more than anything. Tony, who actually approved of Julia, had warned me about getting too close with a woman. He had said to me a million times that 'love can cause you to be too cautious and cloud your judgement'. I think he was right. That carefree manner I used to have was gone. At first I told myself it was probably the news of Paws that was eating away at me. But I knew it was my desire to give Julia a life that she deserved. She deserved a man who had a reasonable shot at surviving a normal day.

Before Paws fucked up, Tony had told us to lay low because undercover DEA agents were setting up a gangster type in the city for a fall. Well, that 'gangster type' turned out to be a Sicilian guy, Vincenzo, who was running more angles than a protractor. He found out they were DEA agents before they busted him. He didn't like being played for a fool, so he killed all three them.

If he wanted to kill them, he should have done it quietly and make them disappear. At least that way there might have been some doubts in the minds of their superiors; they wouldn't have been the first undercover guys to disappear with a couple of million in drug money. But not Vincenzo, he not only killed them, he tortured them and left them to be found as a message to any other potential undercover guys.

The result wasn't what he had in mind. The city swarmed with more Feds and DEA agents than ever, and they were putting pressure on a lot of people. I thought for sure that the family would have whacked Vincenzo, but they didn't, they sent him off to a private compound in Sicily owned by the mob. No one could touch him there. Back in the city we were sweating bullets, the press was on and we were all under the gun.

The streets of New York were covered in blow. From what I heard, Denni was bringing in ten times more blow than we were. In addition to Denni, scores of small independents were buying four or five Ks in Florida and making the run to New York with the blow in the trunk of their car.

Everyone seemed to be snorting cocaine: lawyers, doctors, crooked cops, musicians, barmen, tradesmen, even garbage men; it was the 'in' thing. Guys who couldn't afford it stole from employers, friends and family to get it. No doubt women did the same, but in many cases they found that sexual favours got them what they needed to get high for the night. Many guys who were selling the shit turned would-be nice girls into outright whores. In every city in America, once-respectable people were getting caught up in this mad hysteria and sinking into a terrible abyss. It was all a bit crazy for me and I wanted to run, and I probably could have – but I didn't. It was my loyalty to the guys, not Tony, that kept me there.

Another unforeseen problem was the degeneration of a large percentage of made guys in the mob. All the bosses were pissed off. Half their crews were fucked up on the shit and out of control. They were making big mistakes. It was only a matter of time before some of them took a pinch and started singing like canaries to save their asses.

In less than ten years, this cancerous powder was destroying the fabric that had held together many old traditions, not just in the gangster world, but in the business world and the political world.

I'm not sure I could have articulated all of these thoughts at the time, but I knew the constant tension welling up inside my soul was a result of the chaotic world I was surrounded by.

I was sitting in a local restaurant with Julia, eating the best veal scaloppine I'd ever had before or since, when John the Ace came running in. He looked pretty shook up.

'Marco! You've got to come with me right now, it's important.'

Julia looked a little shocked. She had never met Ace before. Actually, aside from TC, Uncle Tony and Cristo, she didn't know any of the guys. I was a bit pissed off with Ace. He knew I didn't want her to know anything.

'John, I'm fucking eating here.'

'Marco, listen, it's Paws, he's back, but it ain't really him.'

I just about shit myself. 'He's back? What do you mean it ain't him?'

'I'm telling you, it's Paws and he's got no fingers and no mind. He says he's going to kill his daughter and Susan and everyone else if he doesn't get his money.'

I couldn't believe this, it sounded like a Saturday afternoon creature feature on TV. 'Where's he now?'

'He's at his house. Shawn and I were over there hanging with Susan and Jessica, and he just came in ranting and raving about Susan betraying him and us fucking him out of his share of the money. He grabbed the kid and put a knife to her throat, says he wants to talk to you and TC.'

Julia looked pretty upset, but I didn't have time to explain. I had to think.

'All right, listen. TC's at the clubhouse, go and tell him the deal. Tell him to bring a hundred thousand out of the safe, that should calm Paws down for a couple of hours. And if you see Tony or G, don't say a fucking word.'

John nodded in agreement and went out as fast as he came in. I turned to Julia. Her face was pale and the hurt and betrayal in her eyes spoke louder than any words could.

'Honey, I'm sorry you had to hear that. There's a lot of things I've wanted to tell you, I was just hoping to do it next January, when I'm out of this thing for good.'

'I think you better tell me tonight, but right now I think we have to go.'

'No, you can't come with me, honey. I'll tell you the whole deal tonight, I promise.'

Julia abruptly pushed her chair back, stood up and grabbed her bag. 'I'm coming, or there won't be a tonight.'

I knew she wasn't going to budge on this one. But I couldn't lose her, she was the only contact I had with reality. 'All right, but just don't say a word and stand by the door when we get there.'

It was a short drive; we were there in five minutes. I pulled in the driveway and we went to the side door. It was unlocked. As we entered I could hear Susan quietly sobbing. I called out so as not to startle Paws. 'Paws. It's me, Marco.' I could hear him moving in the living room.

I entered the living room slowly. On the couch to my immediate left was Shawn. His nose was bleeding and the right side of his face was swollen. Susan was on the other couch against the wall on the far left of the arched doorway I was standing in. Paws was across the room, right in front of me, sitting in a reclining chair, holding Jessica. She looked a bit frightened but seemed calm.

'Hey, buddy, how you doing?' I knew without asking that he wasn't well. He had a crazed look in his blue eyes that suggested he wasn't exactly the same guy I knew. He also had a strange twitch that made his neck and head move in a creepy sort of way.

'I'm not good, kid. Your fucking Uncle Tony and his fat fucking pal Donnie tied me down and cut my fingers off.' Paws' eyes welled up like he was going to cry, but he didn't. He just rubbed his daughter's head and took a deep breath. I was getting nervous, I had no way of telling where this was going. I tried to calm him.

'Hey, buddy, it's OK, you made it. We just got to get you sorted out with some cash and get you out of here. In a couple of months I'll bring Susan and Jessica to see you.'

This was the wrong thing to say, he got real uptight.

'Don't bring that fucking bitch anywhere near me. She told them, that's how they found me, I should kill her right now!'

Jessica started to cry; she was only eight years old. I had to try a different approach. I raised my voice and took a step towards him. 'Now you listen to me real good, pal. Susan loves you, every person in this room loves you, you got caught because you were stupid, you never should have gone to Vegas and you—'

'She's the only one I told, no one else knew, no one else knew.' Paws began rocking back and forth and put his arms around his daughter. Aside from being afraid, I never felt so sad in all my life. I think he was only half there.

'Listen to me, buddy, you got caught because an uptown bookie saw you and called Tony.'

Paws looked at me incredulously, like I was Judas himself. 'You knew?'

'Tony told TC and me afterwards. There was nothing we could do then, he said you were dead.'

'Fucking A. Did he tell you how he cut my fingers off and stole my money? He thought I told people things, he thought I was going to go to the Feds and rat you guys out. Every time I answered a question, he called me a liar and cut another finger off. And when I had no more fingers,' Paws turned his palms outward, revealing his hands; all the fingertips from the knuckles up were gone, 'he told me he would kill me quick if I would tell him where my cash was. He thought I had millions. I spit in his face.'

Paws dropped his head and quietly sobbed. I think everyone in the room had tears in their eyes. It was a confusing moment. I tried to compose myself and think of something to ease his tension but Paws went on talking.

'Then after I spit in his face, he said, "Now you don't get to die quick", and he told his buddy, fucking Donnie, to take me for a scenic ride in the desert and bury me.'

We heard the side door open and TC and John came in. I put my hand up to TC. 'Easy, T, everything's going to be all right. Did you bring some cash for Paws?'

TC walked up to just a few feet from Paws and dropped a bag on the floor and opened it. 'There's two hundred grand in there, Steven, I'll make sure we get you more in a month or so.' I had never heard anyone, except for Susan, call Paws by his real name, but it seemed appropriate.

Paws didn't acknowledge the money or TC, he just kept on telling his story. It was almost like he thought by telling it, it would change the reality of the situation.

'So that fucking Donnie, he takes me for a ride through the desert, tied to a rope that was tied to his fucking jeep. It seemed like forever and my face kept getting scratched from the brush and I hit a bunch of rocks. Then I passed out. When I woke up I was in a hole in the ground and he was burying me alive. That fucking Donnie! But he didn't know I was awake, I just laid there, face down, and he threw the sand over me. I waited a long time and then I put my hands under myself and I pushed myself up. It was really hard, but I did it.' He paused for a moment, I could see his sadness turning into anger.

I was getting worried again. 'That's unreal, Paws, it's a miracle.'

'Yeah, it was. I walked the rest of the night, and the next morning it got so hot I guess I fainted, but some guy found me in the desert and took me to the hospital. I didn't wake up for two months, the doc said I was in a coma, said I lost so much blood I should have been dead. He figured I only survived because my fingers had been cauterised.'

I didn't understand that bit. 'What do you mean cauterised?'

'That sick fuck of an uncle of yours explained it to me while he did it. He said the Special Forces taught him. After he cut off the first one, he grabs this blowtorch that he had on the table next to the one I was on. He used it to heat up this little metal test tube shape thing, that he held with big pliers. Then he said, "You see, pal, if I don't cauterise the wound, you bleed to death before I'm finished. And we can't have that now, can we?" That Tony's a sick fuck.'

Everyone in the room was silent. What do you say to that when it's your uncle he's talking about? Paws just started talking again, it seemed like he was actually calming himself down as he talked.

'Yeah, the doc said he'd never seen anyone as tough as me. He used to sit and talk to me. He waited a month before he told the police I was conscious and he brought me some clothes, a pair of gloves and a couple of bucks. He said I should probably head out before the cops got there, if I wanted to. He figured the guys that did this to me probably had ways of finding me and finishing what they started. He said he didn't want to see that. He even dropped me at the train station. He was a nice guy.'

TC was the first to speak. 'You got to get out of town, Paws. There's two hundred grand here, just give us some time and we'll make sure you're OK. There's a farm upstate I inherited, it ain't much, but you'll be safe there until we get this figured out.'

Paws just nodded. 'OK, T. It sounds good, thanks.'

'Ace, it'll be dark in an hour, can you take him? I'll draw out the directions. It's easy.'

'Yeah, sure, T. No problem.'

Susan gave Paws a big hug and told him she loved him. He just kept crying and telling her he was sorry. It really wasn't his fault.

His mind was a bit shot but it was still Paws. Maybe with time he'd be OK. At least that's what we hoped for.

The ride up to the farm was about four hours, so we didn't expect Ace to return until the morning. After we all said our goodbyes, I took Julia back to my place. She didn't say one word the whole way home. I had a lot of explaining to do and knew this was where I might lose her.

She went right to the wine cabinet, grabbed a bottle of wine, sat at the dining-room table and opened the bottle. The hard stare I received was one of anger, hurt and weariness.

After what seemed an eternity, she broke off her stare and sipped from her glass of wine. I sat down across from her. I still hadn't decided what tack to take, I hadn't had much time to think about it. I knew that whatever I said she might leave, so I figured the complete truth was the best road to take. Before I could start, she fired off the first question.

'So, Mr Builder, how long have you been in the Mafia?'

Her tone was curt and there were tears damming up in her eyes, but I knew she didn't want me to see them.

'I'm not in the Mafia, and I've never been in the Mafia, and I can promise you I will never be in the Mafia.'

'Oh, I see. Susan's sitting over there with half of her husband because the construction business has got a little cutthroat, has it?'

Her hurt was quickly accelerating to anger and I couldn't see any way out of the abyss.

'Listen, I know this isn't easy, but I'm in the drug business.

The seven of us used to sell pot, then Uncle Tony came to us with this deal, we move some cocaine for him and some of his people, and we make some serious money . . . I know that's not what you want to hear, but it's the truth.'

'Uncle Tony! We go to his fucking house for dinner and sit at the same table as that monster. How can you even look at him? Does your aunt have any idea of how horrible he is?'

'No, I'm sure she doesn't. She probably loves him for all the same amazing qualities that I grew up loving him for . . . I didn't pick him for an uncle, you know!'

'OK. So when you found out what he was, why didn't you walk?'

I took a long pause, got up to get a glass of Scotch and sat back down.

'Look, I know it sucks, but I'm smack in the middle of this thing; getting out isn't an option right now. Before we got into this with Tony, I knew there was a side of him that was scary, but I still got into it. So there's no one to blame, Julia. If you have to walk, I'll understand. It's not what I want. I love you more than you'll ever know. But I cannot walk away until next year. Then I'm out for good. We could buy a bigger boat and sail off for a couple years. Maybe we could—'

She cut me off quick before I could finish my off-into-the-sunset spiel.

'Why next year? Leave now, right now, tonight. If you think I'm going to listen to this every year until you end up like Paws, or worse, you're out of your mind!'

'Listen to me! And I mean, listen . . . to me.' I had to get firm or she'd think I was just selling her some story. 'I can't walk out tonight or tomorrow night, I can walk out after the New Year. We made a pact, I owe it to the guys. Not to mention, if I leave right now, I forfeit my share in the business, which is millions, and I didn't go through all this shit to walk away from it. But even if I was willing to let the money go, I might end up like Paws, or worse.'

'TC and Cristo would never hurt you – would they?'

'No, of course they wouldn't. But we have partners, guys that are probably a lot worse than Tony. I'm stuck right here and that's not going to change. If you stay, and I hope you do, I can't offer you anything different than the life you know I have right now – not until after the New Year.'

Julia poured another glass of wine and sat biting her lip; she seemed to be trying to make a decision. I figured that was a good thing, at least she hadn't already decided to walk. After a couple of minutes she put her glass on the table and looked at me with those beautiful eyes that seemed to be so sad and yet so full of love.

'You know, Marco, the truth is I always knew you guys were up to something but I just figured it was numbers and betting. Even if I'd known you were selling drugs, I might've turned a blind eye to it, because I do love you. But seeing Paws tonight, that scared me, it scares me still. I don't know how I could survive if that happened to you. I want to be with you. I want to have a family with you . . .' The tears started cascading down her drawn, beautiful face, but she took a deep breath and continued. 'Can you promise me that won't happen to you? Can you promise me that you'll be out after the New Year, for ever?'

'No. I can't promise you that that's not going to happen to me. I can tell you that I don't think it will. Tony wouldn't do that to me, and anyone who might, wouldn't because of Tony, TC and Cristo. The only promise I can make to you is I'll be out after the New Year and we can go wherever you want to . . . and that I will love you with all of my heart.'

The tears started rolling down her face again and I got up to wipe them, but she just stood up and hugged me so tight I thought nothing could ever separate us now.

We sat and talked for hours and decided that after I was out we would go upstate to the parcel of land I'd bought and build a house, a home and a life. We made love and slept comfortably in each other's arms.

*

The next morning I made Julia breakfast and she went off to work. Before she left I asked her to quit her job. I explained my financial position and I figured now that she knew the truth, there was no reason for her to work waiting tables for shit money. She could be a big help in getting things in order for the move in the New Year.

When she left, I got in the shower. I thought I'd take a long one, I had a lot to think about.

That's when I heard this loud banging at my door. It had to be the cops. No one who knew where I lived would ever come over without a call first. I got out, dried off and thought for a minute. There was nothing in the house they could pinch me for. I doubted they'd ever find my safe. I had my gun, but I had a permit for it. Anyone who didn't have a police record and owned a business could get a permit to carry, no problem.

When I got to the door in my bathrobe, I was surprised. It was Tony. When I saw his face I wished it was the cops.

'Hey, Tony, how you doing?'

'I'm not fucking good! Sit the fuck down.' I sat at the kitchen table. I didn't offer him a coffee, I didn't think he needed it.

'What's up?'

'Did that overgrown, stupid Mick show up last night?'

I knew better than to lie. 'Yeah, he did. But he's far away now, don't worry about it.'

'No he's not. He's over in Donnie's fucking kitchen, dead as a doorknob, along with Donnie!'

My heart sank.

The first time you hear someone's dead, it's tragic. But when they come back from the dead and die a second time, it's really unsettling. I sat at the table and had to make myself focus. The news troubled me, but I knew I was going to be catching some shit from Tony and better have my game face on.

'What the fuck happened? We sent him upstate with Ace to lay low until we could get him someplace far away.'

133

'I don't know what happened to Ace, but Donnie's wife called me at five o'clock this morning to tell me someone came through the window and attacked Donnie. By the time I got there, the cops were there with the coroner. They killed each other. Now the question I have for you is, why the fuck didn't you call me to tell me right away? What if he'd come to my house and killed my wife?'

I was getting uneasy and had to think before I said anything. 'I don't know, Tony. I thought he was going upstate and then far away.'

He was as mad as I've ever seen him, but I couldn't help but think of what he did to Paws; I felt like telling him to go fuck himself but knew that it wouldn't be conducive to a long life. I'd just got done telling Julia that Tony would never hurt me, and here he was in my kitchen, madder than a snake and ready to strike. I couldn't stand the idea of her coming home to find me dead. I had to control my emotions and eat some serious shit; maybe I'd get through it.

'You thought he was going to just drive off into the sunset, start a new life? Sell insurance maybe? Are you fucking stupid? Of all you shit heads, you're the one I've always relied on the most, and now you've let me down. You've passed your expiration date, son.'

I wasn't thinking so much about telling Tony to fuck off now, I was thinking of what I could say that wouldn't piss him off even more and make him lose his temper completely. I was also wishing I was dressed and had my gun with me.

'Uncle Tony, listen. You know I'm loyal to you. And you know Paws and I were great friends – like brothers. I never would have sided with him and gone against you; I know you know that. I was trying to save his life and keep things moving without disrupting the business or pissing anyone off. I'm sorry, it won't happen again.'

Tony took a long pause and gave me a stare that I didn't like. It was obvious he was boiling over. Aside from me and the guys not telling him about Paws, he'd just lost one of his oldest and closest friends — but maybe that would stop him doing something we'd both regret. He'd just lost a good friend, he wasn't going to kill another of his closest friends — me. At least that's what I was hoping.

'You know, kid, we're family, you don't ever choose friends over family. You really pissed me off. You better toe the fucking line, son. Do you hear me? And another thing, when you divide up your little empire, I want half of Paws' share. Consider it payment for the loss of one of my best soldiers. Not to mention, if I ever hear of another incident of you taking someone else's side, I'm going to deal you a rough hand. Right?'

I didn't like Tony threatening the guys and me and my temper flared a bit — I think I must have had a moment of temporary insanity.

'What are you going do, Tony? Cut my fingers off and drag me through the desert?' I couldn't believe I said that. It was clear Tony didn't like it. He got quiet and leaned forward and started speaking in a low, very controlled, terse manner.

'Let me tell you something, kid. What I did to Paws was civilised compared to what I've done to some people. And I'll tell you something else, you and my wife are the two people I love the most in this world, but you should also know this. I'm playing for Team Tony, and I don't lose. I don't lose because I understand the most important principle of war: acceptable loss. Nothing is more sacred to me than me. So you watch yourself, kid. I'm only giving you a pass because I know the guy was your friend. Your problem is you're too fucking soft. You might want to rethink that one. Now you get your shit together and never fuck up like this again. And you make sure no one in your crew ever tells anyone that Paws was seen. It don't make me look good that my two nephews didn't tell me something like that. Right?'

'Yeah, Uncle Tony, I'm sorry, I didn't see this one coming. And I'm sorry for what I said here. It was disrespectful.'

'Don't be sorry, just don't be stupid. I expect a lot more from you, *capisci?*

I just nodded in agreement and he left.

I sat there for about an hour and wondered how in the fuck did it get so nuts? I might have sat there all day, but the phone rang. It was TC. He said Ace had called and told him that Paws had asked him to stop at a truck stop to take a piss. When they stopped, Paws whacked Ace on the head and knocked him out. He left a note telling Ace he was sorry and would he give the money to his wife.

TC came over and I told him about my meeting with Tony.

'Sometimes you're a stupid bastard, kid,' was all he said about that.

We met up with Ace later and took the money to Susan and explained the bad news. On the way over I felt so terrible that I just went dead inside.

When we arrived, Susan knew immediately that something was wrong. Luckily Jessica was out in the backyard. Before TC could say anything, I went off into a robotic monologue, starting with what had transpired after Paws left and ending with an offer to help arrange the funeral. Susan knew we were shaken pretty bad and did us the favour of putting on a brave face until we left.

It wasn't a good day.

A shooting star can be classified as a meteor, or a meteorite. The meteor burns up upon entry, before hitting the ground, whereas the meteorite, which makes for a brighter 'shooting star' because of its greater mass, survives the atmosphere, and impacts the earth. I was starting to think that we were meteorites, and we would make impact, very, very soon. I was just hoping that the impact wouldn't destroy everything we loved.

14
A Surprise Visit

We all dream about going back in time, a second chance to do it over. Paws' death was enough for me to want to go back. I'd seen more of this lifestyle than I cared to. The funeral for Paws was very difficult but it brought Susan and Julia together as friends. Julia, who was really taken aback when she came home and heard the news about Paws (only twelve hours after me telling her the truth about my business and how there was nothing to worry about) was on high alert – worry time. Every time I walked out the door, there'd be questions, or looks of dread. I just kept my head down and took care of business, trying to avoid the late-night card games with the guys, just so I could get home and ease her mind.

The funeral for Donnie was the day after Paws', and I dreaded going, but knew I had to do it. It was a bit uncomfortable; I went to school with his two sons and they knew Paws was my friend and that I had gone to his funeral the day before. It was like I was being disloyal almost. I was fed up with all the shit and just said my hellos and goodbyes and left after the service. I was also trying to cut a wide berth around Tony that week. I knew he'd be a bit edgy and I didn't want to clash any more than we already had.

By September I was counting the days until New Year's Eve. I figured that if I could get through this last stretch, I'd survive, and maybe, with enough time, I wouldn't feel the desire to go

137

back in time but would have the strength to go forward. I waited for that day, I hoped for that day.

We put Paws' death behind us, again. Things were back to normal, we were moving the same amount of blow and making the same amount of money but something was very different; the sense of ease and calm that we had once had around each other had disappeared.

TC was a grumpy bastard and Cristo was quick to snap at anyone who pissed him off. GG, well, he was out in some other place. He was busting our balls about his two cousins, Vito and Donato. He figured with Paws gone, we could bring them into our crew, but none of us were interested.

GG also thought we should start breaking up more Ks to sell in ounces. With all the heat around the city, it was a stupid idea. We just wanted to keep things the same. After Paws' death, Ace and Shawn kept their heads down. I think they harboured some ill will towards us because of Paws. I didn't really blame them in a way – I mean, we didn't kill him, but one of ours did. He fucked up and paid an overly unfair price for it. But at the same time, Tony was one of ours, and if he could do that to Paws, he could do it to them.

I guess you could say there was an unseen line that had been drawn that separated us, and out of respect we all made sure not to cross it. It was the little things; before, we'd had amazing arguments over card games, now we'd just shrug our shoulders and tend to stand down. TC, Cristo, GG and I didn't want to get too hard with Shawn and John, and I think they were doing what they could to avoid getting whacked out – I'm sure they were counting the days as well. I guess it was about the second week of September that things started getting even more fucked up.

I was supposed to make a five K run with Cristo, but I had an appointment with a Jewish numismatist who was going to trade me $2,000,000 of $500 and $1,000 bills for $2,200,000 in $10 and $20 bills. It was a bit expensive, but it was money well spent.

It was six large bags of small bills for one smaller bag of big bills. This made stashing and moving the cash so much easier.

The biggest upside to the swap was that we would be less inclined to cash the big bills. After 1975, to cash a five hundred or a thousand, you had to take it to the bank and maybe answer questions. No one needs that publicity. It's kind of stupid paying a premium for large bills if you're just going to blow them on foolish shit, which meant we might start saving a little more of our profits.

Every day we were all busy running our business. Tony and G always left on Saturday or Sunday, returning with the blow on Sunday or Monday. Then it had to be cut, reconstituted and packaged so it could be distributed. There were 'counting days' when we just counted money and doled out each share. Then there was the 'crew cut' which had to be invested. And let's not forget meetings with lawyers and accountants, and the occasional bank manager. In the midst of all this we had to find time to relax with our women and maybe the occasional late-night card game.

Originally TC and I were supposed to meet the Jewish guy on Friday afternoon, but he called to say he couldn't make it until later in the evening, which fucked up me going with Cristo on that run with the five K. But the guy couldn't do another day and I knew it would take at least four or five hours to count all the cash and make the trade.

TC had told Cristo to put the deal off until late Friday, but that fucked up the guy buying so Cristo went alone. It wasn't the first time one of us did a big deal alone, but we all preferred having someone for back-up.

It must have been about midnight when Cristo came back. TC and I had finished up with the Jewish guy and were having a couple of beers and watching the Marlon Brando classic *On the Waterfront*. Cristo was covered in blood and had a rag pressed to the right side of his head.

We both jumped to our feet. 'What the fuck happened, Face?' TC asked.

Cristo, true to character, just sat down and calmly replied, 'Got shot in the head, T.' He let out a chuckle and continued with a big smile on his face, 'The bullet bounced off my head. I guess my mother was right. I'm hard-headed.'

TC went to the bathroom and got a wet towel. I tried not to overreact.

'Who the fuck did this, Face?'

'Three spicks got me at a red light. They knew I had the cash.'

TC cleaned up his head. There was a good sized gash just above his right eye. The bullet had just missed his temple and grazed him. TC kicked into command mode.

'Marco, get me a clean, white towel, and then call Dr Fletcher. Tell him we'll be coming by.' Dr Fletcher was a retired doctor in the neighbourhood, who had a small surgery on the side of his house. He could be trusted. Cristo voiced his dissent. He didn't like doctors or hospitals.

'Fuck the doctor, T. Get me a fucking beer and a Band Aid. This ain't shit.'

TC looked at me and nodded to the fridge. 'Get us all a beer, kid.' Then he turned back to Cristo. 'OK, tough guy, tell us what happened and who stole our money.'

'No one stole our fucking money, T. It's in the trunk of my car under the spare tyre.' I handed TC and Cristo a beer. Cristo drank his in one long swig and I got him another. TC was getting impatient.

'Just tell me what the fuck happened before I shoot you myself.'

Cristo laughed and began his story. 'I went way uptown to Hector's place and I did the deal. I counted it, left and put the cash in the trunk. I checked to see if I was being followed and it all looked clear. Everything seemed fine until I stopped at the light on the other side of the bridge. I looked in my mirror and saw these two guys running up to my car. I would have driven off but there was a car in front of me and the guys were coming quick. Like always, when I'm doing a deal, I had my gun

140

in my lap. So I rolled my windows down and got ready. The first guy went behind my car for the passenger side and the guy behind him came straight for my door. He got to my window a second before the other guy got to the passenger door; they both had guns drawn.' Cristo finished his beer and held up the can. I took it, went to the fridge, got him another and he continued.

'So as this guy gets to my door, I shot him in the chest. I think that scared the other guy, because he had his gun aimed right at my head when he pulled the trigger. He shot, and I shot back. I think I might have got him, but he ran off and I'm not sure. The car in front of me took off when I fired the first shot so I got out of there as fast as I could.'

'What about the first guy you shot?'

'I told you, T. I shot him in the chest from three feet away. The fucker is deader than dead.'

I started seeing the big picture. The cops were probably at the scene in minutes and most likely someone got the licence plate number of Cristo's car. We had to act fast if we wanted to clean this thing up.

'Cristo, give me the keys to your car.' He gave me the keys. 'T, come out and get the cash, I got to take care of this car. Face, where'd you park?'

'Next door, in TC's mother's driveway. I wanted it to be off the street in case someone got the number plate.'

TC and I went next door and got the bag in the trunk. 'Where're you going to dump this thing, kid?'

'I'm not, not yet anyway. I'm going over to Bobby Lamatina's house and getting him out of bed.'

'What the fuck is Bobby the Lamb going to do?'

'T, if the car disappears, it's going to look suspicious. I'm going to have Bobby find another car, exactly the same as this one, and have him change the numbers.'

'What does that do?'

'It gives Face a car with no bloodstains or any other possible

141

evidence. In a couple of days, when Bobby's done, I'll park the car some place safe, and take off the number plates. When the cops come looking for Cristo, we say he's been out of town but expect him back in a few days. When he gets back he takes the police to where I leave the car and they see his car without any blood, bullet holes or licence plates. They assume someone with the same make and model stole the plates for some scam. In the meantime, you better get him to lay low for a couple of days.'

'Good point, kid. If the cops question him with his head looking like that, it won't look good. I'll take care of it. I'll leave this cash in the safe here in the clubhouse and you can move it to the warehouse when you get a chance.'

'No problem, T . . . Hey, T, call Bobby and tell him I'm on the way.'

TC nodded and went back to the clubhouse, I headed for Bobby's place.

Bobby Lamatina had an auto body shop just around the corner from his house and by the time I got there he was awake and dressed. I had pissed his wife off for coming over so late but he didn't mind. We always paid him extremely well for his services. Once the car was inside the garage, I explained the situation to him.

Finding another car was no problem. Bobby had it the next morning before ten. He did a lot of business with several used car dealers in the five boroughs and could make things happen fast. When there's plenty of money around, you can make anything happen fast.

I went to pick up the new car late Saturday afternoon, and paid Bobby in full. He asked me what I wanted to do with the old car. I told to him to strip it and sell anything that wasn't traceable, which was most of the car, and then scrap the rest in the junk yard. What was left would be crushed by Tuesday morning. I told Bobby any cash he got from the parts he could keep as a special thanks from us.

It was rush hour when I left Bobby's shop with the new car, which meant more traffic and confusion, and less chance of a cop spotting the car. I drove it to Cristo's Aunt Ginny's house where the car was registered to. She had a large driveway that went around the back of the house. I took off the number tags and went inside to make sure she had the story straight. When I went inside, the story about the shooting was on the six o'clock news. She didn't ask too much, but she knew something was up.

'Is Cristobal all right, Marco?' She spoke with a broken Italian American accent that I really liked.

'Yea, Zia Ginny, he's fine, no problem.' I started to call her Zia – Aunt – Ginny, at her insistence, after I left home. She knew I had left just before my fourteenth birthday and she tended to mother me.

The poor woman, she watched all the men in her life get killed. She lost three uncles, a husband and her two brothers, two in the Second World War, and the rest to the streets.

Unlike her brother Vittorio, her husband, Giuseppe, was a pious man who had no connections to any side of the underworld. After Mussolini went in with the Germans in the war, the two of them, like many American Italians, felt ashamed and volunteered to serve. The government had gathered up all of the Japanese living in America, particularly the ones living on the West Coast, and there was a fear in the Italian community that the same might happen to them after Mussolini decided to get into bed with Hitler. So off they went to fight for their new country. Neither came home from the European front.

Her three uncles never made it to America. They all died in Sicily carrying out vendettas. Back in the early days the highest death rate in Sicily of any male above the age of twelve was a result of attempting to carry out a vendetta, or someone getting you for the same reason.

It's fucked really; if someone kills your brother, you swear a vendetta to get the guy. And in many cases, you get the guy's brother and maybe even his sons, just so they don't get you. It's one big fucking circle.

As for Aunt Ginny's younger brother, Cristo's dad, he was a heavy hitter who had been working the streets since he was a kid. He was dead a month before his thirty-fifth birthday. As far as we know he was shot by a cop on a heist in Jersey. He was brought to the emergency room by an unknown man whose description fitted Tony, but the man left before he could be questioned. No one knows the real story, except maybe Tony, but he'll never talk – the two were like brothers and he still feels the loss.

'Sit down, let me make you a plate, I just made some nice gravy.'

I really didn't have time but I realised I didn't have a ride back. I asked if I could use the phone and called Ace. He said he'd be there in thirty minutes which gave me plenty of time for a nice meal.

While she was in the kitchen, I sat and watched the TV. The reporter was interviewing the local district attorney and the chief of police. The chief didn't mention any names. He just said that all he could report, at that time, was that one unidentified man was dead, he believed another was wounded and the driver of the black Continental in question was being sought for questioning. I knew the chief was on the take and would wait until Tony got back the next day before he made a move on Cristo.

So far so good. Maybe we could skate on this one. I had a great meal and when John pulled in the driveway I thanked Aunt Ginny.

'It was great, Zia Ginny. Now remember, if the police, or anyone, asks, Cristo dropped the car Friday morning. And thanks again for the wonderful dinner.'

'*Prego*. You boys take a care of yourselves.'

'Don't worry, Zia Ginny.'

'That's what they all tell me, but I still worry.'

I kissed her cheek and left.

Ace and I went back to the clubhouse but there was still no

sign of TC or Cristo. I was getting worried, maybe the bullet did more damage than we thought.

The first thing to do was to go and see Doc Fletcher. The last I knew, that's where they were heading. He lived just a few blocks away; I told Ace to stay and wait until I got back, in case they showed up.

Doc Fletcher was a nice old guy, I'd known him since I was a small boy. He greeted me with a warm welcome and I started to relax immediately. If Cristo was in bad shape he wouldn't be so cheerful.

After some small talk, Doc Fletcher told me what had happened. 'I took care of Cristo's little problem, and they were on their way. TC's left a letter for you. He said if you didn't come over by this evening I should call you on the number on the back of the envelope.'

He went to his desk and returned with the envelope. I opened it and read it immediately. I suppose I looked a bit puzzled, because Doc became concerned.

'Is everything all right, Marco?'

'Yeah, forget about it. We appreciate all the help, Doc. I'll see you later.'

As I walked towards the door, the Doc spoke to me in a way he never had before. It was kind of a fatherly tone.

'You know, Marco . . . I always thought you were smarter than the rest of the boys. With your talents and good looks you could do something special. I've watched a lot of kids from the neighbourhood end up in a bad way. You should be in a music conservatory, or a college. You're still young, just walk away, son.'

My first reaction was to tell him to mind his own fucking business, but I didn't. The truth was he was right and he was just trying to help me. I felt embarrassed for even thinking of such a rotten reply but I was also unable to show any gratitude for his concern.

'Yeah, thanks, Doc. I'll see you later.'

I turned and walked to my car without looking back. I could

feel him watch me walk away. When I got in the car, he was still standing in the doorway staring at me with a dismal look.

I went straight back to the clubhouse where Ace was watching TV. I pulled out the letter.

'What the fuck's that?'

'It's a letter T left with the Doc. Just listen.' I read the letter out loud. 'Hey, kid. Face is fine. Doc says just a scratch. Face and I went to Atlantic City on Friday afternoon, if anyone asks. See you in a few days.'

'What the fuck are they doing in Atlantic City?'

'I don't know, John. Maybe TC's gone fucking batty.'

'So who's going to help us with all this shit we have to move?'

'We are. Call Chop and set an appointment for tonight, the usual place.'

I went to the safe in the floor and opened it. It was packed to the hilt. Aside from the hundred grand that we kept for emergencies, there was $2,000,000 from the Jew and the $165,000 from the deal that Cristo had done. I couldn't leave it all in there. TC would've had a fit.

It was the only safe all of the guys had the combination for so I had to move it. Not to mention, we still had twelve Ks of blow to move, plus the new shipment that would be here with Tony and G in the morning. That would have to be cut, packaged and all the rest of the shit that goes with this crazy business.

Luckily Shawn dropped by the clubhouse to put some money in the safe before he went home. I explained what had happened the night before and that we'd need some help. He just said, 'No problem. I'll take a shower and be good for another twelve hours.' I figured the shower was only part of it. I knew he was snorting quite a lot of blow those days. I think his habit got worse after Paws' death. Like all of us, he was starting to lose his grip on reality.

15
Hanging from the Rafters

Tony and G arrived the next day with the new shipment. I explained what had happened and Uncle Tony listened intently. I told him what I'd done with the car and showed him the note. He actually thought we handled it OK. He only saw one flaw in the plan.

'Atlantic City was a good cover. We know plenty of people there that will vouch for Cristo. The only thing that's going to be tough to explain is the gash in his head. But we might get around that. Right now I have to put a couple guys on the street and find out who the dead guy was and who his friends are. We'll want to talk with them.'

G and the guys did real good over those couple of days. Between us we got almost everything sold, under control and on schedule. I even managed to get a few hours' sleep before I met up with Tony the next day to deliver his weekly shipment of cash from our business.

As usual, Francesca had a beautiful lunch prepared for Tony and me when I arrived. She left us in peace and we ate in silence.

Tony's face was drawn and lined. I could see that he hadn't got much sleep the night before. In all the years he'd been a wise guy, no one had ever tried to rob and murder someone under his wing, and he didn't like it.

The thing was, though, it was all changing. Everyone from

junkies to crooked crops to street punks was willing to risk their neck for a couple hundred grand. It wasn't like the old days when things seemed so easy, back when we sold a little pot and made a little money – it was much safer then and I didn't have a woman to worry about. Not to mention, I still couldn't sit and eat lunch or have a glass of wine with Tony without thinking of what he did to Paws.

After we finished lunch, Tony started with his questions.

'Who's the guy that Cristo made the deal with?'

'A Spanish guy that's done well. His name's Hector, he lives uptown.'

'Is it possible that this Hector was in on this?'

'Sure, everything's possible, Uncle. But I doubt it very much.'

'So you know this Hector then?'

'Yeah, I usually make the drop with Cristo. I just couldn't change the thing with the Jew.'

'Yeah, I know that, but what do you know about Hector?'

'He's about thirty-five, got a reputation as one of the toughest guys from Spanish Harlem, a real straight shooter. I never had a problem with him.'

'All right, I want you to go down the street to a payphone and call our Spanish friend Hector. You tell him I want to meet with him today at four o'clock.'

'OK, Uncle, you got it.'

'You meet him at four and bring him to your warehouse. Right?'

'Absolutely, Uncle, I'm on it.'

I started to get up but he signalled me to sit back down.

'I got something for you, kid.' He reached inside his suit jacket and pulled out some photos, and handed them to me. They were pictures of a real nice piece of property on the ocean somewhere.

'What's this?'

'That's a picture of the five acres of land I just bought for you. The property abuts the new ranch I just bought. It's in Belize.

The area's close to Pelican Bay; I thought you might like it down there.'

I didn't really know what to say to that – what can you say? 'Thanks, Uncle Tony, that's really great.' I got up from the table to leave. 'I'll see you at four at the warehouse.'

I felt distant and confused with Tony after what he did to Paws. Tony was my hero when I was a boy, but as the years passed by, I started finding myself disagreeing with a lot of his policy and decisions. I knew Paws had played a big part in his fate, but if he had to die, Tony could have had someone else do it, and he didn't have to torture him to find out where his stash was. I guess the more I thought about it all, the more unhappy I got. So I figured it was best not to think about it. They say time heals all. I'd take that tack. In the meantime I'd try to remember the Uncle Tony that I'd loved so much as a boy and try not to confront the monster that was emerging before my eyes.

Hector met me right on time. He looked like he was going to shit his pants. Just the fact that he showed up was enough for me to believe his innocence. I explained to him that searching him for a weapon was a necessity and not a sign of disrespect, because I had my orders. He understood and complied; he was clean.

Tony arrived right at four and sat down at the table without introducing himself.

'So you're Hector?'

'Yes, sir, I am.'

'Well, Hector, what can you tell me about the guys that tried to kill one of my nephews?'

'The guy that's dead was Jimmy, he and two of his boys were buying a couple of ounces a week from me. I knew Jimmy for a couple of years, the other two I don't really know well. One of the guys was called Juan. I don't know the other, he never came in, he just sat in the car during the buy. I think they were both Mexicans from LA. I don't think they been in the city long.'

'Are you ex-military, Hector?'

'Yes, sir, six years. Rangers. I did two tours in Vietnam, that's where I learned how to sell drugs. How did you know?'

'Well, you can't spot every guy that was ever a soldier, but the ones that were good soldiers never lose what the service gave to them. I'd say you were probably a good soldier. I'd even go as far as to say that you're telling me the truth.'

'Yes, sir, I was a good soldier, and I am telling you the truth.'

'That's very good for you, Hector, because I have your two Mexican compadres over on the Jersey shore. They tell me it was all your idea.' Tony gave Hector a hard look.

'That's a lie, sir. I never discussed my business or associates with them, and I never would have got involved in anything like that, sir.'

'OK, so how do you think they knew who to hit and, more importantly, when?'

'I don't know. I can only make a guess.'

'OK, Hector, let's hear your theory.'

'Jimmy called me Thursday afternoon and said he could move four ounces that day. That's good business for me but I didn't have any product. I told him the earliest I could do anything was late Friday night, probably after midnight. I'm guessing they waited and watched for Face. Spotting him coming into my building wouldn't have been hard. The guy stands out in a crowd.'

'Very good, Hector, because that's exactly what I think, but we still have a problem. I've got these two Mexicans over there in this fishery, hung from a ceiling, and they keep telling me you were in on it. So we're going have to take a ride, Hector.'

Hector looked pretty shaken but I think I was more afraid than he was. I knew Tony didn't bluff. Hector replied quite calmly for a guy in his shoes.

'Yes, sir, I understand . . . I told you the truth.'

'I believe you did, Hector. Don't you worry about it, I'll get the truth out of those two.'

There was a big, black stretch limo with tinted windows

waiting for us in the parking lot outside. GG got out of the back of the car.

'Hey, Tony, what's going on?'

'Don't worry about it, G. Thanks for bringing my driver and car down.'

'Yeah, sure, Tony, where are we going?'

'I want you to go inside and wait for me here, G. *Capisci?*'

'Yeah, right, OK. Where's TC and Face?'

'Forget about it, G.'

The look on Tony's, Hector's and my face was enough for GG to know that he should just drop it and do what he was told. He turned and went into the warehouse.

We all got into the big car. Tony told Hector to sit on the seat facing the rear window, Tony and I sat on the rear seat facing the driver. I wasn't sure where this one was going, but I didn't think I was going to like it.

We crossed the Brooklyn Bridge and cut through the city to the George Washington Bridge. When we got to the other side, Tony pulled out a large black cloth and handed it to me and then he spoke to Hector.

'Hector, I want you to put this over your eyes. I'm sure you can understand why I don't want you to know exactly where we're going.'

Hector looked a bit nervous. Tony sensed this.

'Hector, if I wanted you dead, you'd be dead. If I intended to kill you when we get to where we're going, I wouldn't need to blindfold you. It's for your own good. You don't ever want to know where this place is, trust me, Hector.'

Hector did as he was told and tied the blindfold to his head. About thirty minutes later Tony picked up a telephone attached to the console next to the cassette player, and dialled a number. 'Yeah, it's me, how's our guests? Good, that's good. I'll be there soon. Take one small toe apiece.' He put the phone back in the cradle. 'You see, Hector, if you take off a small toe from a hanging man, he slowly bleeds to death. It takes quite some time, but the pain, Hector, it's un-fucking-believable. Your heart beats faster and harder, trying to get the blood back to the respiratory system to be oxygenated, then every muscle in the body becomes intensely sore. Most people would give anything at that point to just die, to be released from the pain.' Tony leaned forward to insert a music cassette. It was Vivaldi. 'Just enjoy the music, Hector, we'll be there soon.'

After another twenty minutes or so of twisting and turning roads we came to a large industrial-looking complex on the water. The car pulled up to an overhead garage door. The door opened and we drove in.

The garage area was quite large, big enough for two or three tractor trailer trucks. We got out of the car and Tony led Hector, who was still blindfolded, up a small flight of stairs that led to the loading dock. From there, we passed through a large metal door. Tony took off Hector's blindfold once we got inside. If Hector was shitting himself, he was doing a good job not showing it.

We walked towards the rear of the building. On the right was an overhead mezzanine with big glass panels for looking down over the warehouse. I could see Denni up there on a telephone. He gave me a strange look, a sardonic grin like that of an overlord; it suggested to me that he had a kind of God complex.

I could hear voices, moans of pain and jovial laughter coming from the same room. It was eerie. We stopped for a moment as Tony waved to Denni who waved back nonchalantly. Then Hector and I entered the storage room where the creepy tones of pain and humour came together. Tony said he'd be in shortly.

The storage room was about twenty feet wide by thirty feet long with fourteen-foot ceilings. There was a large card table with five guys sitting around playing cards. I recognised three of them. One was the guy that had come out of the kitchen at Denni's sister's restaurant. The other guys were part of Tony's crew, Rocco and Paul.

To the rear of the room two guys were hanging from the rafters. They were naked, except for their soiled and bloodied underwear. Both were missing their small left toes. They were both tied with rope around the wrists with their arms pulled towards the ceiling, and their legs were tied together just above the ankles; their feet hung about four feet above the ground. The air in the room was a bit foul but there was a large extraction fan sucking out the worst of it. A couple of feet from the two condemned men was another table, more like a workbench really. On the bench was a blowtorch attached to hoses that led to the oxyacetylene tanks, and a large set of bolt cutters, used to cut locks and chains.

I knew these tools well, I had used them several times for their intended purpose, but I'd never considered what destruction they could do to the human body. The Mexican on the left, who I assumed was Juan, the so-called brains of his outfit, was making threats in Spanish to the guys at the card table, who I assumed were the ones that cut off the toes. I didn't speak Spanish, but it's similar to Italian and I got the gist of it. He was basically saying that their mothers were all whores and their fathers were all faggots. The guy had a lot of testosterone and hate. The other guy just hung there, sobbing and moaning.

The guys at the card table kept taunting the two Mexicans, saying shit like, 'Hey, spicko, I'm going to fry your balls in about ten minutes if you don't shut up!' They were laughing and joking, totally unaffected by what was happening. My guess was they were trying to psyche them out. Maybe scare them into telling the truth.

Hector just stood straight and stared at the Mexican who was running his mouth. Then he calmly walked over to the workbench and picked up the bolt cutters and started speaking in Spanish to the loudmouth. Then, without hesitation, Hector applied the bolt cutters to another of his toes and deftly cut it off. The bolt cutters seemed to cut through the toe effortlessly. Juan screamed so loud that I thought he was going to die right then. The five card players went quiet and seemed to take a little more notice of Hector, who was now yelling in Spanish at Juan. At this point Tony returned. He had changed into overalls and seemed content to let Hector lead the way. Hector noticed Tony enter and switched his tirade to English.

'You piece of shit, you tell the patron the fucking truth.'

Juan was fading, but the stubborn bastard just spit at Hector and gave a curt retort. 'Fuck jou, Egtor.'

Hector got real upset at that and tore the underwear from Juan's body and placed the bolt cutters on Juan's cock.

'Fuck me, Juan? I'll cut your fucking cock off right now, I don't fucking care.'

Juan was finally broken, he started to sob.

'Please, man, don't do that.'

'Did I have anything to do with that fucking robbery, Juan?'

Juan started to shake his head from side to side. He was crying.

'No man, it was my idea, I'm sorry.'

Hector wasn't showing any pity. 'Yeah, well, I'm not fucking sorry, Juan!' With that he violently squeezed the bolt cutters together, cutting off Juan's penis. Blood gorged out from Juan's body and covered Hector's right shoulder and Juan let out an ungodly scream that sent shivers through my body. His co-conspirator fainted.

One of the guys started laughing and said, 'Ha, ha, he cut his fucking cock off.' The other guys at the table just laughed and resumed playing cards. Tony nodded his head.

'OK, Hector, you get to go free.' With that he pulled his gun out from under his overalls and shot the other Mexican in the head. Juan's body was still convulsing but he was unconscious. Tony put a slug in his head as well.

I felt nauseous and the smell in the room was getting worse. Tony started giving out commands. 'Paul, you and Rocco go and get that cement mixer going, split one pour between the two barrels and make another batch. Stevie, where's Den keep his fucking chainsaws?'

'Tool shed, Ton.'

'All right, get two of them in here and let's finish this job up.' Tony noticed the sickened look on my face. I didn't know why he'd brought me here, he knew I didn't have the stomach for this kind of shit.

'Marco. You go to the car and tell the driver to run you down and grab a couple of bottles of whiskey.'

'Yeah, all right Tony.'

I went to the loading dock, gave the driver instructions and got into the back of the big car. Being alone, I usually would have put the privacy window down and talked with the driver, not wanting to appear like a snob, but after witnessing such a bloodbath I just wanted to sit alone and think.

It wasn't just the violence of the whole thing that disturbed me, but the complete lack of humanity that they all seemed to display. They wore their hardness and cruelty like badges of honour.

I didn't know how, or if, I could go home and face Julia. The episode with Paws had caused her to waver but she accepted my life for what it was with the understanding I'd be out of this thing soon and we'd move away. I was afraid to face her and I didn't think I could bury this night deep enough inside so she wouldn't sense it.

When I returned with the whiskey, all the guys, including Hector (who seemed to think he was on a job interview) were working away. Paul and Rocco were still mixing cement in the main room of the building, while the others were bringing red-stained cloth bundles out from the storage room.

The terrible smell in the air was now putrid. Also in the air was the exhaust of the chainsaws. They were quiet now, sitting to one side, covered with blood and tissue, like obedient servants having a well-earned rest.

Tony was manning the squeegee, pushing the remaining blood and bits down into a floor drain that emptied directly into the sea, which was just below that part of the building. The others were wrapping the last of the body parts in old rags before taking them out to the two fifty-five-gallon drums that sat just next to the cement mixer. I went back out into the main room and opened a bottle of whiskey.

'Hey, Tony, where can I find some cups?' I yelled loud enough for him to hear me; I didn't want to go back into the storage room. He popped his head out and pulled down the white mask, which all the guys were wearing, and pointed towards the mezzanine. 'Up there, kid. Get enough for all of us. Oh, and get some ice out of the freezer.'

I went up the stairs and went through the door on the landing into the large office. The room was full of file cabinets and desks that were normally occupied by a small staff during regular work hours. Denni was the only person in the room; he was sitting at the main desk going over what looked like accounts of some sort.

'Hey, Marco, how are you, kid?'

'Hey, Denni, what's up? I'm looking for some cups and ice.'

He pointed to a large closet in the back of the office. 'Just in there, kid, everything you need.'

'Yeah, thanks, Denni.'

He gave me a funny look; he knew I didn't like him and it seemed to bother him, but I didn't give a fuck. I was sick of the whole thing. I wasn't even twenty-seven years old and I felt like an old man. I was tired and afraid of what I was becoming. I took a package of plastic cups and a bag of ice from the freezer and left the office without a word. Denni looked up for a moment and then went back to juggling his books.

Paul and Rocco had just put the last of the concrete in the two big drums and were fitting the covers. The other guys were taking showers in the industrial bathroom in the other half of the building. To my relief, the smell had dissipated, thanks to the sea breeze that came from the large windows that were now open at the far end of the building. I put the cups and ice on one of the many large stainless-steel tables and poured a huge drink. I wanted to get some air and started for the open windows. Paul and Rocco were just finishing up. Paul was washing out the cement mixer while Rocco wiped down the drums that were now serving as two caskets.

'How the fuck you going to move those fucking things?'

'Forklift. They go on a pallet of diesel fuel drums for the boat. When they get out to sea, there's some place that's like three or four miles deep and off they go. Ain't nobody ever finding these fuckers.'

I just nodded and kept walking towards the windows. I had my cup and one of the bottles. I didn't want to go home that night. I didn't want to face Julia. I'd sleep at the clubhouse and be alone to absorb the horrors of this day.

I was hating Tony more than ever. I'm sure in his sick and twisted way he felt he was showing me how he looked after us. But I also think he wanted to let me know that he didn't like the way I stood up to him in my kitchen on the morning of Paws' death, and how I should think twice next time I decided to get on a morality kick against him.

The next day I awoke with the first real hangover I'd ever had. Don't get me wrong, I'd had plenty of nights when I drank way more than enough, but when you're young the body metabolises quickly. I don't know exactly how much I drank, but I was sick as a dog and decided to stay on the couch at the clubhouse for the rest of the day. I had called Julia and told her I was all right. I said that a couple of the guys got carried away in Atlantic City and I had a lot of work to do on my own. She didn't mind, she was just happy I was OK.

That night TC and Cristo returned from their little trip to Atlantic City. Neither one of them had shaved, TC had a black eye and Cristo had a bandage on his head along with a black eye that wasn't there the last I saw him.

'What the fuck happened to you?' TC asked me.

'I got friendly with Jack Daniels,' I said in a barely audible voice.

'You shouldn't hang around that guy, kid, he's bad news.' They both laughed.

I got up and went for the coffee machine. 'What the fuck happened to you two? You both look like shit.'

TC motioned for me to sit down and went to make the coffee and began his tale.

'We spent the weekend in jail down in Atlantic City.'

'Today's fucking Wednesday! What the fuck were you doing in jail?'

Cristo laughed and sat down on the couch and let TC continue.

'After we left Doc's, I figured Face was going to need an alibi for the shooting. You had the car thing under control, which, by the way, worked like a charm, so we went to Atlantic City. I called Jimmy – you know, the owner of the club near the Boardwalk – and told him if the cops came in and asked, to say that Cristo and I were in there earlier and he threw us out because we were drunk and rowdy.'

'So how'd you get arrested for that?'

'I'm trying to fucking tell you here.'

'Yeah, yeah, so go ahead.' My head was still thumping and I didn't want to know.

'Well, like I was saying. We get to Atlantic City and we go to the little motel that Louie and Johnny own and check in and tell him when the cops arrive to tell them we checked in about seven the night before. He didn't ask any questions.' TC looked at me like he was Einstein but I was hung-over and still didn't get it.

'Yeah, and?'

'Well, it was three in the morning so we went to the Boardwalk and started a fight.'

'With fucking who?'

'With each other, you fucking retard. We starting yelling and screaming and punching the shit out of each other. Someone called the cops and they locked us up for disturbing the peace. We went to court Monday morning, paid our fine and left. We went back to the hotel and I called Tony. He told us not to come back until this afternoon. So when we came back, we went to get

Cristo's car and his aunt said the police were by and asked a lot of questions and wanted to look at the car. She told them Cristo had called Saturday to ask her to send some money because he was in jail. The cops called Atlantic City and our story checked out. They just said Cristo should contact them as soon as he returned. We went to the cop shop and answered a bunch of questions and they let us go. Face is in the clear.'

I was feeling like shit, but I was happy it turned out OK.

'Well, that's great, I think you two should shower and shave because you both look terrible. Hey, Face, did you give him the black eye?'

He laughed and beamed a big smile. 'Yeah. I took it easy on him, though.'

'Yeah, well, while you two were out having fun, we've been working our asses off and there's plenty more to do, and I'm going back to my house to sleep so I'll leave you to it.'

TC sat down on the couch and got serious. 'The other night when I talked to Tony he said he was taking care of our Mexican friends. What happened?'

I gave them the short version of the night before and of those visions of hell in an abandoned seaside factory somewhere in New Jersey. I wanted to get to my own bed and see the only person that made sense to me – Julia.

The next couple of months were more of the same shit. Move blow around, move money around and start all over the next week. It was the third week of December before the shit started flying again and I began thinking that not only was going back impossible, going forward with any kind of a normal life would be impossible as well.

16
The Last Lap

In horse racing it's not necessarily the start that decides the race, it's the last lap that often counts. You see horses start strong and waver at the end or get bumped and fall and don't even finish. I'll take a strong final stretch every time, that's where I want my horse to shine. New Year's Eve was just two weeks away and I felt like a horse on the home stretch. The difference was, I didn't care about winning, I just wanted to cross the finish line.

It was about nine on a Saturday morning and I had just finished clearing the newly fallen snow from my driveway. I went inside to have breakfast with Julia. I usually got a little free time on Saturdays and sometimes on Sundays as well, depending on when Tony got back with the new shipment. I was planning on taking Julia out for a nice lunch, do some Christmas shopping and then we were going to go to an afternoon matinee. Julia loved Christmas and she looked so beautiful and content, I beamed inside just looking at her. It didn't take a lot to make Julia happy, she never complained, she just wanted to spend more time with me.

I got up from the table and kissed her forehead.

'Thanks, honey,' I said as I went to refill my coffee.

'What are you thanking me for? You made breakfast.'

'I know, I'm just saying thanks for all the times I didn't and should have.'

She smiled and blushed. She liked it when I did pleasant little things like that.

I took my coffee and went to the living room to check the weather on TV. It would be at least an hour and a half before she'd be ready to go so I turned on the television – and got a shock that made my head reel. On the TV screen was a picture of GG. I reached to set my cup of coffee on the small table next to my chair but missed the table and it spilt onto the deep shag carpet.

The reporter was relating the 'sketchy facts' of the breaking news story. I listened for a couple of minutes and got the basic details, then shut the TV off and went for the telephone to call TC who answered after the fourth ring.

'Hello!'

'T, it's me. You up?'

'No!'

'Well, get up now and meet me at the clubhouse in twenty minutes.'

'What the fuck's going on?'

'We got some real fucking shit, T. Twenty minutes. I'll call Cristo.'

'Right, I'll be there.'

I hung up the phone and called Cristo with the same message. The next problem was Julia. I went upstairs to the bedroom and sat on the bed.

'Honey, something came up, I can't go with you today. I'm really sorry.'

She looked gutted and I thought she might cry, but she didn't.

'Listen, sweetie. Why don't you call your mom and sister, take them out for lunch and then spend the day shopping, spend as much as you want. Take them to the best place you can think of, you can even take my new Cadillac.'

'I'd rather be with you.'

'Me too, honey. This is just real important.'

'Are you sure you want me to take your car?'

162

'Yeah, I'm sure, it's a much safer car for driving in this weather.'

She smiled, sighed and kissed me. What an amazing woman. I turned and went downstairs, grabbed a jacket and ran out the door. Running out the door seemed to be the only thing about me that Julia really knew. I hated doing this to her, but sometimes you can't change things.

I jumped in one of the new trucks in the driveway and set out for the clubhouse. There was about five inches of snow on the ground so when I arrived, the pristine, snowy sidewalk let me know I was the first to show up. I went inside and turned up the heat, put on the coffee and went back out to shovel the walkway. I didn't mind shovelling the snow, I actually liked it. It took my mind off all the shit that was running through my head

When TC arrived, I was back inside, sipping coffee.

'What's going on, Marco?'

'G's been picked up at his place.'

'Oh fuck. What happened?'

Before I could recite the facts that I knew, I heard a key in the door. It was Cristo; he looked liked he hadn't slept much.

'All right, so what the fuck's so important that I got to get out of my warm bed and go out in this shitty snow?'

'GG's been pinched.'

'For what?'

'The only thing I know is they raided his house last night and arrested him on suspicion of murder.'

TC and Cristo sat down.

'The news is reporting that he's the guy that whacked out those three DEA agents. And they found a bunch of blow and guns.'

'How much blow?'

'I don't know, T. They didn't say. Three counts murder, blow and weapons, that's all I got so far.'

'Did you call Uncle Tony yet?'

'You call him, T. Aside from the fact that he likes to sleep in before a run, he's going to have a fucking nutty when he hears this.'

Cristo got up for another coffee and paused.

'Hey, wait a minute. Those agents were killed by that Sicilian kid, Vincenzo. And they said they were killed on a Sunday?'

'Yeah. So what's the point, Face?'

'Well, GG's always with Tony doing a run on Sunday. It doesn't matter if they leave Saturday or Sunday, he's never here on a Sunday. He couldn't have been involved.'

I didn't have a lot of patience. 'Face, we know GG didn't do it. But he can't go to court and tell them "I was in South America picking up a bunch of cocaine with documents I got from my CIA buddies", can he?'

'No, I was just—'

The telephone rang and Cristo picked it up.

'Yeah, hey, Ton, how you doing? . . . Yeah, I just heard it from Marco . . . TC and Marco are here with me now . . . Right, see you then.' Cristo hung up and turned to us. 'That was Tony; be here in ten minutes.' The knot in my stomach tightened. This was going to be a big problem, I could feel it.

Tony came in with a look in his eyes that was a bit scary. I didn't bother to offer him coffee.

'Do you fucking guys have any fucking idea how many headaches this thing's going to bring?'

No one replied.

'How many fucking times have I told him, all of you, keep it simple! Why the fuck does he think he's got to live like King fucking Farouk?'

TC was the one to break the silence. 'Have you spoken to G, Tony?'

Tony took off his jacket and sat down at the table. 'No, but he called his dad last night who got him a lawyer. The lawyer called me this morning and gave me the scoop.' Tony looked off into space, as if running something through his head, then continued.

164

'The cops got three Ks of blow and—'

'Yeah,' I interrupted, 'but all our shit's sold and paid for. G, like usual, took a K and paid for it. I don't see how they got three Ks.'

'Well, if you quit interrupting me . . . Anyway, he told the lawyer that, aside from a couple of ounces that was his, the cops planted the blow and two of the three guns they grabbed.'

'Why do they want to set him up?' I asked.

'I don't know. But G can be stupid, he might have fucked with someone uptown that had some clout. I'm looking into this thing. I got an appointment with a judge I know, maybe there's a way to do some kind of backroom deal. Aside from GG's shit, I have to find someone else to make this run with me.'

I wasn't feeling very optimistic. Unwisely, I added my two cents of caution. 'Hey, Ton, why don't we just postpone this shipment for a week and get our shit together and figure this thing out?'

The glassed-over look on his face was one I'd never seen before; he had some deep thought running through his head. He spoke slowly, as if to himself, not us.

'Sun Tzu believed a good general, when faced with adversity, needed to create change and manipulate that change to his favour. You never walk into a baited trap but you let the enemy assume you intend to walk into the trap. If there's an enemy, he'll need time to bait his trap.'

We all just listened, not sure what his point was. TC's curiosity got the better of him.

'So who's the fucking enemy, Ton?'

'I don't know. What I do know is GG's sitting in prison for three murders we know he didn't commit. He couldn't have because he was with me, and we all know Vincenzo killed those guys.'

'Maybe they went in for the blow, found the guns and just made a ridiculous connection. It will get thrown out when they do the testing shit they do,' TC said, sitting back in his chair, feeling like he scored a point with Tony for his keen insight. Tony shook his head and started tapping his index finger on the table.

'No, T. For starters, GG told his lawyer that the guns weren't his. He wouldn't lie about the guns to his lawyer, he doesn't have to. Next, if they went in for blow and found a couple of guns, they'd have to run tests that would take days or weeks to come up with a connection. Then consider this. If they went in for the blow and found the guns, he'd be out on bail right now.'

'Yeah, but there's no way they could have the gun or guns that were used in those murders, Vincenzo would've made them disappear first thing,' I said, trying to follow a straight path of logic.

'The thing is, kid, they arrest him in the middle of the night, and next morning the news has his face on the TV as the shooter. There's no way they could know those guns were the ones used in the crime. This is a set-up, be sure of that.'

'Yeah, but it won't stick,' I persisted. 'There's no way the guns they have are the right ones. We wait for the tests and GG's in the clear for the murders.'

Tony lit a cigar and put his elbows on the table.

'Let me tell you a story . . . Do you remember Danny Legs?'

'Yeah, of course, Too Tall Jones,' I retorted, getting a quiet laugh from T and Cristo. It's what we called Danny behind his back because of his unusually long legs and short torso.

'Right, that's him. Well, when the cops got him for whacking out that two-bit bookie, they caught him with the gun and the silencer that was used and he was fucked, but we got him off. Do you know how that happened?'

We all shook our heads.

'The district attorney had two eyewitnesses that had seen Danny walk into the back room of the bar that the shit-ball bookie owned. These eyewitnesses said Danny entered the back room and five minutes later the barmaid goes back to ask the shit-ball a question and finds him dead. One bullet in the head, two in the chest. She calls the cops and gives a description of

Danny and his car. She had seen him around and knew the car. You see, she wasn't supposed to be working, the regular girl normally worked alone. But the shit-ball bookie had hired her that very day. So she sings like a canary before anyone can get to her and explain to her that her health is more important than the shit-ball. Anyway, she gives the description of Danny and the car to the cop, who calls it in. It turns out Danny is four blocks away in a car accident and the police are on the scene. Well, bada bing, bada boom, he gets new bracelets and a free stay in the city jail.'

Tony paused to relight his cigar and wipe a small bead of sweat from his forehead. 'So, the district attorney has the new barmaid and some out-of-town tourist as eyewitnesses, along with the gun and silencer. Danny's fucked. I go to see the judge, who's a friend of mine, to see how much it's going to cost to put the fix in. The problem, my judge friend tells me after examining the case, is if he throws the case out of court or calls a mistrial, it'll be suspect because the strength of the evidence is so overwhelming. Meaning the chances of the DA getting a retrial with a new judge are guaranteed. Well, I wasn't too happy about that, but the judge tells me that if there were some kind of tainted evidence involved, he not only could declare a mistrial but could guarantee the case would never be retried. He then went on to explain that all I needed was an inside cop to contaminate the chain of evidence, and we'd be in good shape. Well, that was no problem, we have half the force on the take.' Tony paused for a minute and poured a glass of wine from the open bottle on the table, took a sip and continued with his story.

'So when this thing goes to court, Danny's lawyer calls a weapons expert to the stand to testify. He's given exhibit A and exhibit B, the gun and the silencer. The lawyer explains that according to his client, Danny, he admitted to owning the gun, but had never owned a silencer. Then he asks the guy if the silencer was a standard silencer, one that might be found readily on the streets. The guy looks at the gun and the silencer and tells the court that this particular silencer isn't compatible with this gun and it's one normally used by SWAT teams and government agencies. The whole courtroom stirs at this revelation and the DA is starting to shit himself. Now Danny's lawyer presents exhibit C, the three slugs pulled from the shit-ball's body, allegedly, and asks him if the slugs in question have a deformity consistent to other slugs he'd seen pulled from a human body. The guy says they're not consistent with others and, in his opinion, they look like they were fired into a cement wall, which would make it difficult to prove if these slugs were even fired from the gun in question. The lawyer asks the judge for a recess, in which the DA, the judge and Danny's lawyer go into the judge's chambers. Twenty minutes later they come back and the judge declares a mistrial. Danny walks out free as a bird.'

This was all a bit hazy to Cristo; he looked at TC, then at me, with that dumb look he gets on his face when he doesn't see the joke. 'Yeah, but Ton, how's that help G?'

'It don't. All I'm saying, if the game's fixed, those test results are going to prove that the guns at G's are the murder weapons, and if that's the case, we've got a big problem, because it means we're not just up against the cops but someone else that knows how to play the game.'

'So what's the plan, Uncle Tony?' I asked.

'Whoever's doing this will need time to break G. Months at least. We just got to make sure his lawyer gets a bag full of money on Monday. When G hears his lawyer is happy, he'll relax. Meanwhile, I'm going to make a few inquiries and see if I can find out who's trying to send G up the river. Right now, I'm calling Tommy Vaccaro, I'll get him to make the run with me. I can trust Tommy. So stay sharp, we're still in the game, boys. Next week we'll have a clearer picture of what we're up against.'

Tony got up and went to the door, stopped and turned.

'And keep an eye in your rear-view mirror at all times. You know the rule, if you think someone's following you, make three consecutive right turns. If they're still behind you, lose them. I'll see you when I get back.'

With that he walked out the door and we all just stared off into space for a moment. I think we all sensed the changes coming. TC was the first to speak.

'Marco, you better go to the safe and get three hundred and fifty grand for G's lawyer and get it to him first thing Monday morning. Leave an IOU with G's name on it for accounting. Me and Face will go downtown and see if we can get in to see him. I know a couple of guys down there that might be able to pull a few strings. If nothing else, I'll make sure they get some cigarettes, booze and the basic shit to him.'

TC and Cristo got up and left. I sat there for a while and pondered the big picture. I didn't give a fuck what anyone else wanted or what happened, come New Year's, if I was alive, I was out of here.

17
Exit Strategies

The following Monday morning I went downtown and dropped the money off to G's lawyer then headed up to the Bronx where I had lunch. From there it was less than an hour's drive to the executive airport where I had to pick up the new shipment of blow that Tony was bringing in.

The whole monotonous exercise was driving me out of my mind. Driving back with the blow I had my eyes in the rear-view mirror the whole way. I figured that if I took a pinch then I'd probably end up doing seven years of a ten-year bid. Before that happened, I decided I was going to have one more beautiful meal at my favourite restaurant on Arthur Avenue.

Technically, I was supposed to do one more run the next Monday or Tuesday, but I was going to invent some reason why I couldn't do it. I'd ask T or Cristo to do it. I'd never asked them to do that before so I figured one of them would say yes.

Panic attacks are funny things that don't play by a set of rules. For one thing, you can get an attack that starts in the chest, which feels like a heart attack, or you can have an attack that starts in your mind. This is where you get this overwhelming sensation that you're losing your mind and your head's about to explode.

Then there's the mother of all panic attacks. This is an attack where you suffer both symptoms simultaneously, which is exactly the type of panic attack I suffered while making that run, right before I had my beautiful lunch on Arthur Avenue.

It turned out that I didn't have any problems, aside from the first and worst panic attack I've ever had, which left a mark on me and, in a strange way, gave me the courage to stand up to the guys I'd always been so loyal to.

The panic attack also made me change my distribution routine. Instead of going to the warehouse and storing half of the blow and taking the rest to Queens, I went straight to the two houses in Queens where we always cut and packaged the shit up.

GG had never been there. He didn't even know where they were because he never got involved with that phase of the business. Whenever he got back from a run with Tony he went straight to the city for a couple of days of R&R.

I didn't really think that G was going to rat us out, but I didn't know who was setting him up. For all I knew they'd been watching him for months before they got him. If that was the case, the warehouse would be compromised.

After I got the blow safely stashed and ready for Lena to get out her boots, I tried calling TC but I couldn't find him anywhere. I tried Cristo and got the same results. Feeling nervous, I made a command decision. I was getting all the cash out of the warehouse and clubhouse. There was the better part of $5,000,000 tucked away in that old jeweller's safe and the floor safe. I had a huge safe hidden very well in a concrete wall in the garage at my house. I thought the money would be more secure there. I made two trips and got it all with no problem. I could have done it in one trip with my van, but if something happened, like an accident or an arrest, at least we wouldn't lose it all. I left a note in the warehouse safe for T, along with a key to my house, my safe combination and the code for the house alarm. I could just imagine him going into the safe and finding it empty, he would have had a heart attack. But until we knew what was up with G, we had to take precautions.

I went to the clubhouse and waited for someone to call. Ace

and Shawn not calling didn't bother me. They knew it would be a day or two before the new shipment was ready to move and were probably relaxing a bit. But not hearing from T and Cristo was bothering me.

Julia was out with her mother for the day and not due back until late in the evening, so I kicked back on the couch, stuck a Vivaldi tape in the stereo and tried to work out some of the kinks that were troubling me about the weeks to come.

Listening to Italian opera was another one of those little things I picked up from Tony when I was a boy.

When I was six or seven we'd sometimes drive to his house upstate and go fishing for the weekend. He'd crank the record player so loud that it echoed over the lake. I'm sure most people who lived up that end of the lake could hear it loud and clear. Then we'd stand out on the dock with our fishing rods and he'd use the time to educate me, Tony style.

He explained the need to have certain types of music on for contemplating certain types of serious problems. For Tony, the music for serious problems was, in most cases, a violin concerto by Vivaldi.

We never threw a football or a baseball around. Our sessions were always simple, like fishing or sitting at a table playing cribbage or chess, always with some type of calm cerebral music in the background. Whatever the activity or music, they where just ambient devices used to set a tone that Tony felt was appropriate for sharing his wisdom with me. For example, he taught me the importance of history early on.

'You see, kid, anyone that tells you they can see the future is running a con on you. No one can see the fucking future. But the Greeks, a couple of thousand years ago, they had it figured out. Their take on the whole thing was this: if no man can see the future, which they already established as a given, then the only intelligent thing any man can do, concerning the future, is to turn his back on it. Now I know that sounds a bit retarded, but think about it for a minute. If you turn your back on the future,

173

you see the past, but not just your past, everyone's past – man's past, civilisation's past. There's an abundance of information at your disposal that can be used to make choices concerning the future. Look at General George Patton, one of the most successful generals in history. His success was due to his abundant knowledge of history. You see, kid, we're all creatures of habit, and we don't really change too much. We all strive for the same shit, generation after generation, and we all make the exact same mistakes, over and over again. Why? I'll tell you why. Lack of information. Most people make some of the biggest choices of their lives without enough information. So when you have to make any decisions in life, you look at the past. That's why I've bought you so many books, they're full of information, kid.'

That, like so many other lessons Tony imparted to me, became a useful tool in my life. Not everything he did for me was like a gift I didn't want. So as I kicked back on the couch listening to soothing tones of Vilvaldi, I considered all of my possible options and played out several different scenarios about escaping from the drug trade. Each path included a tremendous amount of danger. Frustrated, I dozed off into a deep sleep that offered momentary peace.

A couple hours later I awoke to the shutting of the door. It was TC.

'Hey, T, where you been?'

'Long fucking day. Let me get a drink first.'

Instead of a beer or wine, TC went into the liquor cabinet and grabbed a bottle of Scotch. This was a sure sign that he was stressed. As he got the ice, he turned and gave me a positive nod and said, 'I stopped by the warehouse to pick up some cash. That was a smart move, kid, moving all the cash. Well done.'

'Thanks. I got the shits today thinking about all the possibilities.' I paused and thought now would be a good time to mention next week's run. 'Hey, by the way, I got this thing next Monday or Tuesday. Can you or Face make the run for me?'

'Yeah, sure, kid, I'll do it.' He gave me a curious look. 'Moved all that money across town by yourself, and now you got a thing Monday or Tuesday? You really did get the shits today, didn't ya?' TC said it with a smile on his face. He knew I was sweating bullets.

'Thanks, T, I really appreciate it.'

'No problem. So, where's the safe in your house? Is it hidden away like all the other ones?'

'Oh, yeah, that would've taking you a few days to figure out. You go to my workshop in the garage. You know the workbench on the far wall?'

TC nodded.

'The bench and the back that all the tools hang on are all built together and the whole bench has swivel wheels. On the right-hand side you'll see three bolts that look like they hold the whole work bench to the wall, but they don't. The top bolt, that's about eye level, turn that twice to the left with a pair of pliers or a wrench, and it unlocks a latch. Then you just grab that corner of the bench and pull it out. The left side of the bench, and the plywood back with the tools on it, are hinged to the wall. Everything opens up like a door and there's the safe.'

'Where the fuck do you get these ideas from, kid? You should start a safe installation company or some shit like that.'

'Not for me, T. I'm going to drive off into the sunset with Julia and build houses or become a garbage man. Anything that doesn't involve safes, guns or Uncle Tony.'

TC looked at me with a long, weary sigh. I could feel it coming.

'That's something we got to talk about, kid. We need you to stick it out for a while. With Paws and G out of the game, it's going to be a handful.'

I jumped up off the couch. 'No fucking way, T! As of January first, I'm out, finished. I promised Julia I was getting out.'

'Take it easy, kid, I'm not saying years, just a couple of months until we get it straightened out.'

'Yeah, well, I'm saying never, not even for a couple of fucking hours.' TC went quiet; I was just getting started. 'Do you know what was going through my head today, T, while I was moving that fucking shit?'

He didn't reply, so I kept going.

'I was thinking I'm going to get popped and end up right next to fucking GG. What happens to my life then, T? I lose the best woman I'm ever going to find. I lose my freedom. And what about all that money I worked for and risked my life for? It does me no fucking good to be dead or in prison, and it definitely don't mean a fucking thing if I lose Julia. I promised her, T. I promised myself. You can all fuck off, and if you don't like it, fucking kill me – if you can.'

That one got a reaction. TC's eyes glazed over and his body energy lit up like an A-bomb. 'Don't ever talk to me that fucking way again, kid! The only brothers I've ever had are you and Cristo.' He was right in my face. 'So what you got to do, you do, but don't run that shit at me again or I'll knock you the fuck out. You fucking try me!'

I could see in his eyes that he hated arguing with me. But I just stared right back into his without an ounce of fear.

'I ain't fucking staying, T, and if you want my advice, you should walk away too, and don't waste time about it. We've had a real good run, let's get out while we can. This is the fast lane and we're driving a new Ferrari with bald tyres, sooner or later it has to crash. After next week I'm gone.'

I turned to grab my jacket and leave. I'd said what I had to say and didn't want to keep kicking it around.

The rest of the week went fairly smoothly. We were all stressed, but managed to maintain a bit of composure. Tony didn't want to make a run on Christmas Day, or the day after, so he left on Wednesday night and returned Friday, Christmas Eve.

TC said he'd make the run for me, but we both thought it would be Monday or Tuesday, so I figured I'd have to do it. I got the call Friday morning from Tony to tell me the blow was ready to pick up and, much to Julia's disapproval, I headed for the warehouse.

I stopped by the warehouse to get the '24 HOUR EMERGENCY SERVICE' van I always used when doing that particular run. It was basically a plumber's truck but it was a good cover, not to mention, what cop's going pull over some poor bastard that has to unplug someone's toilet on Christmas Eve?

When I got to the warehouse I was surprised. TC was sitting in the van wearing similar attire as myself, green overalls and a green cap. I parked my truck and went over to the driver's side of the van and TC rolled down the window.

'What are you doing here, T?'

'I called your place twenty minutes ago; Julia said you just left. I figured that thing you had Monday or Tuesday probably got changed to today.' He said it with a smile.

I figured I was here so I might as well go with him. 'Jump over, I'll drive.'

'Fuck that, you drive like an old lady.'

'That's my point, T. Move over.'

TC laughed and hopped into the passenger seat. I was glad not to be going alone.

I put on the radio and drove off to the sounds of Burl Ives singing his version of 'Frosty the Snowman'. TC tapped along to the music and didn't say anything until the tune finished. Then he turned to me with a calm look on his face. 'You know what we talked about the other day, you sticking around for a while longer?'

'Yeah.'

'Uncle Tony's the one pushing that thing, you know.'

'Yeah, I figured that.'

'I just thought you should know he's going to push that one hard. He figures it's your goofy, creative ideas that probably kept this thing going as smooth as it did.'

'Yeah, T, if my ideas are so goofy, why are you dressed up like Joe Shit the fucking rag man? You could've worn a suit and tie and took your car tonight.'

'All right, they're not fucking goofy ideas. I just have to say shit like that so you don't get a bigger fucking head than you already have.'

'What's your point, T?' I wasn't in the mood for bullshit.

'Listen, I talked to Cristo, him and me will do all the runs and all the big deals, Shawn and John the smaller ones. If you can just be there with Lena while she cuts and packages the shit. And maybe help out with the financial shit, just for five or six months, it'll be a big help.'

'And then what? I get sucked back in for "just another five or six months"?'

'No fucking way, I promise. Cristo and I got some things worked out, we're going to get out soon too.'

'Get the fuck out of here, T. You can't bullshit a shitter and you definitely can't scare an old whore with a big dick. How many times did Tony tell us that?'

'I ain't fucking with you, kid. We're going legit.'

'What the fuck are you two going to do that's legit, T? Provide sound managerial advice on how to be drug dealers? Maybe do a motivational speaking tour at the Ivy League schools?'

'Don't give me that shit, kid, you ain't the only one with dreams.'

'All right. I'm fucking kidding, T. What'd you have in mind?'

'Forget about it.'

'T, come on, it's Christmas, lighten up.'

'Well, I want to buy a vineyard, and Cristo wants an olive farm . . . in Italy.'

'A fucking vineyard? What, because you grow nice tomatoes in your backyard you're a fucking horticulturist?'

'You got a big head, kid, don't make me squash it on Christmas Eve.'

I could see he was getting pissed off, but I was trying to make light of things. 'Look, T. All I'm saying is, what do you guys know about vineyards and olive farms?'

'We can learn.'

'T, we're talking about Cristo here. Don't get me wrong, I love him, but do you remember when he was arrested his first time, and he thought he was going to jail for two years?'

'Yeah, I do. He said he was going to leave the country.'

'That's right. I asked him where he'd go. Do you know what he said?'

'No, what?'

'He said he was going to Florida.'

TC and I both laughed and it eased all of our tension. I asked him another question, more serious this time. 'How much do you guys need to move?'

'Between me and Cristo, about five million should do it.'

'Wow, did you guys stick that much away?'

'Well, that's the thing, kid, we don't have shit between us. But since you're getting out soon, we're going to have to sell some of the properties to cash you out. The price of houses is on the move, so it's probably a good time to sell most of the real estate we got and split it up between the six of us. I'm sure GG's problems are going to cost some serious cash as well, so he'll need his cut. Not that he deserves it. According to the pact, he's lost his nest egg, but he's not going to do the time with his mouth shut if we don't pay him.'

I nodded; it was easier to just cash him out.

I liked the idea of this. If we liquidated most of the property, it would be easier for everyone to get out and walk away. Maybe I would stay and help out another six months after all.

'I'll tell you what, T. You and Cristo take care of all the runs and deals, and I'll keep the status quo over in Queens with the cutting and packaging and take care of moving the money around. But, first thing we do after the New Year is put a bunch of property on the market and dump it. I walk away forever come June first. What do you say? Deal?'

179

TC nodded his head and put his hand out and we shook on it. I didn't know how Julia was going to take it, but I felt it was the best terms I was going to get that involved me getting most of my investment back, and I wouldn't be moving the shit around any more.

10
Bobby and Dave

We all had good Christmases that year. It was the first time we all had steady girlfriends at the same time, and together we spent a couple of great days enjoying each other's company.

We stopped by Susan's house with lots of gifts for her and Jessica. We all pitched in and gave her $50,000 and told her she'd have more by summer. She was very thankful.

We missed having G around; even though he was a bit of a fuck-up, he was still like a brother.

I told Julia that I'd agreed to help out in a financial capacity. I explained that for me to get the seven or eight million I had tied up, I was going to have to stick around for a few months, and that by the summer we'd go upstate and build our house. I promised her that I wouldn't get involved in any runs or deals and she was relieved to hear that. On the nights I stayed in Queens with Lena, I would say I was counting money, not watching the drugs getting cut and packaged.

New Year's arrived and the five of us remaining toasted to Paws. TC and I explained to the guys the new arrangement and that the majority of the property would go up for sale, the money split six ways. Susan and Tony would split what Paws was owed and I would walk away for good by the first of June. Everyone was satisfied with this and I was very happy to find a way out. Life seemed to be getting better but the real problem was getting

GG out of jail and figuring out who was setting him up.

Tony and Tommy Vaccaro returned from South America a couple of days after the New Year. Between Christmas and New Year's they made two extra runs, which meant we all had to work double time to have it cut, packaged and sold, leaving Tony with little time to deal with GG's problems. Later that same day, Tony called and asked me to bring his cut of the cash to his place. He'd been too busy making the runs and dealing with the holidays to take care of accounting, so I had four shipments worth of money for him. Like usual, he wanted the cash delivered to his house and expected me to stay for lunch.

The next day I arrived at Tony's and pulled in the long driveway ten minutes early to drop off the money. Aside from Tony's Lincoln and Francesca's Delta 88, there was a black Ford LTD that I'd never seen before. It looked like an undercover cop car.

I left the money in the trunk of my car and went to the side door. Francesca gave me a big hug and told me to go into Tony's study. In all the years I'd been making these cash drops, there'd never been anyone else there so it seemed a bit strange, but I shrugged it off and entered the study. As soon as I opened the door I saw the two men sitting on the large sofa. I recognised them both from a long time ago. Tony stood up to greet me then turned to his guests and pointed.

'You remember Bobby and Dave?'

Both men stood and put out their hands to shake.

'Yeah, I remember. How's things, guys?' I used to go fishing with Tony and these guys when I was a kid, but I hadn't seen either of them for at least ten years.

Robert Stockland didn't look like he was a day over forty, but I knew he had to be at least fifty. His black hair was short and curly with only the lightest touch of grey. He was about six feet tall and had a thin athletic appearance that suggested he was extremely fit. Unlike his friendly smile, his blue eyes gave the impression they were attached to an inner iceberg, incapable of warmth or feeling.

David Simms was close to fifty and he looked it. He stood about five foot six inches tall and seemed to be almost as wide, but he didn't have an ounce of fat. If David Simms' appearance was in contrast to Stockland's, his aura wasn't.

'Sit down, kid. Glass of wine?'

'No thanks, Tony, I'm fine.'

'Well, as I'm sure you've surmised, these are our business partners.'

'Yeah, I figured that much.' The truth was, I was shocked that these two were our guys. Don't get me wrong, it made perfect sense, I just couldn't believe I hadn't worked it out before.

'They're here in the city to have a look around and see if they can get a handle on what's happening with this GG thing. They can penetrate places that would be difficult for us. So they're going to ask you some questions and you try and help them out.'

'All right, Uncle, no problem.'

Simms did most of the talking. 'Marco, do you know the people in Manhattan that G's been doing business with?'

'Yeah, most of them.'

'Do you know how to get in touch with them?'

'Most of the business he did that side of the bridge was with the queers in the Village. G's not gay, but those guys got plenty of cash to throw around and it was easy business for him. He used to rob some of the out-of-town crowd that came in from up north.'

Tony jumped in at that. 'What do you mean, he robbed them?'

'You know, grifter shift, short con, sell a couple of ounces to a couple of fags and follow them when they left to go back home and rob them at a restaurant, hotel or a gas station. Sometimes, after doing a few deals with a guy from out of town, he'd rob them before he sold them the blow. He'd have two guys, his cousins, rob them at the hotel a couple of hours before he showed up. When G arrived he'd tell them he felt bad and would cuff them half as much as they'd planned on buying but would have to charge more per ounce. A week later they'd be back for more and to pay him what they owed.'

Tony looked pissed off. 'What the fuck was he thinking? How'd you find out?'

'One night he told us, bragged about it. TC, Cristo and I told him to knock the shit off; as far as we knew, he did. There're a hundred guys running the con out there, Uncle; G wasn't the only one.'

The other two just sat and took it in. Then Simms turned to Tony.

'Do you think there's any connection? Maybe one of them caught on and called some queer lover in one of the agencies.'

Tony shook his head. 'Who the fuck knows? Better check it out.'

Simms looked at me to continue his questioning, but I was getting a bit buggy. Every time he was about to ask me a question, he did this weird, almost robotic thing with his head and mouth. First he would turn his head to the right and breathe in with a terse, non-smile, and then begin his question. I probably wouldn't have thought much of it, but Uncle Tony did a weird thing with his eyes when he questioned someone. Tony would look away and then stare straight at you and his eyebrows would drop.

Stockland did a strange thing as well, he would kind of lean back and turn slightly to the right and bring his head forward, meeting you with his penetrating eyes as he delivered his gaze.

I had never really thought much of it before, but then again I was never questioned by the three of them at the same time. Maybe it was nothing, just personal oddities, but I couldn't help but think it had something more to do with some kind of a military type of training. Whatever, I felt very uncomfortable. Stockland, who had just been listening up to that point, interrupted Simms.

'Marco, maybe you can spend the afternoon in the city with

us, just to familiarise us with the Village and give us a list of the names you know.'

'Yeah, sure, Bobby. I can introduce you to a guy that knows the ropes over there.'

'Good, that's good, Marco. We'll be back in about an hour and a half to pick you up.' Stockland stood up, followed by Simms. They both put on their jackets and said their farewells. Tony and I had our lunch in quiet, both lost in thought.

When I finished my lunch I got the cash from my car and we went through the accounts. That done, I had one question for Tony. 'So, Uncle, how come you never told me Bobby and Dave were our guys in South America?'

Tony thought about it for a minute and replied, 'To be honest, kid, I always thought you had figured it out.'

'No, I had no idea.'

'Well, we wouldn't have told you if we really believed you had no idea. But, the thing is, if this thing ever goes tits up, you should know all of the parameters. Like I've always said, information is paramount to survival.'

Paramount to survival? I didn't ask because I didn't want to know. I already knew that I was in way over my head and had slim odds on getting out in one piece with Julia. But I had to deal with what was in front of me for the moment. If I just paid attention, and thought through it all, maybe I'd be OK.

When Simms and Stockland pulled into Tony's driveway, I left without a word.

I sat in the back of the Ford LTD which was being driven by Simms. Conversation was non-existent until we crossed the Brooklyn Bridge and entered Manhattan.

'What's the plan, Marco?' Stockland asked.

'Get us over by the park, just above the Village. I know a valet over there who will park the car for us. You two can go into the bar there and I'll walk down to the Village and make contact with my guy, and then I'll bring him over to you. If people in the bar see you two where he works, he might not want to talk so much.'

Stockland just nodded his head and went back into his own world.

After we parked the car, Simms and Stockland went into the bar. I made my way down into the Village and went straight for GG's local. It was one of those queer-straight places where most of the crowd was as full of shit as you could get. I went to the bar and was instantly recognised by the barman.

'Hey, Marco, what brings you here? What's all that shit with GG? We haven't heard any real news since they got him.'

'Yeah, he's hanging in there. He'll be all right. Hey, listen, I'm looking for GG's pal Anthony, do you know where I can find him?'

Phil just turned his head towards the far corner of the bar and pointed to a booth where Anthony was sitting alone.

'He's right there. He starts his shift in twenty minutes. Can I get you a drink?'

'No, I'm good, thanks a lot. Oh, by the way, Anthony's going to be a little late starting his shift today. Can you cover for him?'

'Yeah, sure, Marco, no problem.' He smiled, but I knew he was a bit nervous.

I walked over to the table where Anthony was and sat down. Anthony was about thirty and was one of those spoiled rich kids who couldn't support his lifestyle on the monthly stipend given to him by his father, so he ran bullshit scams and worked part-time behind the bar to earn some extra bread. I never liked the guy and he knew it.

'Hey, Marco, how's things?'

'Yeah, I'm all right. Listen to me, I want you to come up the street and meet two friends of mine. They're going to ask you a bunch of questions about GG. If you're smart you'll tell them anything you can. And don't fuck around with these guys, Anthony, they'll kill you as soon look at you. You got me?'

Anthony was nervous, and quietly said, 'I'm supposed to start my shift soon.'

I leaned in close towards him. 'The shit-head behind the bar's going to cover for you. I'm not asking you, Anthony. I'm telling you.'

Anthony looked a bit shaken but nodded his head in agreement. I thought it best to reassure him – just to loosen his tongue up a bit.

'Listen to me, Anthony. You got nothing to be worried about. These guys don't give a fuck about who you robbed or any other shit. They just want to know everything that G's been up to the last few months before he got busted.'

I walked Anthony up the street to the bar where Simms and Stockland were and introduced them. I sat down for ten minutes. Anthony was answering questions without reservation and I figured I wasn't needed, so I said I'd get a taxi back over the bridge and see them later. I didn't have any misgivings about offering up Anthony to Simms and Stockland. Whatever Anthony had coming to him, it wasn't my problem. It was his bed and he had to lie in it.

Once outside, I had an idea. I thought it might be the only opportunity I would have to get a picture of Simms and Stockland. Even if I made it out, I figured it might help the other guys to know who our partners were. Like Tony had said, information is paramount.

I went a couple of blocks down to another bar that I was vaguely familiar with. It was a real dive where a lot of the dregs of the Big Apple hung out. Inside I scanned the room until I found a face I knew; her name was Loretta, she was a hooker and she knew Anthony.

'Hey, Loretta, how's things?'

She gave me a hard look. 'How's things? Well, let's see. My husband's a one-legged junkie who sometimes thinks he's still in Vietnam, my sixteen-year-old daughter's working the streets and I have to sleep with disgusting men to pay the rent, which I'm still a hundred short on this month. Yeah, things are just fan-fucking-tastic, Marco.'

I knew Loretta's bitterness was, aside from her shitty life, a lot to do with the fact that I knew her before her life got turned upside down, and she was embarrassed.

Loretta and her husband Joey were from my neighbourhood before he went to Vietnam; they were a real nice, normal family. After spending ten months 'in country', Joey lost his left leg and spent a year in a military hospital. When he came home he got into heroin as a supplement to the morphine and got Loretta hooked as well. It didn't take long before they had to sell the house and move into the slums. That's when Loretta began her new profession. Whenever anyone that knew her from the past saw her working the streets, it embarrassed her. The way she dealt with this was to respond as harshly as she could.

I got straight to the point. 'Well, how about you help me out, Loretta? It'll only take ten, twenty minutes, and I'll make sure you get the rent sorted and a couple of bucks extra as well.'

'That sounds good to me. What do you want me to do?'

I explained to her that Anthony was just up the street in the bar with two guys and that I wanted some pictures of them. And that if they caught her taking pictures, they might do something really bad to her. She wasn't fazed in the slightest by the potential danger.

'Honey, every night I walk out onto these streets I'm surrounded by danger. This is a walk in the park.' She laughed briefly and then got serious. 'The problem is I don't have a camera.'

'That's not a problem, I'll go next door to the hotel gift shop and grab one.'

She looked incredulous. 'They'll charge you an arm and a leg in there.'

'Don't you worry about that. Just finish your drink and I'll be back in five minutes with the camera. And find someone half respectable to take with you – they can pose near Anthony's table. I'll pay her separately. It's dark in there and you'll need a flashbulb.'

188

Once I had the camera, film and flashcubes, I set it up and went back to get Loretta.

When I arrived back at the bar, she was out front waiting for me with a young beauty named Valerie who was dressed nice-perfect. I went through the routine with her

'Now listen, girls. If these guys know that you're trying to get their picture, they could get very violent. So just be quick and not too obvious. Valerie shouldn't stand too close to their table. In fact, I think you two should get a table across the room from them and have Valerie sit with her back to them. Then Loretta you take a couple of pictures of Valerie with these guys in the background; I'll have the pictures enlarged later.'

Loretta nodded. 'No problem, Marco. We'll be back in twenty minutes.' And off they went.

Thirty minutes later the girls returned and were calm and casual. Loretta handed me the camera.

'I got three pictures. They were only ten feet away so they should be good shots. I didn't get a good shot of Anthony, though. He was sitting with his back towards us.'

'Don't worry about it. Were they suspicious of anything?'

Loretta shook her head. 'No, they were in a real serious conversation with Anthony. Valerie and I were laughing and sounding like a couple of girls having fun.'

'Good. That's really great; I appreciate it.'

I gave Valerie a hundred and she thought she'd hit the lottery. When she left, I gave Loretta five hundred and she almost cried.

'Thank you, Marco, you always were good.'

She got up from the table and kissed my cheek. As she turned away, I grabbed her hand. 'Loretta, if you ever need anything, you know where to find me.'

'Thanks,' was all she could muster. I guess when someone like Loretta falls so far into the abyss, feelings and emotions are job hazards that must be avoided at all costs.

Three months later Loretta was murdered in Central Park, her killer never caught. Joey, her husband, overdosed on heroin within a few weeks after her death, leaving their daughter lost, alone and very bitter. I looked for her but never found her. The word on the street was that after the funeral she caught a bus and disappeared. I can only hope that she found something better than what she left behind. But stories like Loretta's daughter's don't often have happy endings.

The next week was as busy as it had ever been. I had to meet with realtors to put property on the market and change a lot of small bills into large ones. I didn't see Tony until the following week for lunch and to settle up the week's cash.

I knew that Stockland and Simms had kicked a lot of ass for three days. We heard things from uptown and the guys at the clubhouse were talking about it. They'd heard that undercover cops were asking a lot of questions about GG and they weren't being very nice about it. I just listened, not able to explain what I knew and that I had an inside track on it all.

Tony seemed to be much calmer and I thought it was a good time to ask a few questions.

'So, Uncle, did Bobby and Dave come up with anything uptown?'

Tony answered freely, showing no signs of irritation. 'Yeah, I think they made some progress. It seems that G's been muscling a lot of people uptown, him and his cousins. If I get my hands on those two I'll give them a beating. Have you seen them around?'

'No, last I heard they were back in Sicily.'

'If they're smart they'll stay away for a while. It looks like the local DA over the bridge is trying to send a message to the players around town. With three dead DEA agents, he's getting a lot of pressure. I think G will beat the murder raps but he'll do a stretch for the cocaine charges; we're working on that. Tell the guys if they're going to do any business over there to be quiet and don't make any waves.' Tony stood up from the table, indicating it was time for me to go. 'Oh, by the way, tell TC I'll be back next Tuesday; I'm staying for an extra day down there. Right?'

'Yeah, sure, Uncle. I'll see you next week.'

Well, so much for the last lap. Not only didn't I finish, I was still running on this crazy track where the finish line kept moving. It was like one of those weird dreams where you just keep falling and falling. Then when I did wake up, I was still falling. Instead of feeling like a well-conditioned, well-bred steed, I felt like a gerbil running and running on a small round wheel.

19
The Bad Hand

Poker's a funny game. You can have four kings, and the odds of that are awful long, but you can still get beat by four aces or a straight flush. The chances of someone having four aces or a straight flush in the same hand are astronomical odds, but it does happen. I'd beaten so many odds over the years, and I was so close to walking away, I thought that maybe I was holding a winning hand. I had several million dollars coming my way, I hadn't spent a day in jail and, most importantly, I had a woman I loved and she loved me. I just needed to find the right moment to make the right move.

It was late February and things were going smooth. We had all been working hard and decided to go to this after-hours club that did some great parties. I had asked Julia to come with me but she was more of a homebody and wanted to stay at home.

I picked up Cristo and Ace the Mick; we were meeting TC and his girl there. The club was a renovated loft with a huge dance floor and two long bars with tables and chairs around the perimeter. In the rear of the joint was a VIP back room with a pool table and two poker tables, which is where we spent most of our time.

The guy who owned the place, Aaron Connelly, was a friend of ours, a retired dealer who had bought a shit load of product from us in the old days. When he got out of that business, he wanted to start a club. We loaned him $75,000 towards the start-up costs, with no interest. He paid us back in two years and we were still drinking for free whenever we went there.

We got there about midnight, went in, said hello and had a drink with all the locals we knew. We weren't there for the chicks so we made our way to the back room for the card games.

TC, Cristo, Ace and I sat at the same card table with Aaron and another local guy we'd known since we were kids. We enjoyed the banter between us more than the poker itself.

At the other table were a bunch of gangster hopefuls, guys that wanted to find their way into the mob but never made a connection. No Uncle Tony, no father or mentor to show them the ropes and open the doors to that world.

There were a lot of guys like that around. They were mostly petty thieves with too many vices and at the time cocaine was probably the worst vice going. A lot of guys were starting to smoke cocaine and that was much more addictive.

You could spot a base-head, as we called them, by their frail frame and their teeth, or the lack of teeth. Free-basing deteriorated teeth at a rapid speed, as well as the mind. A couple of these guys were base-heads and were kind of loud-mouthed but we didn't pay much attention. Three of the other guys at the table were long-time associates of ours and would keep their eyes on them. We just played poker, drank and laughed.

It was getting late and I had to take a leak. I got up from the table, stretched and headed for the bathroom. I figured I'd play cards for another hour and then head home because I wanted to be back before Julia woke up. While I was in the bathroom I heard an argument break out between two of the guys at the other table. I didn't think much of it. I flushed the toilet and headed back to the card table.

As I opened the bathroom door, I could see one of the base-heads standing up, getting real angry. The guys at my table stopped the hand and watched. The rest happened so quick I don't really remember it so well.

I looked over to TC and the next thing I knew I heard a gunshot. I looked back at the base-head, who was facing me, and saw him pull the trigger of the gun again.

The second shot hit me straight in the chest, just above my left breast. I just remember being on the floor and hearing a lot of shouting. I heard a bunch of people shouting Cristo's name and I thought he must have got hit too but then TC grabbed my hand.

'Marco, take it easy, buddy, you're going to be all right.' I remember thinking that TC seemed more afraid than I was and then I passed out.

When I awoke it was dark and I had no idea where I was. I felt very weak and didn't have the strength to move. I heard a noise and then noticed light along the bottom of a door. The light went out and the door opened. I knew immediately it was Julia, I could make out her silhouette in the moonlight. She came over to my bed, sat down and held my hand. She didn't know I was awake.

'We've got to stop meeting like this, beautiful,' I murmured in a whisper.

Julia was startled and she squeezed my hand, what seemed to me to be very hard.

'You're awake!' She began to cry and kissed my cheek. I tried to touch her face and wipe away her tears, but I didn't have the strength.

'Honey, where are we?'

'We're in the hospital. You were shot last weekend at the card game.'

It started to come back to me. It was a bit hazy, but I was vaguely able to recall the events of that night.

'How long have I been here?'

'Six days. Priest came to give you the last rites after you arrived. The doctor said your heart stopped during the operation – you actually died for a minute . . . They didn't expect you to make it.'

'Don't worry, I'm not going anywhere without you, beautiful.'

Julia just cried softly and kissed me until a nurse came in and interrupted us.

'He really should be resting, his body's had a lot of trauma.'

The nurse gave me a shot of something that sent me right out. I fell asleep with Julia holding my hand and kissing my cheek. I spent a few more days going in and out like that with Julia by my side.

One night I woke up and Julia was sleeping sitting up on a chair with her head on my mattress. I didn't want to wake her so I didn't move at all. I just lay there thinking about what a mess my whole life was.

I was a bit shaken by what Julia had said about me dying on the operating table. I've heard stories about people who have had similar experiences and how they see a white light and relatives that have been long dead waiting for them, but for me there was nothing. I don't remember any part of the experience, no white light, no loved ones waiting. I was troubled by that; maybe I was one of the ones slated to go to hell and that was why I didn't see any of the things others have. Then I just figured I was glad to be alive and would make it a point to protect myself more and make changes in my life. If I was going to hell when I died, I wanted to cheat the devil for as long as I could.

One morning I woke up to a big commotion in my room. TC and Cristo were standing in front of my bed engaged in a semi-heated, hushed debate. They were too preoccupied to notice that I was awake.

'Face, I'm telling you, shut your fucking mouth, he doesn't need to hear that kind of shit.'

'All I'm saying is, that shit's fucked up.'

'Yeah, well, thanks for your medical opinion, Doctor Kildaire, but I think we'll stick with our current physician.'

'T, I'm telling you, they must have fucked up – look at him, he looks like an old man.'

They both looked over at me and realised I was awake. TC gave Cristo a scowling look.

'Look, now you woke him up.'

'It's all right, guys, I was getting up anyway. What do you mean I look like an old man?'

TC gave Cristo an elbow to the ribs and walked over to the bed.

'It's no big deal, kid, you got a little grey hair. Doctor says it's normal with patients that experienced severe trauma.'

I was too exhausted to worry about a little grey hair.

'Forget about it. So how's things?'

'Everything's going fine, we're working our asses off, but things are good.'

'So what's up with the guy that shot me?'

'Don't worry about him, when he gets out of the hospital we'll get him in prison,' TC replied with confidence.

'How'd the guy get in the hospital?'

TC gave Cristo a bit of a look. 'While I was trying to get you to the hospital, Al fucking Capone over there took the gun away from the guy and beat him half to death.'

Cristo's hands went up in the air. 'What, I'm supposed to let the guy shoot everyone in the room?'

Before they got back into another argument, I interjected, 'What about the other guy who caught the first one?'

'Yeah, he didn't make it.'

'Fuck, that's a fucking shame.'

TC went over to a table in the room and grabbed two small wrapped gifts and gave them to me.

'What's this?'

'Just a little something to pass the time.'

I opened the first present, it was a beautifully bound edition of *Crime and Punishment*. The second was a historical book on Florence in Italy and the Medici family. I was quite impressed by the choices and totally surprised.

'That's great, T, thanks. What made you pick these two?'

'I went to the book place and told them my kid brother was in the hospital and needed something intelligent to read. He showed me a bunch of stuff and I picked these two. I don't know, they sounded right.'

'That's great, T, thanks. I appreciate it.'

Cristo walked over to the bedside and handed me a single wrapped present that was quite a bit larger. When I opened it, I was surprised and a bit touched all at the same time.

It was a red fire engine. Not a toy one that you would give a kid, but a collector's edition that was well made with actual miniature cloth-mesh fire hose that you could unravel. I know it sounds goofy, but Cristo's grandfather was a fireman before he was killed in the Second World War, and I always wanted to be a fireman when I was younger. This was something I had never told anyone but Cristo. I was really touched, but TC wasn't seeing the Kodak moment.

'A fucking fire engine! What are you, fucking soft?'

'No, T, it's great, I love it. Thanks, Face.'

Cristo gave TC a superior look, like he won an argument. But TC had to get the last word in.

'First you eat his fucking Jell-O, then you give him a fucking fire engine. You're a fucking retard, Face.'

'You ate my fucking Jell-O, Face? That's the only decent thing I get to eat.'

TC gave Cristo another look. 'Go find him some fucking Jell-O.'

Cristo headed for the door, ranting and raving as he went. 'What, he wants Jell-O? I'll buy him a fucking Jell-O factory. How's that? I'm fucking rich.'

'Don't bother, your head's already full of the shit,' TC retorted.

I knew they were trying to lighten the situation the only way they knew how, and as shity as I felt, the two of them did make me feel a little better.

After Cristo left, I turned to TC and asked, 'Where's Julia?'

'Hey, you got a good broad there, pal. I told her to go home and get some sleep. She's hardly slept for ten days. I told her we'd be here to keep you company until she came back. Face and I got first shift, Ace and Shawn will be here in a little while.'

'That's great, T, I appreciate it.'

'Don't worry about it, pal. You just get strong.'

'What about Uncle Tony, has he . . . or anyone else been here?'

TC knew what I was getting at. I wanted to know if my parents had been here.

'Yeah, sure. Uncle Tony and Aunt Francesca been by every day, they came with your mom and dad.'

That's what I wanted to hear. I hadn't seen my mother or father since I'd left home. Since meeting Julia I'd had a strong need to put that one to bed and start rebuilding my relationship with my parents. Of my six brothers and sisters, the only one I had steady contact with was my sister Maria.

'That's good, T. When are they coming back?'

'After the doctor told them you were out of the woods and was going to make it through this thing, they went back home. They're coming again tomorrow.'

'That's great, T, thanks.'

'You know, I just want to say I'm sorry . . .'

'Sorry for what, T? You didn't shoot me.'

'No I didn't, but I should've stood up against Tony and let you get out after the New Year. You could've been upstate building your house now.'

'T, don't worry about it. As soon as they let me go from this place, I'm going to do just that.'

'Yeah, well, that's good. In about a year I'm out of here too. I've made—'

We heard a loud disturbance out in the corridor. Some woman was shouting, 'What do you think you're doing, young man?'

Then we heard Cristo's voice. 'I'm getting my brother some Jell-O here, he's hungry.'

'You're not supposed to—'

199

'Yeah, yeah, lady, bill me for it.'

With that Cristo entered the room pushing a cart with a couple dozen bowls of Jell-O on it.

TC shook his head. 'Where in the fuck did you get all that?'

'I found it, T.'

TC was about to give Cristo some shit, but I intervened. 'Hey, Face, well done! Bring that cart over here.'

He wheeled the cart over and we both ate three or four bowls apiece. I knew TC wanted some just as much as we did, but you couldn't have paid him enough to eat any.

'Nephew. *Come va?*' Uncle Tony came walking in carrying a small package.

'Hey, Uncle, yeah, I'm doing all right.'

He came over and kissed my cheek and said hello to the guys. Cristo grabbed a bowl of Jell-O and offered it to Tony.

'Jell-O, Ton?'

Tony just gave him a hard look. 'Make sure you fucking guys don't get him over-excited, he's supposed to be resting, not fucking around.'

With that Ace and Shawn came strolling in but as soon as they saw Tony they got real serious.

'Hey, Marco, how you doing, buddy? We thought we'd come by a little early. Do you know, I was holding a queen high, straight fucking flush when that prick shot you. If Face hadn't beaten him stupid, I would have. He cost me an easy grand.' Ace stopped and put a present on the table next to my bed and shook my hand.

Shawn came over and patted me on my head gently. 'What's up, buddy? How's the food?'

Cristo took the opportunity to offer Shawn and John some of his ill-gotten Jell-O that he seemed so proud of. That got TC started again. With all the commotion and noise, an old nurse came into the room and ordered everyone but Tony out of the room.

Tony told them not to come back today or tomorrow. I

assumed it had something to do with my parents coming the next day. After they left, Tony took off his jacket and sat on a stool next to the bed.

'Listen, kid, you know I love you like a son, right.'

I nodded.

'Well, the thing is, when you get out of this place you take that nice girl and go start a new life. This is the wake-up call.'

'Uncle, I didn't need a wake-up call, I've wanted to get out for a while now.'

'I don't mean a wake-up call for you, but for me. I've already talked with the people in South America. At the end of the year I'm shutting this thing down. I'm going to start taking things a little easier from now on.'

I just nodded. I was starting to get tired and Tony stood up to leave. He went over to the table in front of my bed and picked up the small package he came in with and brought it to me.

'Here, keep this out of sight, wait until there's no nurses around.'

'What is it?'

He bent over, close to my ear, like we were talking about espionage.

'That's some of your Aunt Francesca's lasagne. There's a fork inside. *Buon appetito.*' With that Tony kissed my cheek and left.

I was starting to feel like maybe this was the beginning of a better, more quiet life, which was a bit ironic for a guy who felt so weak and ill.

Later that day I awoke and found Julia sitting on the stool with her head in my lap. She was sleeping. I didn't wake her, I just enjoyed her presence.

20
New Foundations

The next morning my parents arrived and I became overwhelmed with regret and guilt. I could see from the looks on their faces that they were emotionally distraught and I was immediately taken with how much they had aged. The last time I'd seen my dad he was a very fit young-looking man of thirty-three but now, at forty-six, he had a small paunch on his waistline and a receding hairline. It was different with Mom, she didn't look any different physically, but she had an aura that you would expect from your grandmother.

Julia was very nervous because she'd only met them briefly while I was unconscious. My father came up to the right side of the bed and my mom the other side with Julia. My mother was in tears as she bent over to kiss me.

'Hi, Mom, how are you?'

'I'm fine, dear, how are you?'

'Yeah, I feel great.'

I turned to my dad, who was like an iceberg.

'Hey, Pops, you OK?'

He just nodded. I knew he wasn't going to say anything while my mom or Julia were there so I didn't let it bother me.

'This is Julia. The love of my life and the woman I'm going to marry as soon I'm back on my feet and can build her a house.'

My mother gave Julia a hug. I knew they were going to get

along fine. I needed to speak with my dad. He obviously wanted to set some things straight before he made any small talk.

'Mom, do you think you and Julia can go down to the cafeteria and get a coffee or something? I need to talk to Dad for a while.'

'I think that's a good idea. It's been too long, Marco. Come on, Julia, let's leave these two alone. I'll tell you how wonderful my son was as a little boy.' She gave the old man a hard stare as she said it. She had always blamed him for being too strict with me, she thought he was responsible for me leaving home so young. The truth was that I was an unruly boy who had more street sense at thirteen than most twenty-year-old men.

After they left, I tried to think of what to say, there was so much to say. I started with the obvious. 'Dad, I'm really sorry.'

'Forget about that shit. I'm not here to get an apology or to give one. I'm here because I love my son and I miss him.' He took a deep breath and held back the tears that were welling in his eyes. 'I'm here because I want to know if you're ready to change your life. Are you ready to take whatever illegal money you've made, walk away and find an honest life with that lovely girl of yours? If you are, I'll help you in every way I know how. If you're not, I'm going to walk out that door and never speak your name again.'

'Pops, listen, I already bought a nice piece of land. It's only thirty minutes from you and Mom. As soon as I'm out of here I'm going to build a big house, marry Julia and fill the place up with babies.'

He sighed a breath of relief and staved off the tears. 'That makes me very happy, son.' Not wanting to get too emotional, he got practical. 'How big's the lot you bought?'

'Two acres, over across the lake from Tony's summer place. It's beautiful, Dad.'

'That's nice property over there. Must've cost you a fortune.'

'Yeah, but it's worth it. I've got planning permission to build a five-thousand-square-foot house.'

'You own the land outright, no mortgage?'

'Yeah, no mortgage, Pop.'

'Then why not build something smaller, something you can do without the bank. If you can start off your first house with no mortgage, your life will be so much easier.'

'I can afford to build without the bank.'

'Really?'

'Yeah, and then I'm going to start up a construction company and start doing some spec building.'

My dad had to pull up a chair. He was very old-fashioned and was having a hard time taking it all in.

'Marco, how much money have you saved?'

'Well, I got about one and a half million in cash at home, a beautiful Victorian monster of a house in the city that I remodelled, and there's no mortgage on that either.'

My dad was awestruck. 'That's incredible, Marco.'

'That's nothing, Pops. Me, TC and the guys have about another fifty million tied up in property all around the city. I own one-seventh of it.'

My father just sat and stared at me, he couldn't have made that much money in ten lifetimes. A worried look came over his face.

'You have to hide that money, Marco. If the IRS finds it they'll charge you with tax evasion.'

'No, it's OK, Pops. I started a business six years ago. We've been buying old houses and fixing them up. We sub-contract most of the work. We've all have been paying taxes for the last six years and we've got real good lawyers and accountants. I made a couple of good choices.'

'Well, that's a relief. You're too young to get on the wrong side of the IRS.'

We talked for an hour or so and when my mom and Julia came back to the room, everything was good. The nurse came in to give me my medicines and I drifted off into a deep sleep with my mom, Dad and the woman I loved sitting with me.

*

When I got out of the hospital, spring was in the air and I felt weak but really happy. I was about twenty pounds underweight and the doctor wanted me to make a concerted effort to put weight back on. He didn't have to worry about that; now that I was off hospital food I planned on hitting every decent Italian restaurant within an hour's drive of my house.

I wasn't supposed to do any physical work, but I could drive and go to meetings with lawyers, realtors and accountants. I wanted to move as much property as I could as quick as I could.

The accountants advised us not to sell too much too quick because the capital gains tax would bury us. He had a couple of different scenarios that had great tax advantages, but they took more time and we didn't want to wait.

We figured the best way forward was to sell sixty or seventy per cent of the property immediately and the rest we could move the following year whatever way the accountant thought was best. With that underway, Julia and I were upstate at our property by the end of April.

The doctor, having warned me against over-exerting myself, suggested it might be good for me to start with a steady regime of light work. Aside from getting tired easily, I felt great and looked forward to a daily routine of work and the pleasure of having so many uninterrupted nights with Julia.

The first call I had made when I got out of the hospital was to an upstate excavating company that I had spoken to when I first bought the property. I sent them the blueprints and asked them to get the foundation in right away.

When we arrived, the foundation was in and the framing crew was half done. I was having a hard time trying to believe that it all wasn't just a dream. We found a beautiful small cabin on the lake to rent until the house was completed. If I needed to go into the city for a meeting with the lawyers or accountants, it was just two to three hours away, depending on traffic.

I bought another small sailboat and we spent long days sailing on the lake, living and loving. I'd have to say it was the best summer of my life. I saw all of the guys from time to time, but TC and Cristo made it a point to come up and visit almost every weekend. According to them things were going smoothly, but I knew that even if things weren't so good, they wouldn't have troubled me with it. There was definitely no ill will from the guys towards my new life or me. In fact they were happy for me and I think they viewed my new life as a prototype of what theirs would be soon.

TC, Cristo and I would spend lots of afternoons fishing and they talked about buying places on the lake as well. We talked about how they could come back from Italy with their children to spend the summers with me and my family-to-be.

The two of them were still set on going to Italy and becoming grape and olive growers. They'd drop little hints to me about how I really should buy a place in Italy as well. I liked the idea and didn't think it would be a hard sell to Julia. But Julia and I were just getting settled into this new life. So I decided I wouldn't mention Italy to her until TC and Cristo were out of the drug business and entrenched in the old country.

The good news was that Tony was only doing two runs a month, which meant a lot less product to cut, package and move. I still urged TC to talk to Tony about shutting the whole operation down, but my advice didn't do any good. TC was a good soldier and would see things through to the end. Not to mention I'm not sure he was ready to give up the life he knew. Not because he loved it, but because he was, like myself, a creature of habit and hadn't figured out exactly what or where his new life in Italy would be. Like many people, TC was leery of the unknown.

By the fall, the house was almost finished. I was building a custom set of oak stairs, and would install oak, maple and cherry hardwood floors when I finished the stairs. Julia spent endless hours finding tiles for the bathrooms and the kitchen. It was around that time Tony showed up for a visit. I noticed he looked really withdrawn and unwell.

'Hey, Uncle Tony, welcome to our new home,' I said as he entered the front door. Julia gave him a big hug and took his jacket – she was trying very hard to put the past behind us.

While Julia gave Tony a tour of the house, I finished fitting the last tread of my staircase. I was standing back admiring my labour when Tony returned.

'Those are beautiful stairs, Marco. You should be proud of yourself.'

'Thanks, Uncle Tony.'

Julia intervened. 'You guys want something to drink?'

'Yeah, that'd be great. We'll be right there, just give us a few minutes, honey.'

Julia smiled and walked off. Tony was still eyeing my new set of stairs.

'Maybe this winter you can build a nice set of stairs like that at my place. I've been wanting to do something nice with that place for years.'

'Yeah, sure I can. In a couple of months I'll be done with things here. Anytime after Christmas would be OK for me.'

Tony looked down the hall towards the kitchen, then nodded and walked to the garage door and I followed. In the garage, Tony closed the door and began speaking in a hushed tone.

'I've got a small problem.'

I didn't think I wanted to know, but I didn't have a choice.

'I was arrested a couple of weeks ago.'

'What! For what?'

'For shooting at two cops.'

'What the fuck were you shooting at two cops for?'

'Because they were shooting at me.' Tony gave me one of those 'what are you, stupid?' looks before continuing. 'Fat Eddy and I were being chased by an undercover unit. They were trying to shoot out the tyres of my car. Fat Eddy was driving so I shot back and blew out one of their front tyres. There was a roadblock waiting for us five miles up the road. They got a bit rough so I knocked four or five of them around pretty good before half the force was on me.'

I just shook my head. I didn't want to know any more but I have to admit I was a bit curious. 'Why were they trying to shoot out your tyres in the first place?'

'Someone got into my safe in my study and you're the only one with the combination.'

Now I was getting a bit nervous. 'Uncle Tony, what's your fucking point?'

'Don't worry, kid, I know it wasn't you. But aside from you, the only other people that even know there's a safe there are GG and Tommy Vaccaro, but they don't have the combination. So I know it wasn't you, GG's locked up and Tommy is as trustworthy as you. It's a bit fucking strange.'

'How did GG and Tommy know about the safe?'

'Because they made the South American runs with me and before we left we would meet at my place and grab the other documents. Your auntie doesn't even know there's a safe in the study.'

'As fucked up as that sounds, I still don't see what that has to do with two undercover cops shooting at you.'

'I was getting to that if you give me a fucking minute here.'

I heard Julia calling and put my finger up to quiet Tony and popped my head out of the garage into the house.

'We're just in here, honey. We'll be there in ten minutes.'

She smiled and went into the kitchen; she knew something was up, but probably figured it was just Tony telling me one of his stories. I turned back to Tony.

'So, the undercover cops?'

'Right. Tommy was away with his family for a few days so I decided I'd get inside to have a look around and see if everything was normal. Whoever went into my safe took all my alternate identity documents but they didn't get the documents they were looking for. By a freak chance, when I got back from the last South American run, before the safe thing, I dropped Tommy at his parents' house. His dad's on his last legs and he wanted to get back to him as soon as possible.'

Tony seemed a bit unhinged. He was always very concise and explained things clearly, but today he was all over the place.

'OK, Uncle, you notice someone's been in the safe. They've taken your other documents, but not the ones that you use for the runs to South America.'

'Yeah, that's what I just said.'

'Yeah, OK. I just want to make sure I got the facts straight in my head. So you see that someone's been in the safe and taken some documents. You figure it wasn't me, even though I'm the only one that knows the combination, but GG and Tommy know where the safe is so you figure it must be one of them. Then you say it can't be G, he's in prison. So then you go to Tommy's to rifle through his house to see if you can find the documents that have been taken. Am I on track so far?'

'Yeah, dead on.'

'All right, did you find anything at Tommy's?'

'Nothing.'

'So you leave. And then?'

'This unmarked car was out front watching the place, we didn't see him until we left. About a mile up the road they stick a flashing light on the roof of the car and want to pull us over. We didn't want to pull over, so they tried shooting out the tyres of my car. I shot back and took out the front right. Up the road there were four cruisers blocking the road and two coming up behind us. We had no choice but to stop. I knock the shit out of a bunch of guys and the next thing I know I wake up in a cell next to Fat Eddy.'

'This ain't a good thing, Uncle.'

'No shit, it's got me baffled.'

'I think it's G. He thinks he's going up the river for life and trying to cut a deal.'

Tony shook his head. 'I find that hard to believe. His case is looking pretty good. And if he rats he's dead, he knows his dad can't save him from me.'

'Then it's Simms and Stockland.'

'No, that doesn't make any sense. If they want to get rid of me, just kill me in South America and get the documents all in one shot.'

I thought about all of it for a minute. I wasn't so sure if I agreed on that point. Killing Tony would never be easy; there's always a risk when you're dealing with Tony.

'Whoever went in the safe was a pro. If they hadn't taken the documents that were no good to them you wouldn't have known. They got by the main house alarm. Right?' I asked, still a bit cloudy.

'You're right. If they didn't take anything, I never would have known anyone had been there.'

I thought for a moment, trying to make sense of it all in my head. 'We both know there ain't a guy in the city with those skills that would have made a move on your house, Ton. It would be suicide. Whoever went in there was looking for documents and thought they found them, or they never would have taken them. It's got to be some government agency or the local boys in blue.'

'It can't be the locals. I have too much dirt on every big player in town, from the police chief right up to a handful of judges. If they knew anything, I would have got a call.'

'The bottom line is, Tony, the game just got dirty, and I think it's time to clean the whole thing up and get away for a while.'

'I'm going to be spending a lot of time up here at the lake. I've already told Tommy we've made our last run just in case he is in on this thing. Fat Eddy's going to make the last few runs with me. I'm moving my stash for the documents as well. It'll be some place close to here. I'll let you know as soon as I figure it out.'

'If it's all the same, Uncle, I'd rather not know where they are.'

'You have to know. If this thing goes tits up, those documents are the only get-out-of-jail-free cards available . . . to any of us.'

The pictures that Loretta had taken popped into my head; I

211

thought it might be a good idea to give them to TC and the guys, but I wouldn't say anything to Tony. 'Hey, I'm out of this thing. I've paid my dues, Tony. If you need me to know, fine, you can always count on me.'

'Yeah, I know that.' Tony gave me a loving kind of slap on the cheek. 'You're a good kid, Marco. Now let's go get that coffee or I'll be sleeping on your couch tonight.'

We went inside and made small talk. Julia told Tony all about her plans for furniture and decorations. I just dazed off into the scary world of 'what if'.

At that time I had no idea that getting shot was the only thing that saved my life. As bad as the last hand was, at least it got me out of the game. I wasn't holding any cards, but I guess you could say I thought it was safe to count my winnings.

The thing about high stakes poker is, more often than not you're not allowed to leave if you're ahead. The other players want a chance to win back what they lost. You have to play until the big losers are out.

Well, I didn't know it, but I was still playing poker. The only difference was, unlike normal poker where you can draw up to three new cards, if needed, to help your hand, this kind of poker I was only going to be able to play the cards I was dealt. I was going to need to learn to bluff real good, and hope that I could make the hand do.

21
Peace of Mind

I finished my house and I was happy to build Tony's stairs for my next project. I thought Julia and I were finished with the chapter of my life that I viewed as ugly and difficult. I set up a workshop in the basement of Tony's and went to work.

The stairs I was building were one of a kind and what I created was beautiful. In my mind, it was the last payment of a debt that I didn't owe. I spent as little time with the guys as possible and devoted my time to the woman I loved, but you really can't hide in this world, it's bigger than want and desire. My new-found peace of mind was about to be rocked to the core.

When I finished the oak stairs at Uncle Tony's, he loved them so much he threw me an extra grand on top of what we'd agreed on. Not that a grand was going to make any difference to me, but to get an extra grand for a bit of hard but honest work was very rewarding. Since it was only March and my hopefully busy season hadn't kicked in yet, he told me that I 'might as well do the spare fucking bathroom as well'. I figured my tools were there and I had the shop set up in his basement, so why not?

'Yeah, sure, Tony. I'll bring by some tile and fixture catalogues for you to look at.'

'Nah, fuck that. You do it, just make it all cobalt blue – what a fucking colour!'

It's better to agree with Tony than question his reasoning. He probably would have given me a thirty-minute lesson on chemical composition and engineering or something like that if I'd asked what was so special about cobalt blue.

Within three weeks the bathroom was finished. It so happened on that spring day that I arrived at Tony's later than usual. Like most days, I drove my new 735 Beamer to Tony's. My tools and shop were in his cellar, why drive a truck when you don't have to?

I knocked before unlocking the door and letting myself in; Tony would expect me as usual and I knew my aunt was still away at their home in Florida but it's all about respect, especially with Uncle Tony. The house was quiet.

He probably had a late one, I thought to myself as I made my way upstairs to the kitchen for coffee.

The kitchen door was closed; something was very wrong. The hairs on the back of my neck stood up and I felt a strong sense of fear. I opened the door and swept the room with my eyes. The wood trim round the back sliding door was in splinters and on the floor. I went up to it and noticed several holes on either side of the doorjamb, three of them filled with lead.

'What the fuck is this?' I said aloud to myself.

'What are you, fucking stupid? They're bullet holes.'

Startled, I spun round. It was Uncle Tony wearing his red bathrobe over blue silk pyjamas. His hair was unkempt and an unlit cigar was hanging out of his mouth. He went straight for the coffee pot.

'What the fuck happened here?'

'Just a little late-night freak show,' he said as he unceremoniously scooped the coffee out of the jar and into the filter. I sat down on one of the stools at the breakfast nook and watched as he added water and lit his cigar.

'Fat Eddy was here last night smoking that fucking cocaine again, the fucking degenerate. I don't know why he can't be civilised and drink whiskey like the rest of us.'

Uncle Tony leaned in across the counter and started speaking in a lower tone, like we're in a crowded coffee shop and he needs the privacy. 'So it's about midnight and we're shooting the shit when one of the motion sensors goes off.'

Tony had the property wired with motion sensors that would be activated if anything bigger than a small dog moved within the fenced part of the property. A small light on the main box in the kitchen, which had a numbered grid for identifying the exact location of the intruder, would flash and a buzzer would sound. Sixty seconds later a large exterior spotlight would illuminate the area where the system was breached. This gave Tony a full minute to react before the perpetrator knew he had been compromised; it was a gadget he had made himself.

Tony re-lit his cigar and continued his tale. 'Now, the thing is, the sensor tells me the perp's right out behind the kitchen window here and I got the light on in here so he can see in the kitchen window.' He points to the window behind him, between him and the end of the counter next to the stove where the coffee pot is.

'So I get below the counter and go to the broom closet, you know, where my Winchester rifle is.'

'Yeah, of course,' I say, nodding as if every normal human being on the planet keeps a Winchester rifle in the broom closet.

'Now, I know it's loaded, so I shut off the kitchen light, go to the window and open it and wait for the outside light to trigger. Well, on comes the light and right there,' Tony points his finger at the exterior wall in the direction of the backyard, 'about two hundred feet from me is this silly fuck all dressed in black with a "I'm a dumb fucking reindeer frozen in the headlights of a Mack truck and about to be flattened" look on his face.'

Tony starts getting into the story, he's lightly chewing and puffing on his cigar and his eyes are fixed on mine.

'I tell the guy to freeze and get on his knees and he does it. Now Fat Eddy, he opens the slider and pulls out his two pearl-handled forty-fives and pulls a bead on the guy, who's on his knees and holding this thing in his right hand. So I tell him to drop it. Well, this fucker does a roll to the left and starts running. So I let a couple of slugs fly, not trying to hit the guy, I just want him to stop. Fat Eddy starts emptying both barrels at him. Thank fuck he was high or he might've hit him. Hence the bullet holes around the door. So the guy gets scared and he drops to his knees, puts up his hands and drops the thing in his hand.'

Uncle Tony gets up from his chair to fill a cup with coffee. He keeps as much eye contact as he can and makes a nod towards the pot to see if I want a cup. I nod. He brings the two coffees and gets right back into the story.

'So now I get out there and there's five of my big floodlights lighting up the whole fucking world. So I figure the best thing is, I'll knock the guy on the head with my gun and get him inside and shut the lights off. I know I'm out here in the middle of nowhere, but them forty-fives make a big fucking noise, you know what I'm saying?'

I just nod my head. I don't want to slow him down; he's on a roll.

'So any fucking way, we get this piece of shit in the kitchen here and we tie him into a chair and wait for him to come round and to see if there's any reaction to all the noise. About an hour later he comes round and I ask him what the fuck he's doing in my backyard.'

'What about the thing in his hand, what was that?'

'Well, if you give me a minute and quit interrupting me, I'll fucking tell ya.' He shakes his head and uses my interruption to re-light his cigar. 'So this thing in his fucking hand turns out to be one of them sound vibration ma-fucking-chines, you know, they point it at the window and it picks up the vibrations of the voices in the house . . . they didn't have that stuff back when I was with the agency.'

'Yeah, I know, I'm with ya.'

Truth is I didn't know shit about it and I still don't for that matter.

'So anyway this little fuck don't want to talk, so we knock him around a little and then, I hope you don't mind, but we borrowed one of your wood clamps.'

'One of my wood clamps?' I think I sounded a bit concerned.

So he says, 'Don't worry about your fucking clamp, we didn't break it.'

I think he missed my point.

After one of his frightening glares he continues. 'So, like I says, he didn't want to talk, so we put the bar clamp on his head and applied a little pressure to his temples. In about five minutes he was singing like Pavarotti.'

'Yeah, right.' I say, shaking my head in agreement. I grab the open bottle of red wine on the counter and fill a dirty glass from the night before – this was getting way past coffee.

'You never were cut out for this shit, kid. Stick with building.'

'No, I'm fine, so what happened then?'

'So anyway, we got this guy's head in this clamp and he's screaming. Then just when he's about to faint he surrenders. I told him that if I took that clamp off his head and he clammed up again I'd nail his balls to the chair with your nail gun. So he nods and I take the clamp off his fucking head. It turns out this guy and three other Feds are camped out in the house next door.'

'Next door?' I said, surprised. 'What, in the new house in the subdivision over there?'

'Yeah, the fuckers. I knew I should've bought that land when I had the chance.'

'So why the fuck didn't his buddies show up? Why ain't you in fucking jail?'

'Well, if you shut the fuck up and listen . . . I'm trying to tell a story here.'

'Yeah, right; absolutely.'

'So it turns out this guy was on night watch, and takes it on himself to hop the fence and get the drop on us. He waits until his buddies are sleeping and pulls a lone cowboy job. Thought he was gonna be the hero. They've been next door watching and waiting for six months, trying to get enough shit on us to bring it all crashing down.'

Tony paused, lit his cigar and got back to the story. 'So this piece of shit tells me that they didn't have enough evidence yet and he thought he was gonna get what they wanted by taking this vibration machine to pick up and record our conversations. Fucking piece of shit . . . These agency people ain't got any respect.'

I nodded in agreement and waited while Tony opened a new bottle of wine, and poured himself a glass and refilled mine as well.

'Uncle Tony, you didn't kill the guy . . . did you?'

He gave me one of his 'what are you, stupid?' looks. 'No, I didn't kill him, we threw him and his sound thing over the fence, back in his own yard.'

'And that's it, end of story?' I said.

'No, that's not it. Before we threw him back he told us that they busted Tommy and set him up.'

'Tommy Vaccaro?'

'Yeah, Tommy. It turns out they were gonna send him up the river hard if he didn't co-operate. Tommy told them about the altered badges and passports and the location of the safe. The Feds got one of their own safe-crackers to hit my safe. The guy gets in my house, opens the safe and sees a pile of documents and assumes he's hit the jackpot. He doesn't realise his mistake until he gets back to wherever, and by then the Feds know I'm going to know something's up, so they don't bother making a second attempt at my safe.'

'Right. But what about when you broke into Tommy's safe and shot at the cops? If the Feds were on to you back then, why didn't they press charges then? If nothing else, they had you for shooting at the cops and assaulting five officers. I know you have a few judges in your pocket, but why did they drop the case without a fight? They just let you walk.' I was starting to get confused.

Tony clarified. 'Well, that's right, kid, I knew something big was up because of the way they let me go that day in court. I just didn't want to fuck your head up and worry you until I had more facts. When I went into court that morning, it was just an arraignment. I made some inquiries with a couple of judges and they said they'd work it out. I wasn't too worried. That day should've just been the declaration of formal charges and the court date set, in and out, no big story. But that's not what happened. I got called and my lawyer and I presented ourselves and the bailiff reads the charges: attempted murder on two policemen with a firearm and five counts of assault and battery on officers of the law. Well, four of the five cops I stomped are there and looking real full of themselves and giving me the eye. So, anyway, for some reason that my lawyer or myself can't figure out, the judge is passed a note, he reads it and asks the district attorney if he would join him in the judge's chamber. My lawyer stands up and requests he be present. The judge tells him to sit down and not to disrupt his court again. I mean, I'm no lawyer, but I know something ain't right and I'm getting a little edgy. Well, the fucking judge and the DA are gone for twenty minutes, and the cops, who are still all fucked up from the beating I gave them, are getting real confident that I'm going down. So they start giving me the evil eye and acting like shit fucks. So I shot them the bird and fucked with them a little, just to pass the time and have a laugh. Anyway, the judge and the DA come back from the judge's chamber, the DA's face is beet fucking red and he doesn't make eye contact with me or the cops. He just goes over to his desk and sits down. The judge tells us to all rise, and I'm thinking this isn't right, he can't set a trial date without discussing it with my counsel. Then he just looks up and says, "Based on new information that has just come in, the district attorney and I feel it's in the best interest of the state to dismiss this trial at once." He slams his gavel down, tells me I'm free to go and calls a twenty-minute recess.'

I hated to interrupt but it was all a bit much. 'That's not

fucking normal, Uncle. What did the cops do?'

'The cops were shitting themselves and rushed the DA like they were going to lynch him. The DA just brushed them off and walked out of the courtroom. My lawyer's looking at me and says, "You must have paid that guy a fortune." I tell him I have no idea what's going on. The two judges I spoke to told me we'd make a plan after the trial date was set. Something big was up, but I wasn't sure what. But our little visitor last night might have something to do with it. He passed out from the pain before I could get any of that out of him. I'm working on it as we speak. Simms and Stockland are meeting me tonight. I'll know more then.'

This was getting weirder by the minute and I was getting a knot in my stomach that I didn't like.

Tony took a deep breath through his terse smile and said, 'So what do you think of that, kid?'

I was getting anxious, this was way bigger than anything I could have imagined. I knew by Tony's whole demeanour that this story was packing one fuck of a punchline.

'I'm not liking it, Uncle. Where's this thing heading?'

Tony could see the deep concern in my eyes and tried to relax me a little. 'Don't worry, kid. For the moment we're all right.'

'Yeah, OK, but what about this shit last night? Why haven't they come to arrest you yet?'

Tony gave me a hard, serious look. 'That's the big question, kid. I was expecting them hours ago.' Tony chuckled to himself and said, 'Fat Eddy's in the guest room sleeping. We waited up for them to come. They never showed.'

'That doesn't make any sense.'

'No, it doesn't. I'm gonna make some inquiries this afternoon and I'm going to play hardball with Simms and Stockland tonight. I haven't heard much of them lately. I think they might be able to shine a little more light on this Greek fucking tragedy.'

I didn't bother hanging around at Uncle Tony's any longer that day. The thought of waking Fat Eddy wasn't pretty. He was a bear in the morning. It was a nice spring day and I thought I'd pick up Julia and take a ride up to Newport and spend the day sailing. Maybe we'd even spend the night and try to get away from this thing that kept following me around.

22
Can't Keep Running Away

Two days later, Julia and I headed back home. We left before the sun came up to beat the traffic. I loved Newport and I loved my little sailboat there and it was always hard leaving. But I had to finish a few things at Uncle Tony's and there was still a lot to do on my own house. If I'd known it was the last time I'd ever see Newport I might have stayed a little longer.

I also felt a pressing urgency to get Julia back home and make a trip into the city. I needed to talk to TC. If Tony hadn't told him anything yet, him and the guys might get blindsided by this thing.

I got to Uncle Tony's by nine and went straight downstairs to work. I wanted to finish the job and get my tools out because I didn't like the idea of the Feds next door. I got as far as the bottom step before I heard my name being called.

'Marco, come on up for a minute, we have to talk.'

I didn't reply, and went upstairs straightaway; there was something in Tony's voice that made me feel edgy. He was standing in the living room at the top of the stairs. The look on his face was like stone.

He took a long breath. 'I want you to take that car of yours back to where you bought it, and sell it. Then—'

'What? What are you talking about?'

'Listen to me . . . Then I want you to go and see your lawyer

223

and give your sister Maria power of attorney, so she can take care of things for you.'

'Power of attorney? Take care of what?'

'Well, she'll have to sell your house and other properties for starters.'

'I don't know what you're talking about, Tony, but I'm not selling my house or—'

Tony stopped me with one hard stare. 'I spoke with Stockland yesterday and the shit's hit the fan. The Feds know for sure that someone in one of the government agencies is working with us and giving us the ability to move in and out of the country with the cocaine.'

'Holy shit. How do they know? You think it was G?'

'It's possible. I hope not, but they might just be going on the possibility that because of my time in the Special Forces, I made my own connections. Bottom line, we got trouble.'

'No, Tony, you got trouble. I've been clean for more than a year. I'm not involved any more.'

'I know what you're saying, kid. But you have to get the fuck out of town before people start showing up dead.'

'Like who? Who's gonna show up dead?'

'I don't know . . . me, you, maybe everyone.'

'Why the fuck is anyone gonna kill me? I'm not involved with this shit any more. I build fucking houses!'

Uncle Tony could see I was getting upset and took another approach.

'Look, kid, you have to leave, or I'll have to kill you myself.'

Now that really bothered me. When Tony said something like that, you better listen.

He tried to comfort me. 'Now you know I don't want to kill you, right?'

'Yeah, sure.'

'Forget about Stockland and Simms for a minute. The Feds have been camped out next door for months, you've been here almost every day lately, you're driving that expensive car, you own expensive property on the lake and, to add insult to injury, you're my nephew. They're going to assume you know plenty, and they'd be right. They're gonna set you up with some crime you didn't do or a truck load of drugs and then you're gonna talk.'

'I ain't no fucking rat, Tony.'

'I'm not saying you are, kid, but you ain't gonna do twenty years of hard time for something you didn't do. Look, if the Feds don't get you, Stockland and Simms are definitely going to get you.'

'Fuck them. I never did anything to them except make them a lot of fucking money.'

'That's not the point. Aside from me, you're the only one that knows them. Even GG, he never met them. He waited outside when they were in South America. It's you and me, kid, the only ones that can positively ID them and implicate them. And if they go down, they don't go to jail. The agency couldn't have that kind of publicity. They'll just cease to exist. Trust me, they'll kill you and won't even give a fuck. Basically it comes down to Darwinism and the survival of the fittest.'

The anger was now passing and quickly being replaced by fear. A kind of fear that was unlike anything I've ever known. Tony's eyes reinforced that fear, for they were filled with a deep sincerity and sadness that assured me there was no other way.

'So what do I do?' My heart was numb as I waited for his reply.

He took a deep breath. 'Walk out the door and drive that car to the dealership and sell it. I don't care how much you lose. Just have them cut a cheque. On the way over there, call your attorney and make an appointment. After you sell the car, call a cab and go to the lawyer's and wait for him to see you. You won't wait long because I'll call him and explain to him that it'd be a favour to me. Then, I want you to take a taxi home. When you get there, put your truck, the one with the cap on the back, in your garage and keep it in there until you're ready to leave. We don't want anyone having access to it and sticking a body or drugs in there. I know it sounds paranoid but you can't take chances.'

I was a bit overwhelmed. I didn't know how I could tell Julia, never mind where I was going.

'Where am I supposed to fucking go, Tony?'

'As far away as you can. Someplace where you don't know anyone. Whatever you do, don't tell anyone where, not even me. In fact, pick a place after you leave, it'd be safer. Oh, by the way, I'll be by the house in the morning to pick you up.'

'Where we going?'

'I talked to a friend of mine this morning who doesn't know you. We're going by his place in New Jersey and he's gonna make you new papers, passport, licence, everything.'

'Oh yeah, great, and what about Julia?'

'You have to leave her behind. You'll never make it with the two of you.'

I couldn't breathe for a moment but managed a short plea. 'I can trust her, Tony. She's OK.' My voice was filled with desperation, and I started to feel nauseous.

'I never said you can't trust her. Most guys can't do this thing you have to do on their own, never mind with a woman to worry about. You have to be able to leave wherever you are at any time. She'll want to call home, she'll miss her family. What if you have a beef and she walks? Maybe when she comes back she says something to the wrong person?' He could see I didn't like the scenario. 'Listen, you let two years pass, and if your new life is solid, you call her.'

'Pretty fucking harsh, Uncle, don't you think?'

Tony got quiet and very serious. 'Harsh? Let me tell you about harsh. I have a thirty-year marriage to a woman I love more than life itself. Now if you repeat what I'm about to tell you to anyone, I will kill you myself.' Tony poured another glass of wine and continued. 'In the next two or three weeks, I'm not sure exactly when, my wife and our family are gonna have to attend my funeral. That, Marco, is harsh.'

'What the fuck are you saying? You're gonna let them just kill you? Let's kill them fuckers!' I said the words without thinking. I didn't want to kill anyone, but I couldn't accept leaving Julia behind.

'I wish it were that easy, kid. You know a couple of weeks ago they dismissed the case against me for shooting at the two cops.'

'Yeah, that was weird.'

'No, it's more than weird, it was fixed from the inside.'

'By who?'

'Well, I talked to Simms the other day after you left and told him about the Feds in the house next door.'

'Yeah, what did he say?'

'He said he'd call me back in a few hours and then turned up on my doorstep that night. It turns out the Feds are the ones that got my court case thrown out.'

'Why the fuck would the Feds get you a pass?'

'Because they got a boatload of cash invested in their investigation in me, and if they convicted me on that case, which was a state case, their new investigation goes in the toilet, and in the worst case scenario, I do three to five in the pen.'

'Yeah, so that's what they want, isn't it?'

'No. Simms says this new investigation is a federal case and they want to try me for murder, drugs and organised crime. I'll get life if convicted.'

'Holy shit, that is harsh. So who's gonna kill you then?'

'No one's gonna fucking kill me! What are you, retarded? We're going to stage my death. Stockland, Simms and I worked out the details last night. That's why I need you alive. With you out there in no-man's land, they can't do the dirty and really kill me. That's why I'm leaving every document and any other proof up in a freezer buried in Pa's field. You're the only other person besides me that knows about it.'

Now I fully understood what Tony was talking about when he said those documents were the only 'get-out-of-jail-free card' if everything went tits up.

The enormity of my situation began to settle in and I grabbed one of Tony's cigars off the coffee table and Tony poured me a Scotch. If I stay, the Feds probably set me up and make me a rat, in which case I definitely get whacked by Stockland and Simms. Even if I don't rat, I definitely get whacked in prison via Stockland and Simms because they can't take the chance that I might change my mind after a year or two, in the event I couldn't do the time. Maybe Tony was right, I had to get out of town and keep my head down.

I stood up and looked at my uncle. Over the years, he hadn't changed much, at least not physically, I thought about how he was when I was just a boy, loving, caring, always trying to educate me with some valuable lesson. It had taken years for me to really understand him.

With each year that had passed he'd been sliding lower into the abyss, and I wondered how much deeper he could go. How far can anyone go before they hit the point of no return? I wondered when exactly I'd stopped loving him and begun to hate him. Because at that moment I felt more hate than I've ever felt in my life. I'm sure that didn't happen overnight.

As I turned and began pacing the room, a disturbing thought rocked me: what if Tony had been this way all along? Instead of falling into the abyss further and further with each passing year, what if he'd reached this level, or maybe a much deeper one, before he'd ever come back from the service? In all the years since his return from military life, Tony hadn't talked too much of what he'd seen or done. What if all this time he'd been operating in his comfort zone? If that were the case, how far could he, or would he, go? What little I had seen with my own eyes was more than enough to put the fear of God into my being.

One thing I knew about Tony, and I think I knew him better than anyone, was he never lived on the edge. He liked to keep everything he was involved in well within his control, never letting things get too close to breaking point without having an escape route. Had he foreseen all of this? Had he taken precautions? As I considered these questions, I suddenly realised that, for Tony, this was his comfort zone and he hadn't been pushed even remotely to the brink.

I gazed into the dark fireplace and drank my drink in silence, bracing for the panic attack that was welling up inside. I would have to go away without Julia and hope that fate would be kind to our future. There was no way I could fight Tony; if I went against him, we wouldn't have a future at all. If I went against him, how far had he already prepared himself to go?

I put the empty glass on the coffee table and looked down to meet his gaze. 'I'll talk to you later, Uncle. I got a lot of shit to do.'

'Yeah, you do. See you in the morning,' was all he said.

As I left the house, my heart ached. I had no choice; I had to be a good soldier and follow Tony's orders. Actually, fuck good soldier, I had to go if I wanted any chance of surviving.

The first thing I did when I got back from selling the car and seeing my lawyer was to call TC and tell him to meet me at our place. He knew that was a truck stop about halfway between me and the city; I figured we'd both be there in just over an hour if we hurried.

Then I picked up the phone to call a taxi, but thought better of it. If anyone was following me, they'd know I was on to them if I took another taxi with two brand-new trucks in the driveway. I didn't like going against Tony's wishes, but I knew it was the best move. I put the truck that I would use to get out of town in my garage and took the other to meet TC.

I arrived at the truck stop in my van about an hour and ten minutes later and parked it right in front of the window so I could see it. When I went inside, TC was sitting there, drinking a coffee. Just the fact that I'd asked him to meet me there was enough for him to know something was up, but when he saw me, he realised something big was happening.

'The shit's hit the fan and I've got to get out of Dodge soon, we got big problems, T.'

He looked concerned. 'What shit? How soon?'

'All the shit, T. It's over. This thing's going to be ugly. I'll be running with the wind in less than forty-eight hours. I think you and the boys should do the same.'

TC tensed and stirred his coffee. 'OK, kid, you got all my attention. What the fuck is going on?'

I explained the whole story and told him that Tony was coming by to see him tomorrow. If he had any fears, he didn't show them. He just sat there and listened, without one interruption, with a stoicism that rivalled the likes of Hercules and Ulysses. When I finished the tale, he sat back and looked at me with his amazing stare and then leaned in real close.

'All right, kid. You stick with what Tony told you to do. It makes sense. I'll talk with our real estate people and tell them we want to dump everything for a song. Wait, if you're not here, how am I going to sell what's left of the property?'

'Don't worry, T, it's all set. I went to see my lawyer this afternoon, and I gave my sister Maria power of attorney for all my affairs. She'll do what's needed.'

'Good, that's good, Marco. Now, do you remember that little town I told you about with the winery I wanted to buy?'

'Yeah, of course I do.'

'I took you there once, we stayed in Giuseppe's café.'

'That's right. I remember.'

'Did you tell Tony?'

'Never a word.'

'Good. In two years, I'll be there for your birthday. If I can't make it, I'll be there for mine nine months later. If for some reason there's too much heat, I'll be there for the following year, and if you can't make it, each year until you do. Worst case, I'll tell the guys the millennium anniversary is still on; that should be more than enough time for all this shit to go away. Sound good?'

'Yeah, I got it. It's like a bad fucking dream, T.'

'More like our worst nightmare. You OK with money? I know you spent a fortune on the house.'

'Yeah, I'm flush. I'm going to leave Julia with a small duffel bag filled with enough to hold her over for a couple of years and then some.'

'All right, that's good, kid. Once I move whatever property I can, I'll leave half of your cut with Maria and I'll personally deliver the rest when I see you. Maybe this thing will blow over in a couple of years and we'll be all right.'

'Let's hope so, T.' I reached into my top pocket and pulled out the picture of Simms and Stockland that I had paid Loretta to take and handed it to T.

'Here, it's not a great shot, but it gives you an idea of what Simms and Stockland look like. I've written down the little info that I know about them on the back of the picture.'

TC studied the picture and gave the back a cursory glance. 'Thanks, kid. This might come in real handy. Don't tell Tony that you tipped me off or gave me this picture, he might throw a nutty.'

'Fuck him, T. I'm getting tired of his shit. He should have shut this whole thing down after G went down.'

'Should have, could have, but didn't. Don't get caught up on that one, kid, it's a sucker's game. The only way forward right now is to do what Tony told you to do. In a couple of years things will quiet down and we'll all be in Italy spending our hard-earned cash.'

'Yeah, let's hope so.'

TC and I sat and talked for another hour before parting ways. It was almost as hard as leaving Julia; I loved TC. He looked after me when I left home and, aside from being cousins, he was the older brother I didn't have.

I sat in my van and watched him pull out of the parking lot in his Mercedes. He gave me a wave and a smile like he would any other day, like I was going to see him tomorrow.

I pulled my head out of my ass and got on the road. I had to have all my wits about me if I was going to do this thing right.

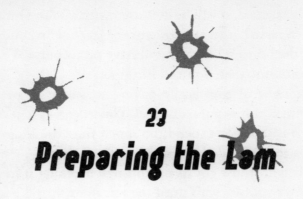

23
Preparing the Lam

The next morning Uncle Tony picked me up and we made the two-hour trip to New Jersey. The guy we met was not a man of words. He took my photo and told us to come back in five hours. We had time to kill so we made our way over to a local Italian restaurant to have some lunch. After we ordered our food I had some questions. The first was: how do you go about staging your own death?

'I'm not sure yet, Simms is still looking for a body.'

'That sounds like fun.'

'Yeah, well, this is their party too. If I can walk away from my wife and family, they can get their hands dirty.'

'So they get a body, and then what?'

'I don't know. We don't have the whole plan yet. We can't move until we can get a temporary doctor in the hospital for the death certificate and we can get guys on the payroll to drive ambulances. We can get helicopter evacuation guys for the airlift anytime. As you know, the funeral parlour's not a problem, but none of it works without a corpse.'

'Who's gonna ID the body?'

'After my death, Stockland and Simms, who have been working in New York lately, will hold and ID the body, claiming that it's me; their number one arch enemy. Your aunt Francesca won't be able to see the body until it's released. Of course when

233

the body is released, it will be confused with a John Doe and sent off to be cremated at the expense of the state. The family will be livid, but the bottom line is they'll have no recourse. Things like this happen more than you can imagine.'

The thought of my family having to suffer all of this was painful. 'Fuck, this is gonna be bad, Uncle.'

'Yeah, it is, but don't spend too much time thinking about it. You have a tough road ahead so keep it together.'

'I'm all right. I just got to get through breaking it to Julia.'

'Whatever you do, wait until the last minute, it'll be easier to walk out the door.'

'I've got tickets to see Fleetwood Mac tomorrow night, I don't think I can sit through it and enjoy it.'

'Here's what you do then: have your sister Maria take her to the concert. Tell Julia you got to meet with a big client. After they leave you, pack the truck and then go. Maria breaks the news to her when they get back from the concert.'

'That sounds pretty shitty, Uncle.'

'I know it does. But sometimes it's easier. Another thing, when you leave, I want you to drive through a quiet neighbourhood and look to see if you're being followed. If you see any head-lights—'

'I know, make three consecutive right turns,' I interrupted. I'd heard that one a thousand times.

'That's right. If the same car's still behind you after three turns, you know you got a tail.'

'And if I do have a tail?'

'Stop at a gas station that has a phone booth that you can pull up next to and call me. I'll take care of it; I'll come run them off the road with my jeep if I have to.'

'Thanks, Uncle Tony. What about TC and the crew? What kind of shit are they looking at?'

Tony hesitated and gave me one of his typical burning stares. In an unpleasant situation it usually meant the person on the other side of the table wasn't gonna like what he said.

'I'm holding three hundred grand of fuck-you money for TC, and I assume he has a boatload more. I'll give them all the skinny, and then they're on their own.'

Fuck-you money was something we all had. You never knew when you needed to get out quick, so the smart move was to have at least two reliable stashes with easy access. Unfortunately, I didn't have as much of that around as I did when I was in business. This was because I didn't think I'd need it any more, but I still had a million I could put my hands on and I knew more would come when TC dumped the property and my house was sold.

'How much heat's coming their way?'

Tony let out a sigh. 'I think if they don't listen to me, and try hanging around, they'll be fucked. They can't start thinking they're super fucking heroes.'

I just nodded in agreement. The only reason we never caught any real static was because of Uncle Tony. No one wanted any of the heat that he was capable of dishing out. If he was getting out of town, via his staged death, I knew things were going to get bad.

'The problem is, I can't tell them I'm about to set up my demise. So they're gonna think I'm still in the corner for them. And one thing I know about Simms and Stockland, they mop up situations better than anyone does. I'd say once I'm out of the picture, they better be far away. And the Feds could get them any day, you never know.'

'You got to tell them to get the fuck out, they got to know.'

'I told you I was seeing TC tonight. I'll stress the point. Then it's up to them.'

I hesitated and gave Tony one of those looks that suggested I was about to tell him something he didn't want to hear. He gave me a nasty look and scowled. 'What? What the fuck did you do?'

'I met TC yesterday. I had to at least see him before I left.'

Tony looked like he was going to blow and I was glad we were in a public restaurant. But just as quick as he got angry, he calmed down.

235

'What did you tell him, Marco?'

'I told him everything, except about you dying and where I was going to go.'

Tony looked relieved, but he was still a bit pissed off.

'Well, thank fuck for that. I expected you to call TC, in a way I guess I'm glad you did. Maybe it'll make it a little easier to get them to listen to me. But you're sure he knows nothing about me shitting the bed?'

'Absolutely. I said nothing, nothing at all about that.'

'Good, that's all right.' Tony got up from the table. 'I have to take a piss,' he said and threw a fifty on the table. 'Get the cheque.'

I got the girl's attention and asked for the cheque; somehow the waitress reminded me of Julia. I thought about the day we'd met at the small restaurant where she worked and how we had come so far. Now it was all going to blow up and I wasn't even going to tell her about it before it did.

The truth is, I had no idea what disappearing was going to be like. I figured Tony was probably right about it being much harder to do if I brought Julia with me. The thought of driving off into the sunset, with no destination in mind, was terrifying. Not to mention starting over without family and friends. That's the one that would've broken Julia, I thought; she couldn't leave her parents. I decided I would stick with Tony's plan, at least for the time being, and then, if things quieted down and I was established, I could send for Julia.

Tony emerged from the bathroom and sauntered across the small room like he hadn't a care in the world. He didn't bother sitting back down, he just picked up his sunglasses, put them on and looked down at me. 'You ready?'

I nodded and got up to leave. My head was starting to reel. My father would never forgive me again, I was sure of it. And Julia, how was she ever going to manage this one without me here?

Tony and I picked up the documents: passport, driver's licence, birth certificate and a social security card. Tony was right, the guy was good. My new name was Robert Pino and I was thirty-one, about two and a half years older, and had a birthday under the sign of Taurus. All the documents were perfect.

He charged us five grand and Tony picked up the bill. I had the money to cover the expense, but you don't look gift horses in the mouth. I didn't feel indebted to Tony, it was a small price to pay for the millions we made for him.

When we got back, Tony asked me to come in. I figured since it was probably the last time I was gonna see him, he wanted to have a drink. We went into his study. He poured a couple of whiskeys and said a toast to good fortune in Italian. Then he went into his safe, took out a money belt and threw it on the table in front of me.

'What's this, Uncle?'

'It's a money belt. Put it on. There're seventy-five one-thousand dollar bills in there. As far as I'm concerned, that's my money and I don't want you to use it unless you're in real trouble. And if that's the case, I want you to come and find me.'

'That'd be like looking for a needle in a haystack, wouldn't it?'

Tony paused, and began to speak in a hushed tone.

'Now listen to me. I'm gonna tell you something that can get you killed, so don't fuck up.'

He told me the name of a village in South America that was a private community for the Mafia. He said it was heavily guarded and if I needed him in the next two years, that's where he'd be. Then he made me memorise a password in Italian that I would have to give when I tried to enter. If I got it wrong, I'd die, no questions asked. He also gave me a number for an answering service where I could leave a message and he'd be able to get back to me.

I said my goodbye to Uncle Tony. It was harder than I thought. Even though I was angry with him, I had to accept my own responsibility. I could have left years ago before things really got crazy; I chose not to. I had to put my anger away and take this thing on the chin; the bottom line was, his life was about to get turned upside down more than mine. As angry as I was with him, I still couldn't show it. He was going to be my only link to my new world, and I was going to be his; we needed each other. This was the first moment when I realised just how real it all was. Now I had to make it to tomorrow night.

That night I arrived home before Julia did. She had had a busy day down in the city with her mom, and she didn't get back until late, so she was tired, which is probably the only reason she didn't notice my uneasiness. I had prepared dinner for her and as we ate she enthusiastically talked about the Fleetwood Mac concert the following evening. It killed me to have to bust her bubble.

'Honey, I've got some bad news – well, it's good news as well.' I guess my tone was a bit dark because she braced herself. 'I got a call from a friend of Uncle Tony's, he's coming up tomorrow afternoon and wants to meet with me about building him a new house; it would be a great contract for me to get.'

She looked relieved but saddened at the same time. 'So I guess that means we can't go to the concert tomorrow.'

'No, not at all. It just means that I can't go. I called Maria and asked her if she would go with you; she was excited about getting out of the house and away from the kids for a night.'

Julia warmed to the idea quickly and returned to her naturally content and positive state of being. 'That sounds great ... I mean, I'd rather you were going, but we'll have a great time.'

We finished our dinners and went to bed early. We made love and she peacefully went to sleep in my arms. As I lay in my bed, I stared at her wonderful face and tried to imagine a possible scenario that could change what I had to do, or that could enable me to take her with me. None of them was very realistic. It came down to one thing: time. If we could get through the next six months or a year, maybe we'd be all right. If not, I'd be heart-broken forever.

The next night came quickly. Maria came by after lunch and picked up Julia for some shopping before the concert. I felt like shit not saying that I was leaving that night and she might never see me again. But Tony was right, if I said anything, it would have taken a week to convince her to stay behind.

I left her a letter explaining things and that she should sell the house as soon as she could and keep as much of the money as she needed. There was a list of instructions and $18,000 in our joint account for her. That and the duffel bag with another one hundred and fifty grand would be enough to pay the taxes and bills on the property for a year or two and still leave plenty to live on.

I knew the house would sell sooner than that, but I wanted to be sure. I had also just bought her a new car a few months before. If nothing else, if she decided not to join me later, she'd be able to live comfortably for at least two years after the house had sold, until she sorted herself out.

I watched her drive off with Maria, who kept such a straight face she could have won an Oscar for her performance. I had six hours to kill before I left. I wanted to leave after the rush hour, just as the sun was going down, and drive through the night. So I settled down on the couch listening to Vivaldi and began working out the kinks.

The truck was packed, the two gas tanks were full and I was behind the wheel. I turned the key, drove out of the driveway and took one last look at the home I had built. I drove away and it was the last time I ever saw the home that I built for Julia. Sometimes I wonder if those beautiful stairs are still there, gleaming with a new finish, or if they were carpeted over by the next owners who might have had different ideas. It is certainly strange, the things you think about in the most difficult times of your life.

I followed Tony's instructions and went through two neighbourhoods, repeated the three consecutive right turns twice, always looking for headlights behind me. There was nothing there, it was all clear. I put a cassette in the tape player and got on the interstate heading west.

The first hundred miles seemed to take an eternity as I thought about who I was and who I was becoming. It was a whole new frontier out there. I could start over, be who I wanted to be, no one but me to decide, no other considerations; it was a lonely thought but exciting. I was thirty-one according to my new passport and new driver's licence, and the world was new and waiting out there in front of me.

The only thing that came to mind was college. I hadn't really applied myself in school but I knew that I could've done well if I had given it a chance. Maybe I'd study physics or history; both subjects interested me and, if you think about it, who's gonna look for me in college? Even my family wouldn't guess that one.

Maybe I'd find a new life, a better life; only time would tell. The only thing I knew was that the miles were flying by, separating me from the past. I was making great time, I just didn't know were I was going.

After driving a thousand miles I was dead tired, burnt out from too much coffee, and was in need of sleep and a shower. The first stop I made was just west of St Louis. When you cross the Missouri River you pass the great arch known as the Gateway to the West. Somehow I found comfort in this and thought it would be safe to get a hotel.

I had one more chore to do to separate myself from the past. I had to sell my truck to my new self, and get insurance and licence plates in the new name. Tony thought it would be better to do that in a different state. When selling a vehicle that's relatively new, the title has to be turned in and a new one is issued and mailed to the buyer. If I did it in New York, Tony was afraid it might leave a trail to my new identity. This meant I would need a mail service that would give me an address. Then I could send the mail forwarding company my address when I got settled, and I could do the process again in my new state. Finding such a service proved very simple. Within thirty-six hours, I was rested, showered, a resident of Missouri and back on the road heading north-west with my new Missouri licence plates, driver's licence and new name.

After three and a half days of driving across the plains and over some of the most beautiful mountains I'd ever seen, I found myself in Astoria, Oregon, a picture-postcard seaside city bordered by the Columbia River to the north.

I checked into a motel, bought a local newspaper and began my quest for a temporary house for rent. I wanted to get a feel for the area before I bought a house. Within two days I found furnished lodgings and I moved in.

Nearby was a small college and I signed up for a fall course. I took the SAT tests for placement and found that I was in serious need of understanding the English language. The upside was I got an almost perfect score in math. So the focus for that summer would be the correct use of the English language. I also found a small sailboat company that rented boats by the hour or the day which was a great perk. I felt selfish for getting excited about my new life in the Pacific north-west. Who knows, I thought to myself as I daydreamed about the possibilities, maybe if things stay quiet, I could send for Julia or, even better, return home?

24
Phoning Home

A month passed by and I was missing Julia, the guys and my family more than I could have ever expected. It was as if they'd all perished in some bizarre tragedy. But actually I knew, deep down, it was me who had perished in the tragedy.

Feeling incredibly low and lonely, and against Tony's instructions, I drove an hour down the coast, found a payphone and called my sister Maria's house. My heart raced as I dialled the number. I didn't know what to expect.

'Hello?'

'Maria, honey, how you doing?'

'Sweetie, is that you?' It was Julia.

'Yeah, it's me. How you doing, honey?'

She began to cry. It tore my heart out to hear her upset. 'I miss you so much, are you all right?'

'Yeah, I'm all right.'

'Oh, I have terrible news.' I braced myself for news about Cristo or TC getting whacked.

'Your Uncle Tony was killed in a bad car accident. I'm so sorry. I know how close you were.'

Now I didn't know what to think. Did he really get in an accident? Or was this part of his plan?

'When?'

'Two weeks ago. It was the biggest funeral I've ever seen.'

I had to find a way to grill her for details without her catching on. 'Did he suffer at all, or was it quick?'

'They said he died instantly. But then the FBI wouldn't release the body for a couple of days, and somehow Tony's body got mixed up with someone else's and he was cremated. Francesca's a mess.'

As bad as I felt for Francesca, I knew that Tony was still alive, but I wasn't sure if I'd rather he was dead. 'Jesus, that's terrible. How's the family managing it?'

'Oh, it was awful, the whole family's taken it hard.'

'Wow, I can't believe it. It's just awful.' I tried to sound upset. 'Marco, where are you?'

'I can't tell you that right now. Just try and be patient, I'll come get you.'

'I can't wait for you. I want to see you now.'

'That's not possible, Julia. If you find someone else, I'll understand.'

'I don't want anyone else.'

'I know, I know. I can't stay on this phone long. I'll try to call again next month; same time, four weeks from today . . . I love you, Julia.'

'I love you too. But wait, Maria wants to talk to you.'

Maria picked up the phone upstairs and Julia hung up the receiver.

'Mom called me two days after Uncle Tony's funeral and wanted to know exactly how tall you were and how much you weighed.'

'Why? What are you talking about?'

'The cops pulled three bodies without hands or heads out of the fucking drink. We've been worried sick.'

'Where?'

'Two from the East River and one out by the Verrazano Bridge. They haven't identified them yet. We thought one of them might be you.'

'I told you I was leaving.'

244

'Yeah, I know, but you could have spent a quiet month downtown. Who would have known?'

'Yeah, I guess. Well, I'm all right. You didn't tell Ma anything, did you?'

'No, I haven't said anything to anyone.'

'What about TC and Cristo, are they all right?'

I held my breath, I didn't know if I wanted the answer.

'I haven't seen them since before the funeral, but I haven't heard anything else. Why, should I?'

'No, I was just wondering. I got to get off this phone, I'm not supposed to call anyone. I love you, Maria. Take care of Julia for me.'

With that she hung up the receiver. I knew from her voice her feelings were hurt because my tone was a bit harsh. I couldn't help it; my mind was racing in overdrive. I missed my family, I missed Julia more than I ever imagined.

I was trying to think out the news on Tony and make sense of what she'd said about the guys and, just for extra kicks, I was worried about the call being traced. It was the beginning of a sadness that never went away. With time it slowly hid in the depths of my inner self, but twenty years later the intensity of that sadness and that moment still remains firmly planted.

The summer passed quickly and I began to feel at home in my world. I managed to call my sister and Julia once a month. It was during one of those phone calls that I learned the first real bad news.

It was about three months after I left home and settled in Oregon. It was a late Sunday morning. I called Maria, knowing that Julia would be there, as previously arranged. We kept the calls short and sweet.

Julia answered the phone. After a few minutes, Julia got quiet and I knew she had something she really wanted to say. I could sense it was upsetting her and would upset me. I was sure she was going to tell me that she'd met another man, but that wasn't it.

A couple of weeks earlier, Shawn's house had been set on fire. It was a definite case of arson. Shawn and his girlfriend Linda were in bed asleep at the time and both died of smoke inhalation before the fire department arrived.

Of the six other original crew members, Shawn was the one that I was the least attached to, but we were still good friends. It all seemed so senseless; the fact that whoever it was could have killed Linda, a woman who never did drugs or anything wrong in her life, except get involved with Shawn, was devastating to me; what would they do to Julia if they knew that I was still involved with her and she might know something?

Why hadn't he left town? It didn't make any sense. Shawn had more fuck-you money then a Federal Reserve Bank. After TC dumped most of the property and Shawn got his split, he must have had fifteen, twenty million, counting his personal property and stocks. The guy could have disappeared with Linda without a trace and never been found again. Something wasn't right. But the most disturbing part of the phone call was that none of the guys showed up for the funeral. No Ace, no TC, no Cristo. Now I know that the plan was to disappear, or at least lay low. But I really thought Ace, if anyone, would have sent flowers or got word to someone.

I was getting a bit concerned. I toyed with the idea of going back and checking things out for myself. But I figured if the guys were alive, I wouldn't find them anyway. On the other hand, if it was the worst case scenario and everyone was dead, it meant that Stockland and Simms were doing a clean sweep and not taking any chances. They'd be paying people off on the street to keep their eyes open. No, if I went back I could only endanger my family. I had to wait and wonder . . . or did I?

I made arrangements with Julia and Maria to call again in ten days' time, just so I knew she'd be around and because I couldn't discuss what I was thinking on the phone. I was due to start college in a few weeks and I figured I'd take a little trip to

Vermont. With my new identity, no one would have any idea I was on the move.

The first thing I did when I got off the telephone was write a letter to Julia. I knew it wouldn't be safe sending it to our house or my sister's, but I could send a letter to her mother's address. The next morning I went to the post office and sent it by express mail. It would get there in two days, then add a day or two until she went by and visited her parents, which she did all of the time. She'd have it by the weekend.

I kept it short. I told her to take the train from her parents' house in Brooklyn into the city, and I stressed the importance of not taking any clothes, make-up or anything, just a hand-bag. Once she was in the city, she should go to the train station and get a ticket for Florida on the Amtrak. Having previously checked the timetables, I knew everything I needed to know.

The following Tuesday the train for Florida departed at 8:15 p.m. The Chicago train left at 8:05 p.m. If anyone was following her, they'd find out that she'd bought a ticket to Florida and would wait until she was in a quiet part of the train before they made a move to question her, or maybe just follow her until she met me. Either way, they'd get a ticket for Florida and be relaxed as they waited for the train to depart. What she had to do was inconspicuously take note of the track that the Chicago train was on and wait until it was ready to depart. If she timed it right she could be the last person on it, with several possible stops to get off at. Once the train was on the move, she should buy a ticket from the conductor and get off at the last stop in upstate New York, which is only a few hours by car from the airport in Vermont, where I would rent a car and drive down to pick her up. I couldn't see why it wouldn't work, at least once.

The next Monday I flew out to Vermont and rented a car. I didn't get a hotel, but decided to drive down to the western border of New York and get a hotel there. I wanted to be early rather than late, and figured I'd be so anxious the next day I'd have a hard time concentrating.

The next evening at 10:45 the train pulled into the station and I was there waiting. When Julia walked off the train, my heart went into my mouth; I had missed her so much. Before she was in my arms she was in tears, and after she was in my arms, I was in tears.

When I'd composed myself and given her a long kiss, I stopped and looked at her. 'Hello, beautiful. It's so good to see you.'

'Hi,' was all Julia could manage for a minute. I dried her eyes and she pulled herself together. 'I never thought I would see you again. I was so afraid.'

'It's going to be all right, honey. Come on, let's get out of here. Are you hungry?'

'No, I just want you.'

We got into the car and headed back to the hotel. It was only fifteen minutes away. Julia slid up next to me, put her head on my shoulder and held me tight.

'Did everything go all right? Did you follow all my instructions?'

Julia nodded and looked up at me as if afraid. I just figured she was tired and emotionally burnt out.

'What did you tell your parents?'

'That I was going to Philadelphia for the week to visit my girlfriend from college.'

Once we got in the hotel room I opened a bottle of wine and found a nice radio station that was in the middle of a romantic set list. We never touched the wine, we just made love for hours and laughed and cried until we both collapsed in each others' arms and slept.

It was the best sleep I'd had since I'd left home. The next morning we made love again and ordered room service. It arrived while Julia was still in the shower. I had no plans to leave the room that day so I set it all up for breakfast in bed; I thought she'd appreciate it.

When she came out of the shower she was wrapped in a towel. She didn't seem to notice the breakfast. I knew from the look on her face that something bad was coming. She went over and sat in the chair next to the television.

'Marco, I have something really terrible to tell you. I probably should have told you last night, but I just couldn't bear it.'

My heart sank, I had every possible scenario running through my head. My dad or mom died, Julia found someone else, something had happened to one of the guys. I just sat stone-faced and waited for her to get up the courage to tell me.

'You know the three bodies found in the river a couple months ago? I didn't want to say anything, because they hadn't been identified at that time. The heads and hands were missing. But two of the three bodies have now been identified.'

My heart sank into my stomach and all the joy I'd woken to was stolen from me in an instant.

'Yeah, go on, honey, it's easier to just get it out . . . Who were they?'

'One was Ace, and the other was Cristo. It was a positive ID made from their tattoos.'

This news numbed me to the bone. I couldn't believe how this nightmare just seemed to keep on going.

'And what about the third body? Is it possible it was TC?'

'No, your cousin Mary, his sister, viewed the body. Definitely not TC. They think it might be Cristo's cousin. He went missing around the same time.'

I couldn't help but think of Aunt Ginny; my heart was aching for her. Two more men in her life gone – Cristo, how she loved Cristo. I was numb just thinking about it. It didn't seem real somehow. On the flight to Vermont I was thinking that this was all probably really stupid, this sneaking around and hiding out shit. Everyone was overreacting. So much for that theory. This thing was every bit as real as Tony had said it was.

We both went silent for a while and neither of us touched any of the food. I couldn't stop thinking about Cristo, and when I finally did, I thought about Ace.

I had really got close to him over the years, especially after Paws died. We'd both looked up to Paws like an older brother and we missed him badly. That was the thing about the Micks that I didn't get in the beginning, they had the ability to show their feelings and express themselves openly. Whereas TC and Cristo, might have loved me like a brother, they did it in that real John Wayne macho man's way. I guess that's why Ace and I got so close.

After about an hour of silence, Julia raised her head from my chest and gave me another one of those looks that said she had more bad news.

'What is it? Just tell me and get it off your chest, honey. None of this is your fault.'

'I've been followed lately. Sometimes I see them, but sometimes I don't, but I know they're there. It started just after Tony's funeral.'

Now that got me going, I was on my feet and heading for my gun. 'Don't worry, they didn't follow me here. I lost them at the station.'

'What? Julia, who'd you lose at the station?'

'This big guy. Well, he's not tall, just a guy with a really big chest, blond brownish hair. I'd say he's about fifty.'

Simms, it had to be him. I started feeling a bit tense and thought I'd have a glass of wine to stave off the panic attack that was brewing in my chest. 'OK, the train station – before the train station. Tell me what happened.'

'I got to my parents' house and went shopping for them, like I always do, but there wasn't anyone following me then. I'm sure of that.'

'What happened when you first arrived at your folks' place? Tell me everything you said and did.' My tone was emotionless and hard.

Julia looked a bit frightened. I felt like shit but I needed to know the truth if I was going to be able to keep her safe.

'Well, there's not much really. I went in and told them I was going to Philadelphia to visit my friend and I'd be back in a week or so. My mother thought that was a good idea and asked me if I had time to pick up a few groceries before I left. I went shopping and came back. There was no one following me at that point. That's the part that's strange. I didn't see the big guy until I got to the train station. It was like he was there waiting for me.'

'Are you sure he was following you, and it's not just a mistake?'

Julia shook her head. 'No, it wasn't a mistake.' She sounded certain. 'I've seen him before, sometimes in Brooklyn and sometimes upstate by our house. Anyway, I pretended not to notice him and just went and bought a ticket, went to the ladies' room, using that for an opportunity to take a walk and find out where the Chicago train was. Then I came back and sat down.'

'That's strange, he wasn't following you before you got to your parents, but he was at the train station . . . That's it! They've got a wire in your folks' house. They're listening to their conversations. What have you said to your parents?'

'Exactly what you told me to say. You were away in Ohio building a church and couldn't get home a lot. When I stay at your sister's place, they think I'm in Ohio with you.'

'That's good. You can't ever say anything at their house until this thing goes away. They can't keep looking forever.'

Julia looked like she was going to cry again. I gave her a hug and kissed her forehead. 'So what happened after you sat down in the station?'

'Nothing at all, not until seven fifty-five when I went to board the Florida train.'

'OK, so you went to board the train . . . and?'

'I figured the best thing to do was to actually get on the train. So I did, and I made sure he saw me get on the train. Then I waited for him to get on, which wasn't difficult because it's easier to see out the window than it is to see in, especially through a crowd. I watched him go in the same door I did – I was further up at the other end of the same car. As soon as he came up the first step, I quickly moved forward. He hadn't seen me, so I knew I was OK. I went all the way to the front of the train and got off, ran to the front of the engines and crossed the tracks over two platforms.'

She said it so calmly. I was amazed at her actions.

'Good, honey. That's real good, smart. Put two trains between you and the one he was on. He'd never see you.'

'Well, it seemed to work. Once I got over the first platform and onto the next, I ran as fast as I could to the Chicago train and stood just inside the door, only looking out enough to see if he was coming after me. Three or four minutes later the train left and I knew I was OK.'

'You're a remarkable woman, Julia. They don't make too many like you.'

She smiled and started to relax again, then kissed me with the most tenderness I've ever experienced. All of the bad thoughts disappeared for the moment and I fell into her beautiful world.

I awoke several hours later feeling refreshed for an instant. Then reality came rushing in and seized my heart and soul, leaving me saturated with hurt for my buddies and terrified for Julia.

I didn't want to wake her, so I quietly got up and ate some of the cold, untouched breakfast and poured myself a glass of wine. I had to put off any emotion until Julia was back home and safe. I needed her to be relaxed and not get pulled into my world of pain. I figured this might be the last chance I had to be with her, I couldn't waste it making her upset.

I also needed to think things out. Was Julia in danger? Was it better if I took her with me? Maybe she should just disappear for a while as well? How far were Stockland and Simms willing to go to bring me down and get the fridge full of documents that they wanted so desperately?

Julia was still asleep and I managed to finish a bottle of red wine without any effort. I went into the bathroom to uncork the second. As I sat back down I felt like I had covered all the bases.

Julia would be safest back at home. If I took her with me, and they found me, they'd probably kill her as well. What's one more body to guys like that? But they wouldn't hurt her if it wouldn't bring them to me, and they knew I'd never tell her where I was. She had to go home. They also knew if they hurt her, they'd turn the hunted into the hunter.

I've never crossed that terrible line, taken another human being's life. But I'm sure Stockland and Simms knew that if they hurt her, and I was still alive, I'd walk right over that line and take death to their doorsteps. After all, I was Tony's protégé and a force to be reckoned with in my own right. No, they'd play the patience game, it was the safe bet.

As I sipped my wine, I found a temporary inner peace as a result of my decisions. Now I could spend the week with Julia and give her all the love I was capable of. Somewhere beneath that temporary calm were Shawn, Ace and Cristo. I shuddered when I thought of what Tony did to those Mexicans that shot at Cristo. What Cristo and Ace got was probably much worse.

25

A Visit from an Old Friend

It was horrible imagining the end that my good friends must have met. It's strange, though, when you are not there to mourn the body of your loved ones it makes the grieving process more removed, and harder to process. For me, I went back to Oregon, bought a small sailboat and spent endless hours sailing and thinking.

Of the seven of us that had started our wild ride fourteen years ago, only TC, GG and myself were still alive. At least I hoped TC made it out of New York alive, but I had no way of knowing for sure. I'd have to wait and make it to the rendezvous point with him in a couple of years. It weighed heavy on my mind. Until then I wouldn't know where to start to try and find him if he was still alive.

It was now fall and I began my course at the local community college. Most of the classes were great – history, anthropology, science and math. I loved them. The only class that bothered me was English.

My SAT test results had shown a very poor understanding of the use of the English language. My vocabulary and reading skills were strong but I just had no idea how to string sentences and paragraphs together. I was put in a special class with a bunch of foreigners, I was the only actual citizen of the United States in the class. This didn't do much for my confidence.

The administration thought I was a bit of an oddball. They said my math scores were in the highest percentages ever seen and that I had a special, natural gift with numbers. They re-tested me and asked me to sit with the math professors, whom I didn't mind, but I had no desire to make a life as a mathematician.

Sitting in a special class learning what a verb and a conjunction are at my age didn't make me feel very special. The math department hounded me but I just blew them off. I was really enjoying the other classes and concentrated on those.

I met a lot of really nice people quickly and got invitations to parties and dinners. But I had to keep my guard up. I couldn't let anyone too close, yet. I was still trying to get used to responding to the name Robert, or Bobby as a lot of people called me. I was also very conscious of the fact that I constantly had to lie about myself. It's not a great way to start off a new relationship. I found the easiest way to do this was to stick as close to the truth as possible.

I told people I was a carpenter, loved music and loved to sail. All these things were true. Then I would try to keep conversations going in a direction I felt comfortable with, sticking with topics such as politics, history and travel in general. I also had a lot of great experiences that I had shared with Julia. I could talk about a lot of my life with her fairly easily; except for the fact that it was still very painful, it came freely and played true. My whole approach to new people was simple: keep them at arm's length and stay guarded.

One day in late October I was on my way home after school and forgot to stop at the grocery store, so I parked the truck in my driveway and headed off to the corner convenience store for milk and a few basics. It was only a block away. I'd got to know the guy that worked there and liked him. We weren't good buddies or anything. We just made polite small talk and the occasional joke. I walked over to the fridge and got my milk, eggs and bread.

'Hey, Bobby. There was a girl in here looking for you.'

'Yeah, right. I wish.'

'No, I'm serious, a pretty little thing with brown hair and nice knockers. She had a picture of you and her and asked if I'd ever seen you.'

I was speechless. 'Don't fuck with me, man.'

'For real. She was driving a new blue T-bird with New York tags.'

That was the same make and colour car I'd bought Julia . . .

'What did she say?'

'She showed me the picture and asked if I'd ever seen you. I said you come in a few times a week and then she asked me to tell you she'd be here tonight at seven o'clock.' He handed me a small piece of paper with a phone number on it and said, 'She said to try and call her there if she misses you.'

I couldn't believe it, I was in shock. I put the items I had in my hands on the counter, took the phone number and walked out without another word. It was the last time I ever went in that store.

It was three thirty in the afternoon and the first thing to do was find a payphone, which I did immediately. Julia picked up the phone on the first ring, probably expecting the front desk.

'Hello.'

I didn't have time for pleasantries.

'Listen to me carefully. I want you to hang up the phone, pack your bags and check out. Then get in your car and drive to the store where you met the guy that knew me. When you come under the bridge, don't pull into the store's parking lot, keep straight on, you'll see me in my truck. Don't wave or even look. Continue for about a mile and pull off to the side of the road and wait. I'll be along in a couple of minutes. I'll pass and you follow. Do you understand me?'

'Yeah. Is everything OK?'

'I just need to be sure you're not being followed. How long will you be?'

'I don't know. Twenty minutes, I guess.'

257

'All right, honey. Remember, drive past the store a mile, pull over and wait.'

I purposely told Julia to come under the overpass because if someone were following, the embankment on either side would obstruct their view and they wouldn't be able to see me standing there on the side of the road. I was in a bus stop enclosure next to where the truck was parked. If someone was following her, I wanted to be able to follow them. It was a rural road with open farmland, a great spot to force them off the road into a ditch and get Julia out of there.

About twenty minutes later I watched as Julia's car came through the underpass and drove past me. Like I instructed her, she didn't look or wave. I eyed the immediate line of traffic that followed. None of the cars fitted the profile. Back then the Feds weren't very creative and they were easier to spot. If it was Simms or Stockland, I'd know them instantly.

I hopped up into my truck and could just make out Julia's car. She was six cars ahead of me. About a mile up the road she pulled off to the side and waited for me. I waved as I passed and she smiled back. As mad as I was about the danger she put us in, I was excited to see her. I drove for another twenty minutes just to be safe and pulled into the clubhouse driveway of a local golf course. We could have a drink in there and make plans. After a rather passionate greeting, we made our way inside to a quiet corner table. There was so much to discuss.

'I can't believe you drove out here by yourself!'

'It wasn't that bad,' she said with the innocent look of a child.

'I find it hard to believe you weren't followed. If they were gonna watch anyone, it'd be you after that episode at the station.'

'Oh, they've been watching every move I made since I duped them at the train station. But I was really careful about everything I said and did. I made a plan then waited for the right moment.'

'What do you mean?'

'I took the hundred and fifty thousand in the duffel bag and

the ten thousand I found when I moved your library to Maria's.'
She gave me a look. She never liked the fact that I kept so much
money in my books. I thought I had got it all when I left town.
'So anyway, every day I put a small amount of cash along with
panties, stockings, and basic stuff in my bag before I left the
house and then casually stuffed them under the seat of the car
when I was at a red light, or whatever. Within a week I had a
travel kit in my car with travel money, and I never even went to
the bank; the guys following me never knew.'

'That's smart, but how'd you beat the tail?'

'Well, you know I drive fast anyway, and always pass trucks
because I hate not being able to see up the road.'

'Yeah.'

'So I just waited. One day I was on the way to get my hair
done and I passed this truck on a two-lane road. I only just made
it, so the guy following couldn't pass, because of all the oncoming
traffic. It seemed like a good time to give it a try. Then, just for
good measure, I ran a red light and took a turn down the back
roads. I was on the interstate twenty minutes later with no guy
on my ass.'

'But the big question is how did you find me?'

'That was a little harder. First of all, you love the sea and said
you were sailing a lot. And I know you don't like sailing on a lake.
Then, one time on the phone last month, you said you like it
over here. If you were in a place south of New York, you would've
said down here, so I knew it was the West Coast. Plus you
mentioned the mountains were close by. You also mentioned a
big river nearby; that was a big help. So I just got out a map and
looked for a place on the West Coast near the mountains with a
big river. And I see Astoria, which made sense to me, because on
our first date you told me you wanted to move out west someday.
I asked where, and you said Astoria, Oregon.'

'Well done.'

'Then, when I got here, I went to all the places you might go
to: the golf course, sailboat rental place, the local college, and I

showed everyone I met a really happy picture of you and me. And now I have you back.'

She started to cry. She was an amazing woman with so much love to give. I didn't deserve her. No, it wasn't that, she didn't deserve to live a life on the lam without her family and friends.

'We need a plan. The first thing to do is pack up my things and get out of here. We need to find some place temporary until I can get Maria out here to drive you back.'

'What? I just drove three thousand miles to be with you, I'm not going back!'

'If you can find me that easy, they can. I have to leave here and start over. No more golf, no more sailing, I have to change everything I do. There's no way I can take you. It makes it easier for them. If I can make another year, then maybe we could try it; they have to move on some day. But right now it's still too dangerous and you have to go.'

Now she was really crying and I felt like a piece of shit.

'Listen to me, I love you and I want you, but it won't work, it's too hard now. We'll spend a couple of weeks together, and then you have to go.'

The idea of spending a couple of weeks together calmed her a little, but she was still upset. She was calm enough for now, but I knew that our love affair wouldn't last under these extreme conditions. I told her it got harder, not easier with time. After a couple of months of this life she'd resent me and anything that we might have. I told her she had to go back and start over. Period. If she met someone else, I'd understand; I wouldn't like it, but I would understand. Who knew? Maybe in a year or so, things might change.

Julia and I spent a glorious three weeks in a mountain chalet not far from Astoria. I liked the area and went to see a realtor one morning when I went out to the store. He showed me a well-built log cabin that had never been finished off, for a price of only $25,000. I left a $1,000 deposit and told him I'd be back in two days to finish up the deal. I told Julia I took a ride to check out the views; I didn't want her to know I was buying a place there. You never knew with her. She could show up again out of the blue, so I kept it to myself.

It was getting to that time when I knew I had to send her away. I dreaded the thought, but I couldn't see any other way. If she stayed with me, I'd have to focus all my energy on making sure she was safe, which was almost impossible without totally removing her from her name and family. It would take months and it was only a matter of time before she fucked up. I already had a lot of experience with this kind of living and I fucked up – she found me. Not to mention I knew Julia had to have some kind of contact with her parents and that she should live near them because they were old and might not be alive much longer.

We discussed having my sister drive back with her, or me taking her most of the way and flying back. But Julia refused to have me, my sister or anyone drive back with her. She said she wanted the time to think and get used to our situation. She was a stubborn woman and in the end I watched her drive away not knowing if I'd ever see her again. Would she evaporate into the mists of lost dreams and murdered friends?

26
The Wilderness Years

My new life in the mountains was lonely, but great. I told Julia I wouldn't be making phone contact with anyone for at least a year. But I couldn't live in a bubble of isolation; if I couldn't have my family and Julia, I had to live a life that included someone. I still went to school every day during the week, and then escaped to my mountain retreat to spend the weekends. I always enjoyed cooking so I started inviting people from school to dinner parties and meeting other women.

A year passed quickly and without any major upsets. I met some nice people, who might have become great friends if I had let them get close. But it's difficult getting close to anyone when you're not who you say you are – celebrating your birthday on some strange day and receiving birthday cards and gifts with a strange name on them. I felt like a fraud.

During those times I just got through the days the best I could and tried to get the most out of my new education. After a while I dropped my guard and got close to two people who I had met at school, two people I told the truth to, or as much as I could: Jack Steeple and Tammy Bennet.

Jack, Tammy and I were older than most of the students. Jack, a typical aspiring novelist, was a neurotic megalomaniac with a multi-faceted personality; we got along great. Tammy, she was much different. She jumped into the deep end of the education pool, trying desperately to atone for her ill-spent youth.

We had some common interests, like history and law, and started hanging out a lot. That fall the three of us celebrated my real birthday together and one thing led to another. The next morning I woke up in her bed.

A few months prior to this new development I called home for the first time since Julia had left. Maria answered the phone and I almost hung up. Sometimes it's easier not knowing things. 'Hello? Hello?'

'Hey, Maria, how's things?' The uneasiness in my stomach was almost unbearable.

'Marco! Are you all right? We've been worried sick about you.'

'Yeah, I'm fine . . . I'm sorry for not calling sooner, it's been hard trying to adjust to this situation.'

'Well, Mom asks about you every day, she's really upset. You should call her and talk to her.'

That was a dime I couldn't emotionally afford; the guilt I felt for putting all of them through so much bullshit was overwhelming. 'That's not going to happen any day soon . . . So how's everyone else?'

'All right, the boys are getting big, they ask about you a lot. They—'

More pain, more regret. I interrupted Maria before she could continue. I needed to move on and get off the phone; too much reality was rushing in and strangling my heart.

'What about Julia? Is she OK?'

There was a short silence and my stomach began to knot up even more.

'Ah, well . . . Julia never came back after she went to see you. She's . . .'

I went paralysed inside. 'What happened to her? Where is she?' My voice was full with desperation.

'Relax, she's OK. After she left you she was in a car accident just a couple hours away from where you are, a town called Caribou; she wasn't hurt. After the accident she met a local guy

264

there. It took a few weeks to fix the car and I guess she fell in love before the car was finished . . . She's married . . . She hasn't really told me too much. But she just had a baby boy last month. I think she's happy.'

I was standing in the telephone booth wishing that I could sit down because my legs had gone to jello. 'What? Who the fuck is this guy?'

Maria knew she needed to reason with me and deflect me from the anger and hurt that was welling up inside.

'Listen to me, Marco! You have to let it go. She used to call me night after night crying for you. She's not to blame here. Let her be happy.'

'Who is this guy, Maria?'

'His name's Dominic Miller and she says he's a really wonderful person . . . You've already made a mess of your life, Marco, let this go and just find a way to get yourself together. We all love you very much and still hope that things will be back to normal someday. Just let her go. If you love her, you will.'

I didn't know what to say, I just had to get off the telephone.

'Listen, I miss you guys and love you all. But I can't talk right now. I'll try to call in a couple of months.'

'Wait a minute. Your house sold six months ago. What am I suppose to do with all of this money?'

It wasn't the best time to talk about it. 'I don't know. I'll call you next week and we can work it out. I have to go.'

'Take care of yourself, Marco. Don't let this make things worse than they already are . . . We all love you.'

'Yeah, me too.'

I put the receiver down and walked back to my truck in a daze. The little hope that I had had inside had been taken away with one small sentence from Maria, 'She's married'. I resisted the strong urge to go and look for Julia. This wasn't the time. I needed to digest this new tragedy.

After a couple of weeks, I found myself driving through Julia's area more and more, hoping to bump into her by chance, but it never happened. I suppose, at that time, it was probably for the best. I wasn't ready to accept this reality yet.

For a couple of months after my birthday party I spent more time at Tammy's house than my own. I guess I was trying to move forward and thought that Tammy could put me back together. But, like all the king's horses and all the king's men, in the nursery rhyme, Tammy was unable to mend what remained of my fractured shell and its fragile contents. The harder I tried to make things work, the further away from inner peace I found myself. In a last chance attempt at emotional survival, I asked Tammy to marry me. She saw the folly of such a union and declined; we quickly drifted apart.

After Tammy turned me down, I put the cabin on the market. I decided to spend New Year's Eve alone and I found myself thinking of all of those New Year's Eves spent with the guys. It was the first time in a long while that I really let myself sink into the abyss of those memories.

As I struggled with the darkness of memory lane I stumbled on some thoughts that disturbed me greatly, but as troubling as they were, they offered some light.

I had to release the ghosts of my fallen brothers from my thoughts and remember them as they were. I had to accept my failure to rebuild the bridge that would have led me to my parents and my family, and hope that maybe someday I would find another path that would take me to them before it was too late. And most of all I had to find a way to be happy for Julia and let her be happy and alive in my heart again, not an unwitting jailer that kept me prisoner.

I had to face her and let her go without any remorse. Then I had to find TC. Don't get me wrong, Uncle Tony was prepared to jump through fire for me, but the resentment for him that burned inside me could only be quelled with distance and time. No, the only way forward was to find TC, he was the one person I could turn to who could really understand my loss. The only person I could share my burden with. The only person who would offer to help me carry it – and who I would allow to help me.

My next birthday was ten months away and I would be thirty-one. I was lost, but I had a plan. It would be the second year since I'd last seen TC. We had said we would meet in two years on my birthday. Next week I would sell my boat and I would drive back to the east and find a temporary place to stay, where I could leave my truck and personal belongings. Maybe I'd have a quiet summer before I made the trip to Italy and hopefully meet up with TC. Seeing him again might give me a new focus on life.

The wintertime is a good time to sell a log cabin; I sold it in less than two months. But it's not a good time to sell a sailboat. It only cost me five grand so it wasn't a big deal. I offered it to my crazy writer buddy Jack; he thought it would be great to have, but could only come up with half the asking price. I was happy to see him get it and not lose out on the total investment.

Everything was set; I had the truck packed and ready to go. There was only one more stop, and that was two hours away to the east. I had to see Julia and release myself from these internal chains.

Finding Julia was very easy. Maria had told me the name of the town and after my second cup of coffee in the local diner I mentioned her husband's name, Dominic Miller, and had their address in moments. I left the coffee shop and took a deep breath. She was only ten minutes away and I didn't have any idea what I would say.

The driveway up to Dominic Miller's house was almost a mile long and lined with banks of snow either side. As I came around the last bend in the driveway, the house came into view.

It was a monster of a log cabin that couldn't have been more than five years old. The snow on the ground and the smoke coming from the chimney, with the mountains in the background, made it an impressive sight.

I stopped the truck and immediately saw Julia. She was off to the side of the house lying in the snow making snow angels with a well-bundled little bambino lying on her chest and a huge smile on her face. It was a rough moment for me but I was happy that she looked so happy. She sat up, looked over and recognised the truck immediately. She looked at me with a sad smile.

I noticed a big guy making his way towards me. I got out of the truck and approached him.

'Hi, are you Dominic?'

'You bet, how can I help you?' he said with an amazing, friendly smile on his face and such a gentleness in his manner that I liked him instantly. I could see how he'd ended up with the best girl I ever met.

I reached out and shook his hand. 'Marco Bolzani, pleased to meet you.' It struck me as odd hearing my name. It had been almost two years since I had heard my full name spoken.

Dominic looked a bit startled and tensed at my name. I didn't want him to be alarmed and quickly put him at ease. 'No need to worry, Dom. I just stopped by to wish you both the best of luck before I head back east.'

He quickly relaxed and smiled. 'Why, thank you, that's mighty kindly.'

Dominic stood about six foot two, an inch or so bigger than myself, and looked like he was well built. His black hair had a touch of grey which, along with the lines around his eyes, gave me the impression he was about forty-two. I wasn't surprised. Julia needed an older guy who was settled. The chances of her finding someone her own age that could give her the kind of life we had were slim.

'Here she comes now.'

I turned and saw Julia holding her little package and walking towards us. I knew from the look on her face she was about to cry. Maybe it was a bad idea, but I couldn't drive away now without at least saying goodbye.

She didn't say a word, she just repositioned the baby to her right side and hugged me with her left arm. I could feel her warm tears on my cheek.

I half choked trying not to cry. 'Hey, Julia, how you doing, honey?'

She smiled and nodded. 'I'm good. Really good,' she said, wiping her face with her mitten.

She cleared her throat and composed herself before she spoke. 'This is my husband Dominic, Dominic Miller.' There was a pride in her voice when she said his name that assured me my first impression of this man was accurate

'We just met,' I said with a reassuring smile. 'You guys have a great place here.'

She didn't respond to my comment about the house. She just pulled back the hood and hat that engulfed her little baby's head. 'And this beautiful little guy is Marco.'

Well, if that didn't make me feel awkward. I tried not to show my uneasiness and reached out to take him in my arms.

'Hey, Marco, I'm your Uncle Marco.' I felt stupid saying it, but I didn't know how else to respond. I hadn't come here to interfere with their lives, I just wanted to see her one last time and say goodbye.

The baby was beautiful. He had big hazel eyes and black hair and he was built like a truck driver. His demeanour seemed very happy and balanced. I felt like I was in some dream, a strange moment that there was no easy way out of. Julia was just staring at me with a big smile and she started crying again, while Dominic stood there looking as uncomfortable as I was feeling. He was the first to break the ice.

'What are we doing out here? Come on inside, Marco, and have something to drink.'

'No I can't, really. There's a storm coming in and I want to be on the other side of the mountain before it gets too bad.' This was true, but even if the weather had been perfect I would have declined his kind invitation.

Julia looked sad. 'Are you sure you can't stay, just for a while?'

'Yeah, I'm sure. As much as I would like to, I can't.'

I handed little Marco back to Julia and shook Dominic's hand.

'It was nice to meet you, Dominic. You're a real lucky guy.'

He just shook his head in agreement and smiled. 'I know I am. You take care of yourself and watch them mountains. If you come back this way, make sure you stop by and see us.'

'I'll do that, Dom. You take care.'

I turned to Julia to kiss her goodbye. She pulled little Marco's hat back so I could kiss his cheek. I didn't want Dominic to feel bad but I couldn't refuse. As soon as I kissed him, she handed Marco over to Dominic. 'Take the baby inside, Dom. I need to have a minute with Marco – if it's OK?'

'Sure it is. Have a safe trip, Marco,' he said with a smile on his face. He took Marco and started walking towards the house, waving the baby's little arm goodbye at me as he went. The guy seemed like a saint. At least I didn't have to worry about Julia.

She turned to me and gave me a bear hug that took my breath away.

'I've missed you so much. I think of you every day.'

'Me too. I try not to, but I do.'

Julia wiped her face again and gave me a brave look. 'So where you off to now?'

'I'm going back east, probably to the north. Find a little house for a temporary hangout and head off to Italy in the fall. I'm supposed to meet TC there for my birthday.'

'Have you heard from him?'

'No. We made plans just before I left to meet two and a half years later in Italy. I'm just hoping he's there.'

She looked worried and I thought she might cry again.

'When you get back . . . and when you get all of that craziness behind you, will you come back?'

'What, here?'

'Yeah.'

'Oh, I don't know, honey. I don't think I could be too close without being with you. You're married, and the baby, it would just get messy.'

'No it wouldn't. Just trust me. When you get it all figured out, come back, we'll be waiting . . . Promise me you'll come back.' With that she gave me a long sweet kiss, a quick hug, and looked up into my eyes. 'Do you promise?'

Reluctantly I nodded my head. 'Yeah, I promise.'

With that she turned and ran towards the house before I could say any more. I just stood there in shock for a moment, and watched her shut the door. When she got inside she waved and stared out the window. I got in my truck and gave her one final wave before I drove off.

As I began my long ascent up the mountain, I actually thought about turning around and going back into town to get a hotel so I could meet with Julia the next day and try to understand what she wanted from me.

I would've given her anything, I would've taken her away right then and there if I'd thought it possible. I decided to keep on driving. I probably just read it all wrong. I was never good with reading emotional moments with women. They say one thing but mean another more times than not. I stuck a Vivaldi cassette in and turned it up loud. I had a lot of kinks to figure out.

27
Italy and Back

I left Oregon far behind and started thinking about what was ahead. I couldn't go back to New York because it was too risky. Running into Simms or Stockland in a busy New York was a long shot but they might have paid guys to be eyes and ears for them. These guys would be expecting me to make contact with family and friends.

You see, not many people can just walk out of their lives and never look back. Most guys that got out of the drug trade went straight for a few years, but eventually they wound up right back where they started. Where else can you make that kind of money? For me, the answer to that question was one word: construction.

The economy was very strong in 1987 and I had a lot of the money I took with me when I first left, and the money from the sale of my cabin. Not to mention the money my sister was holding for me from my house that sold the year before. I just needed to find the right place to make my new start.

I hated starting over again. It would have eased my soul just to know TC was alive. I knew him better than anyone, how he thought and what he felt. If he was there, in Italy, waiting for me, I wouldn't have to think twice. I wouldn't bother going through the headache of starting over again in America, I'd just go straight to Italy. But the rendezvous with TC was still eight months away and I needed to get myself set up and solid before I went in search of the unknown.

I passed from Iowa into Illinois; the miles were piling up as I sped onward, pondering the possibilities of the future. With each state line I crossed I felt as if I was going somewhere, doing something. That's the beauty of travelling, you feel like you're making great progress even when you have no idea where you're going.

By the time I hit the New York state line I had decided on the state of Maine for a new, temporary home.

I found a small city near the coast of Maine and settled in. I bought a small 'fixer upper' and set in to making it everything that I thought it could be. With that done, my next move was the purchase of a small, ten-lot subdivision. The planning for ten houses was already approved and I just needed to get started, which I was more than anxious to do. The only thing that made sense to me was to throw myself into a rigid work routine and try to build a new life alone. I decided that the tack I took in Oregon was wrong. As much as I'd enjoyed the college life, it had allowed me too much free time, and free time can be dangerous. It had allowed me to fall into bouts of depression and wallow in the loss, pain and danger that permeated my existence.

By the end of September I'd finished five of the houses and had poured the remaining five foundations. I had used all of the money I had with me and would have to contact Maria soon. And with my birthday only three weeks away, I had to make preparations to get to Italy and, hopefully, find TC.

The best way to contact Maria would be by post, but I wanted to see her, and her boys, for an emotional fix. Aside from needing the money that she was holding from the sale of my house, I hadn't had any contact of substance with anyone and was feeling despondent. Don't get me wrong, I talked to subcontractors that I hired, but I kept them all at a distance; I didn't even drink with them. I basically lived like a reclusive workaholic. I was actually feeling rather optimistic at this juncture and had a two-point plan. One: if I did find TC when I went to Italy, I'd come back, finish the remaining houses and get right back to Italy for good when the houses sold. I didn't want to feel the pain of leaving anyone behind again. In Italy I'd sit tight and wait for Simms and Stockland to drop the ball and take themselves out of the game. They couldn't chase me forever. Two: if I didn't find TC, I'd come back to Maine, work hard for five years and build a solid life that I could be proud of. Then, when it was safe, I'd return to my real life with my head held high.

I booked my flight to Italy via Canada. I would drive to Montreal, post the letter to Maria using a return address of a friend of Maria's who lived in Montreal, and then catch my flight. The letter read as follows:

Hey Maria,

How you doing?

I need to pick up that cash you got. On Saturday, the twenty-eighth of October, take the four boys to the zoo at 10 a.m. and go inside like you're going to spend the day. Arrange to have a limo pick you up at 12:45. That will give you enough time to let the boys have a look around and get some lunch. It's also enough time that, if you're tailed, they'll go back to the car and wait for you in the parking lot. Have the limo pick you up at the delivery entrance in the back access road.

Talk to Cousin Mike, he'll arrange to get you family passes for the day, and get you access to the rear entrance. Tell the limo driver you want to go to the New Haven Marriot Hotel. I'll be in the lounge. It's about a 90-minute drive. Bring a movie cassette or two for the boys to watch. When you reserve the car, request one with a TV and VCR. Don't use Uncle Sal's limo service, call one of the downtown executive services. Use another name and pay cash. If you can't make it Saturday, come on Sunday; I'll wait. I really appreciate it, Maria. I'm looking forward to seeing you all.

Love,

Marco

P.S. Don't make any of those calls from your house; use a payphone.

After posting the letter to Maria, I spent a night in Montreal. The next day I would leave for Italy. My birthday was in five days and I'd need a day or so to get to the north of Italy where I'd arranged to meet TC. Then I could come back to see Maria, get my cash, then start building my future again. A complicated plan, but what isn't complicated when you are living a life on the lam?

I had been to Rome several times over the years and still found myself overwhelmed by the city. As much as I wanted to stay and appreciate the ancient beauty, I had to rent a car and make a move. I had the better part of ten hours' of driving to do and wanted to get settled into a hotel and wake up in Cassiopeia, the town where TC and I arranged to meet.

Cassiopeia is a very old, lovely village set in the foothills. Too far away from the sea for me, but I wasn't the one planning on living there, so it didn't affect me. The next morning I went into the village to the cafe that TC had chosen.

The owner of the cafe, Giuseppe, had made us feel very welcome years before when TC and I had passed through the area and spent the night there. He ran the restaurant with his wife and four sons and they were all very friendly. I hadn't returned to Cassiopeia since the first time with TC, but TC had been back several times looking for a property and became good friends with Giuseppe and his family.

As soon as I entered, he recognised me. Unlike the rest of his family, his English was pretty good.

'Hey, Marco, how are you?'

'Giuseppe, nice to see you, how's things?'

'Very well, my friend. Have a seat. Cappuccino?'

'That'd be fine, thank you.'

It was still very early and there were only two other customers sitting there. Giuseppe set the cappuccino on the table and sat in the chair across from me, looked around the almost empty cafe and leaned in towards me, speaking in a hushed tone.

'You're looking for Tommaso, no?'

My heart raced and I almost let myself begin to hope that TC might already be there.

'Yes. I'm supposed to meet him here tomorrow. Have you seen him?'

'Yes, I've seen him. He was here two years ago and said he'd be back in a couple of months. He said he was coming back to the villa here and, if you came, I should tell you he was here. He's in trouble, no?'

I couldn't answer right away; I had to think. Was two years ago before Tony's funeral or after?

'Giuseppe, exactly when did you see him last?'

He paused for a moment, remembering. 'Two years next month. I remember because the cold was early and it was very cold when he came.'

'Are you sure?'

His hands were waving in true Italian fashion. '*Absolutimente, amico mio*. I can still remember the Great War, so of course I can remember two years before. I'm sure.'

I was relieved. It meant that TC had got here in October, after Tony's funeral. The guys disappeared only days after the funeral, which was September. The thought of seeing TC again was like a glass of cold water after a week in the desert without a drop in sight.

'Thank you, Giuseppe, this is good news. But why did you think he was in trouble?'

Giuseppe sighed and looked around the room again before speaking.

'Because he buy a big villa with olive farm just outside town

277

and say he come back in a couple of months. And he say, you'll come looking and I'm supposed to tell only you about the villa or him coming back. But he doesn't come back. I think he's in trouble . . . I think maybe you're in trouble . . . no?'

'I don't know. I don't know anything. He told me to be here tomorrow, that's all I know.'

'Yes, he tells me you coming now. He gives me a letter for you and says I must give only you the letter.'

This really took me by surprise. 'Where is the letter? Do you still have it?'

The desperation in my face must have been very obvious because Giuseppe took offence at my suggesting he didn't have it.

'Marco, I'm an honourable man. Of course I have the letter.' He placed both hands on the table and waited for my apology.

I made one instantly and in my best Italian.

Before I had finished he was on his feet heading for the back room and looking over his shoulders as if some unforeseen danger was lurking in the shadows. I wondered if TC had told him about what was going on, which I doubted, or if his suspicious manner was a condition brought on by living through that terrible war of so many years ago.

When he returned he didn't sit back down. He handed me an unopened letter, which had my name written on it, and went back behind the bar. This was to give me privacy. To many Italian gentlemen, like Giuseppe, respect is everything. I opened the envelope, took out the single page inside it and began to read.

Marco,

If you're reading this, it means more than two years have passed and I haven't returned. Cristo, Ace and Shawn didn't make it out. I tried getting Cristo to listen to me, but you know Cristo. He thought there was enough time and he could survive the shit anyway. Before Tony's funeral I made a trip to Amsterdam and moved some money around for me and Cristo. When I got back, Cristo and Ace were missing and Shawn was dead. I knew something was wrong, but had no idea what had happened at that point. I left immediately and came here to buy a house and get set up. A few weeks later I called back home and found out that Cristo and Ace had been identified.

I can't stay here and wait for you for two years, I have to go and find the fuckers that did this and settle the score. If I have too much heat on my back, I won't return for a while; I'll have to lay low. I still have a shit load of big moves I need to make to get our money out of the country and back here, my new home. The only thing I can say is don't stay where you are too long. If I'm not there by the night of your birthday, get out. I think the place is safe, but if I try and whack these guys out and don't succeed, they're going to come looking for you with all they got and I'm not sure who knows about that place from the old days. But no one knows about you being there for your birthday. So plan 2: do you remember the name of the village where we rode the hairy whales? Try to be there in the month of June, and your birthday each year. I know that might not be possible every year. So every year I can make it, I will.

You take care of yourself and keep it together. Stay away from Julia; I think they'll keep a close eye on her.

T

I waited until the following evening but TC didn't show. I said my goodbyes to Giuseppe and his family. Before I left he gave me the address of TC's place and the set of keys that TC had left with him. I wrestled with myself about going to see the place, and in the end I decided not to. I just drove off into the night towards Rome, thinking how good it would be to see Maria and the boys when I got back. Not finding TC was troubling me, but I had to stay focused and not let it get to me.

I got back to Montreal a week before the meeting with Maria and enjoyed an easy drive south, stopping for a day of sailing in Bar Harbour and then again the next day further down the coast in Camden Maine. It was cold, but it was the last sailing I'd be able to do that year without heading south.

I knew Maria would be there, even if she'd had other plans. We've always been very close, and I knew she missed me as much as I did her. When Maria sold the house she got $375,000. It was worth $500,000, but the lower price persuaded the new buyer to put $150,000 in cash into the deal. From the $225,000, the sale price on paper, the bank got $90,000 for the construction loan I took to make myself not stand out to the tax people. That left $135,000, less six per cent for the realtor's fees, and I couldn't get to that money without a trail. So I told Maria to buy another piece of property upstate, at least a couple of hours away. If you don't reinvest within a year of the sale, you have to pay capital gains tax.

Like I knew she would, Maria arrived as arranged. I was disappointed when the door of the limousine opened and only the two older boys, Tommy and John, got out with Maria. I had expected all four of the boys, but she said she left Donnie and little Sal with our mother. I was overwhelmed with emotion but for a few brief hours I actually felt normal, a condition that now seemed alien to me.

We spent the afternoon enjoying the unseasonably warm October Indian summer in a local park, where I had planned a great picnic. After playing football with Tommy and John, we ate lunch and then the boys went off exploring the small pond just a couple of hundred yards away. It was home to frogs, small turtles and all of the amazing wonders that such a pond can offer an eight- and ten-year-old boy.

Maria and I caught up on lost time and discussed events I'd missed at home. The one topic she pressed relentlessly was the whereabouts of TC; that was one I tried avoiding until Maria finally pushed the topic to the front of the discussion and basically demanded an answer.

'I don't know, Maria. The only thing I can say for sure is that he was still alive after Tony's funeral and the identification of Cristo and Johnny the Ace. After that, I can't tell you anything.'

She didn't look very convinced, but I couldn't tell her that TC was hell bent on whacking out Simms and Stockland; she had enough grief and fear to deal with already without thinking of the countless possibilities that came with that scenario.

'So can you tell me when this nightmare is going to end? When can you come home? Where are you going now?'

'I don't know how or when this all ends. The only thing I can do now is bury myself in work and keep a low profile. Maybe in a couple of years things will change – that's my hope.'

'Where? You must have some idea of where you're going?' she said with more than a little bitterness. 'You must have some kind of plan?'

I let out a long sigh. I knew I shouldn't say too much, but I had to put her at ease.

'I can't tell you exactly where I'm going but my plan is to go up north and build some houses. I have to do something productive with my life. I have to put the past behind me, Julia – Mom and Dad, Uncle Tony, all of them, and you guys, for a while anyway. And the only way I know how to do that is to work as much as I can. With any luck, it will all go away eventually and I can try to pick up the pieces. What else can I do? Do you have a better idea?'

My tone was a little harsh and I regretted it instantly. Aside from making Maria cry, all of the easiness I'd experienced earlier in the day was evaporating. 'I'm sorry. I'm sorry that this whole thing has got so messed up, I just—'

'I'm not mad at you. I'm not crying because you won't tell me where you're going, I know you can't do that. I'm angry because my sons are growing up without you being there, but that's not why I'm crying either. I'm crying for you. I can't imagine how you're getting through all of this, I just wish you could spend more time with us. Months go by and I just sit and wonder if you're ever going to call again, if I'm ever going to see you again; it's an awful feeling.'

I leaned over and hugged her. One because I wanted her to stop crying, but also so that she wouldn't see me crying. The whole damn thing was too much. I just wanted to get in my truck and drive north and go back to work.

As soon as I got back to Maine I'd work harder than I'd ever worked before, just so I wouldn't have the strength at the end of the day to feel any more of this sadness. I knew that if I wasn't careful, I could wash over the looming precipice and never survive the fall. I had to toughen up.

We tend to take the best things in our lives for granted, especially the normal things. You can bitch about your family, or your lovers, or maybe your friends. But can you imagine not having any of them, losing them all instantly and you're the lone survivor of the only life you've ever known? And then travelling to some strange place where you don't know anyone? Add a new name and birthday to that scenario, along with the loss of the love of your life, and the word normal slips out of your vocabulary. Just a few short hours of hearing your real name again and having a few loved ones to hug can hit you like a sledgehammer and make you feel again. And feeling is, in itself, a dangerous thing.

We spent the rest of the day like a normal, happy family. It was like a Norman Rockwell fantasy for me. But, as all good things must, the day came to an end. The boys cried and wanted me to come home with them. Maria cried and just said goodbye. I still think about all the pain I caused my family, never mind the pain I inflicted on myself. Could I ever be with them again and make it up to them?

20
Europe

As the Paris-bound 747 headed for its destination, I stared out the window trying to find a bright star to hang my hopes on. It was the summer of 1992, I was almost thirty-six years old and I was still lost.

I had made a mess of things in my life so far and I had to redeem myself. I tried calling my dad, but he still didn't want to talk. He had a hard time believing that I hadn't got involved in the drug business again back when the shit hit the fan. I tried explaining it to him, but I couldn't tell him the truth about Tony being alive, and I didn't have the heart to tell him that my life was as fucked as it was.

It was better to let him be mad; that way he wouldn't worry as much. If he knew I'd spent almost a million dollars in the last four years he would've been really disappointed. But the thing that would have hurt him the most would be to know I drank myself into oblivion for the better part of two years and then spent almost a year in rehab.

When Dad wouldn't talk to me, there was only one other call I could make for advice: Uncle Tony. It was good talking to Tony, but he gave me a lot of shit for not calling often enough. I still harboured a lot of anger towards him and hadn't learned how to deal with it at that point, so I didn't call very often.

Tony told me that GG had got a twenty-year bid. That would

make him about fifty when he got out, forty-six if he made parole. I hoped he rotted in there or, even better, maybe someone would shift him. I wouldn't lose any sleep, and it would save me from having to do it myself.

The real troubling news I got from Tony was that Stockland and Simms were still hell bent on finding me. Tony said he had an inside connection on Stockland and Simms and that they were into some serious shit. They were running scams in South America, Europe and back at home, so if I was lucky they'd fuck up and I'd be in the clear. But they were more organised and powerful than ever. The only good news I got from Tony was that they never found Julia and assumed she was with me. Tony was the one who suggested I go to Europe; he thought the old country would do me good. I took his advice and now, here I was, with my head up my ass at thirty-five thousand feet, heading for Paris.

I tried to sleep, but the demons were haunting me a little more than usual. Sometimes, just for fun, they'd give me the grand tour of my past: dead friends, lost family, losing the love of my life, not to mention the wasted years and shattered dreams. A condition once remedied with a bottle of Scotch and a handful of Valium was now dealt with by deep breaths into a paper bag and a mild, over-the-counter sedative. Before the sedatives kicked in, I thought about Gina and how I broke her heart. She knew I was unhappy and she tried so hard to make things better. I'd tell her it wasn't her but I'd keep on drinking. She couldn't understand and I couldn't tell her the truth . . . I guess, in a way, I'm writing this down for all the people I hurt just as much as I am for myself. But I'm getting ahead of myself; I suppose I should give a brief account of what happened after the last meeting with my sister Maria and the boys.

The game I was playing didn't even have set rules, never mind instructions. So how was I supposed to know that when I declared all the profit from the ten houses I'd built in Maine, the taxman was going to ask my accountant questions? In the past I'd always declared large amounts of profit, but that was over the years and that was as myself, not Robert Pino, a guy with no history at all – a small oversight on my part that would bring yet another of my lives to an abrupt end.

Apparently the IRS were always looking for guys, particularly construction guys, who worked under the table on the black – according to my accountant, who, after the flags came up, assumed I was one of those guys.

'If you're going to come clean with the IRS, you do it over many years. The more "funny money", the more years. Why didn't you tell me you never paid taxes?'

I told him I'd spent my early twenties in college and then spent the next five years helping my dad build his big house and barn. And that my dad gave me the funds to start this business venture. I then assured him we could get all the documents to support this, and asked him to set an appointment with the IRS as soon as possible so we could clear it all up.

Now that was a load of shit. I didn't know how much trouble I was in, but I did know my accountant had to reply to the IRS quickly and positively, offering to make a full disclosure and rebuking them for the imputation of an impropriety. If he didn't, they could freeze my assets and then I'd be fucked.

I left the accountant's office and found myself in disappear mode. I didn't have much time and there was so much to do. I had to find a way to get my money out of the bank, sell my house, get a new identity and sell my trucks and tools. How was I going to do all that?

I wanted to disappear that night. I was afraid if they dug too deeply into Robert Pino's life they'd find it rather strange that a man in his early thirties had no traceable past. I couldn't take the chance.

The next day my accountant informed me that I had a meeting with an IRS agent in nine days.

Getting the money out of the bank wasn't too difficult. I had set up a corporation back in Oregon that I'd used to buy the cabin. One of the company bank accounts was in the Cayman Islands. I would transfer most of the funds in my Maine bank account to the offshore account in the Caymans, but not yet, I had another move to make first.

The house was difficult. If I put it on the market, people would become suspicious; I had a great thing going as a builder, why would I up and sell overnight? Not to mention, it takes time. No, that wasn't the move.

I called one of the local banks I did business with. I had financed a dump truck through them to establish credit and that truck was paid for in full. They had been trying to win me over from their competitor across town. I was doing big business and they wanted in. So when I spoke with the loan officer about taking a mortgage on my home, he was happy to get right on it.

I filled out the forms and three days later was informed of my approval. I borrowed half of the value of my house, which covered all the cash I had put into it. I could have borrowed more, but I had become part of the community and didn't want to leave anyone holding the bag. When I disappeared and stopped making the repayments, the bank would repossess and easily get their investment back.

I put the money into an existing account in Maine, then transferred it to the Caymans the same day. Now I could go across town and transfer the funds from the big account to the same place.

Within five days of the meeting with my accountant, I'd sold most of my tools and equipment to an out-of-town rental store that was privately owned. It was a great deal for him and a one-stop deal for me.

The money was in the Caymans, two of the three trucks were sold to the dealer I'd bought them from, and my personal belongings were in the truck. I would be driving out of town the next morning.

I tried to sleep that night but found it difficult. The thought of leaving again was intolerable. Another attempt at finding peace whisked away in a flash. More lost memories, more what ifs, more despair. But something kept me going. I guess it must be the survival gene I seem to have been born with. So, with sleep nowhere to be found that night, I got out of bed, dressed and got on the road, accompanied by Vivaldi.

Florida was my destination, for two reasons. First, it's a place where a lot of gangsters and other seedy characters vacationed and even retired. I could broker a deal on a new identity with a guy who was out of the New York loop; it would be more expensive but was much safer. Second, I had plenty of money that could be traced to the Caymans and needed to take some time out to make a new plan that wouldn't go tits up again.

Joe Castellaccio was an old New Yorker and a friend of Tony's who knew his way around Miami. For health reasons he'd relocated there. He fucked a bookie back in the Big Apple for a hundred large and thought he'd live longer if he disappeared. He changed his name and made a living selling new identities, mostly to Central Americans. Tony had given me his number before I left home.

I told Joe I wanted two passports, two very different names and an age difference. Getting two passports and all of the supporting documents to go with them was expensive, but I didn't know what future lay ahead of me and thought I'd better get an extra passport just in case. Joe said he needed three days to get them together, but otherwise there'd be no problem. So I took a long drive down I-95 to the Keys, and used the time to relax.

One of the other reasons I chose Florida for a temporary residence was the weather. I wanted to buy another boat and sail the Caribbean. I had done a lot of flying in single- and twin-engine aeroplanes in the past, and thought I'd get my pilot's licence as well. I also wanted to lie on the beach for a couple of days of reading.

After three days of much needed R&R, I paid Joe and he gave me my new papers. My new name was Michael Cooper and I was a Pisces. Now that I had my new name, I needed to go to the

Caymans so Robert Pino could take his money out of the bank and Michael Cooper could put it into another.

But it's not that simple. Cayman bankers are like Swiss bankers but not as effective. The US government has some authority there and they can make things difficult. If the IRS were to find Robert Pino's money transfers to the Caymans, they'd find the withdrawals, so they'd just check the other banks for a new account, opened soon afterwards with a similar balance. If they found that, they found me, Michael Cooper.

Most people think that once you have the money in hand you can just jump on a plane or a boat with your suitcase full of money, but it's not that easy. Whether it's a plane or a boat, you run a risk. If the authorities catch you with that much cash, you have to explain where it all came from, why you have it and, most importantly, why you haven't declared it. That was a game I didn't want to play.

I had a couple of hurdles that needed hopping. One, Robert Pino had to fly to the Caymans, withdraw his money and disappear. Two, Michael Cooper, a few days later, had to find a safe home in the Cayman Islands for his money, and get some of it back into the US without a trace. I was gonna need a little help and I knew the perfect guy to give it.

Those who knew Philip Healey referred to him as Captain Cocktail. Captain because he was a pilot in the Vietnam War, Cocktail because he spent more time on the floor of the local bar than he did in a plane. He'd seen too much death in the war and, like many vets, used alcohol to dull his visions of horror.

I had first met Cap years ago with Tony. We were on a two-week fishing and R&R trip in Fort Lauderdale and Cap decided to show us around the Caribbean. He owned an old Second World War B-5, a big twin-engine cargo plane that he used for delivering supplies to island resorts and the like. I remember hitting the party hard in Haiti and waking up in a hut in Jamaica two days later.

Finding Cap was pretty easy, if you knew where to look. There was a small airfield just outside of Fort Lauderdale where he kept his plane when in the area. I just had to ask the other pilots; someone would know where Cap was and when he'd be back. As it turned out, Cap's plane was in for general maintenance and I was informed Cap was making use of the couple of days off in a local bar. When I found him, he was true to form.

He stood six foot two, weighed a fit 195 pounds and his head was shaved. Sporting a Fu-Manchu moustache and dressed in jeans, he wasn't particularly handsome but had a huge presence. To look at him you'd think he was a biker guy, or maybe a neo-Nazi without all the tattoos. But behind his piercing blue eyes was a mind that was razor sharp.

Cap was sitting at the bar with three attractive blondes who were eagerly listening to one of his crazy stories. He didn't see me come in, so I just sat down and listened to him tell his tale.

'So anyway, everyone else in the plane's dead, or dying. Three of the four engines are dead, the plane's about to run out of fuel and there's nothing but ocean below.' He pauses for a moment and makes contact with his dedicated audience before he continues. 'Then I see them, a squadron of fucking Japs coming in for the kill. Now I know it's all over, there's no way out of this one.' Cap pauses and sips his large tropical drink with a worried look on his face.

The girls are waiting intently for more, and one of them eagerly asks, 'So then what'd you do, Cap?'

Cap looks at them with a strained face. 'What do you think I did? I shut the fucking TV off! That movie was fucking scary.'

The girls broke out laughing and Cap did as well. That was the thing about Cap I liked, he had faced death several times and had real stories that would terrify you, but he preferred to make people laugh, even if it was at his own expense. Cap hugged one of the girls and then saw me sitting a couple of seats down. I hoped he wouldn't make too much of a fuss and say something like, 'Marco.' It was probably safe here in the bar, but I still worried about those things.

But Cap didn't do that. He turned to the girls and said, 'Girls, my ride's here, I got to go.'

They were all disappointed but Cap bought them another round and said his goodbyes, promising to see them again soon.

He walked up to me and said, 'I'm ready.'

We walked to the door in silence. Cap staggered a bit, he looked like he had been at the bottle hard, but when we got outside he transformed himself into a sober man.

'How much shit you in, kid?'

'Who says I'm in shit?' I wasn't sure how much I should say to Cap.

'Listen, I'm the one that flew Tony out of here after his death. And I know your new name's Robert Pino. Tony told me to keep an ear and an eye out for you, so give it to me straight.'

I waited until we got in the car before I spoke. 'I'm not in any real shit, I just need to go to the Caymans and move some money out of one bank and spread it around in a couple of others and get a couple of hundred grand back here without no one noticing.'

'Why? Name change?'

'Yeah, the IRS wanted to know how a guy with no past work history reported more than half a million in profit last year.'

'You should've known better, kid.'

'Yeah, well, next time I'll know.'

'Aside from that, you OK?'

'Yeah, I'm all right. Tired.'

Cap drove in silence for ten minutes, obviously deep in thought, and then offered a solution to my problem. 'Listen, I can get you to the Caymans tomorrow. You get the money out and keep it in your room and stay there for five or six days. If you want I'll take a couple hundred Gs out for you, I'll take a hundred tomorrow and another hundred when I pick you up. I can't take too much, it'd be a risk.'

At first I wasn't sure what to think, but deep down I knew I could trust this crazy old fucker. 'Sounds like a plan, buddy.'

The trip to the Caymans went off without a hitch. I got $200,000 out in cash and I put the rest in two new separate accounts, in two different banks on two different days.

When we got back to Florida I checked into a huge suite at an upscale hotel on Miami Beach. Cap stayed for a couple of days and we caught up on old times. I paid for everything, it was the least I could do; Cap only charged me $1,000 to cover fuel and expenses. That was nothing for what he did for me. I paid him with ten $100 bills.

He took out a pen with black ink and signed all of them Captain Cocktail, and put them in his pocket. It was something he'd been doing for years. He always took signed hundreds with him to the Caribbean and spent them. So if you ever get a hundred in the Caribbean signed 'Captain Cocktail', you'll know where it came from.

After my little party at the hotel I packed up my new car. I had sold the truck to a Ford dealer for short money and bought a new Mercedes 560 sedan at a local Mercedes dealer. I got on the highway and headed for the west coast of Florida. The west coast is predominately a retiree community, it's very quiet and I'd be a bit bored, but it would be safer there.

I found a sensational house for rent right on the beach, with a pool. It was a bit expensive, $2,000 a month, but I figured what the hell. I needed to lay low and make a plan, a year there would do me good. Not to mention, now that I knew Tony confided in Cap, I looked forward to spending time with someone who knew me, and he was someone I could talk with.

The first weekend I went out in my new neighbourhood it was to a little wine bar called the Fountain. It was one of those eighties yuppie joints that, five years before, I wouldn't have been caught dead in. I didn't realise it then, but I was changing. I guess my situation demanded that I change. I had to be more serious, more informed. Exchanging raunchy bars with pool tables for wine bars was part of that evolution.

At the Fountain that night I met a wonderful woman named Virginia Darcy. She was a few years older than I was, highly educated and very beautiful. I bought a bottle of great wine and we spoke for hours. Virginia was an interior decorator and self-employed. After five years of college and a degree in business, she married a man she had met in school. Seven years of a long-distance relationship was more than they could bear, and they called it quits. The biggest problem between them was her inability to have children.

That night Virginia, or Gina as I came to call her, came home with me and we stayed up all night talking and anticipating the arrival of the sunrise; she ended up staying for three days.

During that time she decided I needed her to decorate my unfurnished home. So off we went to buy furniture, curtains, art and everything that was known to man. I'm not sure if it was her expensive taste or my need to feel secure, but I spent over a hundred grand in those three days. I had never got the chance to finish furnishing the house I had built back home so I made up for it.

The following week she thought my wardrobe wasn't up to par, so once again she offered her shopping services. Between the new Mercedes, the week-long party at the hotel with Cap, the clothes and the furniture, I had spent almost three hundred grand. I hadn't spent money like that for a while; it felt great.

A couple of months passed quickly and I felt pretty good about things. I was living in a sleepy little retirement town and I minded my own business. No one would find me there. Gina was spending most nights at my place and I liked it. When I felt the urge to be wild I'd call good old Cap and he'd fly in and pick me up at the local airfield. We'd fly off to wherever he was delivering something and we'd get drunk.

It bothered Gina when I went with Cap. I knew she loved me more than I loved her and she was afraid I'd meet some young beauty, but it was never like that; it was a guy thing for Cap and me.

I think Cap liked the idea of looking after me. He was about old enough to be my dad and didn't have any family. No parents, siblings or cousins. He had no one else. The big thing for me was, on our excursions I got to be me. It didn't matter what the name on my passport was and I didn't have to watch what I said to Cap. That's it in a nutshell. The worst part of living on the lam is the having to be someone else. It makes it so hard to get close to someone new. And it's not fair to them, because they don't get the whole you. They get a new twisted version of who you were.

The first year of my new life in that Florida retirement community went smoothly. It wasn't until the end of the second year that I really sank into the abyss. Gina was a driven woman and consumed with her work but I just enjoyed life. In the beginning I told her that my plan was to have an easy year and then get back into the building game. After a year she began to wonder why I wasn't getting into the swing of things; she also started asking lots of questions about my past that were difficult to answer.

I couldn't express to her the fears I had of running a company, the danger of selling homes to the public. It wasn't likely I'd run into someone I didn't want to see, but it was possible, certainly a lot more possible there than in the middle of Maine.

What if they found me and killed Gina too? What if I had to disappear into thin air again? It was thoughts like these that started to corrode my soul and sent me into a tailspin that drove me deep into a seemingly endless bottle of Scotch, a bottle that took me more than two years to get through.

One day I just woke up and decided I would stop the drinking and the drugs. I checked myself into rehab and as soon as I felt strong enough, I boarded the Paris-bound jet. And that's where I found myself now.

I didn't spend any time in Paris. I had been there two years before with Gina and didn't want to deal with the memories of how I hurt her. I caught the first train to Amsterdam and, for the first time in a long time, was excited. I had been there on a few occasions several years before, moving cash around. The idea of going to Amsterdam as a non-practising drunk seemed a bit like an obese person on a diet going to an open house at McDonald's. But I had already decided that I was going to keep myself straight and wouldn't let booze or drugs be a problem.

29
One More Time

Amsterdam is a city of amazing vibrancy. Even in winter, with the cold and endless rain, you can feel the electricity of its pulse. I spent the first two weeks in a hotel enjoying all that the city had to offer, excluding the prostitutes, drugs and booze. Then I found a small apartment that I could use as a home base and settled in, before going on a ten-month Euro-road trip.

I figured that while I was out and about seeing the sights, I could pop into Italy and wait for TC during the weeks of his birthday and mine as well. I half hoped I might bump into him in some strange place. I know it sounds ridiculous, but sometimes you have to create hope just to keep going. The millennium meeting at the clubhouse was almost eight years away; I wanted to find TC long before that.

I returned to Amsterdam after I finished my road trip just in time to enjoy the short Amsterdam summer and indulged in the many non-booze-related activities that the amazing city has to offer. Joining the chess club was the biggest event since my return from the road trip. It wasn't until the following spring, in 1994, that I met Christine and fell again into Cupid's line of fire. This time with an arrow that would wound me almost as deeply as the wound I received when I met Julia.

Amsterdam had more English bookstores than any other foreign city I'd been to. I'd buy a book and sit in cafes for hours just reading and meeting interesting people, and that's how I met Christine. I was sitting at a table in the corner of the cafe when this stunning woman with blonde hair entered. She looked over at me and gave me a polite smile, then went over to the bar and talked with the girl who worked there. I didn't think much of it but about ten minutes later she came over to my table with a coffee and asked if she could join me. I welcomed the company.

'I hope you don't think I'm rude, I just didn't feel like sitting alone.'

'No, not at all, I was getting bored with myself, actually. Michael Cooper.' I offered my hand and she politely shook it.

'I'm Christine Van Allen. It's a pleasure to meet you, Michael. Are you American?'

'Well, I was born there, but my parents are Italian.'

'You look Italian, but Cooper doesn't sound Italian.'

I couldn't believe I'd fucked up in the first two minutes. I had to think quickly.

'Yeah, when my family came to America they landed in New York's Ellis Island and the name was changed. It happened to more immigrants than not.' At least that part was true.

'That's terrible,' she said, and then instantly it hit me, that overwhelming sensation you get when you meet someone who sweeps you off your feet. It was the first time I had been taken with a woman's beauty so completely; the fact that I had been living in a bubble of seclusion for four years and hadn't been romantically involved for so long probably enhanced the moment. I suddenly realised I was staring at her and it was my turn to say something.

'Were you born in Amsterdam?'

'Yes, I was born here in Amsterdam, but my family now live in a small village to the west.'

'And you? Do live with them?'

'No. I have a small flat here in the city; very small,' she said and laughed.

When she laughed I felt an overwhelming sensation come over me. I knew I was a goner.

'Do you work?'

'Yes, I finished school last year and began my new job a couple of months ago. I'm a psychologist.'

I couldn't believe it, a shrink, just what I needed. 'Oh, that's great! Are you going to start your own practice?'

'Eventually. At the moment I'm working for the city of Amsterdam, counselling prostitutes, battered women and people who suffer from addiction. Eventually, someday, I'd like to have my own practice.'

The conversation went on like that for three more hours and I asked her to join me for dinner. She agreed. She ended up spending the night with me. I got the full brunt of Cupid's arrow this time and found myself lost in a sea of love that was so deep I never thought I'd come up for air. Living in two small separate flats was difficult so we decided we wanted to live together and I found something bigger.

On one of the canal streets was a small, two-bedroom house that was in need of serious remodelling. The owner was a young guy who I met in a cafe. He'd inherited the building and didn't have the money to carry out the necessary work. We quickly came to a deal. I would buy the material and do the work in lieu of cheap rent, 600 guilders, about $300, a month for ten years. In the end I got a beautiful place to live on the canal for a short investment.

We were proud of our new home and began having dinner parties, usually with her friends. I didn't know many people at that time, but Christine's friends were nice people, and they were shrinks as well, she had met them all in college.

There was a group of us, five couples, and we often had dinner with each other, and even went on a couple of holidays together. Of the ten of us, six were shrinks, two were happy little homemakers addicted to Xanax and wine, and one was an ex-prostitute. And let's not forget me, a recovering drunk who was

297

on the run from a host of bad guys who held day jobs as good guys. You never knew where the dinner conversation was going to start, but it always got to, and remained on, psychotherapy.

After a year and a half with Christine, I found myself with a little too much time on my hands. Now that the house was remodelled I fell back into the cafe groove and Christine felt uneasy with it. I wasn't doing anything wrong, but it made her uncomfortable. So one day she brought a girlfriend home from work, whose father owned a construction company. When she saw the work I had done in our house she called her dad and made an appointment for me to meet with him.

I met with Jan the following week. He gave me the address of the project he was working on. I looked around and was impressed with the scope of things. Jan was buying historical buildings in the centre of Amsterdam and, under Dutch regulations, putting them back the same way they originally were. He was particularly interested in my knowledge of timber-frame roof construction.

We agreed to a two-week trial period to see if it worked out for the both of us and it did. The two other lead carpenters were both in their sixties and I was able to relieve them of a lot of the physical stress that the work demanded.

After the two-week trial period, Jan offered me a full-time position. But in Holland, like many European countries, a foreigner is not allowed to take a job away from a Dutch person. The only way a Dutch employer can hire outside of the Dutch work pool is if the position can't be filled by a local person. Like many cities in Europe, craftsmen were on the decline in Amsterdam and not many young people had the experience or the desire to learn. So within a month I was legally working and totally enjoying it. That was the beginning of what I thought would be the rest of a quiet, stable life.

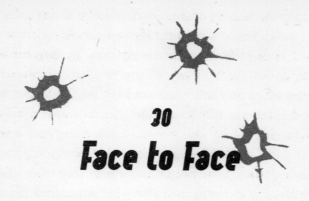

30
Face to Face

It was now March 1997, twelve years since I'd begun this life on the run, three of them spent with Christine in Amsterdam. I loved Christine but that's not always enough. She made me her psychoanalytical guinea pig and as a result I became her hobby. I didn't talk about my past for my own reasons and she assumed I was repressing a tormented childhood. She was determined to draw me out of that dark abyss and save my grieving soul.

After two years of being grilled, I stopped coming straight home from work. I started having a couple of beers with the guys from work because I needed my own friends who had normal conversations devoid of Jungian metaphors. I didn't seem to fall off the edge with just wine and beer, but I didn't push my luck; I stayed clear of Scotch and all the other spirits. It didn't make any difference to my lovable little shrink because she got angry with my new-found freedom whether I drank or not.

Her first line of defence against my unacceptable, insubordinate behaviour was to redirect her psychotherapy. She would augment her rigid hard-line psychology with a double dose of guilt. I didn't buy into that tack at all, but her second line of defence, the termination of our great sex life, had an immediate effect. Not the one she wanted, though.

The way I see it, if a woman is capable of using that as a

weapon, she has changed the playing field of sexual equality, moved the goalposts and torn up the rule book.

I left Christine within the week. She underestimated my resolve and had no idea of my ability to shut off emotions that cluttered my mind and soul. She couldn't have known, because I didn't tell her about my past. She didn't know my existence depended on my being able to shut any door and never look back.

I let Christine keep the house and everything in it, and I took what I could carry in a suitcase. The only stipulation I made was that I would store my tools in the attic rent-free for as many years as I needed to. She couldn't believe I was actually leaving, I think she really believed I'd be home in a week. I wasn't. She insisted I keep my keys, but I never once walked through that door again. For the first time since my quick departure from New York, I felt like I was strong enough for anything.

I stayed with Ricky, a guy I had met at work, for a couple of weeks until I found a small one-bedroom downtown that was clean and furnished. I took it right away. Then I asked Jan, my boss, for a couple of months off so I could regroup.

Jan wasn't thrilled about me taking it off, but he agreed to it on condition I worked three more weeks to finish the job we were on. It took us five weeks to finish, but then I was free for two months to gather my thoughts and heal my emotional wounds. I found a great little bar, just twenty yards from my house, that was frequented by all the street performers, and I had a good time having a laugh with the crazies. I must admit, I enjoyed that bar more than any other drinking establishment I've ever been to.

I met David there. He was about forty and looked like a biker guy. He had all the tattoos and a long ponytail with a great big beard on his face. It was crowded that night. I had just walked in and got a beer and the last table available. Ten minutes later this big guy walks up to the table.

'Excuse me. I heard you order your beer. Are you American?'
'Yeah, you?'

'Yeah, man, San Francisco,' he said with a big smile.

'Great, I'm from Maine. Have a seat, I haven't talked to anyone from home in months.'

He sat across from me and put his hand out. 'Name's David.'

'Hey, David, I'm Michael, nice to meet you.'

'Yeah, same here, Mike. You here on business or pleasure?'

'Oh no, I live here now. I fell in love with a Dutch beauty and never left. I live just twenty yards away near the corner. What about yourself?'

'Just pleasure, man, I'm celebrating.'

'Great, what you celebrating?'

'I just sold my software company to one of the big guys for seven figures.'

It all made sense. San Francisco is near Silicon Valley, a lot of computer guys dress a bit funky and I'd read of a couple of small guys in that business selling out for huge profits so I didn't give it another thought. We had a few beers and some great conversation. He was very intelligent and quite interesting. It was nice to talk to another American, kind of like seeing an old friend.

After about an hour and a half, he said, 'Mike, what do you say we get some dinner, my treat.'

I hadn't eaten anything yet and usually I was the one picking up the tab. 'Sounds good to me. What do you like, Chinese, Italian, Vietnamese?'

'Do you know somewhere good that does huge steaks and mashed potatoes?'

'I know just the place.'

The restaurant was located in the infamous red light district, where almost anything is possible. I liked the area, it was swarming with wild pubs full of mad people from all over the world. On any given night you could find every walk of life there. On the way we got into a conversation about New York. I lied and told David I had only been twice. He had spent two years there at college.

After a few bottles of wine, I was feeling nostalgic and I

was reacting to the big black hole in my heart that not seeing Christine had put there. Anyway, I started telling this guy my story. I didn't mention names and I tried to change things, but it was pretty much all there. I guess after so many years I needed to get it all out.

David listened intently and hung on my every word. I must admit, hearing my epic journey vocalised for the first time was something of a shock. I guess I had never really absorbed the whole thing. Almost immediately after I finished my tale, I regretted having doing so. I knew I had made a mistake.

We finished dinner and I got up to go. David offered to buy a bottle of champagne but I lied and said I had to work the next day. To make me feel even more insecure, he said he was around for a few more days and asked me to join him for a couple of beers at one of the bars I'd told him about.

We made plans to meet, but I knew I wouldn't be there. The whole walk home I had a bad feeling about telling him my story. I decided to take the longer way home up the shopping street. It was lined with shops the whole way and I could use the reflection from the glass storefronts to make sure I wasn't being tailed.

The next day I hung around the house, not wanting to go out, when I got a call from Gary, a guy I worked with. He had the next day off and wanted to know if I'd help him frame a wooden roof on the garden shed he was building. He built a lot of these sheds and used some kind of African hardwood because of the moisture in the garden and always brought the scrap wood to my house for the fireplace so I figured it was the least I could do. Since I was going to work with Gary the following morning, I decided I'd stay in that night as well.

In the autumn Amsterdam gets dark early so we finished up about four. I filled two heavy-duty yellow bags with some scrap wood and started my walk home. It began to rain but I had my rain jacket and didn't mind so much.

When I turned off the canal and onto my street, I saw a white van parked there. It didn't make sense. I eyed the vehicle suspiciously for anything abnormal about it.

The first thing I noticed was the tinted, almost mirror windows. We hardly get sunny beach weather in Amsterdam so that was definitely out of place. The next thing I noticed were the three small antennas on the top of the van. Was that some kind of communication system? And it was parked with the back of the van looking down my street, giving a perfect view of my door and the two small streets that ran into my street.

I walked past the van, looking slightly away, as if trying not to get hit in the face with rain, then took a left towards the bar where I had met David. I made sure not to make eye contact with anyone inside the bar, which was easily done with all the pedestrians walking alongside me. I passed the bar and went to the end of the street and made a right. I was going to take another right up the next little street and head back towards my street for a better look. I wanted to be sure I wasn't overreacting.

As I made the next right, I saw a guy standing in the doorway on the corner. I don't know if it was the clothes, shoes or the haircut, but I knew this guy was an agent on a stakeout and I would have bet the ranch he was an American.

That's when I made the first of a series of mistakes. I looked him right in the eye. This gave him the chance to ID me. I tried to regroup and just nod a polite hello in Dutch. I then turned my head to the opposite side of the street and scanned the glass store-fronts. I could make out the guy's reflection and saw him reach into his pocket, pull out a small radio and put it up to his mouth.

I didn't panic but I had only two hundred yards or so to make a plan and there were a lot of people bustling around in the rain. Luckily the street turned to the right about halfway up and once I passed that bend, he wouldn't be able to see me. I figured he'd signalled either the guys in the van or someone on foot and they'd be looking for a guy in a yellow raincoat carrying two yellow bags. I sauntered on calmly for another thirty feet past the bend until I found what I was looking for.

On the right side of the street was a set of stairs that went to a basement below street level. I threw the bags down there along with my raincoat. I had my winter jacket on below the rain jacket and put on the wool cap I had in my pocket; and just for good measure I put my driving glasses on. The switch only took me half a minute.

As I came to the end of the street, I put my head down, as people do when hurrying through the rain. I could go left, away from the van, or right and get a better look. I went right.

I could see the van just ahead, about two hundred feet away. About halfway to the van, I stopped at a storefront for a look around. Anyone watching would have assumed I was window-shopping, but actually I was using the reflection to get an idea of how many guests were at this little party.

It was easy to spot the two guys watching the corner because they both looked ex-military. They had a disciplined, military look in their eyes and a stiffness in their posture, unlike undercover agents who are trained to fit in. Not to mention they were both staring at the corner I had come from, anticipating my arrival.

I walked, with my head still down, towards the van. Passing it was a bit tense, it was the best place for them to grab me, but I walked right by without any problem. On passing, I noticed the registration plates were German. I found a small cafe on one of the canals and got a coffee.

It wasn't hard to figure that telling my story to David two nights before was what had brought this all on. How he was involved I had no idea but feared I would find out. I needed to regroup and sort out the facts. There was no Vivaldi on the jukebox so I had to make do with some light jazz.

Back at the table, I began my list. First, were they definitely here for me? It certainly looked like it, although being on the lam for fifteen years can make a person a bit paranoid. Second, if it was David who gave me away, how did they get here so quickly? If the agency were doing this legitimately, they would have to have co-operation from the local authorities and that takes time. Third, why did the van have German tags? That was the question that really stuck out.

In a way, it answered all of the questions. It suggested to me that they were there for a snatch and grab, a kidnap. And that in turn suggested it was me they were here for. They wouldn't want to take me in locally, I'd make too much noise. I was a tax-paying citizen with no criminal record in any name I've ever had. And, no matter what they tried to pin on me, they'd need time. That would give me a chance to pitch my story to the press, a story they couldn't afford to get out globally. The more I considered the facts, the more I was convinced I was right.

There are several American bases in Germany and a lot of army and air force cargo planes that come and go with no customs check. Not a bad way to hide a problem passenger you don't have clearance for. Not to mention, Stockland and Simms could probably muster a small army of guys off one of those bases and get all kinds of services for a small bag of cash.

The only thing I couldn't figure was why not just kill me right there? When the guy on the corner spotted me, he should have called ahead and had the two other goons come down the street for me. I would've been fucked. A simple push from one of the two coming at me and a needle from the guy behind me was all it would have taken to render me helpless or induce a life-ending heart attack. They say, 'Excuse me,' and keep walking, no one pays attention and ten minutes later I'm be on the ground dying. No one would ever know.

The only thing that made sense was that they needed me alive to get the evidence that would put them all away – the badges and documents Uncle Tony had left with me. They didn't know if I'd left them with TC or someone else or just stashed them somewhere, which made me think that maybe TC was still alive.

It was a good thought, like a small light in a dark tunnel, but it didn't show me a way out.

31
The Lion's Den

My heart was racing in that cafe as I considered my limited options. I knew I had to go back and try a different tactic, one that wouldn't get me caught or killed.

I went to a local store and bought a new rain jacket with a big hood and a pair of khaki trousers that were a size too big. If I got into a scrape I didn't want to be restricted in any way. Then I went to a small pub where I changed my jeans and had a whisky to relax. I didn't like the idea of leaving Amsterdam and starting all over; I was so tired of fucking running, but I couldn't see any other option.

I decided to walk right back into the lion's den. I passed the van and walked straight on until I came to a small shop almost directly across from my front door. It was a shop that sold tobacco, beer and miscellaneous crap. I had a friend, Cathy, who worked the late-day shift there; she'd be a good extra pair of eyes and the back door in the shop gave me a second way out if needed.

The front window of the shop provided me with a clear view of the opposition. The two ex-marine types were still positioned out front, basically in the same spot, about thirty feet apart. One guy was two doors down from my door, almost directly across from the shop I was in. The other was on the same side, standing there looking at his watch occasionally, like he was waiting for someone.

I spent an hour in the shop with Cathy and it was nearing closing time but the two guys and the van were still there. Then a group of four guys came in for cigarettes and I said goodbye to Cathy and walked out with them. The street was less busy now and walking out with four other guys gave me a little extra cover. I really needed to get into my flat. Aside from the $20,000 in Dutch money, I had a few personal effects that I really wanted. Most of my belongings could be replaced, but my money belt with the seventy-five one-thousand dollar bills Tony gave me for an emergency was essential, and my pictures couldn't be replaced.

Once I was in, I had an escape route. I could climb out my rear window and up the fire escape to the roof. Then I just had to run along the ridge of a couple of houses and I could come back down to an apartment that a friend of mine was remodelling. Its front door would give me an exit on a different street.

My street was still a little busy so I walked around Amsterdam for an hour until it quieted down around eight o'clock. I approached from the opposite end this time and the first thing I noticed was that the van was gone. I scanned the doorways and shop fronts but I didn't see anyone.

I quickened my pace and headed for my front door with the keys in my hand. I got the key in the door and opened it, thinking to myself, so far, so good. Now I just have to—

An arm, a very powerful arm, went round my neck and pulled me back. Then my assailant's free hand was on my mouth with a wet cloth that had a strange smell. The first thing I thought was not to breathe. Then I bent forward, almost doubled over, bringing the attacker off his feet, and I spun to my right so my back was facing the doorway. With all my might I pushed off my feet, throwing his body against the granite corner of the recessed entrance. I heard a loud gasp and felt the grip on my neck loosen. Before I could turn and confront him, a second guy came at me.

It was happening so fast, I didn't have a lot of time to think.

I bent forward a little, getting a deep breath of fresh air into my lungs – that's probably what saved me.

I think the guy coming at me thought I was succumbing to the chemically laced rag that the other guy put over my mouth so he approached me less cautiously. I waited until he was just about two feet away and I lunged at him. The front door key was still between my thumb and index finger, and I thrust it forward into his cheek with all the strength I had. I felt the key go through his flesh and I yanked it back towards me, slicing his face from the cheekbone to the corner of his mouth. When he screamed in pain, his mouth looked about five or six inches wide. Then I hit him with a sweeping, open-palmed blow that seemed to move his nose to the left a couple of inches and he went out immediately. The other guy was still on his ass with his back up against the granite. He had a large gash on his head that was bleeding pretty bad and I kicked him straight in the face twice, putting him out cold as well.

I heard a vehicle and turned. The van was coming down the street, only a hundred yards away. I wasn't about to press my luck. I closed the front door and ran up the stairs to my flat. I put a huge iron security bar, typical in A-dam, across the door. If they tried coming up, it would take at least ten minutes to break through. I stopped for a moment to collect my thoughts, my head still dizzy from the small amount of shit I'd inhaled from that rag the guy stuck in my face.

First thing I did was wash off all the blood on me from my assailants, and change my clothes. Money belt, Dutch money, family pictures, documents and a change of clothes, that's all I could take.

I went to the window and cautiously looked down into the street. The van was nowhere to be seen but I was sure they'd left someone to follow me. I grabbed my bag and took a last look around – the pictures of my life here in Amsterdam, the first-edition books I'd been collecting, the hundreds of movies, I had to leave it all. I had one last thought: I couldn't leave the pictures.

If they came back and got in, I didn't want them to have any current pictures of me or, more importantly, any of Christine.

I got another duffel bag out of the closet, took pictures off the wall and put them into the bag. Then I went to my desk and gathered all the photos stored there, and anything else that I thought could identify me. I decided it might be a good idea to take the bloodied clothes as well. With a great sadness and not a small amount of fear, I headed to the window and climbed out onto the fire escape.

I had to climb two storeys up before I could start walking across the rooftops towards the apartment that was being renovated. It was slippery from the rain, but I made the trip without any problem. I had to break the window on the balcony door to get in but I left fifty guilders on the counter to pay for the repair.

I walked out into the hall and down the stairs to the front door. Out on the street I found an alley with a dumpster and threw away the bag with the Amsterdam pictures and bloody clothes; I only kept one picture of Christine. That done, I hailed a taxi to the airport.

I wasn't going to the airport, but the driver had to call in the location of his fare. I was probably being over-cautious, but fuck it, I was scared. I didn't dare take my truck, they could have asked around the bar and found out a lot about me, like where I parked it, and waited there for me as well. That left the train, but they might have the station covered too. The fact was I didn't have any idea of how many guys were involved or where they might be.

I waited until the taxi was halfway to Schiphol Airport before telling the driver I'd changed my mind and wanted to go to the nearest train station. He just shrugged his shoulders and did as I asked. I didn't care what station, just as long as it wasn't Amsterdam's Centraal Station. They couldn't stake out every place.

I paid the guy and went inside to check the timetables. There was a train for Brussels in twenty minutes. Perfect.

I spent that night in a dumpy hotel just fifty yards from the train station in Brussels. To say I was feeling down would have been an understatement. I couldn't sleep, so I just sat in a chair and thought about who I was and who I wanted to be. I hated the whole new city/new life thing. I was exhausted. I was really missing the quiet life I had had when I lived in Maine. It seemed every time I tried to interact with the world, something collapsed, always from within.

I felt an ever-growing weight on my shoulders that was pulling me dangerously low, to some place I didn't want to be. I'm not sure if it was the repressed anger that was welling up inside or the constant pressure of living in fear. Whatever it was, I'm sure the fact that I didn't have family or friends in my life, there to pick me up occasionally, added to the ever-mounting tension that resided in me. I fought off the strong urge to get a bottle of whisky.

I don't know if I hated Tony or myself more. It seemed to be a pretty close call. The violence that had ensued when those guys tried to take me really scared me. Don't get me wrong, I was glad to be there in that shithole of a hotel and not tied up in the back of a van, but I felt filthy. I had always been an able fighter, ever since I was a kid, and that didn't really bother me. It was being so efficient at it, without any real effort, that made me not want to know what lay dormant inside in my soul. I guess it was fear of that unknown quantity that made me avoid confrontation whenever possible.

I just sat in that hotel replaying the scenes of my life. Would this madness ever end?

The next morning I checked out of the hotel and headed for the train station. I had no idea where I was going, but I thought Italy sounded good. At the ticket counter I learned that the next train for Rome wouldn't leave for two hours. So I bought a newspaper and caught up with the news while I waited.

After a week in Rome I decided that I'd head for the little

311

town where TC and I rode the hairy whales, a reference to two girls who didn't shave their armpits, as some European women don't, who we spent a night with so, so many years ago.

On arrival I had a sensation of coming home. Aside from the time I had spent there with TC, I had been back two or three times as well. It was a small fishing village that still had most of its old-world charm and, best of all, memories of TC and myself back when life was good. Within six hours I found a small, furnished house that was for rent and started my new life there.

As usual, in the beginning I didn't interact with many people. I stayed home, cooked and read a lot of books. There was an English bookstore in a nearby city that had a great selection of new and used books and great staff who enjoyed mingling with the customers. I also bought another small sailboat and when the loneliness and boredom started to corrode my soul I would take off for days on end.

Things went on like that without any real change for two years, by which time the new millennium was only six months away. If TC didn't show up for his birthday in June, and if he didn't show up in the fall for my birthday, I'd go back to New York and hope he showed up for the millennium meeting that we'd set so long ago. I wasn't very optimistic.

He didn't show up in June, but then things changed one sunny July afternoon.

I returned home from three days of sailing down the coast and back, and thought it would be nice to go to the local cafe for a beer and a newspaper to catch up on the three days of news I'd missed.

I arrived at the cafe and it was quiet, as it usually was in the early afternoon. I grabbed a beer, paid for my paper and made my way over to an empty table overlooking the sea. When I sat down I was startled to hear a familiar voice.

'Where the fuck you been? I've been hanging around for three days.'

I spun to my right. He looked the same, the only real

difference was his hair was white, which gave him an air of respectability somehow. Tony had aged gracefully.

'How'd you find me?'

'What, you think I'm stupid like those other fucks trying to find you? I could give you a three-year head start and you'd never be able to hide from me. I know you too well.' Tony laughed and sipped his glass of red wine. 'How are you, kid?'

'I'm OK, Uncle. But . . . how the fuck did you find me?'

'Relax, kid. You're doing a good job staying low. TC told me you might be here.'

That got my attention. 'TC? He's all right, you see him?'

Tony took another sip of his wine and sighed. My hopes started to fade. 'All I know is he came and saw me after he tried whacking out Stockland. That was a real fucking mistake which might not have been so bad if he'd succeeded, but the bullet just took off Stockland's earlobe and he had to have plastic surgery. I can't say I wouldn't have done the same thing when I was younger, but it was a mistake nonetheless. After he left my place he sent me an occasional postcard, but I haven't heard anything for five years.'

'He tried whacking out Stockland?'

'Yeah, he found his house in Baltimore and tried taking him out with a rifle. The only thing he did was intensify Stockland's resolve to kill the both of you.'

'I would've thought he would've made one attempt at the both of them together. Even if he'd succeeded with Stockland he would have had Simms on his ass.'

'No, I think if he'd succeeded, Simms would have called it a day, he doesn't have the resources Stockland does. Stockland's the one with the big inside strings.'

'Do you think they got him, Uncle?'

'No. I think he realised the shit storm he'd created and put as much distance between you and him as possible. He probably found some place to bunker down and ride out the storm. Stopping all contact was the smart move.'

313

I drank down my beer and went to the bar for another round. As good as it was to see Tony, I really wanted to see TC.

When I got back to the table, Tony lit a cigar and gave me a long stare. I wasn't sure what it meant, so I just sat and waited for him to get around to what was on his mind.

During the silence I noticed for the first time how old and tired he looked. In a strange way, he looked more terrifying now than he did twenty years ago. He still had that strange power that emanated from within. After what seemed like a lifetime he started.

'You know, I didn't hold a gun to your head when I asked you to move that white poison around. I figured you guys were moving pot already and would've made the transition on your own, but I got to tell you, kid, I was wrong. I fucked up all your lives and mine as well. Fucking mine up, well, that ain't so bad. I fucked that up long before we went down that path. I killed a lot of men, more than I care to mention. Most of them probably deserved it, but a couple didn't. But I don't lose any sleep over that. That's for me and God to work out. What I do lose sleep over is fucking up you kids, because I had a choice in that. I should have kicked you all in the ass and made you all fly straight.' He paused to re-light his cigar. I felt a bit uncomfortable, I'd never heard Tony apologise to anyone, never mind admit he was wrong. He took a slow sip of wine. I felt like I should say something.

'The thing is, Tony, we probably wouldn't have listened anyway. We were fucked-up kids living in a fucked-up city at a crazy time. I don't think you could've saved us.'

'Maybe not, but I didn't have to put you in the deep end either.'

'What's done is done. There's no going back.'

'That's exactly what I'm trying to tell you, kid, you have to go forward.' Tony gave me one of those looks that used to send fear into the furthest reaches of my soul, but I wasn't affected in the slightest. I'd travelled too many hard miles and didn't know that kind of fear any more. But I realised that this whole dialogue had a purpose, and he was preparing me for something. I just sat and drank my beer without emotion.

'The thing is kid, GG's made parole. He got released last week.'

Now that kindled some emotion in me. I started to burn with anger and decided I better get a whisky and try to quiet the dragon that still lived inside me.

As I waited for the barman to pour the drinks, I began to understand why Tony was apologising to me. He knew I was going to be incensed with rage and want revenge. He was trying to shift some of it towards him so I wouldn't do anything stupid.

When I got back to the table, he was a bit edgy.

'Listen to me, Marco. You have to let it go. In another five, ten years this thing will be old news. You just—'

'Five, ten years? What, are you fucking kidding me?' I knew interrupting Tony was a forbidden thing, but I didn't give a fuck about him or his old rules at that moment. 'Another five, ten years living in the shadows while that fucking two-bit fuck lives it up large? Fuck that, Tony. Cristo's dead! Ace, Shawn and Paws, dead. And TC, who knows where he is or if he's alive or dead. Fuck that! G's not getting a pass from me. I don't have anything left, Tony, no family, no friends, no Julia. Why the fuck should he get a pass from me?' I was almost screaming across the table at him.

'For starters, Marco, lower your fucking voice and quit thinking with your heart. Now I'm not saying he should get a pass, kid. I'll whack him for you. I just need to get the time right. I can't exactly go walking down the street in broad daylight back at home, can I?'

'No, fuck that, Tony. Thanks, but no fucking thanks. I made a promise. We all made a promise to each other. If someone fucks one of us, we settle it.'

Tony started heating up a little and leaned in towards me real close, eyes blazing with life, fire and brimstone.

315

'Listen to me good, kid. I didn't fly halfway around the fucking world to get into it with you. And don't let the white hair fool you. I can still kill you and everyone else in this bar right now and have a nice dinner on another continent by sundown. That's what I do. I'm only here because I was afraid you might find out from Maria, or whoever it is you might keep in contact with. The bottom line is, if you're going to whack GG, I can't stop you. But just remember, once you cross that line, and take a man's life, your soul's not your own . . . And let's just say you pull it off and make it back here to your little life, it's only a matter of a couple of months, maybe a year, before it starts to eat you up inside. Killing a stranger's not easy. Imagine what killing a childhood friend who was once like a brother would do to you. It would slowly destroy you.' Tony sat back in his chair and relaxed a bit. I tried to do the same, but the anger inside me was seething and I didn't know how to let it go.

Tony was right. Even if I was able to do this thing, and pulled it off without going to jail or getting killed – which could happen if I froze up and GG was prepared – it was probably going to eat me alive, but I didn't care.

A few months before, I'd gone to Austria for a couple of days. I wanted to call Maria. She had told me that my father had had a massive heart attack and was practically bedridden. I felt so guilty about not being there that sometimes I'd pace the floor for hours trying to figure out how I got so fucking lost. Maria also told me that she still heard from Julia from time to time. Julia's husband had died.

As far as Maria knew, Julia and her son Marco were still living alone up there in the mountains and that hurt me more than the news of my father. I wanted to go rescue her and take care of her and maybe somehow be a family, but my life was so fucked. I could only bring them danger and pain.

These were the thoughts running through my head. What did I have to lose? I could still have a great life, nice houses, nice boats and enough money to live out the rest of my days, if I wasn't too careless. But inside I was dead. I felt nothing but heartache and pain every day. I didn't even want to meet another woman. I could only bring her a broken heart and who knew what else. Tony was right, but I was going for GG. I meant to take from him just what he took from the rest of us: life. I leaned in towards Tony, calmly. My mind was set and I was firm.

'Uncle, I didn't mean any disrespect to you. I appreciate you coming all this way, and I know what you're saying is all true. But this is one thing I have to do. If it gets me killed, fucked up or whatever, I have to do it. I'm almost forty-three years old and I've spent half my adult years running. I'm fucking tired, Uncle, I don't care any more. Everything I love is dead to me. That's not living.'

Tony gave me a hard look of disappointment. 'Listen, Marco, you don't even know where he is. The only way for you to find him is to go out in the open and that means exposing yourself on the street. You don't think that Stockland and Simms don't have ears on the street? This ain't going to be one, two, three parties over. If you have to do this, let me help you.'

'No, that's where you're wrong, Uncle. I don't need your help to kill G, and I do know exactly where he's going to be for the millennium.'

'And how the fuck do you know that?'

'Because we made a pact back in the old days. We all promised to be at the clubhouse at midnight for the millennium.'

Tony shook his head. 'I think you've been out in the sun on that boat of yours too long, kid, because you're fucking nuts if you think G's going to show up there after all the shit that's gone on.'

'Maybe you're right, Uncle, maybe he won't be there. If not, nothing to worry about. And maybe I am fucking nuts, and maybe killing GG will make me certifiable. I just know I have to try. If I don't, I definitely will go nuts. Besides, TC might show. We all made the pact, I have to try at least.'

Tony sighed and shook his head. He knew I was just as

stubborn as he was. 'If you're going to go, I ain't going to stop you. But I wouldn't count on TC showing up. I don't think he's made contact with anyone back home. They all assume he's dead.'

'How do you know that?'

'I have someone back at home that I talk with. I like to make sure Francesca and the family are all right. Anyway, all I'm saying is don't be surprised if you're there alone this New Year's.'

'Yeah, I know.'

Tony stood up, grabbed his jacket and motioned to the door. 'Listen, let's get out of here. I'm hungry.'

'Yeah, sure, I could eat. I know a great place a couple of miles down the coast.'

'Yeah, I'm sure you do, but I know a better one.'

'OK, where?'

'Palermo.'

'Sicily?'

'Yeah, fucking Sicily. What else you got to do?'

I shrugged my shoulders, he was right. I didn't have anything I had to do; it'd be nice to have the company.

As it turned out, we spent two weeks in Sicily, and two more in Rome. Tony tried to change my mind about going back, but I wasn't listening.

When I said goodbye to Tony, he asked me to come and live with him down in Belize. I said I'd think about it. I couldn't even consider that just now. I needed to make my plan and get my head right for this thing I had to do. I had four months until the New Year, time for a lot of Vivaldi and some of the biggest kinks I'd ever had to work out.

32
Millennium

Passing customs at JFK is always nerve-racking when you're on the lam and using false documents. But this time really gave me the shits. I had left the country as Michael Cooper, which had been compromised in Amsterdam, and was now returning as Steven Thompson; I didn't know if it would make a difference. I didn't think I'd make it in without at least being questioned, but I passed right through like I was just another guy returning from a business trip.

I suppose I shouldn't have been surprised. My passport was clean and Stockland and Simms had no idea of my new name. Now if I could just get to GG and do what I had to do, maybe somehow I could come out on the other side. I didn't dare to hope beyond that. However, if TC fulfilled our twenty-year pact and showed up, it would be a consolation for what I felt was the right thing to do.

The cold air hit me like a slap in the face but it was good to see snow again. Driving the rental through the old neighbourhoods was strange. It looked the same but it had lost that family atmosphere that I missed more than anything else.

As I passed my childhood home a touch of nostalgia washed into me. I tried to dismiss the sensation as soon as it came because I needed to be focused. I quickly did the math and realised that it had been thirty years since I had stepped foot in that house.

I wished that somehow I could go back and talk to young Marco in a way that my father had been incapable of doing. That was the thing; I could always be reasoned with, but start throwing punches around and I became as unreachable as the planet Neptune.

As I was leaving the neighbourhood I passed the Dagostinos' small store. The façade was remodelled and it looked like whoever owned the shop was prospering. I thought of TC, and what he did for Mrs Dagostino, and even though it didn't feel right to smile about a man's death, I smiled to think about that little lady who was able to keep her livelihood, a woman who knew the law of these streets and understood its moral code. I kept driving; as much as I wanted to, I couldn't stop for a chat.

It was getting dark and I began to relax a little more with the cloak of night. After my trip down memory lane I shot up to the Bronx to see if the old warehouses we used for our operation were still standing. Strange, I'd felt more secure moving a truckload of pot or 20 Ks of coke in broad daylight when I was a kid. Now I needed a beard, a different style of clothes and the cover of night to drive down the streets that I had once called home.

The warehouses were gone, replaced with two six-storey condos that must have been put up in the nineties. I pulled in and stopped for a moment, and thought about the old times. I tried to picture us driving around without a care in the world in pick-up trucks and dump trucks, loaded with enough illegal cargo to put us away forever. We must've had balls of steel, or perhaps just brains of lead. I held the memory for a moment and then drove off for the clubhouse just five blocks south on T Street.

It's funny how some things you learn as a kid stick with you for life. Without even thinking about it I made the first pass by the clubhouse without turning my head. If there was anyone in a car or house staking the place out, that's what they'd be waiting for. They'd be watching to see if anyone slowed down and looked.

So I passed without slowing down and just glanced out of the corner of my eye. I stopped at the STOP sign in front of the clubhouse and put on the inside light. I picked up a piece of paper, read it and kept looking around. If someone was watching they'd think I was lost and reading directions. But really I was checking out all the parked cars and the surrounding houses to see if anything looked out of place. It also meant that I could make another pass in the next five minutes and if there were eyes watching, they'd just think it was the moron who was lost. And that's exactly what I did. On the second pass, I went a little slower and had a better look.

Everything seemed OK from T Street so I thought it would be safe to have a look from Bacon Place at the back, a small cul-de-sac that ran parallel to T Street. The last house to be built on Bacon Place was right behind the clubhouse, and a little-known footpath ran alongside it, giving access from Bacon Place to T Street. From the footpath I could get to the back door of the clubhouse without being seen from T Street.

Driving up Bacon Place was a real blast from the past. I could picture TC and myself fighting on the lawns, fights that would last for hours, starting at one end of the street and ending at the other. I always lost because TC was older.

Everything looked fine so I parked about halfway down and walked back to the metal gate. As I expected, it was locked. I just hopped over it. The bushes looked as if they hadn't been trimmed in twenty years and a lot of small trees had popped up.

As far as I could judge from the street light, the stone walls of the clubhouse, the slate roof, wooden shutters and the door all seemed to be intact and in reasonable condition. As I navigated my way through the overgrown vegetation, a sudden feeling of dread came over me. Something didn't feel right. But I was compelled to go forward. I had to see this through.

I put my key in the lock and it turned. After twenty years, locks tend to freeze up. But this just opened without any resistance. Inside I instinctively reached for the light switch, not expecting that the electricity would be on after all these years. To my surprise the lights came on.

I shut the door and stood quietly in the tidy kitchen. It should have been covered in an inch of dust but this looked as if it had just been cleaned. The bathroom was on the right; I opened the door and put on the light and it was clean too. This wasn't normal. No one besides GG, TC or myself could have been here. We owned it, under the name TCMG Inc. Years ago, TC, myself, Cristo and GG decided to buy it jointly because it was our childhood hangout, it had nothing to do with Shawn, Paws or Johnny the Ace. Maybe our property attorney had been paying a maintenance guy to look after the place for us all these years. I couldn't think of another explanation for the clubhouse looking so tidy. The truth was, I had no idea how much property TC had sold and what we still owned. But the clubhouse was the only property the three Irish didn't have a stake in.

I walked through the small kitchen and into the main room, put on the light; this room was clean as well. The couch covers, the carpet and the seven chairs round the oval table were all clean. The four wooden swords still hung on the wall. They looked so small, so old, and I thought, how did it all come to this? Then, just to really fuck me up, on the table was a framed picture of the seven of us, a bottle of 1976 Barbosa wine and two empty wine glasses.

Now I didn't know what to think. Could it be possible that TC was still alive and here for the reunion? I suppose anyone could have got inside and left the wine and glasses without too much bother, but not the picture and that particular bottle of wine, here, now, the night before a meeting set almost twenty years ago. It was all pretty fucking weird. I couldn't help but feel that I was walking into a trap.

I was thinking that I'd feel a little better if I had a gun. That would be the first thing on my list of things to do tomorrow morning. Then I thought of the safe. The safe might have some answers, and also one of my old guns. It should also contain a key to the outside gate.

The safe was located in the cement floor under one of the

kitchen cabinets. I took out the large pasta pot and removable shelf that concealed the safe, and dialled the combination.

One to the right, three to the left, five to the right and seven to the left. I turned the handle but it didn't move. That's when I remembered. We changed the combination after GG was arrested, so I tried again. One to the right, three to the left, seven to the right, seven to the left. I reached for the handle and turned.

The handle moved freely and I opened the door. It was dark, the light we'd installed under the cabinet didn't work. So I put my hand in and began pulling out the contents. The first item that came out was a sealed, bulky manila envelope. The next was my old .45, a gun I'd never liked. Unlike a smaller calibre weapon, it tended to leave the recipient of its wrath dead or maimed for life. Not to mention it was too damned noisy, and in my old line of work you wanted something that wasn't going to alert half the city. But it meant I wouldn't need to buy a new gun after all – it would do just fine for my purpose.

I felt around inside the safe for the gate key and found it. I closed the safe, put the key in my pocket and took the rest to the table and sat down. The clip in the gun was full and aside from needing a good polish and oil, all the parts moved fluently. The manila envelope was labelled 'MARCO'. I pulled out three banded stacks of bills. Two stacks were one-thousand dollar bills, and the other one five-hundred dollar bills. All three stacks looked to be complete, which would be two at $100,000 and one at $50,000.

This was an unexpected cache; if I survived this thing I might use the money to buy a bigger boat, but I wouldn't think about that now. I'd have plenty of time to worry about changing the bills and spending it later, if I was still alive and not locked up.

The other item in the envelope was a smaller envelope. It contained a US passport and a driver's licence, birth certificate and social security card. The passport and the licence both had my picture on them, a much younger me. I looked at the expiration dates; they were still good for three more years. The driver's licence and passport were only valid for ten years – a good sign. There was also a letter. I opened and read it.

Marco,

Hey kid, how you doing? Things are fucked. I tried whacking out Stockland and failed. I'm sure they'll figure out it was me pretty quick, so I'm trying to get out. I sold the rest of the property and divided it by three, fuck GG, he started this shit and he's probably never getting out of the can alive anyway. I gave Cristo's cut to his old lady for his kid. I know two hundred and fifty grand isn't much, but it's the best I can do in cash on short notice and limited space; I have to meet a guy in Texas to buy large notes, then I can move it all north, over the border and get a boat from there. I'll go and see your guy in Amsterdam to redistribute it safely. I don't know if I'm gonna make it, but if I do, I'll see you at the same place I mentioned in the last letter; if you got the last letter? The town where we rode the hairy whales – month of June, or the week of your birthday. I'll try to make it as soon as I can move freely. If not, I'll try my best to make the millennium reunion. Take care of yourself.

T

P.S. Those documents are the real thing. I hope you make it, kid.

I read the letter again. It was definitely TC's handwriting and the millennium reunion, that was tomorrow night. For the first time in years I felt a weight lift from my chest. I really wanted to see TC again. Don't get me wrong, the idea of two or three million sitting in some safe place waiting for me in Europe sounded great to me; I just figured I'd think about that later, after the New Year; tomorrow was enough to worry about. There was no need to wait around the clubhouse, tomorrow night things would play out, for better or worse.

33
End Game

As I headed downtown to Manhattan for a hotel room I tried to make sense of everything so far. Fact one: GG was out of prison and laying low. He hadn't been on the street in almost twenty years and a lot of people were blaming him for many deaths, he couldn't walk around freely. He had to live in the shadows and wouldn't have any real resources or friends. When Tony and I were in Rome, he told me that GG's dad had passed away and left him a small inheritance, but that and his father's connections wouldn't be enough to buy his way out of the bad books of the locals.

Two: one of the crew was definitely alive, aside from GG; who else could have got into the clubhouse and left the framed picture? Three: TC was still alive as of seven years ago, when the documents he left in the safe were issued. And finally, the real kicker: someone had put on the electric and oiled the locks, put out two wine glasses, bought the right bottle of wine and created the illusion that everything was fine. If it was T, why didn't he leave a note in the safe?

If GG set the scene at the clubhouse then he was either up to something or had lost his mind in prison. If he showed, his only chance at getting a pass from me was for me to lose my nerve. As per our pact, I had to kill him for his betrayal. He must know that, whatever prison had done to his mind. Maybe he was working for Stockland and Simms. But why? I would've thought GG would've been avoiding those two like the plague, not working with them to kill me. Not to mention, Tony had said that GG had never met Stockland and Simms. Nothing made any sense.

After all these years I would have thought Stockland and Simms would have given up by now. The amount of time and money involved must have been outrageous. Surely they knew that I had no desire to reawaken the past and that I just wanted to be left alone. I was only here in the hope that TC was still alive and because, like the other six, I promised I'd be here and I had to fulfil an obligation that we'd all made to each other.

The only thing to do now was get a bed and sleep. Tomorrow was going to be a long day.

The next morning I paid for another night and went back to my room. I figured it was better to pay for the room and have it and not need it than to need it and not have it. It was New Year's Eve and I only got the room as a result of a last-minute cancellation. I hoped I would need it, I wanted to welcome 2000 with a smile, or at least with a pulse.

It was possible that this would be the last day of my life. So I went back upstairs and read a book. It was probably the best thing I could do to take my mind off the meeting. Not to mention going out wasn't safe, it was possible I could bump into someone I didn't want to see, like Tony's old friend Denni. He was probably long dead from heart disease, but you never knew.

Back in Rome Tony said that Denni had taken a bad heart attack and wasn't expected to survive the year. I wouldn't miss the fat bastard, with his creepy God complex and arrogant attitude. In fact, I was sure the world would be a better place without him.

After a great dinner from room service I sat in the tub for two hours and got dressed about eleven. On the drive to the clubhouse I couldn't help but think I should have accepted Tony's offer to meet me here just in case something came up.

When I got to T Street I did the same routine as the night before and parked the car on Bacon Place. It's funny how a dramatic moment can intensify your surroundings. As I walked towards the black gate, I seemed to notice every detail of the Victorian houses that lined the street and was particularly taken with the beauty of the snow-laden branches of the trees that decorated so many lawns. I wondered if they had always been that beautiful.

My stomach knotted as I unlocked the gate with the key I had retrieved. I didn't let the extreme cold or the snow that was beginning to fall again upset me in the least. I felt so alive, yet I was sure I was about to die. It was a confusing feeling. As I walked to the back door and got out the key, I heard music. I stopped and listened. Unable to make out what it was, I moved to the door and put my ear against it. I knew the tune immediately, 'Summer Wind' by Frank Sinatra. That was TC's favourite tune.

I turned the knob and entered, expecting to see TC with a glass of wine and a big smile on his mug. I wondered how much he'd changed in seventeen years.

The kitchen was dark, as was the bathroom, but the light from the main room was bright. Just to be safe I pulled out my gun and made my paces to the main room without noise. As I got to the doorway I could see him. He was sitting at the table with his back turned to me. He caught my reflection in a mirror and slowly turned.

'Hey, kid, how you doing?'

I recognised him right away, but the face was different. So hard, so old, and he was mostly bald. But it wasn't TC. I tried to hide my disappointment.

'Hey, G, what are you doing here? I thought you're supposed to be doing life? What kind of shit did you pull now?'

I tried to mask my anger and intent. I wanted him relaxed, not on edge anticipating my vengeance. I'd let him think he was out of the woods and forgiven, then I'd kill him, but for the moment I kept my gun drawn.

He lowered his eyes and shook his head in agreement. 'Yeah, I know. But the thing is, kid, seventeen years in that shithole and you'd sell your own mother to get out.'

I didn't like the overtones of that comment but didn't offer any retort.

In the old days G was always a bit high-strung, now he seemed to be devoid of all inner life. Lethargically he picked up the wine bottle and filled the two glasses. He set one glass across the table from him and motioned with his head for me to sit down. I hesitated and then lowered the gun that I had fixed on his chest. I tried to look forgiving and even sympathetic to his statement; I had to give him a false sense of security.

As I contemplated sitting down, I felt something was wrong. He was sitting as if he expected me to just drop the gun and give him a hug; not an ounce of fear. If he wasn't afraid then he had something up his sleeve.

Sensing my uneasiness, GG slowly raised his hands.

'Easy, kid, I'm not packing. I'm gonna stand and slowly turn so you can see. If you want to frisk me, that's fine too.'

GG was wearing tight jeans and a T-shirt, he looked clean and I believed him. But I still held a firm stance.

'It's all right, sit down, Marco. Fuck it, at least have a glass of wine with me.'

I tried to regroup, relax myself. 'I was hoping TC was still alive. When I heard the music, I thought it was him in here.'

GG shook his head. 'Yeah, I know, I always thought he'd beat them too.'

My stomach knotted. Did G know something that I didn't?

GG lifted his glass and drank. 'That's a beautiful wine,' he stated and swirled the remaining wine in his glass.

I waited for him to continue. I knew he was leading up to something.

'The thing is, kid, he was alive for two years after the shit hit the fan.'

My heart sank and my anger started to arouse the dragon that resided inside my soul, but I thought of the documents T had left in the safe and relaxed a bit. I casually took a sip of wine and tried not to show my emotions. 'How do you know that, G?'

He knocked back the remaining wine in his glass and poured himself another. He was obviously uneasy about what he had to say.

'I'll get to that in a minute. They got him in Florida. He was gonna whack out Stockland and Simms, but they got him first. Fucking T, he should have just let it go. He'd probably be here now if he had.'

I knew this was gonna go bad and the best thing to do was just shoot GG and get the fuck out, but I needed some answers.

'How did he even know who to look for? TC didn't know what Simms or Stockland looked like, or their names.' Now I knew that wasn't the case; I gave TC the pictures of Simms and Stockland myself, but G didn't know that.

'Yeah, well, after Face, Shawn and John the Ace were whacked, TC made contact with Tony. Tony gave him the names and maybe pictures as well, I don't know the whole story.'

None of this made sense to me; GG wasn't telling it straight. One thing bothered me, though: how did G know any of this information, like Stockland and Simms' names? And how could he know that TC tried to take them out, or that Tony was alive? I was getting uneasy.

I knew they didn't get TC in Florida. For starters, TC's attempted hit on Stockland was in Baltimore, and Tony saw TC after that. Not to mention, the documents that he left in the clubhouse safe proved he was alive at least five or six years after he attempted to take out Stockland Or did they get TC in Florida later? I hoped not. I needed to know more. If this was a set-up, there was someone outside waiting for me anyway. I wanted to at least get the truth before I tried finding a way out of there alive.

'Well, the big question is, how the fuck do you know all this, G?'

GG tensed and took a cigarette out of his pack and nonchalantly tapped the filter on his gold Zippo lighter.

'Well, I would've thought you figured that one out by now, Marco.' He lit his cigarette, took a long inhale and let the smoke out without making eye contact with me. 'But fuck it, I'll tell ya.'

As he took another long, nervous drag off his cigarette, he looked like a stranger to me. It was G all right, but a different G. For all the shit he caused, I couldn't help but think that he had paid twice for his mistakes. Uncle Tony was right, I'm too fucking soft; I had to suck it up and do this thing, G needed to make the final payment.

I knew if we kept on talking, I might not be able to kill him. But I really had to have some answers, so I sat silently and waited for his revelation, fingering the trigger of my gun which now sat in my lap.

GG lowered his eyes, took another sip of wine and began. 'After I got arrested, they told me they had enough evidence to put me away for three lifetimes – two murders which, as you know, I didn't commit, plus drugs and money laundering.'

'Yeah, I got all that, G,' I said impatiently.

'Right. The deal was, I do all the talking and all seven of us get to walk. The Feds just wanted a case against two rogue agents, Simms and Stockland, but I didn't know them then. So the only way to get them was to stake out Tony and wait for them to make contact with him. But before they can do that, Simms and Stockland find out that I've made a deal and there's an internal investigation trying to root out these rogue agents.' GG laughed. 'Wait till you hear this. When the agency keeps hitting walls and getting nowhere with the case, Stockland and Simms get themselves assigned to the case and go undercover to find the two rogue agents. God bless America, huh?'

I just nodded my head and tried to breathe.

'So Simms and Stockland come and see me in the joint, but at that point I have no idea they're our partners, so I try to co-operate, thinking we're all gonna walk away from this thing without too much time. I tell them everything, even about the pact and the millennium meeting; I figure it couldn't hurt. I guess the FBI stakeout at Tony's was starting to get them closer to a bust and Simms and Stockland knew that you could ID them. So they start killing everybody, hoping you'd left the documents with one of them, but you and TC got out and that was a problem. So they came back to the joint and told me that it was them all along and if I didn't help them find you and T, they'd put the dirty story out in the prison that I was a rat. And I'd spend the rest of my life in prison in solitary confinement, unable to go outside, eating alone. No one can do that kind of time, kid.'

I almost felt sorry for G, but the problem was, no matter how you stacked it, everyone's life had been fucked because of him. And now he was telling me he'd made a deal with Stockland and Simms. Just a couple of questions and I'd do what I came here to do.

'So where are we now, G? How'd you get out?'

'Well, that's the thing, buddy, they got me out on parole. They just want to make a deal and they'll go away.'

That's when my bad feeling got really bad. I should have listened to Uncle Tony.

'So they got you out?'

'Marco, they're out front now.'

I started to stand up, thinking that maybe I could make a break for it, then thought better of it and poured myself a glass of wine and sat back down.

'Relax, there's two guys out back covering the back door, and Simms and Stockland out front. They have a bug on the place, they're listening to everything we say.' From the look on his face I really think he believed he was going to get out of this mess.

'You fucking prick, G!' I said incredulously.

'I'm a fucking prick? You came here to whack me out, and I'm the prick?'

My mind was racing and I didn't really listen to what G was saying. I had to find a way out.

'Marco, listen to me. They just want the documents. Then we walk, it's that simple.'

'That simple, huh? I hand over the documents and we just walk? You got to be fucking kidding me, G. They're gonna fucking whack us both.'

That's when the front door opened. It was Simms. He was much older and looked different, more refined, but it was Simms all right. He stood five feet away to my left, next to the door, and kept his gun on me.

'Marco, how's things?'

I looked him straight in the eyes. 'You tell me, Dave.' What else do you say to a guy who's been trying to kill you for seventeen years?

'We just want the documents, Marco. You give us what we want and you get to go wherever you want. We'll even clean your record of all the false charges and warrants for your arrest. You'll be able to start all over again like nothing ever happened.'

The prick had the nerve to actually look and sound sincere as he spoke. I couldn't believe he said 'like nothing ever happened'. What about my dead brothers and all the years stolen from me? And if he wasn't going to kill G, I was. The temptation to raise the .45 above the table and shoot the piece of shit there and then was strong, but I figured Simms would shoot me, so I held back. I'd wait for a more opportune moment.

'Well, that sounds simple, Dave, doesn't it?' I released the grip on my gun and put my hands on the table, leaving the gun on my lap. Maybe Simms would drop his guard.

He smiled easy and replied, 'It really does.'

GG didn't say anything, but watched and listened carefully. I didn't have a plan, so I thought I'd keep Simms talking until I could think of something.

'Even if I give you the documents, Dave, who's to say I haven't made copies of the badges and given them to someone else?'

Simms' face glazed over as if in disbelief.

'You don't even know what's in those documents, do you?

332

It's not the badges we want. Anyone can make false documents these days.'

I just shrugged my shoulders and tried to put on a good poker face.

'You see Marco, if you don't know what Tony's put in there, you're not a threat to us.' Simms' tone was far too sincere and as he continued, he lowered his gun and tried to reason with me. 'Why don't you just give us the documents, and we'll be on our way. You and GG can have your lives back and everyone's happy.'

I didn't believe a word of that bullshit. But I figured I'd buy some time. 'Right. OK, sounds good, Dave,' I said, hoping that might stall things.

'Good Marco, I'm glad you agree. Now, where are they?'

'Nearby, in a buried freezer, about two feet below the ground.'

'Exactly how nearby?'

'I don't know, about fifty feet. There should be some shovels in the shed out back, but you're going to have a hell of a time busting that layer of frost out there.'

It was a total lie. The buried freezer was still upstate.

Simms nodded his head. 'Good, that's good.' He pulled a small two-way radio from his jacket and spoke into it. 'Three, this is two, over.'

There was no reply from three, whoever he was. Simms looked baffled.

'Three, this is two, over. Where the fuck are you?'

No reply.

'Four, this is two, check on three; I've lost communication, over.'

Once again no reply. Simms was looking nervous.

The front door opened and in walked an older and somewhat fatter Robert Stockland. He gave the room a cursory look and turned to Simms. 'What's up?'

Simms didn't reply. He spoke into his radio again. 'Team three, team four, this is two. Do you copy?' Static was the only reply.

Stockland slowly drew out a cold, black 9mm handgun and raised the radio to his mouth. 'Three, four, this is team leader, do you copy?'

Nothing.

Stockland turned to Simms. 'Check out back.'

Simms turned and started for the back door. Stockland looked at me and pointed his gun at my head.

'What do you know about this, Marco?'

I tried to stay cool. 'I don't know, maybe the guy's taking a fucking piss.'

After a deep stare, Stockland nodded his head.

'Yeah, maybe. What about you, GG? Anything you want to tell me?'

GG didn't even raise his eyes, he just shook his head. 'No, boss.'

I heard the creak of the door as Simms opened it. I couldn't see him because the wall between the living room, where we were, and the kitchen was in the way.

Simms called to Stockland, who still had his gun drawn on me, 'They're not at their posts—'

I heard a moan and something hit the floor. Then I saw Simms' hand, with the gun still in it, on the floor in the doorway. It didn't move. I hadn't heard a gunshot, but I was pretty sure he was dead.

I had no idea what was happening. I wanted to reach for my gun which was sitting in my lap, but Stockland was looking panicky and still pointing his gun my way. It was a hard fucking call to make. Do I? Don't I?

Stockland suddenly grabbed GG, who was closer to him. He put his forearm accross GG's throat and pulled him to his feet and closer to the front door. Using GG as a body shield, he turned his gun towards the back door. That gave me the break I needed.

I grabbed my gun, stood up and pointed it at Stockland. Stockland put his gun to GG's head. 'Put it down, kid, or I'll kill him right now.'

GG spoke up. 'Don't do it, Marco. Fuck him.'

Before I could do anything a piece of plaster popped off the wall behind Stockland. It was a bullet fired from a silenced gun. The unknown gunman obviously didn't have a clear shot because of the kitchen wall.

Stockland turned the gun in my direction then to the rear door and put his back against the wall, sliding slowly to his right until he was next to the front door. The small entry wall partially blocked his view of me and limited my line of fire at him, but he had a clear view of who was coming through the back door without being in direct sight.

Stockland whispered to GG, 'Reach down and turn that doorknob and open the fucking door. Right now!'

GG did as he was told and opened the front door.

Then I heard two footsteps from the back and a voice – a voice I knew well.

'Put down the fucking gun, Bobby.' The tone was ice-cold and steady.

It was Uncle Tony. I felt a little better, but I knew it could still go bad. Stockland pulled himself together and went straight into negotiations with Uncle Tony.

'Step out of the door and place the weapon on the floor, Tony, or I'll shoot the both of them right now, and I still might get you. Put the gun down and we all get to walk out. Do it!'

Very calmly, Uncle Tony replied, 'Bobby, you know me. If you don't let him go and put the gun down, I'm gonna kill you, and if you shoot my nephew before I kill you, I'm gonna spend the next couple of days killing your whole family.'

Stockland was sweating now and he repeated his demands.

'Tony! I said step back, place the weapon on the floor and kick it away.'

I could hear footsteps approaching. Uncle Tony wasn't stopping.

'Tony, step back or I'll blow his fucking brains out.'

I'm not sure what I heard first, the silenced report of Tony's weapon, or GG gasping for air. A slow stream of blood began staining his shirt. I looked at G and he looked at me, then his eyes went shut.

Tony entered the room from the kitchen. I'd never seen him in this mode, he had an aura that would have stopped the greatest of warriors in their tracks. Stockland, still holding up GG's body and obviously feeling the strain of his dead weight, kept his gun levelled at Tony.

'Well, Bobby, that's one hostage down, and your other one has a .45 levelled at your head. You're not doing too good, friend. If you shoot him you know you're fucked. The best piece of advice and deal I can offer you is to walk out of here without shooting my nephew and disappear for ever. If I ever hear that you've popped up your head, I'm going to spend the rest of my life hunting you and your family down.' Tony's voice was even and precise; if he had any fear I couldn't hear it or see it.

Suddenly Stockland threw GG's body forward and leapt for the open door. Uncle Tony got two shots off; one hit Stockland in the upper left shoulder blade, the other lodged in the doorjamb. GG's body crashed into the table before hitting the floor.

Tony walked over to the front door and watched Stockland get into his car.

'Another day, Bobby, another day.'

Tony closed the front door and walked over and checked G's pulse.

'Is he dead?'

'Yeah, he's gone.' Tony stood at the table across from me and took out a cigar from his long black trench coat and lit it.

'Why'd you shoot him?'

'Because I knew you wouldn't, and rats have to die. Besides, it was the best way to defuse the situation. I took away his bargaining chip and burdened him with G's dead weight.'

I didn't know what to say. I just stood there and looked around, my mind in a fog.

Uncle Tony looked up at me to speak, and I realised how old he was getting. The lines in his face seemed so deep tonight.

'So what are you gonna do now, kid?'

I shrugged my shoulders. 'Go back to Europe, I guess.'

'Where are you staying tonight?'

'Downtown at a small hotel. Why?'

'I want to see you tomorrow afternoon. We have to talk.' Tony gave me a stern look and I got the feeling that whatever we had to talk about was something unpleasant.

'Yeah, sure. What time? Where?' I said, unable to feel or care about much of anything.

Tony walked over to the small table where the phone sat and grabbed the pen and paper there. He wrote the name and room number of his hotel and passed it to me.

'Tomorrow at five o'clock. It gets dark after four so you'll be able to drive across the city with less chance of being spotted.'

I put the paper in my pocket and shook his hand. Tony issued his last orders of the evening.

'I have a lot of cleaning up to do here and Johnny G. is down the street waiting for me to call and give him the word. It'd be better if he didn't see you. Go straight to your hotel and stay there until tomorrow night. Order room service and don't leave until after dark. I don't want anyone to spot you; you don't want anyone to get any ideas when GG's reported missing. As it stands, when I'm done here, they'll never find the body; they'll just think he's another con that broke his parole conditions and skipped town.'

I nodded my head in agreement and shook Tony's hand again. 'I'll see you tomorrow, Uncle.'

As I turned to go, I noticed that the framed picture had been knocked to the floor when Stockland threw GG's lifeless body into the table. I bent over and picked it up. The glass was shattered from the centre out. Just like our lives, I thought to myself. I put the picture under my jacket and walked out without looking back. I wanted to leave this night behind me and move on.

The rest of the night passed slowly and I found myself pacing the floor in my hotel room. The mental image of GG's body lying on the floor in the clubhouse was more disturbing then I thought it would be. And Tony's request to meet with him the following evening was unexpected; I was feeling tired and emotionally drained. The sun had been up for a couple of hours before I finally passed out on the couch.

When I left for the meeting with Tony, I packed all my things and took them to the rental car. I paid for another night just in case Tony needed me to stick around, but if not, I wanted to get the first plane out of JFK and get back to my little village. The first thing I would do when I was back would be to get in my boat and sail off for a few days; that usually eased my soul.

I called Tony's room, from the lobby at five o'clock sharp and he told me to come up. He was unshaven and had no shirt on. His undershirt clung tightly to his well-defined chest and stomach; his physique would have been impressive for a thirty-year-old guy – he was almost seventy. I walked into the suite and he pointed to the dining-room table where an opened bottle of wine sat.

'Sit down, have a glass of wine.'

I poured out two glasses and waited for him to start.

'You know, I was out in Oregon last month.'

That remark caught me off guard. 'Oregon? What were you doing in Oregon?'

'I went to see Julia. I stop in and check on her and little Marco from time to time. Now that her husband and parents are dead she looks forward to the company, and it's good for me to have someone that I know from the past to talk to.'

'She never remarried?'

'No. I think she's still waiting for Marco's dad to come back.'

'Well, unless Dominic is related to Lazarus, she's got a long wait.'

'You know, for a guy that's as smart as you are, you can be pretty fucking stupid. You're the father.'

My heart froze. I couldn't process the information; it didn't make sense to me. I just stood there. Tony could see that I was lost for words and decided to clear things up for me.

'When you sent her back home, she was already pregnant, she just didn't know it yet. Then she gets in the car wreck and meets the guy. Before she gets romantically involved with the guy she finds out she's pregnant and tells the guy that she's carrying your baby. It turns out he's a real decent guy and really cares for her. They were married before little Marco was born. She didn't want to tell you back then. And I wasn't going to say anything last summer because I knew you'd go and rescue her and your son, which might have got you all killed.'

Hearing Tony say 'your son' hit a real nerve; at first it scared me, but then I felt a warm glow in my stomach.

'So, what do you think about that?' Tony asked and took a sip of wine.

I wasn't really listening, I was thinking of Julia and the son I hadn't seen since he was a little baby.

'You know something, Uncle. I'm going to Oregon to see Julia. Even if we can't work it out, I'll make sure they're OK.'

Tony nodded and smiled. 'Kid, she'll greet you with open arms. I told her to watch out for you this year.'

'Why would you have told her that?'

'Because I thought this would play out this way. I knew back when you told me you were going for GG that I'd be here. I've had it planned for months. I had two guys tailing Stockland and Simms since they arrived in New York last week. Don't forget, kid, I always make sure I'm the smartest guy in the room. Oh, by the way, that fat shit Denni died last month, I thought you might like to know that.'

I didn't give a fuck about Denni when he was alive; I certainly didn't give a fuck now.

'Sounds like his problem. Is there anything else, Uncle?

339

Anything you need before I go?' My heart was throbbing and my stomach was knotting up. The idea of seeing Julia and my son was overwhelming.

Tony gave me one of those looks that meant I wasn't going to like what he said.

'I don't think it's a good time to take Julia and Marco back to Italy with you. I think you better lay low for a while and see what Stockland does. There's still a chance he'll make a move on us.'

'He's not that stupid, is he?'

'Yeah, he is. He could relocate his family and put a crew together to make a shot at it. I doubt it though.'

'It's always something, isn't it? I'm sick and tired of all this fucking shit, Uncle. How long do I have to wait before I can see them?'

Tony emptied his glass and poured another.

'I'm not saying don't go and see them. Stockland's going to be shitting his pants and trying to regroup right now; this is a perfect opportunity to go and spend some time with them, just keep your guard up. Give it ten or twelve months and make sure I've got Stockland in check before you let your guard down.'

I wasn't going to get too upset. I wasn't even sure Julia would be willing to make another go at it. I'd at least go and see her and feel out the situation and have a talk with my son.

I could tell that Tony still wasn't finished; there was something else on his mind.

'There's something else I didn't tell you last summer . . . I know where TC is.'

This was another shock I wasn't expecting; I just sat and waited for Tony to continue.

'TC's in Houston, Texas, doing a ten-year bid in prison.'

'Prison? How the fuck did that happen?'

'After he tried taking out Stockland, he came to see me, as you know. He had to lay low for a few years before he made any moves. When he thought it was safe, he had a couple of million in small bills he was trying to unload on the quiet, and he went

340

to see that Jew Bernie that we used to buy the bills from. Well, it turns out Bernie was under investigation and they all took a pinch. TC got done for tax evasion and money laundering. He still has another couple of years to go.'

'If he's in the can, how come Stockland and Simms didn't get him on the inside?'

'He's using a clean identity. He's in prison as Joseph Costa. I'm the only one that knows, and I certainly can't go visit him; it'd be too dangerous for him and me. I've been sending money to him via the attorney he hired to defend him. I don't want you going in to see him either, it could cause problems for both of you.'

The thought of TC doing hard time with no outside connection really bothered me. The only thing that gets you through is the contact from the outside and visitors.

I finished my glass of wine and stood up. I wasn't in the mood for any more talk. I just wanted to get to Oregon and see Julia and Marco, then I could figure out how I could get to TC and help him out.

'I got to run, Uncle. I need to figure some things out.'

Tony got up and gave me a hug. 'Take care of yourself, kid. You know, you could always come down and live in banana country with me.'

'I know, Uncle. I'll think about it.'

'Remember what I said, stay clear of TC and keep your head down and eyes open out there in Oregon.'

I opened the door and gave Tony a nod before shutting it. All this information had knocked me sideways; I was going need some Vivaldi for the trip.

As much as I wanted to see my parents, I went straight to the airport and landed in Oregon the next morning. I grabbed a taxi downtown and found a car rental agency where I hired a four-wheel drive SUV. I didn't like the idea of driving into the mountains in a car because the thought of getting stuck in a snow bank didn't appeal to me.

The whole drive I braced myself for the worst. I had to be realistic; after all these years, would all my love for Julia be enough for her to forgive me? I had put her through so much pain, I really couldn't expect her to just drop everything and come with me, but maybe I could stay with her.

Tony seemed to think Stockland wouldn't bother me again. But you never knew with these things. Maybe Stockland would seek his revenge on Tony and then come after me. It was too much to think about so I just popped in the Vilvaldi tape and watched the mountains rise as I got closer to Julia and little Marco.

The sun was just setting and a snowstorm was kicking up as I made the left turn into the long driveway that would lead me to the most important moment of my life. I eased the truck down the driveway gently, not wanting to rush the moment. I wanted to savour those waning minutes that still held hope.

I pulled up in front of the house. It looked just the same as the last time I visited all those years ago. As I hopped down from the truck and shut the door, I saw Julia. She was standing at the front door, peering through the fogged glass.

When I reached the front steps, she opened the door. I stopped and stared at her, almost afraid to move any closer. She was wearing dungaree overalls with a white turtleneck sweater.

It seemed like forever passed twice before either of us spoke. Her beautiful blue eyes were moist with tears, but she was smiling. Her eyes and the soft kiss said everything I needed to know. I was home at last.

Epilogue

Within a month I made plans to see my family and introduce my son to them. As much as I wanted to return to Italy, we needed time all together before we could make a move of that magnitude. And the time would give me a chance to think about what I wanted to do with the rest of my life. I could be a builder, maybe a handyman, it didn't matter as long as I had Julia and my son. And I just wanted to be a good guy.

While we were visiting my parents I took a drive out to the piece of property that was once owned by my grandfather. I had to see what Tony buried there and destroy it. I removed the small layer of topsoil and opened the reluctant freezer lid. Inside were two automatic weapons, a small wooden box containing a dozen hand grenades and an old leather satchel. I had to laugh; only Tony would think to leave such a care package.

Inside the satchel was a large envelope with fifty grand, the passports they'd used and letters containing the details of some of the dirty scams that Tony had pulled with Simms and Stockland. I now understood why they were so hell bent on trying to kill TC and me. If that information was passed on to the right people, they'd never see a courtroom, they'd just cease to exist. At that moment I realised that the drug business and killing people was just a sideline for them, the fun stuff. Their other endeavours were frightening and once I burnt all of the

343

evidence, I put it out of mind forever. I didn't want to know.

As I drove back to my parents' house, I thought about the future and considered all of the possibilities. It all looked great. Only one thing really bothered me – TC. He had another two years to do and the thought of him rotting away in a cage troubled me. Maybe I could break him out . . . But that's a story for another day.